AGENT 13™ THE MIDNIGHT AVENGER

VS.

THE BROTHERHOOD

In 1907, a gifted child was kidnapped and taken to a place known as "the Shrine," the ultra-secret headquarters of the sinister "Brotherhood." The child's real name was erased, and he was given the number 13. As memories of his parents faded, he was trained in the arts of power. An exemplary student, he seemed destined to become a great agent of the Brotherhood. Instead, 13 learned the true nature of the Brotherhood, and fled.

Thus began a deadly cat-and-mouse game between Agent 13 and the Brotherhood.

What is the Brotherhood?

The Brotherhood has existed since the dawn of civilization. For millennia, it guided mankind down "the bright path." But then Itsu, the Hand Sinister, seized power and converted light to darkness. Now, in the 1930s, the Brotherhood lusts for global dominance and intends to throw the world into a debilitating war to gain it.

Only Agent 13 stands in their way.

A midnight avenger, Agent 13 is a master of disguise, an invisible operator, and a ruthless destroyer of evil—committed to toppling the Brotherhood through any means. And the Brotherhood fears him, for many of the members have been discovered dead, with the number 13 branded into their foreheads.

Essentially a loner working through a network of informants, Agent 13 has come to trust Maggie Darr, the only person who has seen his real face. Daring and beautiful, Maggie looks as good with a Thompson submachine gun as with a smile. She and 13 are allies, not lovers, but were Agent 13's lifelong mission any less compelling, things might be different. . . .

Join Agent 13 in this fast-paced, action-packed adventure reminiscent of the popular 1930's pulps.

#1 — THE INVISIBLE EMPIRE

#2 — THE SERPENTINE ASSASSINS

and look for

#3 — ACOLYTES OF DARKNESS

AGENT 13™
THE MIDNIGHT AVENGER

#2

THE SERPENTINE ASSASSIN

by Flint Dille and David Marconi

Cover art by Jeff Butler

TSR™
TSR, Inc.
PRODUCTS OF YOUR IMAGINATION™

AGENT 13™, The Midnight Avenger

Book #2

THE SERPENTINE ASSASSIN

Distributed to the book trade in the United States by Random House, Inc., and in Canada by Random House of Canada, Ltd.

Distributed in the United Kingdom by TSR UK, Ltd.

Distributed to the toy and hobby trade by regional distributors.

First printing: April 1986
Printed in the United States of America
Library of Congress Catalog Card Number: 86-52198
ISBN: 0-88038-282-1

9 8 7 6 5 4 3 2 1

TSR, Inc.
P.O. Box 756
Lake Geneva, WI 53147

TSR UK, Ltd.
The Mill, Rathmore Road
Cambridge CB1 4AD
United Kingdom

THE STORY SO FAR. . . .

AGENT 13™ THE MIDNIGHT AVENGER AND THE INVISIBLE EMPIRE

In 1937, a sinister hooded figure, known only as the Masque, sends the President of the United States film clips of three disasters—the destruction of a train carrying carloads of helium, an explosion and fire at the Westron aircraft factory, and the destruction of the German airship, the *Hindenburg*.

Unless the United States is prepared to meet his demands to begin military disarmament, the Masque threatens even more terrorist attacks. The President, of course, refuses to allow America to be blackmailed. In retaliation, the Masque sends a band of Serpentine Assassins to slaughter everyone present at a meeting of the National Security Council. There are only two survivors—Kent Walters, National Security Advisor, and Agent 13.

Agent 13 sees a terrible pattern in these disasters. The Masque, he believes, is a member of the secret, powerful organization known as the Brotherhood. And, if that is true, then these disasters and the Masque's demands are all part of a much larger scheme for total world domination!

Aware that another disaster of major proportion is imminent, 13 and his beautiful associate, Maggie Darr, work to thwart the Masque's plans. The mystery is further complicated by the Brotherhood's sudden interest in Dr. David Fischer, developer of a unique and powerful weapon known as the Lightning Gun.

When the Lightning Gun, Dr. Fischer, and a host of celebrities—including the beautiful Brotherhood agent, China White—board the luxurious liner, the *Normandie*, 13 believes he knows where the next disaster will strike.

It is up to him to stop it. . . .

1

Eyes of Crimson

1937. A sea lane two hundred miles off the coast of Newfoundland.

The midnight waters of the Atlantic were cold and serene, reflecting the full moon that cut like a beacon through the crystal blackness.

Suddenly, the throb of churning engine screws filled the night as the tall, crimson bow of the SS *Normandie*, the pride of the French liners, sliced through the black waters.

While Europe stood on the brink of an armed conflict that threatened to tear apart the world, the *Normandie* offered a temporary, elegantly appointed haven of peace to those who could afford her.

From a distance that night, the *Normandie* was truly a wonder to behold—one thousand twenty-nine feet in length, fourteen decks high—she was a floating palace of twinkling light. A closer look, however, revealed that something was wrong . . . terribly wrong!

The bars aboard ship were crowded, but no one was celebrating. Rather, they were talking in hushed, sad, or angry tones about the great tragedies they'd been witness to that night.

Security officers were posted around the ship, scrutinizing the passengers closely, for no one knew whether those responsible for tonight's bloody carnage were still on board or if they had all escaped on that mysterious airboat.

On the bridge, grieving, shocked crew members were removing the bodies of their captain and his officers from the bullet-ridden command center of the great ship. Another group was doing the same with the men who had been in the radio room—a room with all its equipment now smashed and blood-spattered.

With most of her officers dead and her radio equipment destroyed, the *Normandie* had no choice but to turn back to New York. The investigation of just what happened had already begun on board. Also sealed off was the garage, where still more bodies lay—bodies of the thugs who had been in on this operation and who had been shot down by escaping comrades.

The fire that had raged in the garage had been brought under control, but too late to save what was rumored to be the prototype of a new and devastating weapon developed by one Dr. David Fischer. Dr. Fischer himself, it seemed, had narrowly escaped with his life. Drugged and only partially aware of what was going on, he had given a rather incoherent account of Nazis trying to kidnap him and his gun.

One person could have told the confused investigators the whole story of the strange, sinister figure behind this near-disaster—the hooded figure known as the Masque, who had engineered this horror in an attempt to blackmail America into meeting his demands. One person, who was—even now—still standing on the deck, staring back out into the dark sea at a tiny pinpoint of flame on the horizon. That spot of flame marked the burning wreckage of a lifeboat—and it marked the burning pain in Maggie Darr's heart.

For out there, in the cold, black waters, had perished the man Maggie loved, Agent 13.

Maggie might have stood there for hours, staring back at the spot of flame that gradually disappeared over the horizon. But the Texan, who had loaned Agent 13 his pearl-handled Colt .45, discovered her standing there.

"Say, little lady, what's this?" he drawled, true concern in his voice. Maggie's blood-stained, grease-smeared evening gown clung to her body. Her long, strawberry blonde hair whipped in the wind of the ship's motion. She was shivering violently, her lips blue.

Grabbing a blanket from a deck chair, the Texan wrapped it around Maggie's shoulders.

"Yer Mrs. Plotkin, ain't ya, little lady?" the Texan said awkwardly. "I heard your husband was—er—lost in the stampede, so to speak. I'm real sorry, ma'am. But, look, standin' here ain't gonna bring him back. Let me take you back to your cabin. The doc'll fix you up somethin' to help you sleep. . . ."

No, thought Maggie wearily, this won't bring him back. Nothing can bring him back. But at least I'll avenge him. At least I'll keep fighting!

Maggie straightened up and gave the Texan a strained smile.

"Thank you," she said in a toneless voice, "you are very kind. I'll take your advice. I'll go back to my cabin. Thank you."

"You sure I can't help you?" the Texan asked.

"No, thank you," Maggie said wearily. "I—I'd rather be alone right now." Seeing the Texan look doubtful, Maggie added, "I'm all right, truly."

The Texan touched the brim of his Stetson. "Glad to be of help, ma'am. Again, I'm right sorry about yer husband, Mrs. Plotkin."

Mrs. Plotkin. Maggie sighed. Would she have to keep up that charade the rest of the voyage? And what about when they arrived in New York? No.

There'd be too many questions. It would come out that Hiram Plotkin had never existed.

Trying to think, Maggie made her way below decks. She had been with Agent 13 long enough to know about disguises. Mrs. Plotkin would disappear along with her husband. Give them another little mystery to ponder. . . .

As Maggie moved along the silent corridors to her cabin, the cabin that would seem so empty now, she passed cabin 48. The number registered in her weary brain. 48. Stopping, she stared at it, trying to remember. . . .

Of course! Dr. Fischer! It was *his* cabin number. Agent 13 had given her a mission—to watch Fischer. She had been successful in preventing China White and the Brotherhood from kidnapping him. She had also managed to destroy his prototype weapon—the Lightning Gun.

Maggie recalled her last glimpse of Fischer. The ship's doctor had been leading the dazed, drugged man away. Had they taken him to the infirmary? Or back to his cabin?

"I ought to check on him," Maggie said to herself with a sigh. But she was tired, so very tired. She only wanted to get to her room, alone.

"But I promised him. . . ."

She knocked softly on the door. "Dr. Fischer?" she called out.

"Who's there?" asked a frightened voice.

"It's me, Mrs.—uh—Plotkin. Remember? We talked in the Winter Garden Room?" she said lamely, wondering how much Fischer remembered about the attempted kidnapping.

There was a moment's silence, then the door opened a crack. Fischer peered out. Maggie was shocked. The man looked terrible! His face was gray and haggard, and it barely resembled the face of the man she had rescued. His eyes still had that glazed expression of someone shaking off the effects of a drug. That must explain why even his voice sounded different, Maggie thought.

"I'm sorry to disturb you," Maggie said gently. "I just wanted to be sure you're all right—"

"Come in," Fischer said, his eyes darting nervously down the corridor. "This has been a horrible ordeal! My nerves are shattered. . . ."

Mumbling, running his hands through his graying hair, Fischer turned from the door. Maggie followed him inside.

He turned and shouted, "Shut the door!" Hurtling past her, he slammed and locked it.

Maggie, alarmed at Fischer's distraught state, suggested, "You really should be in the infirmary." She went to the phone. "Let me call—"

"No!" He knocked the phone from her hand.

Seeing her startled expression, he said, "I'm sorry. I—I didn't mean to be so abrupt. It's just . . . I'm so frightened!" He looked at her pleadingly. "You're the only one I can trust!"

"Dr. Fischer," Maggie said firmly, "I really believe you are safe now. You should go to bed—"

"Oh, but first I have to thank you for saving me!" Dr. Fischer said in a trembling voice. "I have money! Lots of money! Let me give you—"

"Really, Dr. Fischer," Maggie said with a sigh, "that's not necessary—"

Fischer's hand went to his inside coat pocket.

"Yes, it is!" he said. Then, suddenly, his voice changed. "Believe me—it is—very necessary!"

Fischer's eyes gleamed strangely as he stared intently at Maggie. His body no longer trembled, and the expression on his face grew hard.

"What the—" Maggie began, then stared in horrified fascination as Dr. Fischer's hand emerged from his coat pocket, holding a .38.

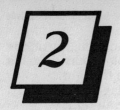

2

FIRES OF FREEDOM

"Dr. Fischer! Are you crazy?" Maggie gasped, watching as the gun, seemingly in slow motion, swung around until it was aimed at her head. "I'm not going to hurt you! I'm not one of them!"

The man didn't answer. Maggie looked into his eyes and saw the glazed, insane stare . . . Fischer's ordeal had driven him over the edge.

Backing up, Maggie grabbed for the only thing within reach—the telephone. Picking up the entire instrument, she threw it at the professor with all her strength. The gun fired just as the phone slammed into his hand, sending the shot wild and the gun from his hand.

Maggie reached for her own gun inside her purse, then remembered it was empty. She had used her last bullet on the escaping China White.

She dove for Fischer's weapon. Sliding on her stomach across the floor, Maggie grabbed the gun and pulled it toward her. But the professor jumped on top of her, pinning her hand and the gun it held beneath her body. Sitting on her buttocks, he wrapped the telephone cord around her neck and began to twist.

Desperately, Maggie fought to free herself and the hand with the gun. But the scientist was strong, incredibly strong for such a frail-looking man. The phone cord cut into her windpipe, slowly choking the life from her body.

Maggie saw bursts of light and pain. For a brief instant, she thought about giving up, to join 13 in that far-off realm. . . .

But something in Maggie refused to surrender. Even as she was beginning to lose consciousness, she remembered an old trick 13 had taught her. She went limp, letting her body fall flaccid. Her head slumped forward. She ceased to struggle.

Fischer quit twisting the cord. Maggie held her breath. Still crouched on top of her prone body, the scientist sat back. With his weight shifted to her legs, Maggie could raise up enough to free her gun hand. Fischer made another lunge for her as he felt her body move, but it was too late. In a sudden, rapid motion, Maggie twisted onto her side.

She raised the gun and fired, point blank. . . .

Dr. Fischer's head exploded in blood and brains and bits of bone. . . . His body, still on top of Maggie, began to convulse.

Fighting back her horror, Maggie pushed the headless corpse off her. Then she realized that the body was growing rapidly hotter! She leaped out of the way just as the corpse burst into flames!

Agent 13's words came back to her. "They are called Jindas, or Serpentine Assassins—the Brotherhood's legendary killers. Before they go out to kill, they drink *mantha*—an ancient drug that causes the body to burst into flame when it mixes with the chemicals of death."

No trace of the Brotherhood's assassins would remain—even after death.

As the last pieces of "Dr. Fischer" burned away, so, too, did Maggie's illusions about the success of her mission to keep Dr. Fischer out of the hands of the Brotherhood.

The Dr. Fischer who had boarded the *Normandie* had been real, Maggie was certain. During the gun battle, China White had apparently substituted her assassin for the real Dr. Fischer. Maggie now remembered the lumpy, ruglike bundle she had seen being transferred to the airboat.

The Brotherhood thought of everything, Maggie realized grimly. If the *Normandie* had been sunk by the torpedoes Agent 13 had stopped, the disappearance of Dr. Fischer would have never been questioned. But if their plan failed, if there were survivors—the "fake" Dr. Fischer would remain on board for everyone to see. And Maggie Darr would be silenced forever.

Opening the door, Maggie staggered out into the hall, coughing with the smoke.

"FIRE!" a voice in the corridor screamed.

Dully, Maggie looked back. The body was gone, but the room was filled with smoke. The rug was afire and the flames had spread to the drapes.

Someone grabbed Maggie, pulling her out of the way. The corridor outside the room was quickly filling with smoke and sleepy-eyed passengers.

"Get water!" yelled another voice, and immediately pandemonium broke out.

Fleeing the scene before anyone could ask questions, Maggie crept to the upper deck, heading for the one place she was certain she would be undisturbed—China White's suite. Already, baskets of flowers stood outside the door, gifts of mourning for the beautiful opera singer who had mysteriously vanished during the disaster.

No one had seen the black-leather-suited woman board the airboat—no one except Maggie Darr.

Glancing up and down the darkened corridor and finding it empty, Maggie picked the lock and entered the elegant Rouen Suite. Closing the door behind her, she locked it securely. She would wait out the voyage here. Maggie didn't dare turn on a light, but she didn't need one. Lying on the satin-sheeted bed, she stared up into the darkness.

So, the Brotherhood had succeeded at least partially in their diabolical scheme. Though they hadn't managed to destroy the *Normandie*—a disaster that would have had world-wide repercussions—they *had* kidnapped Dr. Fischer. That they wanted him for his Lightning Gun was certain. But why? What did they intend to do with it? And how did it tie into the other disasters and the Masque's outrageous demands on America.

Something had to be done.

As she had stared at Agent 13's funeral pyre, she had sworn vengeance. Somehow she *had* to expose the Brotherhood, tell someone about Dr. Fischer. But what would she say to the authorities? As quickly as she wove together the strands of a persuasive story, it unraveled of its own improbability.

What evidence did she really have? Certainly there were witnesses aboard the *Normandie* to the gunplay and the presence of the airboat as it dropped its torpedoes. But what did it all prove?

That a crime had taken place? Of course.

That criminal masterminds were at work? Not necessarily. Everyone was blaming the Nazis!

That there was a secret 'Brotherhood' trying to take control of the world?

Maggie shook her head wearily and began to cry. They were tears of grief, tears of frustration.

Even in failure, the Brotherhood had succeeded in masking its very existence.

For the first time, Maggie Darr felt the depth of the frustration that Agent 13 must have known.

Gradually, she cried herself empty. But, as she drifted into sleep, Maggie Darr made a pledge.

"Wherever you are, beloved," she murmured, "I swear to you that I will never cease fighting them! Somehow—I'll make someone listen. . . ."

3

HANDS OF LIFE

The prototype Mosquito airboat had left the *Normandie* far behind. Aboard the strange craft, the pilot was cursing about their failure to destroy the ship. In the cargo hold, the drugged Dr. Fischer lay wrapped in a rug.

Near him, leaning back against the metal fuselage of the Mosquito, her sultry beauty evident even in the moonlit darkness, China White was staring out into the night with unseeing eyes.

One of the crew members knelt beside her, clumsily trying to bandage her bleeding shoulder where Maggie Darr's bullet had penetrated.

"Leave me alone!" China murmured viciously.

Still she stared straight ahead, as though listening to a voice only she could hear. Then, abruptly, she rose and made her way forward.

"Turn the airboat around," she commanded.

"What?" The astonished pilot looked up at her. "Are you nut—"

"I said turn it around!" China White hissed.

The pilot stared into her eyes. "Sure thing," he muttered, feeling a chill shake his body.

The fires of the floating wreckage slowly burned out and darkness descended on the ocean. To the semi-conscious figure who clung to one of the larger fragments of wood, death was closer than morning.

Dreamily, he imagined what it would be like to die on top of this bit of wood. His body would bake in the sun. The flesh that had once been Agent 13 would slowly wither and dry.

Suddenly, a harsh white light hit him a palpable blow. Spray washed over him as a roaring sound struck his ears. The waves became larger, threatening to topple him back into the sea forever. 13 hung on to the splintering wood with his last remaining strength.

Then hands were pulling him upward, lifting him into something cold, black. He was encased in metal. He saw faces—eyes and voices blurred in a flurry of images. Moments later, he felt a sharp stinging pain in his arm, and though he tried to resist, he drifted into blackness.

"Will he survive?" China asked coldly.

"I doubt it," the crewman muttered, standing up and replacing the syringe in the first aid kit. "That morphine'll ease his pain, but we need to get him to a doctor pronto!"

"Then do so," China White said, her voice carefully devoid of all trace of emotion.

Biting her lip against the pain, China forced her rapidly numbing hand to scrawl out the location of a hidden airfield near America's eastern coastline. This done, and the crewman on his way to deliver her note to the pilot, China White leaned back again.

Her face carefully expressionless, she reached out and gently stroked the wet hair back from Agent 13's pale face.

The sound of the props reached full throttle as the airboat slowly lifted off the frigid waters. Rising effortlessly, the Mosquito disappeared, unseen, into the night.

4

Dark Meditations

Itsu's throne room had been hacked from the mountain thousands of centuries ago, practically at the dawn of human history. Its cavernous expanse dwarfed all who stood within it.

The high throne rose two hundred feet from the center, with hundreds of steps leading up to it. Status among those who served Itsu was revealed by how high they were allowed to ascend the great marble stairway that led to the black onyx throne. None but Itsu set foot upon the final twenty golden stairs that led from the top landing to the throne. For the moment, none save one figure in the robe of a Bishop stood upon the stairway at all.

It was from this vantage point, two hundred feet above the nave of his dark cathedral, that Itsu, the Hand Sinister, meditated upon the *Normandie* mission. Though his agents had failed to destroy the vessel and his beloved nightingale had been wounded, his master plan could still proceed.

In fact, things had worked out better than the Hand Sinister had dared hope. For he had just heard of the probable capture of the one man in the world who came close to proving a threat to him—Agent 13. But was it really Agent 13, or was it—as had happened many times before—a false report? More than once, 13 had disguised others to resemble him, even as he disguised himself to resemble others. There was only one proof—the tattoo of the number 13 upon the palm of his hand. All agents of the Brotherhood bore similar marks, which only death and the decomposition of the flesh would erase.

The tattoo could be seen in only one way—through a Seer Stone. The Hand Sinister would have to wait for this to be confirmed.

Even as he sat motionless upon his throne, the Hand Sinister projected his consciousness onto another plane. Many times before, he had detected actions of Agent 13 in the astral realm, but had been unable to thwart the Agent, whose spiritual aura was unusually strong.

Now, however, when he detected the Agent's aura, he sensed it changing. Dividing. The two halves of the same entity were moving independently. This unique occurrence puzzled the Hand Sinister.

Nevertheless, he wasn't surprised when he spotted a red-robed minion dashing up the steps to stand on the second landing far beneath him.

"We have confirmation." The servant gasped for breath. "It is he—Tredekka!"

"What evidence?" growled the Bishop.

"China White confirms his identity. . . ."

"Bah!" the Bishop started to argue. "Who can tell without the Seer Stone?"

Itsu smiled.

"*She* can tell," he murmured.

5

MIDNIGHT ECHOES

The Mosquito dropped out of the sky just as the sun was beginning to peak over the horizon.

Skimming along the glassy waters near the Virgina shore, the airboat coasted to a landing, then the airboat turned and cruised toward the large building built partially in the water. Huge doors beneath the structure opened up, swallowing the moving airboat like a whale consuming a fish.

A sign on the building read "Sea Breeze Fish Cannery."

As the airboat taxied to a stop against a stone pier, men dashed forward to help and, before many minutes had elapsed, stretchers carrying three people had emerged from the plane. One was Dr. Fischer, still unconscious. That stretcher was taken to hidden quarters far below the cannery. The other two stretchers were carried to the infirmary where Dr. Colbert Winslow waited. To America, he was a renowned surgeon. To the Brotherhood, Winslow was one of them.

Less than an hour earlier, Winslow had received one of the cryptic phone calls he had come to know so well in his double life. Hastily jumping out of bed, he drove through the night to the cannery's infirmary.

Two patients awaited him. One, he was astonished to see, was the beautiful opera singer, China

White. Weak from loss of blood from a shoulder wound, she had lapsed into unconsciousness. But, after a quick examination, Winslow discovered that her situation was not life-threatening.

The same could not be said of his other patient, a man whose face was unknown to the doctor. Checking his patient who, even unconscious, was being closely guarded by two huge thugs, Winslow marveled that the man was still alive.

"This man needs to be in a hospital!" Winslow barked. "He has multiple fractures, undoubtedly internal bleeding. He's suffering from shock and exposure. . . ."

"Just patch him up, doc," growled one of the thugs. "We'll take care of the rest."

Shrugging, Winslow did as he was told, then turned his attention to China White. Carefully, he removed the bullet from her beautiful shoulder, thinking—as he did so—what a pity it was that such lovely skin would be scarred for life.

"She'll be fully recovered in a couple of days," Winslow told the guards, who nodded silently. "I'm going to make one last plea that you let me take this man to a hospital."

The guards shook their heads silently.

Winslow shrugged, packed his medical bag, and set off for home. The less he knew about this, the better he'd sleep.

As China emerged from the anaesthetic, a disheveled-looking young man picked up a phone, gave a brief report, then hung up.

"What happened to the man we brought in?" China muttered drowsily.

The young man, who had been hastily pulled off guard duty in the tunnels below the fish cannery, shrugged. "We boxed him an hour ago."

"He's . . . dead?" asked China White, shocked

into full consciousness.

"Looked that way to me, lady. Stiff as a board." Then, he shook his head. "Though," he added thoughtfully, "with all the strange stuff I seen around this place lately—" Suddenly, the hood's voice changed. He began to shake and clutch at his throat.

China stared at him, startled at first. Then she recognized what was happening—the brainwashing. The young hood had been wagging his tongue too freely. Now he was getting tied up by it.

The hood's face turned purple as he flopped onto the floor, gagging and gasping for air.

What a nuisance, thought China irritably, looking around for a bell to push to have someone come fetch him. Maybe it was only his first offense and he would come out of it. If it wasn't, he would die, choking on his own tongue.

A wave of sadness swept across China. Not for the gagging hood, but for Agent 13. Even she had come to believe he was immortal. And there was something more—a feeling deep inside her that even the passing of time couldn't subdue.

Pausing, she listened for his voice—that spiritual voice that had spoken to her on the plane, making her return to the wreckage of the lifeboat. But that voice was silent.

Something left her then, as a pleasant dream leaves upon wakening. No matter how hard she tried to fall back asleep, she knew that dream would never come again.

She was empty.

The orderly suddenly slumped into the corner, limp, silent. He was either unconscious or dead.

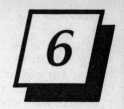

6

THE INVISIBLE GUARD

Crowds thronged the French Line pier in New York as the passengers from the *Normandie* disembarked. Applause clattered over the water as reporters crowded around, chucking questions at anyone who would answer.

"Where's the guy who piloted the lifeboat?" demanded one reporter, crowding the Texan.

"Mind you don't step on mah boots, boy," the Texan growled, eyeing the man irritably. "What do you mean, where is he? Probably bein' awarded a medal by St. Peter 'bout now."

"What about this Mrs. Plotkin? Has she disembarked yet?" another asked.

"I believe she has been in seclusion," said the Texan. "And, if they're smart, they'll keep her away from you coyotes!" Shrugging, the reporters hurried off after another victim.

The authorities, too, were interested in Mrs. Plotkin. In vain, the harassed security officers aboard ship insisted they hadn't seen her. No one had seen her since the disaster. The authorities began to search the ship cabin by cabin.

A small, wrinkled, old Chinese man in dark, wire-rimmed glasses on his thin, bald head stood on the edge of the crowd, peering at all who disembarked intently. "That daughter of mine," he muttered to anyone within earshot. "Always the last to leave. Probably lost her luggage. . . ." His fingers bedecked with several jeweled rings, tapped impatiently on a metal railing. No one gave the old man a second glance.

If they had, they would have noticed that his eyes behind the glasses were much younger than his face. They would also have noticed that he was scrutinizing the face of every passenger who walked down the ramp.

Finally, his fingers ceased their tapping. The old man smiled. His eyes were focused on a middle-aged woman descending the ramp alone. Her hair was gray, her dress was gray, her life was probably gray—the kind of woman who passes through life unnoticed. She was the woman he was looking for—conspicuous by being inconspicuous.

He shadowed the woman closely, his own movements and presence as unobtrusive as hers. His smile broadened as his suspicions were confirmed by the woman leaving the terminal without so much as a piece of luggage.

The woman stepped toward the crowded cabstand and tentatively raised her hand at the passing cabs, but the drivers ignored her.

Sidling next to the gray woman, the old man took off his hat and rubbed his bald head with a handkerchief. The rings on his fingers flashed in the sunlight. An out-of-service cab suddenly went back on call. Pulling over to the curb in front of the woman, the driver opened the door. Startled, the woman stepped back, carefully scrutinizing the driver.

A young Chinese man with a warm, infectious smile, the driver jumped out of the cab. "You get in, lady," he said, respectfully taking her arm. "Not good, you stand in cold like this."

Talking volubly, the young Chinese assisted the woman into the cab quite before she knew what was happening. Bystanders who had been waiting longer glared at her, but she just locked the door and settled back into the seat.

The Chinese boy jumped into the cab and sped off. Replacing his hat, the old man pulled a newspaper from the pocket of his overcoat and appeared to be reading. But his eyes were scanning the nearby area.

Suddenly, he focused on a middle-aged newsstand attendant hurrying toward a double-parked Hudson and jumping in. He saw the man point at the cab as it pulled into traffic.

The old man raised his ringed hand in a quick gesture. A beat-up, rusted DeSoto leaped out of its parking place like a rampaging bull, swerving directly in front of the Hudson.

The Hudson tried to avoid the DeSoto, but it was too late. There was a shattering crash. The Hudson broadsided the DeSoto so hard that it lifted the car up on two wheels. Glass flew everywhere.

The driver of the DeSoto, an ancient Chinese man, jumped out and began waving his hands and babbling angrily. The slightly damaged Hudson backed up, trying to get past the DeSoto, only to be boxed in by the honking cars behind it.

The Hudson stopped, trapped.

Suddenly there was the sound of a siren, and lights flashed on the roof of a squad car stuck eight cars back.

The newsstand attendant and two thugs jumped from the Hudson and dashed wildly away as the police battled their way forward.

When the police finally arrived, they looked helplessly at the two driverless cars, while the symphony of blasting horns played around them.

Smiling with satisfaction, the old Chinese man melted into the crowd.

"Where to, lady?" the driver asked Maggie.

"Just drive around awhile, young man," Maggie said in her best "frumpy" voice. "And please let me know if anyone's following us."

"Following you, lady?" the Chinese boy asked in astonishment.

"My husband's so jealous!" Maggie simpered, patting her gray wig.

"Okey dokey, lady," the Chinese boy said, hiding his grin.

Leaning back in the seat, Maggie was too preoccupied with her own thoughts to notice the skill with which the young man dodged in and out of side streets and took practiced advantage of gaps in traffic.

"No one follow, lady," he finally said.

Maggie started. "Oh, well, take me to Grand Central Station then, please," she said.

Reaching the cathedral-like train station, Maggie paid the driver and watched as he pulled away. Then she entered the station. Occasionally she peered surreptitiously behind her but didn't notice anyone taking an unusual amount of interest in her. In fact, no one seemed to take *any* interest in her whatsoever!

No one, that is, except a small Chinese urchin who was begging for pennies. Maggie purchased her ticket, then walked to the appropriate track. The dark-haired child followed closely behind, dodging with ease in and out of the crowd.

The child watched as Maggie boarded the train, then ran back to the crowded station area.

"Starlight Express," he said in Chinese to an old man waiting for him there, "to Washington. . . ."

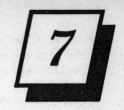

7

JOURNEY TO DARKNESS

The grieving couple stood in the rain, watching as the casket was loaded aboard the airplane.

"Our only son," sobbed the woman, her face hidden by a thick black veil.

"He'll be glad to get back home," said the man, patting her on the shoulder.

Within moments, the coffin was airborne. Inside it, the unconscious Agent 13 was in his most bizarre disguise—one he would never see; he was disguised as a corpse, with two of the Brotherhood's trusted agents as his "parents."

So powerful was the drug the Brotherhood injected periodically into Agent 13 during the journey that it slowed his heart beat to only twice per minute. He breathed only once per hour.

Thus the air in his sealed casket lasted him for days, and even the skilled eyes of a doctor might fail to see the glimmer of life that existed behind the mask of death.

Twice the casket was opened and checked by border guards as it moved across international boundaries where caskets had been used for smuggling. But on both occasions the guards found only what was claimed by the grieving family—the battered body of their handsome son.

On one occasion, the "family" thought they were being followed. To shake off pursuit, the body was buried under the watchful eyes of a priest. But, before the spades had patted the last clods into place, the casket was being hauled down through secret passages built beneath this cemetery long ago for just such fake burials.

Thus, there was no way that any investigator, no matter how diligent or clever, could have followed the path of the corpse from America to its final destination.

After a ten-day journey covering thousands of miles, the unconscious Agent 13 arrived at the mysterious, cloud-shrouded Shrine.

He was taken to a dark, vaulted chamber. There, several grim figures in monks' cowls, their shadowy forms almost indistinguishable from each other, hovered over the unconscious man. Their faces, normally cold and expressionless, gleamed with strange, sinister smiles as they looked through the Seer Stone. Agent 13 had come home.

"I'm not dead" was his first clear thought. If he were dead, his soul would have been liberated. But he knew that it was still chained inside his body. He tried to open his eyes, but his lids would not move. He tried to clench his fists, but his muscles failed to obey. Agent 13 was paralyzed. Where was he? What had happened?

Then he discovered that he could hear and understand people talking around him.

"When was he last given the serum?" The voice hissed like wind whistling through a cave.

"Two nights ago."

"Then soon he should be able to hear me."

"Perhaps he can hear you now."

"He has caused me much displeasure, yet I do not want to destroy him. It will be better to see him destroy himself—and all that he cares for. See that it is done."

13 heard the words. The cold, hissing tones seemed familiar . . . a long time ago. Then the horror suddenly registered—it was Itsu! The Hand Sinister! He was back at the Shrine!

His mind tried to retrace events. His last remembered thoughts were that at least the *Normandie* would live. The Mosquito plane . . . the torpedoes screaming toward the great liner. He maneuvered the frail lifeboat into their path. The moment before impact, he dived into the frigid waters, swimming deep, deep. Then the explosions, then pain, then nothing. . . .

He drifted away again. . . .

Moments, maybe days, later, 13 felt his first physical sensation since the *Normandie* disaster. He felt a pair of fingers upon his eyelids. They were cold and dry, more like bone than flesh.

Desperately, fearful of what he would see, 13 tried to keep his eyes closed, but hands pried the lids open. He stared into a skull! Dark, rotting eyes stared down at him.

Itsu!

The lipless mouth spoke in a hoarse whisper. "Forget not my face. . . . It is life. . . . It is death. . . . It is all!"

Suddenly 13's eyelids closed and he was plunged back into darkness, his very soul shuddering with horror.

It was the face of his nightmares, implanted when he was a child and first brought to the Shrine. He had heard the words then, as well. They were etched on a holy wall erected deep inside him and taken as faith. For though he had fought and won many battles with the Brotherhood, he had never questioned what the skull had whispered, "Life . . . death . . . all!"

Never questioned it, because he knew it to be true!

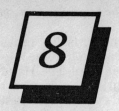

8

SEARCHING FOR PIECES

Washington, D.C.

The lights glimmered brightly over the sleeping city. Somewhere high above a street in the warehouse district, a faint shadow paced past a window, lost in thought.

A twisting smoke plume drifted from the glowing cigarette in Maggie Darr's fingers as she absently eyed the distant Capitol dome.

The almost dark room she stood in was Agent 13's Washington lair, one of several that existed on the 13th floors of abandoned buildings—*nonexistent* 13th floors. The room was jammed with make-up materials, mechanical devices, information.

Maggie recalled the last time she had been in the cluttered lair. 13 had been one of the few to have survived the Brotherhood's attack on the National Security Council meeting where they had slaughtered the nation's top lawmen . . . only to fall prey to the Jinda assassins. Maggie had managed to save him from brutal death. But then they had sailed on the *Normandie*. . . .

Upon her return to Washington, Maggie found she *could not* walk into 13's lair. The things in there were *his* things. *His* presence was still alive in those rooms. Maggie rented a small motel room where she kept to herself . . . and thought.

Locked in seclusion, Maggie gave way to her

grief. Then, one morning, she woke up and knew everything would be all right. She *could* go on. She *must* go on—for his sake.

Now,staring at the illuminated Capitol from the window of 13's lair, Maggie felt the ghost of 13 everywhere, calling her to pick up the flag and continue. She remembered others who had died in his service—the Oriental named Ray Furnow, a strange man who had helped the Agent with many of his inventions. Doc Kendall, the white-haired man who was tailing one of the Brotherhood's agents when he was sliced in two in a "trucking accident." Freddie Dey, Willie Peck, and "Dogs" Kelly. . . . Someday, she knew, the name of Maggie Darr would be added to the list.

She repeated the names over and over in her mind, like an ancient mantra. And, almost unconsciously, she began to pick up the investigation where Agent 13 had left off.

Her first thoughts were of Dr. Fischer. She was the only one to know he had been kidnapped. She ought to report it someone—but who? Who would believe her? Time and again she picked up the phone to call the police—only to put it down again. Finally, she realized she needed more to go on. And it was up to her to find it.

She reviewed what she knew about the events that had occurred prior to the *Normandie*'s sailing. Somehow, they all tied together. Agent 13 had always told her that the Brotherhood plotted their campaigns the way a composer writes a symphony. There is always a repeating motif.

So she recalled everything 13 had told her about the filmed ultimatum delivered to Washington. In that film, a shrouded Brotherhood agent calling himself "the Masque" had threatened disaster after disaster if the United States did not comply with his demands—demands that would virtually cripple the Armed Services.

To back his powerful threats, the Masque had shown film clips of three disasters. First, a train trestle blowing up, sending passenger cars and some helium tank cars tumbling to a fiery end in the canyon below. Then, an armaments factory went skyward in a fiery blaze that destroyed an entire new generation of fighter planes. Finally, the *Hindenburg*—pride of the German dirigibles—exploded while docking at Lakehurst. A film clip of the *Normandie* would undoubtedly have been the next to be shown—were it not for Agent 13's sacrifice.

All of the disasters might have been attributed to other causes were it not for two facts. First, the films of the disasters themselves could have been taken only by ultra-sophisticated camera equipment specially positioned to catch the events on film, and, second, the Masque made sure that his sinister, secret symbol appeared on the film made at every disaster—the Omega and the Star.

The same symbol used by the Brotherhood.

Maggie replayed the disasters in her mind. Allegedly, these crimes were all committed to demonstrate the Masque's power over America, but 13 had been convinced that there was something more to them.

If China White had indeed been the Masque, as Agent 13 had supposed, would her death bring an end to their plots? Maggie doubted it. But there was always the possibility that China White wasn't the Masque. 13 had suspected her, but he hadn't been certain. If not her, then who?

Maggie pored over stacks of papers, clippings, and photographs. A lot of it was research into Dr. Fischer, inventor of the Lightning Gun. Here, too, were the papers Agent 13 had removed from the briefcase of SS Colonel Reinhardt Schmidt, papers showing the Brotherhood's plan to participate in a test of the gun.

A photograph taken during that test suddenly caught Maggie's attention. The test had been conducted for the United States Army when Fischer was trying to raise money to fund his weapon's development.

13, having discovered the Brotherhood's interest in the gun, attended the test firing disguised as a reporter, camera in hand.

The test was a success—the small cannon completely destroyed an old steel tank—but the U.S. Goverment didn't bite. Others did, however, and one interested party paid Fischer's passage to Europe aboard the *Normandie,* making certain that he was on the right ship at the right time.

She carefully studied the photographs of the test. Somewhere was a clue, somewhere an answer—there was General Hunter Braddock, the aging head of the Joint Chiefs of Staff; Fischer; Colonel Joseph Pack, head of the Army's weapons development; Kent Walters, head of the National Security Agency. . . .

Kent Walters! Suddenly it clicked. With the exception of Agent 13, Walters was the only survivor of the Jindas' attack on the meeting in Washington where the Masque's filmed threats had been revealed. But it was also at that meeting that Agent 13 had exposed his identity in an effort to stress the seriousness of the threats!

Walters knew who 13 was, he knew that 13 was on their side. Walters had, in fact, even protected 13's identity when the police had arrested the Agent! Walters would understand the terrible danger they faced! Walters would be the one to tell about Dr. Fischer!

At last, she had something to do, something to think about. Perhaps—even someone to help.

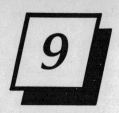

9

SENTENCE PRONOUNCED

The first sensation Agent 13 felt was a slight tingling. Starting in his chest, it spread slowly outward. It was a strange sensation, as if he were being reborn. Soon his heart rate increased, slowly at first. Thirty times a minute, then forty, finally—normal—sixty-eight beats.

The tingling spread throughout his body. As it did, he wasn't Agent 13. He was a small boy. His subconscious suddenly came to vivid life. . . .

A weather-beaten wagon creaked down a rutted jungle road, spoked wheels turning, bumping.

He sat in the back of the wagon, playing with his tin soldiers. He was angry because he couldn't get them to stand up—the wagon was shaking too much. Angrily, he looked up at the two men and a woman sitting on the seat of the wagon. One man was the driver, but the other wore the black suit and white collar of a missionary.

At his cry of protest, the woman turned and smiled at him. Cheered and comforted by her smile, he forgot his anger. She said something to the missionary, causing him to turn around too.

Suddenly, an icy chill ran down the Agent's spine. He recognized the man and the woman—his father and mother!

Slowly, 13 began to hear sounds in his vision. First, the rustling in the jungle, then the whizzing of arrows through the air. He heard a scream and saw his father fall over sideways, an arrow stuck through his neck. It was his mother screaming. She reached back for him. . . .

Everything was wrong! His father's eyes were open and staring. Blood was all over his black suit. The child's mother tried to pick him up to protect him with her own body from the hail of arrows. But he was ripped from her soft arms by stronger hands.

As he was lifted, wailing, through the air, he turned his head to strike out at whatever it was that was hurting him. What he saw made him recoil in horror—the dead-white face of a Puljani warrior! The man's lips were painted bright red, and jagged lines streaked down the cheeks.

His mother's screams stopped suddenly as strange hands carried the boy swiftly into the jungle. The world became a blur of green.

Soon, many miles up the path, they reached a small village. There, the warrior entered a bamboo shack and dumped the boy on the ground in front of a man of indeterminate race with a face as smooth as polished stone.

"The preacher's son?" the Strange One asked.

The Puljani responded quickly in a native dialect, bowing many times.

Apparently the Strange One was satisfied, for he motioned to a crate of rifles on the floor beside him. Grinning, the painted warrior lifted the box and carried it out.

The boy crouched on the floor, watching. With a syringe in his hand, the Strange One came forward and grabbed his arm. There was a sting. . . .

It was then that the veil fell upon the Agent.

A soft bell tinkled in the distance and the Agent felt a twinge of hunger. As if waking from a night's sleep rather than from a drug-induced coma, the

Agent opened his eyes. He was in a small room, nearly as old as time. It had been carved from stone. A jagged slit of light sliced through his chamber. As 13 looked away from the radiance, he realized he had known, even in his coma.

He had returned to the Shrine.

The bell rang, and he was a boy again, this time older, responding to the call for breakfast. For just a moment, he felt the twinge of a deep inner peace that he'd forgotten. He waited, his heart pounding, to be joined by his love, China White. . . . But she never came.

She had betrayed him.

Escaping the Shrine, escaping the evil he had discovered at its core, 13 fled, hunted and pursued like a wild beast. But, because of the training he'd received at the Shrine, he survived his trainer's best efforts to kill him.

Slowly, 13's eyes adjusted to the light. He peered out of the thin crack in the rock wall.

For a moment, 13 thought about escape, then smiled grimly. The Brotherhood would never let him go a second time. He briefly considered suicide, but that would be conceding defeat. He could not do that.

On unsteady legs, 13 hobbled to a door bolted into the rock. He tried the handle. It was open. As he suspected, they would not lock him in. Their prisons were far too subtle for that.

Stepping through the door, his eyes fell upon the sparse, yet rich symbolism of the Cloistered Garden. Composed of nothing but rocks, it was—nonetheless—of surpassing beauty. For each rock was of a different size, a different shape, a different color. And, to the trained eye, each shape, size, color had a meaning. The interrelationship of all formed the harmony of the whole.

Looking down, 13 saw the shape of peace. It

could not exist if it were not outlined by the shape for war, which itself could not exist were it not for greed and aggression, these two balanced by charity and restraint.

It was the garden of his childhood, yet it looked different to him now than it had then. It was as if the forces of Itsu had been disturbing the rocks, shifting the geometries, the way he had shifted the philosophy of the Brotherhood itself.

"Tredekka!" a voice thundered.

13 turned, hearing himself called by a name he hadn't heard in twenty-one years.

Spinning around, he stared into the dark, cold eyes of the Jinda-dii, the legendary High Priest of Serpentine Assassins. It was a familiar face, for the Jinda-dii had been his mentor long ago. It was the Jinda-dii who had indoctrinated 13 into the Brotherhood, teaching him the principles upon which all was based.

The Jinda-dii still possessed the face of a kindly mentor and wise sage—except for the eyes.

The Agent's expression did not change, even as mentally he reeled under the impact of memory and emotion. But the Jinda-dii instantly read the complexities of the Agent's emotions. He knew, at that moment, that the rumors were true. 13 had discovered "the Dark Truths." Those that went against everything—supposedly—he had been taught as a youth. Too late, he saw that his very soul had been twisted into the soul of a power-hungry fanatic. Too late? No, it had not been too late for 13. He had, after all, escaped.

"Jinda-dii," 13 said calmly in the Brotherhood's ancient language, "I assume it is no accident that we meet here."

"Long ago, Tredekka, I taught you that there is no such thing as an accident," the Jinda-dii responded, smiling a non-smile, then bowing.

"Then there is purpose in the fact that I am still alive," the Agent concluded.

"There is purpose to all. . . ."

"What is this purpose?"

"Because you are an initiate of the Brotherhood, there can be no subterfuge between us. It will be up to you. If you want truths, I shall tell them. If you want lies, I shall create them. The decision is yours and absolute."

Heads/Tails. Yin/Yang. White/Black.

There could, of course, be no doubt. "I want truth," 13 said firmly.

The Jinda-dii smiled slightly. "Of course you do, Tredekka. It was ever your shortcoming. Very well. You have been sentenced to the Serpentine Assassins. You will swear obedience to a Pagan Afterlife. You will drink the *mantha*, the oil of fire. When you die, the oil of fire will erupt in flame and consume you, leaving only ashes and a sooted air as testimony of your existence."

The Agent listened calmly. There was nothing he could say. There was nothing he could do. His mentor watched him calmly accept this horrible fate with pride, mingled with sorrow. The Jinda-dii had bitterly opposed this sentence. He felt like an architect watching a building he had spent years designing and perfecting being torn down before his eyes. 13 had been his favorite pupil, his most glowing success, his most horrible failure. Thus, he understood the necessity of the sentence. Thus the Jinda-dii would carry it out.

The blue eyes of the Agent and the dark eyes of the Jinda-dii looked deeply into each other. There was no emotion, both were well trained to conceal such things. But there was understanding.

Agent 13 knew there would no escape. . . .

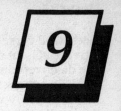

9

FRESH CLUES

A smartly dressed young woman ascended the granite steps of Bethesda Naval Hospital.

"May I help you?" asked a bulldoglike nurse who manned the reception desk as grimly as if it were the Maginot Line.

"Yes, please. I'm Kimberly Wirth, with the *New England Journal*." She flashed a press badge. "I'm here to see Kent Walters."

The nurse studied the woman closely. She was attractive and well-proportioned, her strawberry blonde hair was tied smartly in a bun, and her eyes flashed with a keen intelligence. She certainly *looked* like a reporter.

"Is he expecting you?" the nurse barked.

"Yes," the young woman replied, somewhat impatiently. "I'm certain my editor cleared it."

Reluctantly, the nurse lifted the phone. "This is reception. There's a Miss Wirth of the *New England Journal* here, *claiming* to have an appointment with Mr. Walters."

She paused, then, "Very well," she said in disappointed tones. She turned back to Miss Wirth. "You may go up—he's on seven."

"Thank you."

Inside the elevator, Maggie quickly went over her disguise. Long ago, Agent 13 had forged fake press credentials for Kimberly Wirth. This wasn't the first time she had gone after a story. Having been well versed in writing skills at the expensive private school she had attended in Chicago, Maggie discovered she had a real knack for reporting. At 13's suggestion, she had constructed a more solid cover by working up some genuine stories, and several had been published.

So, the name Kimberly Wirth wasn't unknown in journalistic circles. Phone calls to a few editors with hints that she had an interesting angle on the "Washington Massacre" won her a brief interview with Kent Walters, the National Security Advisor who had been one of only two survivors of the slaughter that had killed the nation's top law officials. Agent 13 had been the other.

Arriving on the seventh floor of the big military hospital, which was also used by important government officials, Kimberly Wirth showed her ID and press badge to several guards. She was then searched for weapons by a female officer. Finally, reluctantly, Kent Walters's aides let her see his doctor, who stressed that she must do nothing to upset the Advisor. Maggie promised and was at last permitted to enter Walters's room.

With her very first sight of the official, Maggie was impressed. Kent Walters was as handsome as the papers had made him out to be. Clad in a red satin smoking jacket, he was sitting up in his bed, going over a pile of reports. He looked up and smiled.

"Miss Wirth?"

"It's a pleasure to meet you, Mr. Walters. Thank you for seeing me." Maggie stepped forward to shake his hand.

"The pleasure is mine, my dear." He smiled warmly. "I was expecting some guy in a battered fedora and ready to devour me like a barracuda. Instead, I'm being interviewed by an angel!"

"Don't be so sure!" Maggie said, laughing. She

had heard that Walters was quite a ladies' man; she might be able to take advantage of that.

"Please excuse me if I don't get up," he said in slightly mocking tones. He gestured toward the heavy bandages on his legs as if they were mere nuisances.

"Of course," Maggie said, her voice unconsciously softening with compassion.

"But you may tell your readers that I'll be up in no time," he said.

"Sounds like a good quote for my story," Maggie replied, making a note.

"And just what *is* your story?"

"I want the exclusive on what really happened the night of the Security Council meeting."

Walters smiled again, only this time it was the smile he used for the press. "You're a little late—you can read the story in any paper."

Maggie raised one eyebrow. "You know, I haven't read one single article yet that mentions the Masque, his link to the Montana train accident or the Westron and *Hindenburg* disasters, or of the involvement of the Brotherhood, or a man known as Agent 13."

The smile on Walters's face vanished. With a visible effort, he regained his affability. "Someone has been filling your head with fairy tales, my dear. I'd be curious to know who."

Maggie was suddenly all business. "That's not important. Let's just say that I know." Maggie paused, then went on. "I'm not really here as a reporter, Mr. Walters. I'm here to give you some important information."

Walters sneered slightly. "Of course. And what is to be the price? A thousand dollars? Two?"

"Your help," Maggie replied coolly.

Walters blinked, then frowned, caught off guard. "Very well. What is your information?"

His voice was now colder.

"Dr. David Fischer has been captured by the Brotherhood," Maggie said.

Leaning back on his pillows, Walters shrugged. "Provided I even acknowledge that I know of this 'Brotherhood's' existence, why should it matter to me whether they have this Dr. Fischer or not?"

"Please don't play games, Mr. Walters," Maggie said sternly. "Time is running out. You are interested in Dr. Fischer because he is the developer of the Lightning Gun—a weapon you and General Braddock saw demonstrated in October, only one day before the massacre at your headquarters."

Walters stared at her thoughtfully. Finally, he sighed and said, "Very well. You seem to know all the answers. Perhaps you can give me a few. How sure are you about Fischer?"

"Very sure." Maggie turned abruptly toward the door. She thought she'd heard someone coming. Lowering her voice, she said, "They took him off the *Normandie*, just before trying to blow it up—" A sudden thought struck her.

"What else?" Walters urged.

"Uh"—Maggie was jolted back to her surroundings. "Oh, yes. I believe I know the identity of the Masque. What's more, she *may* be dead."

"She?" he asked, startled.

"The opera singer, China White."

Maggie had expected scorn at this statement. But Walters only looked grave.

As if reading her thoughts, he said, "No, that information does not particularly surprise me. We have noticed that she is often in the company of the powerful, those 'in the know,' so to speak. In fact, General Braddock was once involved with her." He was silent for a moment, then glanced up at her and nonchalantly asked, "By the way, what do you know of this Agent 13?"

Maggie was about to give a glib reply when the door to the room suddenly flew open.

"Eet ist time vor dinner, Mr. Valters," boomed a voice with a thick German accent.

Startled, Maggie turned to see a large nurse glaring at her from the doorway. The woman's face was odd—it was ugly, but a strange sort of ugliness. Nothing matched. Glowing eyes were contrasted with a pale, splotched complexion. Cracked, chapped lips split over remarkably pretty, pearly teeth. The nurse's hair was gray, her face wrinkled, but her hands looked soft.

"You vill haf to leaf, Miss Virth."

"Dinner can wait, Miss Stahlberg," Walters said coldly. "Miss Wirth can stay the allotted time."

"Really, Mr. Valters—"

"I said she can stay," Walters said in the voice that even Roosevelt had come to know meant "no argument."

With a muttered remark in German, the nurse left the room, shutting the door behind her.

"Do you have any political plans for '39?" Maggie asked Walters loudly, all the while jotting down a note on her pad.

Walters began a long-winded, canned speech, during which he read what Maggie handed him.

That woman is wearing a disguise!

Walters looked at her quizzically. Maggie nodded emphatically.

I'll have her checked out, Walters wrote back. *About Fischer, have you told anyone else this information?*

Maggie shook her head.

Walters wrote again, still continuing to speak on his future political career.

Don't. I have no idea who I can trust anymore.

What can I do? Maggie wrote.

Suddenly they both looked at each other. The

heavy footsteps of the German nurse could be heard, finally walking away from the door.

Meet with Braddock and find out what you can. He might be involved. But be careful! If Braddock is the Masque—he's very dangerous!

Shouldn't one of your people do that?

I told you! I can't trust anyone!

What if he won't see me?

Walters leaned over to whisper, "Then my office will issue you the necessary clearance. I wish I could do more, but I'm stuck in this damn bed. And I'm afraid that without any solid evidence concerning this 'Brotherhood' organization . . . Well, you can imagine what the President's reaction would be."

"What if I could get proof?" Maggie whispered.

Before Walters could reply, the door was thrown open with a crash. The Advisor glared angrily at the nurse, but Miss Stahlberg was armed and ready for him.

"Miss Virth, your fifteen minutes is up!" With a commanding gesture worthy of an opera, she ordered Maggie out.

Walters gave Maggie a rueful, little-boy look. "I can't fight doctor's orders. Sorry. I look forward to reading your article."

Maggie stood up. "You'll be the first to see it, Mr. Walters!" She clutched her notebook to her like a reporter with a scoop.

As Maggie turned to leave, she saw the nurse's eyes go to her notepad, then to Walters, who had nonchalantly spread his blanket over the notepad he had been using.

The nurse glared at Maggie and, for a moment, Maggie wished she had her pistol. But, since she couldn't fire a gun at this strange woman, she fired a phony smile instead, then walked out.

11

Ceremony Of False Hope

Agent 13 was locked in a small, cold, empty room painted stark white. It had no windows, no exits, other than the small door he'd been forced to crawl through. It had no feature of any kind that his eyes could grasp.

He had no idea how long he'd been in the unnervingly featureless room when there was a faint crackling sound behind him. Whirling, 13 saw that the far wall of the small room was on *fire!*

13 ran to the small cell door and pounded on it. But—even as he did so—he knew it was a futile gesture. No one would come.

The flames grew in intensity, though there was nothing in the room to feed them. He huddled by the far wall, then it, too, exploded into flame. Then the third wall, and the fourth—until 13 cringed in the center of the small room, the only place not ablaze.

Walls of heat seared him. The flames flared from all sides, sending the stench of burning flesh—his own!—to his nose. He pleaded to lose consciousness, to end the excruciating pain, but his own innate strength kept him aware, though screaming in horror, as the flames spread over his body. He saw his skin bubble and char, then slough off his raw arms in sheets.

The white-hot flames engulfed his legs, carbonizing them until there was nothing left but blackened bits of bone.

He could no longer hear his own screams. . . .

Suddenly—silence. Gentle, cooling wind . . .

13 was back in the subdued light of his stone chamber. The Jinda-dii sat cross-legged next to him, regarding him calmly.

"You see, Tredekka, the ultimate terror is inside your own mind."

13 looked at his arms and legs, then lay back, gasping with relief. Mental torture. The Jinda-dii was an expert at it. He was, after all, the designer of the Helmet of Truth—a diabolical device 13 remembered from his youth—and from just a few days before, at China White's "office" beneath a New York dive, the Brown Rat.

The Helmet of Truth could reproduce electrically what the Jinda-dii could produce with his own extraordinary mental powers.

Agent 13 felt savage rage well up inside of him. But he quickly repressed the urge to kill his tormentor. The Jinda-dii was the highest of the Serpentine Assassins. He would *know* what 13 was thinking and could instantly send the Agent on yet another journey to the unspeakable hell of Primal Fear.

"You still have a high tolerance for fire, Tredekka," the Jinda-dii was remarking with detached interest. "I remember that, from your childhood. But there are, of course, three other Primal Fears."

As the Agent looked into the Jinda-dii's face, a hideous transformation began. The teacher's skin turned brown and scaly, his eyes became dark slits, his eyeteeth lengthened into fangs. The hissing reptilian head swayed, its tongue flickering out.

His heart pounding, 13 slowly pulled his legs into a crouching position and crept backward, away from the pallet. Then, behind him, he heard another hissing sound.

13 peered back over his shoulder. He was surrounded by cobras! King cobras, the most intelligent and deadliest reptiles in the world! Their hoods spread, the snakes were ready to strike. Slowly, the slithering reptiles closed in on their target, their great, scaly bodies undulating toward him in hypnotic motions.

The Agent knew how to catch a cobra—lure it into striking at one of your hands, then grab it by the neck with the other.

Simple in principle, difficult in practice.

The first serpent struck, narrowly missing the Agent. He grabbed its head as it lunged past. The creature hissed horribly as the Agent crushed its skull with his bare hands, then threw the lifeless corpse away with a shudder.

The second serpent closed in.

Agent 13 had a sudden flash of perception. This is an illusion! He'd been hypnotized again!

13 stood stock still in the snake-filled chamber, an almost sneering smile of condescension on his lips. He was in control now. He would not again fall prey to an illusion!

Then he felt a whoosh of air like a whip streaking past, the sharp sting of two fangs entering the flesh of his leg. Pain shot through his body. His muscles contracted in convulsive spasms. He couldn't breathe.

13 saw an arrow whiz toward the cobra's hideous head as it reared back to strike again. Then the snake twisted and writhed in the throes of death.

Through the pain of his own approaching death, 13 saw the blurry images of three robed acolytes removing the other cobras with forked sticks.

An instant later, the Jinda-dii slammed him to the ground and injected antivenon into him.

13 heard the Jinda-dii murmur, "You must learn to distinguish illusion from reality, Tredekka," as he slowly faded into unconsciousness.

When Agent 13 awoke, his first sensation was remembered pain in his leg from two small puncture wounds. Looking up, he saw—of course—the ever-present Jinda-dii.

"You thought you were safe in the realms of illusion, did you not, Tredekka? Perhaps you are. Did you ever stop to think of that? Perhaps *I* am nothing more than illusion—perhaps this Shrine, everything . . ."

"Then perhaps I will surrender," 13 said wearily. "I will die, then it will not matter."

"No, Tredekka, you will not surrender as long as there is a single ray of hope. It is not in your nature to do so. And as long as you live, you shall see that ray. I will make certain of it. Therefore you will be mine for as long as I want. You will not be killed, nor will you die by your own hand. But, I can assure you, you *will* be broken!"

13 closed his eyes. He could do nothing now but wait.

The Jinda-dii made a sweeping gesture to the ground on which 13's pallet rested.

Sitting up the Agent looked around. It was familiar. It was the scented garden.

His heart ached. Long years ago, he had stood in this garden with the woman he loved—China White. Tredekka was the only name he knew then, and she was Carmarron. As the flowers in the exotic garden bloomed, so too did their love. But then he had discovered the "Truths." He learned of the central dark core of the Brotherhood. He learned that everything he had been taught to believe was a lie.

For long months, he kept his new knowledge a secret from his mentor. He continued to advance in his studies. Believing him to be one of them, they taught him the arts of torture and assassination. They taught him the arts he would someday use against them.

Always, he watched for his chance to escape. And then it came. But he could not go without her. And so, here, in this scented garden, he and his beloved Carmarron made plans to flee together.

Then, "Wait for me here," she whispered. "I must get my things. Then I will return."

His love for her overrode his good sense and very nearly cost his life. He counted the minutes, knowing how long it would take her. Then he began to grow uneasy. She was late. . . .

Still he did not leave. He *could* not go without her. Only when the figures in black—the assassins—appeared did 13 admit to himself that, yes, she had betrayed him. He lingered a moment longer, secretly hoping to die—death seemed so much easier than to live knowing she had given him to them.

But, 13 already knew his mission, and her betrayal just confirmed it. It was to destroy the Brotherhood and everything it stood for.

Agent 13 ducked away in the dark and fled into the snow-covered mountains surrounding the Shrine. Hours turned into days as he trudged through the white landscape. Then a blizzard closed in, and it took all of his skill to survive. But finally, even his will to continue eroded. Lying in a snowbank where he fell, he wrapped himself in illusory warmth and gave himself up to sleep.

His dream was one of great horror. He saw Itsu, the evil divider and slayer of Tog and Nof. He saw the Triad that controlled the Brotherhood of good destroyed, but he also saw hope. . . .

The dream shifted. He was in a sunny villa in Sicily. His body had been completely healed of its frostbite. His mind was clear. Standing over him was a grinning man with Chinese features. The man who had saved his life more than once. The man whose body had long ago been torn apart by sharks. Ray Furnow. . . .

The dream shifted again. Or was it a dream? Was it reality? He was back at the Shrine.

And then, China White appeared, bearing a pot of tea. She set it between the Jindi-dii and 13. Moving with elegant grace in her silken kimono, she knelt down beside them to pour the tea.

Agent 13 stared at her, breathless with longing. This was how he had remembered Carmarron—young, innocent, beautiful. . . . Their hands touched under the transparent china cup. She looked into his eyes, and he knew that nothing had ever changed between them.

As she rose and began to walk away, 13 found himself rising, too, but, after a quick, shrewd glance from the Jinda-dii, he sat back down.

"Life goes in circles," the Agent remarked, sipping the perfumed tea.

"It is the ceremony of false hope," the Jindi-dii replied. "In the last minute, I have reminded you of the one great pleasure in your life. A pleasure that could still be yours. . . ."

"What do you mean?" Despite himself, 13 could not keep a catch from his voice.

The Jinda-dii smiled. "Ah, there you see, Tredekka? You hope—still! It is impossible to torture one who has no hope."

Suddenly, it was dark—totally, absolutely dark. There was no sound, no wind, no light—only blackness. 13 felt the floor beneath his feet. It was curved upward slightly, as if he were standing in the bottom of a giant bowl. Its texture was smooth, cold, and hard to his touch—polished marble or perhaps metal.

Then he had another sensation—that he was not alone. Something was with him in the darkness, something evil. It was silent . . . waiting.

He sniffed the air. There was no smell. Reaching out with his senses, he tested the space around him. There were no vibrations, save for his own. Yet something told him he was being stalked in the darkness.

A chill shook him. He fought to get a grip on himself, knowing well what this was—the test of the Primal Fear of Darkness.

Something leaped at him!

He lashed out at the blackness—

—nothing.

There it was, behind him!

He lashed in another direction—

—nothing.

He began to move. . . .

Suddenly he was slammed to the floor by a powerful, clawlike object. Its stench was bestial, nauseating. He struck in its direction—

—nothing.

He felt a warm, sticky substance running down his face. He tasted it. Blood.

Frantically, 13 whirled about the blackness searching for *anything.* Even the horrid monster of his imaginings would have been welcome compared to this nothingness. And then the feeling of being watched passed. He was alone. Absolutely alone in the blackness. This is madness, he thought suddenly, coldly.

Feeling his way along the floor, he began to investigate the room. Following the floor carefully, he concluded that the room was indeed circular. He discovered that he could crawl perhaps thirty yards in each direction before the upward pitching of the bowl-like enclosure became too steep.

Suddenly he felt "it" again. Its fetid odor approached like a cloud of death. It seemed to be searching. . . . 13 lay flat on the curved surface, trying to be a less obvious target. But then—out of nowhere—it attacked. Grabbing his arm, it yanked with a sudden, violent force.

13 screamed in agony as his bone was snapped from its socket—cartilage and muscle tore, while tendons snapped like rubber bands. The "thing" disappeared into the darkness, carrying with it 13's left arm as a sort of gruesome trophy.

13 went into shock. The blood flowed from his mangled shoulder. Ripping his clothes, he hastily constructed a rude tourniquet to stem the flow of blood. Then he stumbled downward. . . .

And came to hole in the surface.

13 fought against the mists of darkness closing over him. He felt about the edge with his hand. A hole cut in the floor, about four feet in diameter. He put his hand in the hole. He could feel no bottom. He yelled down into hole. Seconds ticked by, then he heard a faint echo. But it was so faint, so distant. Did it come from his own mind?

This was a way out—but would it lead only to death? Wasn't he bound to die anyway? What did it matter?

Hope came the voice of his master. *Hope.*

Minutes ticked by. He waited, trembling in fear. The bleeding stopped. The pain in his arm had vanished. But he didn't notice.

Nothing was real to him. Nothing but the darkness around him and the hole . . .

The Primal Fears. He had faced three of them—fire, reptiles, and darkness. There was one more—

falling.

13 could sit in the darkness forever or he could ease himself into the hole, into the next unknown plane of existence.

Then he felt "it" again, coming back for him. He didn't move, there was no use.

A slimy, fetid clawed hand caressed him, tormenting him, prolonging the inevitable. He struck at the empty air as its rotted breath filled his nostrils. It was everywhere, nowhere. It began to suffocate him with its nearness. He couldn't breathe.

Crawling slowly to the edge of hole, he hesitated. Then, suddenly, he couldn't stand it any longer. The horror was too ghastly. He let go, sliding through the hole. . . .

As he plummeted into the darkness, he realized that it didn't matter if it was illusion or reality. He had made the decision for death.

He had surrendered.

A scream rose from deep inside of him as he fell, a scream of pain and anguish.

From somewhere deep in the nothingness came echoing laughter. "He is mine! He is mine!"

12

FURTIVE MOVEMENTS

The desk lamp shown brightly on the blueprints for Dr. Fischer's Lightning Gun. The light reflecting off the blue diagrams bathed the darkened area in cold, sinister hues.

China White stood in front of the massive desk. Beyond the bright beam of the lamp, she couldn't see to make out any details of the hooded figure who sat before her. She could only see his eyes, when he looked up at her.

"The capture of Agent 13 was worth the minor failure in the matter of the *Normandie*. And, you *did* bring Dr. Fischer in as well," the Masque said. His eyes gazed at the woman who stood before him. She was so incredibly beautiful. . . .

"Remarkable how quickly you recovered from your wound," he added softly, his gaze lingering on her left shoulder.

"The miracles of medicine," China responded coolly, smiling slightly at the lust in the eyes that stared at her. So—even the Masque was human. That bit of information might prove valuable someday. "It's ironic that he thought I was the Masque when he died."

"Died?" The Masque's eyes glittered. "You haven't been kept informed—13 is very much alive."

"Alive?" China's composure wavered.

"He's been returned to the Shrine."

China stared speechlessly at the seated figure. He was amused to see that she was so distraught. So she was still emotionally involved with this man. She would have to be returned to the Shrine for "re-education" after this mission.

"There are those who believe you are dead as well," China said coldly, aware that she had revealed too much of her inner feelings. Deep inside, she feared this man as she feared few others.

Behind his hood, the Masque smiled. "Soon, the entire world will know that I am very much alive." His eyes returned to the blueprints again.

China said nothing. She stood motionlessly, hoping he would say something more about 13 but not daring to ask.

"That is all," the Masque murmured, without looking up.

Turning, China walked, somewhat unsteadily, from the room.

Finishing with the diagram, the Masque glanced at the first draft of a script he had written. Clearing his throat, disguising his voice, he began to read the text from his second—and final—ultimatum. This one had to play well, for an entire nation would eventually hear it—after the investigation into the latest disaster. . . .

13

BACK IN THE FOLD

The Jinda-dii saw the strange irony of the scene being played out before him. Two men sat facing each other, staring into each other's eyes. One was Itsu, the Hand Sinister. The other was Agent 13. One possessed the decomposing face of death. The other, the bloom of life. But the living face was dead, devoid of will. While the dying face was very much alive.

The Hand Sinister suddenly turned his bright, black eyes upon the Jinda-dii. "I read your thoughts, my friend. You are right, this body is dying once more. Shortly, I shall be transported for *Juvita-ta*. But that will happen only when it is safe . . . or when it is absolutely necessary."

The Jinda-dii bowed. His thoughts had betrayed him and caused an embarrassment.

There was no movement or sound from Agent 13.

"As for this one," Itsu continued. "His gaze is dull. Is he ours?"

"Completely."

The Jinda-dii looked at the man who had once been known as Agent 13. His face was sunken and sallow. Though completely well and undamaged—the loss of the arm had been illusion, nothing more—in his eyes was the look of a man who has surrendered. Gone was the spirit, the fight, the defiance. Gone was any trace of the

Midnight Avenger.

He was Tredekka.

The Jinda-dii was overwhelmed with sadness. Though proud of his success—hadn't he broken the best agent the Brotherhood had ever produced?—he couldn't help but contrast the magnificent specimen this man had been upon arrival with the dull-eyed wretch who sat before them.

Itsu had no such qualms. "Will he carry out my mission?"

"Yes. He will carry out any mission. He has consumed the *mantha,*" the Jindi-dii answered.

"Good." Itsu turned to Agent 13. "Look at me, Tredekka." The man's eyes raised reluctantly to the leathery skull before him. "Your mission is to slay the woman who was your companion, your associate, your friend. She is getting much too inquisitive. She is too near the truth." Itsu smiled. "When the deed is done, Tredekka, you will wake up. In your normal mind, you will behold the terrible act you committed."

Tredekka nodded.

Itsu turned back to the Jindi-dii. "You have power over him?"

"Yes."

"Even in his normal mind?"

"No matter where he is, what he is doing—when I call, he will obey," the Jinda-dii said with pride.

Itsu nodded in satisfaction. "After he has suffered to the fullest," the Hand Sinister said, "we will call him back to our service."

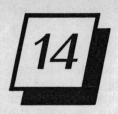

14

WORDS TO SQUIRM BY

As Maggie Darr had suspected, her reporter ruse didn't work when she attempted to gain access to General Braddock. As a result, she was forced to turn to Kent Walters's agency, who supplied her at his orders with the necessary papers.

But the young man who handed her the phony identification papers for Sara Sheldon, investigator for the National Security Council, made it painfully clear to her that she was operating on her own. If anything went wrong, Kent Walters would deny ever having heard of her. Even the National Security Council wasn't in the habit of intimidating high-ranking generals.

In the days that followed, Maggie did her research, trying to find out as much about the disasters and General Hunter Braddock as she could. In particular, she was checking up on the quick flash of insight she'd experienced when talking to Kent Walters in the hospital. As she had expected, disturbing patterns began to emerge. Not so much with the general, but with the disasters themselves.

At the Montana train crash disaster, for example, Maggie discovered through persistent phone calls and research, that there had orginally been *five* helium-carrying tank cars attached to the train behind the passenger cars. Only two showed up in the Masque's film. Only two had been found in the wreckage.

There were also three people missing whose bodies were never found, though all were believed to have been consumed in the fire that followed the collapse of the trestle into the canyon. One of the missing was Dr. Richard Taylor, a physicist, noted for his work in helium and other lighter-than-air gases.

Odd, thought Maggie—Dr. Fischer disappears on board the *Normandie* in the midst of what might have been a disaster. This Dr. Taylor vanishes in the train disaster. . . .

Quickly, she turned to the list of those killed in the Westron factory explosion and in the crash of the *Hindenburg*. Sure enough, the names of several scientists were on both lists. In each case, no remains had been discovered. That could have been explained by the resulting fires, of course. But might there have been another reason? Had anything else disappeared in these disasters, its loss carefully concealed, as appeared to have happened to the missing helium cars?

As Maggie reached for the phone to contact Kent Walters with her new suspicions, she reflected that undoubtedly General Braddock—China White's sometime escort—could shed additional light on the subject.

"General Braddock," the officious-looking female investigator began, "you have the option of reporting honestly to me here, in this informal inquiry, or being summoned officially to appear before the full board. . . ."

"Inquiry into what?" the gray-haired Braddock demanded.

"Inquiry into the Westron factory incident. I must warn you that if you are brought before the board, it will damage your record, regardless of the outcome. We have enough evidence—"

General Braddock leaned back in his chair, eyeing Maggie angrily. "Who the hell do you think you are, barging in here and threatening me?"

Maggie steeled herself. She was bluffing, and if she didn't play her cards just right, she would spend the next twenty years behind bars. Or worse. She recalled Walters's words to her in the hospital—*if Braddock is the Masque—he's very dangerous!*

"I'm with the National Security Council," Maggie said, "and with the backing of the highest authority—the very highest, General—I am conducting an investigation into the Westron factory explosion and other related events. Information has implicated you, General Braddock."

"Balderdash! What kind of information?"

"*I'm* the one conducting the investigation here, sir. But I will say it is substantial, otherwise I wouldn't be here."

"I'll give you five minutes, Miss Sheldon," Braddock growled, "then get out. As for Kent Walters, you can tell that bastard that he doesn't frighten—"

"Certain 'objects' were discovered missing after the Westron explosion. You failed to mention these 'objects' in your report of the incident."

Braddock's already red face went splotchy, with patchy circles of white in his heavy cheeks. He glared at Maggie without answering.

Maggie glanced inside a file folder, then referred back to the pad of paper in her hand.

"One of the projects Westron was working on was the development of a new, secret fighter plane. Several prototypes had been built. These outperformed anything the Germans have in the air. After the explosion, no trace of the plans or the prototypes were discovered in any of the wreckage. The Westron people were told that, in the interests of national security, they were to keep their mouths shut. Now, however, they have become convinced that it is in the best interests of national security to talk.

"What do you believe happened to those planes, General?" Maggie asked coolly.

Braddock swallowed. He looked deflated, like a balloon that has lost its air. "I'm sure your boss has drawn his own conclusions, but I suspect sabotage."

"But no trace of the planes was found. Don't you mean they were stolen?"

"No comment," Braddock muttered.

"Why didn't your report mention that?"

"Because it's a radical theory, damn it!" Braddock exploded. "How the hell do you steal thirteen damn airplanes? We have no evidence, no suspects. The last thing we wanted was a witch hunt. What with this talk of weird characters in masks—"

"Surely that wasn't the only reason," Maggie said, eyeing him sternly.

Braddock shifted in his seat. "Well . . . there had been problems with security at Westron. Suggestions had been made that things needed beefing up a bit."

"Who made these suggestions?"

"Hoover at the FBI. His boys are always coming by and telling us how to run our operation. They're annoying as hell."

"So what was done to tighten up security?"

"I made my recommendations," Braddock blustered. "I assumed the matter would handled."

"Was it?"

"I can assure you that those responsible have been—"

"In fact, they weren't," Maggie interrupted

firmly. "How did the explosion affect the project?"

"It set us back only a year. At the most."

"I see." Maggie pondered as she made her notes. The General was obviously guilty of gross incompetence, but whether of anything more remained open. He seemed to be admitting this all very freely—almost too freely. . . .

Glancing up, Maggie noticed a framed picture of a woman and two girls, presumably his wife and daughters, hanging on the wall behind him. By all reports, he was a happily married man.

"Tell me, General Braddock, are you an opera lover?"

Looking startled at this abrupt change of subject, Braddock snorted. "That screeching and yowling? Fat women in plate armor carrying spears?"

"Then how is it that you have been covertly meeting the noted operatic soprano, China White?"

Braddock's face went from splotchy to livid. "Th-that's a personal matter!" He rose to his feet. "You are stepping beyond your bounds, Miss Whoever-you-are! Tell your boss that. Any further questions concerning Westron, I will answer at your damn inquiry. But I will not be strong-armed or blackmailed by Walters or anyone else. Now get out."

"But, General—"

"That is *all*, Miss." The General turned and scowled out the window.

Maggie gathered up her papers and left. Was his behavior due to the fact that she had discovered a tawdry little affair or was it because of something else? . . .

The pieces were slowly fitting together.

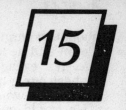

15

THE SERPENTINE ASSASSIN

Everything was familiar to Tredekka. Even the street felt familiar beneath his worn shoes.

It had been a long journey from the Shrine, one that had taken him thousands of miles, across countless borders. He remembered little about the first stages—they had kept him drugged. There were none who knew how to reach the Shrine. Few who knew how to find their way back once they had been there. Tredekka knew that this wonderful secret would be given to him, however—as soon as he had completed his mission.

But, for now he was back in Washington, walking through the streets that he knew so well, even though they were in a life that he recalled as something that happened to someone else. The garish colors of neon splashing across the damp walls and pavements—once this had given him some small enjoyment, he recalled. Once he had found time, even among his larger concerns, to appreciate such things. But no longer.

Everything was now categorized into four classes. Those that would help him to commit the murder, those that were of neutral relevance, those that might interfere with his mission, and those that might actively hinder him if he were not careful. Nothing else mattered.

Mentally, he rehearsed the murder he was

about to commit. It would be simple. He knew his victim and he knew her habits. Simple and savage. Yes, savage. Very savage. His place in the highest circle of the Serpentine Assassins—the Jinda-Gol—would then be assured.

He would need proof, something that would show the Jinda-dii that he had acted without passion, without mercy. Tredekka smiled. He knew what that proof would be. He would bring the Jinda-dii the woman's head. That, as nothing else, would prove his unquestioned loyalty. He would, once again, be recognized as their best. His would be the example for those beneath him to follow.

And there were many beneath him. Very like the sacred stairs that led one up to Itsu, the Hand Sinister, there were stairs leading to the Jinda-dii, the head of the Serpentine Assassins.

At the very bottom, not even really upon the stairs, were the *Jinda-Hai.* Hauled from the streets that were their homes, these wretches would do anything for money, drugs, liquor, or a combination of all. Typically, they would make quick brutal hits that appeared to be robberies or actions in a gang war. They were expendable. If a Jinda-Hai returned alive from his mission, it was a bonus.

Above the Jinda-Hai were the *Jinda-Nuul.* Their expertise was death in the night. They were poisoners—adept with ancient powders that caused heart attacks, viruses that would be transmitted in drinking goblets, and small, venomous creatures that would work their way into warm beds.

Above the Jinda-Nuul were the *Jinda-Gaan*—masters of persuasive killing. Practioners of brutal torture and ritual mutilation, they caused deaths that were meant to be examples to others, and so the killings were done in such a way as to gain as much publicity as possible. The theory behind this was that a single, effectively executed murder could stem or spark an entire revolution, start or prevent a war, bring law or chaos to a fledgling society.

At the apex were the *Jinda-Gol.* Well practiced in the arts of the other Jinda, the Jinda-Gol had a repertoire all their own. They were masters of deception and disguise. Able to change their appearance radically, they could murder with impunity, knowing that no eyewitness would ever be able to identify them.

Tredekka had been raised as a Jinda-Gol. This had given him the skills that made him such a deadly enemy as Agent 13. His abilities to melt into society and assume other identities had frustrated the Brotherhood's plans dozens of times.

Tredekka's capture and "re-education" had caused many of the Brotherhood's agents throughout the world to breathe a sigh of relief. Once again he was in their fold. Once again he was on a mission of their calling. . . .

Tredekka stood silently in mist-filled air of the winter night. Before him was the warehouse, the end of the journey that pulled him halfway across the world. A few feet and a few minutes away, his mission would be complete.

He began to walk briskly toward it.

Inside the warehouse, Agent 13's Washington lair, Maggie Darr sat at 13's old desk, poring over her notes. Her meeting with Braddock had yielded some interesting facts about not only the general, but also the Westron disaster itself.

Braddock had definitely been guilty of a cover-up, but the question was why. Was it to save his face or was it because of direct involvement with the Brotherhood?

And China White? Was the General just a worried man caught in an affair that could wreck his marriage? Was he a minion of China's? Was he her boss?

Maggie knew that there was one way to tell for sure whether or not Braddock was a Brotherhood agent. That was with the Seer Stone—the ancient stone that Agent 13 had stolen months earlier from the dead hands of a Brotherhood agent in Istanbul.

Its purpose was identification. Every top-ranking Brotherhood agent had an invisible tattoo branded on his palm. This tattoo was a number contained within the Brotherhood's symbol, "Omega"—meaning "the end." The tattoos were invisible to every known detection device except one—the Seer Stone. It was the only device that would absolutely confirm a person's membership in the secret, ancient organization.

The knowledge that Agent 13 was in possession of one of the stones had come as a severe blow to the Brotherhood. Thus, Agent 13 had hidden it carefully, telling no one—not even Maggie—where it was.

If only I could find it, Maggie thought longingly. Then, somehow, I could find a way to check Braddock. It would yield the "proof" she needed of Braddock's complicity to bring to Walters!

The phone rang.

Maggie answered, not saying a word—as had been Agent 13's habit.

"Miss Wirth, the National Security Advisor says to tell you that we have received a new filmed threat from the Masque. It is being examined by our department and the FBI. There will be a high-level meeting in two nights at Walters's country estate to discuss it. Please plan to attend."

"Yes, of course," said Maggie.

"Next, Mr. Walters has asked me to relay the information that there is a survivor of the *Hindenburg* disaster you might be interested in questioning regarding your theory—"

"Where?"

Giving her the hospital and the room number, the impersonal male voice clicked off.

Walters was starting an investigation of Braddock, she knew. But he was dubious about its outcome. Braddock was a long-time friend not only of FDR's but of J. Edgar Hoover's as well. Without absolute proof, Walters emphasized, their investigation of the popular general would be squelched instantly.

Hanging up the phone, Maggie stood for a moment, lost in her thoughts. Suddenly, she jumped and whirled about.

"Who's there?" she called out.

There was no answer. Of course not! She was in a well-protected room in an abandoned warehouse on a floor that didn't exist! How could there be anybody here? Shrugging, scolding herself for her irrational fears, she sat down.

But she couldn't shake the feeling. She was being watched—she knew it!

She had known it for weeks. The feeling had been especially strong when she had gone to interview Walters at Bethesda. She had experienced it once again while returning from her interview with Braddock. 13 had taught her the art of recognizing and losing a tail.

She tried all the tricks—stopping to look in store windows, going in a building and exiting through the back, even climbing out a restroom window. But she never saw anyone, and the feeling was always there. Now, here it was, haunting her in the supposed safety of 13's secret lair.

Then she heard the whine of the warehouse's freight elevator. Someone was coming up!

Maggie glanced at her watch. Someone coming to an abandoned warehouse at 1:36 a.m.? Her heart leaped as she scrambled to the back room and grabbed her Thompson submachine gun from the rack.

Maggie knew that the Agent had built escape passages into the lair, but she had never had reason to find out where they were. She had to wait and, if necessary, shoot her way out.

Heart pounding, she heard the elevator stop at the fourteenth floor—the floor above the lair. Then, she heard the special gear being manipulated, the gear that no one on earth knew about! It dropped the elevator down to the unmarked thirteenth floor! There was no time to reach the elevator doors and be ready as they opened for whoever it was. Better to find a safe and hidden spot inside the lair itself. See who it was first.

Maggie quickly switched off the lights, taking refuge behind a large wooden desk in the chemistry lab. Anyone coming through the secret entrance would be silouetted by the light from the fake office by the elevator.

She was the one with the advantage, Maggie knew. But fear of the unknown intruder began to well inside her. Her palms began to sweat, and her fingers fumbled as she fitted the steel drumload into the bottom of gun. The click of it being secured eased her fright a bit, but not much. She leveled the gun at the doorway.

The elevator doors slid open. The floor boards creaked slightly as someone stepped from the elevator into the fake office.

Maggie's finger poised on the trigger.

Wood creaked in the anteroom of the lair—someone walking across the floor. She started to tense her finger, aiming at the doorway . . .

Nothing happened.

For several heartbeats, she sat there, gritting her teeth, trying to keep her hands steady.

Then, the secret door to 13's sanctum flew open.

She almost fired, but 13's disciplined training told her—find out who it is, why they're here, if possible.

She waited for someone to step into the light.

But as abruptly as the door had opened, it closed again! She could see *no one*. Nobody had entered!

Then she heard the elevator start again! This time going back up to the fourteenth floor!

But why? Was it being sent up by the same person, to deliberately throw her off guard? Had someone come and—thinking the room empty—left?

Slowly, ever so slowly, the elevator reached the floor above and stopped, giving its usual recognizable clatter of machinery.

Breathing a sigh of relief, Maggie lowered her Thompson.

Then, a man stepped into the light glowing through the anteroom door. His head turned slowly as he looked around. She jerked her gun up again.

"Maggie?" the man's voice called. He raised his hands. "Don't shoot."

Maggie froze, not believing her ears. It couldn't be! He was dead beneath the Atlantic! No one could have survived that explosion, not even him!

"Maggie? I know you're here."

What could she do? The Brotherhood had tricked her before. What better way than this? But his voice. Having been around 13—a master of deception—she knew how difficult it was to mimic a voice . . . and this was perfect! It had to be him! But how?

Tears flooded her eyes. She had accepted his death, absorbed the pain she never wanted to experience again. And now he stood before her.

She had to know.

Rising to her feet, Maggie reached out to flip on the lights, her Thompson cradled and ready to send whoever-he-was to the afterlife for good. . . .

"Maggie!" he said as he moved toward her, arms outstretched.

It *was* him! She was one of the few to have seen his real face and this was it! Or else it was a clever disguise. . . .

"Stay where you are and keep your hands where I can see them," Maggie commanded, ignoring the tears that rolled down her cheeks.

"Good girl," he said approvingly. He stopped. Then, hands in the air, he turned and walked slowly over to the bookshelves.

"What are you doing?" Maggie demanded.

"Settling your nerves," he replied as he pulled an old book out from the upper shelf.

Keeping his movements slow and deliberate, both hands visible at all times, he opened the book, letting her see inside. The book was fake! It was really a box. Inside, glittering like a priceless gem, was the green Seer Stone.

13—was it he?—lifted out the Seer Stone and placed it on the desk. Then he backed away so that Maggie could get to it.

She walked over and picked up the stone. She held it to her eye, gazing through it at the palm of his right hand, which he displayed for her.

13!

Even if the Brotherhood had faked the tattoo on a bogus agent, only the real Agent 13 would have known where the Seer Stone was hidden.

Dropping the Thompson, Maggie ran into his arms, sobbing, as the tension, the fear, the loneliness ran from her.

"I'm sorry!" She buried her face into his shoulder while holding him tightly. It wasn't proper—the display of open affection for him was a clear violation of all of the unspoken rules he had forged in their alliance. But the man she loved was back from the dead!

She rested in his embrace as his strong arms wrapped around her, tightening in a passionate hug.

They kept tightening.

"Hey," Maggie teased, squirming, "you don't know your own strength—"

She looked into his eyes—and realized something was terribly wrong! His eyes were glare ice, cold, pitiless.

His grip tightened.

"No!" Maggie gasped in horror, struggling for breath.

She kicked, twisted, and fought, but none of her movements had any effect on his trained, killing embrace.

She felt the air being squeezed from her lungs. Her body tingled, not with passion, but with death. She was growing weak. The room began to spin, and darkness closed in. His steely expression, cold and murderous, was her last sight.

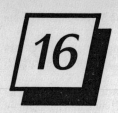

16

THE DEAD RETURN

When his victim had ceased moving for several moments, the Serpentine Assassin relaxed his grip. Holding the carcass of his prey, he felt her neck for a pulse.

There wasn't one. Good.

He let go of the corpse. She slid from his arms to the floor, landing like a pile of rags. He pulled out a sharp knife from his pocket and knelt down beside her.

Suddenly, a dark veil lifted within him.

The essence of who he was flooded back into Tredekka as if a dam had broken somewhere in his soul. He looked down at the corpse. . . .

"Maggie?" he whispered in agony.

Her vacant eyes stared sightlessly at the ceiling. She had died a brutal death. She appeared to have been crushed!

13 looked at the knife he held in hands. He began to shake, torn by horror and confusion.

Looking around, he saw that he was in his Washington lair. But how did he get here? Frantically, he sorted through his memories—the last thing he remembered was piloting the lifeboat from the *Normandie* into the path of the torpedoes. . . .

Or was it? He seemed to remember perfume, a soft voice, dark, sultry eyes, hands pulling him from the water. . . .

Then he knew! The Brotherhood! China had rescued him and given him to the evil organization he sought so hard to destroy! And they had turned him into a murderer!

Frantically, 13 tried all the lifesaving techniques he knew to restore Maggie to life. Again and again he felt for a pulse, to no avail. He put his ear to her cold lips, but there was no breath. Finally, in grim silence, he closed her beautiful eyes forever.

The Brotherhood had claimed another life, this time that of his most trusted assistant. Assistant? Who was he kidding? he asked himself bitterly, gently gathering the limp body into his arms and holding her close. How often had he longed to do this when she had been warm and alive, but he had forced himself to think only of his mission.

13 remembered the first time he had met her, how he had saved her from mobsters' bullets inside a church after she had avenged the death of her young fiance by killing one of their kingpins. He remembered the years she had helped him in his crusade againt the Brotherhood. She loved him, trusted him, and what had he done?

Killed her in the most horrible way possible—crushing her to death in his arms.

"Please forgive me, Maggie!" he whispered, bending his head to kiss her one last time. Then, he saw something—a small sliver, a tiny needle—little more than a thorn—protruding from behind Maggie's ear. The Agent knew what it was.

A blow dart.

A hand touched his shoulder. 13 froze. His eyes went to the hand. It was adorned with jeweled rings. Raising his eyes, he looked into the face of an old man. At least it seemed to be an old man. Or maybe not. The man's features were Asian. His age might have been somewhere between forty and sixty. His eyes were those of both jester and sage.

"Ray Furnow!" the Agent gasped. "You're alive?"

"It seem everybody think everybody dead around here," Ray said, nodding at Maggie's lifeless body. "We all think you dead, but Brotherhood bring you back to life as Serpentine Assassin."

Taking a small vial of brownish liquid from his pocket, he handed it to the Agent.

"You drink."

"What is it?"

"Too long to explain. But it counteracts oil of fire that you have been made to drink."

The Agent downed the foul-tasting liquid.

"I watch Maggie for many weeks now," Ray continued, "ever since she come off boat. She not know, of course. But I had thought you or someone else might come looking for her and the Seer Stone."

"Then why did you let me do this to her?" 13 asked angrily.

"The only way to bring you out of the hypnotic trance was to make you believe she is dead."

"*Believe* she is dead . . . " 13 echoed softly.

"I know well the ways of Hand Sinister and Jinda-dii. I know Serpentine spell lifted when you kill woman you love."

"Why?"

"You feel more for others then yourself. Pain and sorrow much greater, as you can see. He wants to punish you, wants you to hurt very badly. You be easier for him to get next time."

Ray Furnow knelt beside Maggie. "But you must be careful, for until you die and go to next plane or the Jinda-dii dies, he will be able to control you."

Ray pulled the tiny dart from Maggie's neck. Holding it up to the Agent, he said, "Laced with powerful drug, makes person seem dead. Only use small amount. She come 'round soon. She have one hell of a hangover, though."

Agent 13 was silent for a while, staring at Maggie thoughtfully. Then, he glanced at Ray.

"What did you mean—'next time' and 'control me'? How?"

"Many ways possible, but particulars not known. Rest assured, my friend, the Jinda-dii has key to your soul. It buried deep in your brain." He shrugged. "Maybe a gesture, a word. . . . You will become Serpentine Assassin again!"

"Am I—"

"—safe now?"

Standing up, Ray pulled the Agent to a small square cut into the wall. It was actually a window that looked like a normal brick from the outside. Ray pointed to the deserted street below. There, in the middle of the pavement, were two black patches of ash.

"Jindas," said 13.

"Yes. Sons of fifth wife make certain followers cease to follow. Contained within Jindas was most probably key to bring you back to Shrine."

Agent 13 looked curiously at his old friend. "Who are you?"

Ray grinned. "You know who I am. Balding Chinese man on the run from many wives—"

Agent 13 snorted. "Can it! Even that accent's phony! You know more about the Brotherhood than anybody—even me. Join me for good! Help me fight them!"

"The more you understand, the more you will understand," Ray said. "Did not Jinda-dii say that?" He shrugged again. "If not, he should."

"This is serious—"

Ray's grin vanished. "So am I, my friend. I no more capable of direct acts of aggression than Hand Sinister capable of direct acts of kindness. I save lives. I do not take them. I can make shields for you. But I cannot make spears. I can make fireworks. But not guns."

"But the Jindas on the street?" The Agent gestured. "Fireworks didn't kill them!"

"The work of my sons, who have sworn themselves to protect me. They are effective, but they are not the deadly assassins the Brotherhood has produced.

"A day shall come, my friend, when you will understand the reason for what occurs. For now, you must remember that you are the bridge, and in you lies our hope. Your solitude builds strength. Strength you will need on final day."

Ray knelt beside Maggie. "For now, take this as a sign that I am with you in other ways."

Ray's hand touched Maggie's neck in strange, gentle motions. Slowly, she began to move. Her eyes opened. Looking up, she saw 13. . . .

A wave of horror, fear, and rage contorted her face as she leaped up.

"Maggie—"

13 took a step nearer, only to be knocked from his feet by a flying spin kick. Lifting her foot, Maggie was about to smash it down onto his neck when he reached out, caught her ankle, and flipped her back to the floor.

"Ah, see," said a laughing voice, "I tell you, she have terrible hangover. . . ."

13 couldn't answer Ray. He had his hands full. Grabbing hold of Maggie, he tried to pin her arms to her sides.

"Maggie! Stop! I can explain—"

She bit him.

He loosened his grip inadvertently, and she

twisted away, staggering to her feet. He ran after her, caught her, and finally, exhausted, she sagged limply in his arms.

"I won't hurt you," he said softly. "Believe me!"

"Then let me go!"

"I'm going to let you go. But you have to relax."

"I'm relaxed." Maggie caught her breath with a sob.

He let go of her.

Instantly, she lunged for her Thompson.

He didn't stop her.

Grabbing the gun, she spun around and trained it on him.

"Now I want answers!"

"Ray, explain it to her," the Agent said calmly.

No answer.

"Ray?" 13 looked over at where Ray had been standing.

"What kind of trick is this?" Maggie sneered. "Ray Furnow's dead! Shark bait! You should remember! He died trying to save you—"

"Ray!" 13 yelled.

There was no reply. Looking around, 13 saw the room was empty except for the two of them.

"Well, then, I guess I'll have to explain it to you myself. Do you mind if I sit down?"

Maggie kept the Thompson leveled. Smiling at her, Agent 13 sat down. "You've no idea how great you look right now, Maggie Darr," he said softly. "Now, the last thing I remember was being dragged, half-dead, into an airboat. . . ."

"And so," he concluded, looking at her earnestly, "there is every possibility that I might turn into a Serpentine Assassin again—at any time. I might try to kill you again. Can you live with that?"

He sighed, looking down at his strong hands. "If

not, I'll understand. You can leave now, go somewhere where I can't reach you. I'll never bother you again."

Maggie had, long ago, laid down her machine gun. Now, in answer, she rose and walked up to him . . . and into his arms.

The lamps burned late in the lair that night as Maggie Darr told Agent 13 of her investigations into the disasters.

"The newspapers reported China White dead. She hasn't been seen—"

"She isn't dead," 13 said, his tone strained. Maggie—watching him closely—noticed this and sighed. "I remember seeing blood. You wounded her, when you shot her from the ship, but only in her shoulder."

Maggie changed the subject. "The Masque has issued a new ultimatum. There's a high-level meeting at Kent Walters's house day after tomorrow. I got a call from his office earlier tonight."

"I'll go there," he said. "You go to the hospital and interview that *Hindenburg* survivor."

Sighing wearily, Maggie laid her aching head on the table. "This is all so dark, so foggy!" she said. "Do we have a chance?"

"Hope, that's all we have," said Agent 13, wondering why that one word should give him a sudden shivering sensation.

17

GRIM REPORTS

On the first landing below the golden stairs that led to Itsu's towering throne in the Shrine, the Jinda-dii knelt. Raising a sharp dagger high in the air, he cried out, "The penalty for my failure is death!"

There was no answer from above. Bowing, the Jinda-dii put the dagger to his abdomen, preparing to disembowel himself.

The Hand Sinister heard his servant's words but paid no attention to them. His eyes were locked on the cathode image of the Masque that showed on the immense screen that hovered in the air above him.

"Do not worry, your Holiness," the Masque was saying. "Our plans are too far advanced for Agent 13 to be any threat to us. In fact, we might be able to use him."

"Your thoughts are clear to me," the Hand Sinister said. "I am pleased. Continue."

Itsu made a ritual sign. The Masque returned the gesture. Then the black and white picture swirled away.

The Jinda-dii had been waiting for this moment to rip his stomach open. Itsu's attention was now fixed upon him. The Jinda-dii ordered his arms to drive the dagger deep into his stomach. His arms, blocked by an outside force, refused to obey the order.

"Suicide is the act of a coward," the Hand Sinister said.

The Jinda-dii looked up at the being who held sway even over his own body. He tried to respond, but, as his hands were frozen, so too was his tongue.

"You may well die a hideous, screaming death," Itsu continued, "but it will not be by your own hand." The Hand Sinister gestured. "Go now. Continue your duties until you are summoned. Carry with you the knowledge that your work was good, but mighty forces interceded to save the Agent."

With that, the Jinda-dii's muscles went limp. The dagger clattered to the floor, as did he.

Moments later, he gained full control of himself and began his long trek down the staircase. Death might have been preferable, thought the Jinda-dii, than to have to live on under the spectre of failure.

18

Thirty-Six Hours to Doomsday

It was well for the law enforcement agencies that Agent 13 had not turned his superior talents to criminality. As it was, he was able to penetrate Kent Walters's heavily guarded house with only two things—Senator Tom Hanover's face and ID card.

Several years ago, Senator Hanover had faced complete and total ruin. Compromising photographs arrived in the mail, showing him engaged with several young women in certain recreational activities that neither his wife nor his public would condone. These photos would be sent to the papers and his family unless Hanover agreed to vote a certain way on matters of defense.

Hanover was innocent. It wasn't him in the pictures—it was a man disguised as him. But he knew no one would ever believe him. After all, politicians were notoriously corrupt. Yet, he was an honest man. He could no more sell his vote than he could sell his soul. Alone, without anyone to turn to, Hanover took a gun out of his desk drawer and contemplated it thoughtfully. One bullet in the head and he would never live to learn if he might ever be tempted to give in.

Then a man had stepped into his office through a door the senator had thought was locked. He was a strange man with a nondescript face but intense, penetrating eyes.

"Put the gun away, Senator," he said. "If you've got the guts, we can fight them—you and I."

And thus Tom Hanover met Agent 13, and thus began a terrifying race against time through some of the worst parts of New York City that ended in the capture and conviction of a local mobster with ties to War Department contracts. Hanover's reputation was saved. Indeed, he became a hero when his part in the daring capture was revealed.

But he had learned enough to know—as did Agent 13—that this hood was but a pawn in a bigger game. And so Tom Hanover became one of 13's most loyal associates in his fight against the Brotherhood. When 13 learned that Hanover had received an invitation to Kent Walters's top-level meeting, he had called the senator and asked to assume Hanover's identity. The senator had been only too pleased to comply.

The police officer at the door was apologetic. "I am sorry, Senator Hanover, but because of certain extraordinary circumstances, we have been ordered to frisk everyone for weapons."

"What circumstances?" the Agent asked casually, submitting to the search gracefully. The cop did his job well. It would have taken an expert, however, to discover the cigarette lighter that turned into a small pistol with explosive bullets.

"Sorry, sir. I can't discuss it."

"Sure!" Agent 13 shrugged, but he was uneasy. This seemed an extraordinary precaution, when everyone here tonight was here by invitation only.

"Thank you, Senator Hanover," the cop said, motioning him on into the foyer of Walters's home. As more uniformed officers took his overcoat, 13 looked around, absorbing his surroundings. Walters's country house was both tasteful and lavish, he noticed.

Though the Agent's disguise came so near to perfection that even Tom Hanover's own family might not have recognized him, 13 had not had time to perfect the little gestures, facial expressions, the hundred other things that made up Tom Hanover. Therefore, he had to avoid contact with anyone who might know Tom intimately.

As the other guests filed through a corridor to the large study where the meeting was to be held, Agent 13 stayed at a table in the living room, apparently absorbed in a number of files.

"Tom, my boy!" a voice shouted.

Agent 13 looked up. The speaker's face was soft, his face fat and jowly. His eyebrows were raised in an expression of perpetual surprise, and his mouth hung half-open, awaiting Hanover's response, giving him a dull-witted look that contrasted with his keen, intelligent eyes.

He was Chester Hallet, one of the men who had helped Tom Hanover rise in his political career.

Agent 13 sensed danger. What on earth was Hallet—purely a behind-the-scenes farmer politican—doing at a meeting to discuss national security? Rarely was the Agent caught unprepared, but he had never questioned Tom Hanover concerning Chester Hallet. 13 made a casual response, hoping to gather information as well as keep his conversation to a minimum.

"Chester! I never expected to see you here!" The Agent awaited a response, hoping Hallet would explain his presence.

But Hallet only looked at him shrewdly. "Figured *you'd* know—if anyone! C'mon, Tom. Don't play it close! What's the reason behind all this?"

13 hesitated, making it appear as if he was considering whether or not to reveal his information. Suddenly, they were interrupted.

"Excuse me, gentlemen," a police officer said.

"But the meeting is about to commence."

Nodding to Hallet, Agent 13 rose to his feet.

"Guess we'll all find out soon enough," he said with a short Hanover laugh as he walked into the large study that had hastily been converted into a screening and lecture room.

Looking at the group gathered there, however, 13 wondered himself—why had all these diverse people been invited? There were highly placed government officials mingling with pig farmers like Hallet. There were top lawmen rubbing shoulders with military brass. 13 was growing more and more uneasy. He knew that if the Masque wanted this whole group of people dead—dead they'd be, in a matter of minutes.

There was nothing he could do but find a seat in one of the chairs lined up before a lectern. Behind the lectern was a movie screen.

When all were seated, the ambient voices hushed as the door on the far side of the room opened and the Kent Walters, National Security Advisor, entered. He was seated in a wheelchair, pushed by a young, muscular attendant. Though the recently wounded official was doing his best to appear on the mend, 13 noted that a doctor and a nurse hovered at a discreet distance.

The fifty or so guests gave Walters a round of respectful applause. A weaker man, having escaped death by a hair's breadth, would have gone on leave of absence or even resigned. But Walters kept going, seemingly filled with a new resolve.

"Gentlemen, let me begin by assuring all of you that I appreciate your coming tonight. We have done everything in our power to provide the best security available for all of you." An uncomfortable silence blanketed the room. "And, in an effort to minimize the risk, we will keep this meeting short. We'll start with the screening."

As the lights in the room went out, the loud whirr of a projector tickled the air.

The crisp gray lines of a small battle cruiser—the USS *Trent*—appeared against the darker gray of the ocean and sky. It remained in their view for several moments, then the camera shifted its angle to show an incredible-looking weapon. While many faces present registered skepticism, even amazement, at the sight of the weird contraption, Agent 13 stared at it grimly, recognizing it easily—Dr. Fischer's Lightning Gun!

13 gritted his teeth. The Brotherhood had constructed the full-size version of the device much faster than he had expected! Even as he watched, the Lightning Gun fired. The *Trent* exploded in a ball of flame.

At that moment, a hooded face appeared on the screen, superimposed against the burning ship. Whispers of surprise rustled through the room among those who had not seen the Masque before. The enigmatic figure spoke.

"Again I have perpetrated disaster. Will you continue to ignore my demands? Oh, I know you are searching for me. But you have been for weeks, with nothing to show for your best efforts! Fools! Do you think you will be more successful this time? You don't even know who I am! You don't know where I am! And, you do not have one single lead!"

No one moved, everyone in the room apparently transfixed by the mysterious shrouded face on the screen.

"No, you do not have any clue as to who I am. Maybe you have seen me on the street. Maybe some of you even know me! But what must concern you now is this question: where am I going to strike next? I think, by this time, you accept that I can strike wherever and whenever I choose.

"I assure you that it will be in your best interests to give in to my demands. As you have seen, I am willing to kill for my cause. Are you willing to die for yours? Are you willing to sacrifice your sons, your daughters? Are the voters who control your destinies willing?"

The baiting voice was silent for a moment. Then, in a quiet tone, almost tender, the Masque continued. "Sometimes, it takes men of great strength to admit defeat. I ask that you show that strength tonight. I do not want to kill more."

Many of those in the room, 13 among them, looked around uneasily. As if reading their minds, the Masque went on in an amused tone. "Do not worry. You need not fear an attack upon your meeting. It is my belief that you men present here, and you alone, can advise President Roosevelt to listen to reason.

"And now—my warning: During the State of the Union Address on Tuesday night, your President will announce that he will immediately dismantle all aggressive weapons in the United States, or I will unleash a horror upon this nation the magnitude of which has never been seen before!"

The film end flapped and the projector's bright light glared on the screen. The room lights came on. At first, there was silence, then a low rumble of muffled conversation began. A tall, thin man with grayish skin, gray hair, and silver wire-rimmed glasses stepped up behind the lectern.

13 didn't recognize this man, who spoke with a thick, German accent. "Before ve get on with this meeting, ve vill be taking one precaution. Ve vill be checking your fingerprints before you are allowed to leave."

The murmur in the crowd turned to outrage.

"First searched by cops," muttered one, "now this! Do they think one of *us* is this Masque?"

"Who are you?" A challenging voice called to the speaker.

"I am Dr. Arthur Eisenstaadt, Department of Forensics—"

"Take your brownshirt tactics back to Germany. We don't have any use for them here!"

There was scattered applause. The combination of the terrible threat, plus the nervousness of everyone in the room was apparently finding an outlet. Seeing things getting rapidly out of hand, Kent Walters wheeled his chair to the front.

Picking up a gavel, the pale government official pounded on the lectern with remarkable strength for a man so frail. Those in the room slowly fell silent.

"Yes, Senator Hanover?" Kent Walters said coldly as the disguised Agent 13 rose to his feet.

"Mr. Advisor, it will take hours to analyze every fingerprint in the room! Surely you don't suspect one of us of being the Masque? Everybody here knows everybody else. I say that each of us vouches for everyone in the room he knows!"

There was a muttering of approval. Then the crowd was silenced once more by the insistent hammering of the gavel.

"Silence!" Walters glared at them sternly. "There is one element to the assassination attempt at my agency's headquarters that was intentionally left out of the newspaper reports. One other person was present in that room. One other person survived—Agent 13."

The room buzzed—incredulous, curious, disbelieving, dubious, scornful.

So that's it, thought 13 grimly.

"What's that got to do with us?" cried out one.

Walters went on. "As you may have heard, the

Agent is a master of disguise. He could very well have taken on the appearance of any man in this room. In our first encounter with him, he drugged the GS-7 projectionist and took his place. I believe he is in this room right now. And if he is, he knows something—something vital about this case. We want to talk him—now!"

Agent 13 frowned. What was Walters's game? He knew that 13 was trying to help them with the case—he had implied so to Maggie. He knew 13 wasn't involved in the assassinations. Why was he trying to nail him?

"Tom Hanover" stood up again. "Why are you after this Agent 13?" asked the disguised Agent 13. "Aren't there more important things we should be doing?"

"Because it is my belief that Agent 13 is the Masque," said Kent Walters.

Agent 13 sat down. Not often in his lifetime had he been stunned, but this new twist had taken him completely by surprise.

"Bear in mind that I have no evidence that Agent 13 really is the Masque," added Walters. "But, as I said, I believe he possesses valuable information that he has not passed on to us. So let me lay down a challenge to him, if he is indeed in the room with us"—the National Security Advisor's eyes scanned the crowd—"Agent 13, come forward, and I personally offer you immunity from all prosecution. If you are indeed aligned with the forces of good, then you are in good company in this room. Step forward that we might know you."

13 knew now that no one would protest being fingerprinted. He could have been prepared for this situation by matching Hanover's prints by any of a hundred techniques, but he had not foreseen this drastic turn of events. One by one, he

eliminated each idea he had.

Walters sighed. "Let it not be said that I did not give Agent 13 adequate opportunity to ally himself with us. We can only assume, therefore, that he is against us. And, if he is in this room, we will capture him!"

With that, two efficient-looking Army lieutenants stepped up and gestured to the crowd to form a line from the front desk, extending past windows overlooking a beautifully manicured garden. Agent 13 stood next to a grumbling Hallet.

13 had to get out of here! Precious time would be lost while he endeavored to explain to the authorities who he was and what he knew. His freedom was the only chance these people had against the Masque!

He hoped he could escape without killing anyone, but 13 had long ago sworn his Code of Death—if his mission was imperiled, he would kill if necessary for the greater good.

Reaching into his pocket, the Agent felt the solid weight of an expensive cigarette lighter—a real lighter, not the gun. Unscrewing the fuel reservoir of the lighter, 13 pulled it out as he brushed up against a beautiful curtain. Then 13 "accidentally" allowed a thin stream of the fluid to dribble down the fabric. Glancing around, he made certain no one was looking at him. Hallet was scoffing with the Secretary of State over the proceedings. He didn't believe any of it—not this Masque, not this Agent 13.

Good. No one was paying any attention to him. 13 pulled out a pack of cigarettes and proceeded to light one.

Inhaling deeply a couple of times, he then bent down to adjust his shoelace. Swiftly placing the cigarette next to the dampened curtain, he stood back up. The line had advanced forward by several feet. Casually, Agent 13 moved away from the curtain. He had calculated that it would take about one minute for the fabric to catch.

The line moved slowly. Agent 13 glanced at his watch. His eyes caught a small stream of smoke curling up from the curtain. One man, near the window, sniffed, frowning. He looked around. . . .

"Fire!"

Within seconds, the chemically-treated curtain material had burst into flames! The flames spread quickly. As everyone in the room reacted to the fire, 13 ducked back against the wall and inserted one end of a bent paperclip into an empty electrical socket. Again checking to see that no one was watching him, he jammed the other end in with an abrupt flick of the back of his hand. Sparks flew. The lights in the room went out.

In a high, shrill, panic-stricken, Tom Hanover voice, Agent 13 shouted, "My God! It's the Masque! We're trapped!"

Drawing his lighter-gun, 13 fired several shots into the air. That was all that was necessary. Within seconds, everyone was shouting "The Masque! Another massacre! Burned alive!"

In vain, Kent Walters pounded his gavel and yelled for calm. In vain the guards endeavored to stop the surge of terrified men that rolled over them to the door.

Within moments, all was over. The only sounds that could be heard were outside Kent Walters's house—the calls for chauffeurs, the slamming of car doors, the roaring of engines and the shouts of the policemen who were searching the grounds for assassins that didn't exist.

The fire was quickly brought under control, Kent Walters was helped back to his bed and given a sedative after the excitement, and Agent 13 vanished into the night.

19

MAGGIE'S SCOOP

Maggie Darr entered room 417 of the Georgetown University Hospital. A nurse, following her, switched on a soft light. Maggie's eyes fell upon the contours of a body swathed in bandages like a mummy. A moaning sound from down the hall made her shiver, while the ubiquitous smell of hospital disinfectant, which seemed to also carry the mixed emotions of fear, desperation, joy, stung her nose.

Maggie sat down opposite the mummy in a tubular hospital chair. Much to her surprise, the mummy's eyes were wide open. Maggie leaned forward in the chair.

"Mr. Hendricks," said the nurse, "this is Kimberly Wirth, the reporter from the *New England Journal.* The doctor said she could stay five minutes. Do you feel up to talking to her?"

"It's extremely urgent," Maggie said, her voice soft with pity she did not have to feign. "I must talk to you about one aspect of the *Hindenburg* crash. . . ."

The mummy nodded and the nurse left the room, softly shutting the door behind her.

"Now," Maggie began, "I need to know if you remember anything about a scientist named—"

"The cause can be summed up in one word," came a weak voice through a hole in the thick gauze wrapping. "Hydrogen."

"I beg your pardon?" Maggie said, blinking.

"Hydrogen!" snapped the mummy irritably. "If they had used helium, there wouldn't have been any explosion, and I wouldn't be a burned sausage. The blasted ship was designed to run on helium, but the U.S. banned all helium sales to Germany and so they used hydrogen."

"Yes," Maggie murmured, "but about the scientist— His name was Wulfgang Heidelberg. He was an important airship designer, traveling on the Zeppelin. His body wasn't located, and I was wondering—"

"I'm considering suing, you know." The mummy's voice overrode hers. "Over the helium. You can print that. . . ." His bandaged fingers fumbled for a buzzer by his side.

"Here, let me," Maggie said, leaning over to help.

"Thank you," the mummy said. Maggie pressed the button. A soft buzzing sound echoed down the corridor.

"Is there something I can do for you?" Maggie asked.

"The nurse will take care of it," the mummy answered.

The door to the room swung open. Maggie turned slightly—and froze in her seat. Entering the room was the German nurse! The one she had seen with Kent Walters at Bethesda! Instantly, Maggie's hand went for her purse.

"No, no, Miss Darr. I know you are not going for your lipstick."

Turning, Maggie saw the "mummy" holding a Luger with a silencer attached. The bandaged figure motioned. "Put your purse on the floor, slowly. Now, Miss Darr, have no illusions. Bodies come and go out of this hospital every day. Yours would be just one more."

"I don't understand," Maggie said, forcing herself to maintain her cover. "I'm not this Miss Darr! You've made a mistake! I'm Kimberly Wirth! This—this nurse can identify me!"

"I most certainly can, Miss Maggie Darr," said Nurse Stahlberg, stepping toward her, one hand held behind her back. Slowly, that hand emerged. Light flashed off the long, thin needle of a syringe as she grabbed hold of Maggie's arm. . . .

Slowly, Maggie Darr became aware of the low whine of engines, the rumble of propeller blades, and the bumping of minor air turbulence. It took her a few moments to collect her senses. Then she remembered! The nurse! The mummy! A stinging sensation in her arm. . . .

Opening her eyes, Maggie stared up into the face of the most terrible creature she had ever seen! It was a giant! In the semidarkness of the interior of what Maggie realized was a transport plane, the giant's features seemed horribly distorted and unreal.

For a moment Maggie wondered if she were going mad. Could this being really exist? Was it something she dreamed? Was she still dreaming?

Then she saw the giant turn around and heard him shout something into the rear of the aircraft.

Maggie struggled to sit up, but she discovered that she was strapped to a stretcher.

A cigarette seemed to dance in the air like a firefly. Then the cigarette's owner emerged from the darkness of the plane. Even in the poor light, there was no mistaking that stunning beauty. . . .

"Who are you, darling?" the voice asked.

"I'm sure you rifled my purse and know exactly who I am!"

"Ah yes, Kimberly Wirth, ace reporter for the *New England Journal*," China White replied.

Filled with hope, Maggie drew a deep breath. Had China White ever seen her? Hurriedly, she thought back. She and China White had seen each other on the *Normandie*, but there had been the smoke, the shooting—and Maggie had been disguised as Mrs. Plotkin. . . . Maybe China *didn't* know her!

"Look, I don't know who you are or who you work for, but you're not going to be able to keep the *Hindenburg* sabotage secret for long," Maggie said, trying to keep up her cover. "If I don't crack this case, another reporter will. Or maybe the police. My editor knows what I was digging for. If I vanish, he's going to go to the FBI. Hoover himself'll start looking around in this *Hindenburg* thing."

"Oh? Suppose your editor doesn't live to tell Hoover what story Kimberly Wirth was working on?" China White asked in an amused voice. "Suppose, like you, he has an unfortunate accident?"

Maggie swallowed. She had a feeling they weren't discussing newspaper editors anymore. But she had no choice but to keep on. "There are others who know," she said loudly.

China White laughed. It was a strange laugh, at once operatic, piercing, ecstatic, and joyless. "He trained you well, my dear."

Maggie's soaring hopes crashed. China White was playing with her as a cat plays with a mouse before killing it.

"You love him, don't you?" China White said, sitting down next to Maggie and regarding her with a look that was cool, condescending.

Maggie said nothing.

"Do you think he loves you? Because he doesn't, you know. I think you should resign yourself to exile from his heart forever."

Maggie could not let this woman see her weakness. Tossing her head on the pillow, she put on her best Scarlett O'Hara act. "Ah really don't know what y'all are talkin' about, ma'am. I don't share intimacies with folks I've just met. Why, we've never even been formally introdu—"

China's beautiful face hardened. "The tougher you act, the weaker you will become. We need no introduction. You know me. You've seen me countless times. And each time you have wondered if the Agent loves me still. And, in your heart, you knew the answer. Each time you have felt the absence of 13's love for you, you have felt the presence of his love for me!"

Maggie looked at her coldly. "I don't know what you are talking about—"

China ignored her. "I am taking you to a place where they have elaborate tortures. They will ask you where his lair is and you will tell them. Oh, yes, my dear—you'll tell them, anything they want to know. But, right now, I'm going to indulge in a little torture of my own. It will, perhaps, be much more painful than even the Helmet of Truth. I will tell you of my affair with Agent 13."

"Keep your dirty little secrets to yourself!" Maggie said, but she couldn't keep her hands from clenching.

"It was at the Shrine." China's eyes stared out through the aircraft windows. The sky was gradually getting lighter. It was near dawn. "Has he ever told you of the Shrine?"

"It has been mentioned in passing," Maggie responded sarcastically.

Still staring into the distance, China went on, as if in a trance. "It was a wondrous place. Truly ancient. Hallowed. I have no idea where it is. It has been hidden for millennia and will probably remain so forever. Its physical beauty is as overwhelming as the mystical energy that surrounds it. It is a place of dreams . . . but it is also a place of nightmares."

China was silent for a moment. Curious despite herself, Maggie listened in pain.

"All societies train women in the arts of seduction, just as all societies train men in the arts of warfare. Some accomplish their tasks better than others. The Brotherhood—the most ancient society on earth—does both jobs superbly. Rare is the man who could resist me—"

"They must have skipped the courses in modesty," Maggie muttered, to keep up her own spirits. Inside—as China had predicted—she was writhing in agony.

China went on. "As a final test of our skills, each of the female acolytes in the Shrine was given a male to attempt to seduce. It was a deadly game, for if the male were seduced, he would be forced to undergo an ordeal of courage in the desert—an ordeal most did not survive. If the female failed, she was disfigured, becoming a grotesque, hidden operative of the Brotherhood. You met one who failed, in fact. Once Nurse Stahlberg was one of the loveliest women in the world. You noticed she was disguised. Little did you guess why. . . ."

China shrugged and snuffed out her cigarette. Then she went on more briskly. "Be that as it may. I was given the most difficult target—Agent 13. For week, months, I lured him with every charm I had been taught, plus those natural charms I have developed on my own. He resisted me. Then the unforeseen happened. I fell in love with him. I was about to concede failure when, one day, I looked into his eyes in an unguarded moment and realized that he loved me, too!"

Maggie gritted her teeth, forcing herself to lie perfectly still. This woman must not see her pain!

In China's luminous eyes, Maggie could see that first, innocent love reflected there still, undimmed by time.

China sighed softly. "One night, we met in the garden. We could resist our urges no longer. He held me. We kissed. And then, we started to part. But the priests, who had been watching us, leaped out and caught hold of me, accusing me of failure. 13 lied for me then. He told them I had been successful, that he had fallen victim to my lures long before that night." China smiled.

"He lied to spare my beauty. They took him away and sent him into the desert for his ordeal. Do you see what he did, Maggie Darr? He willingly gave up his life for me. But the gods favor those with reckless courage. One by one, he eluded all the men who hunted him. When he returned to the Brotherhood, he was hailed one of the greatest agents ever. But he knew them, then, for what they really were.

"When he had the chance, he came to me, asking me to escape with him. I agreed, of course. When I went back to my chambers, however, the priests were waiting for me. They offered me a choice—love or power. Agent 13 or the world. I need not tell you which I chose."

"Slut!" Maggie shouted. "He may have loved you when he was a boy, but now he is a man! He may have protected you then, but now you've been disfigured by the ugliness around you! He sees you for—"

The palm of China's hand caught Maggie across the jaw. The pain from the blow brought tears to Maggie's eyes, but she had the satisfaction of seeing the beautiful, dark, luminous eyes of the opera singer glisten with tears as well.

20

Intruders In the Sanctum

Late that night, the cab left Agent 13, no longer disguised as Tom Hanover, several blocks from his Washington lair.

"Thanks," he said, stepping out and handing the driver a tip.

"Thank you, boss!" the young Chinese driver said, grinning.

By the light of a street lamp, 13 looked at him closely. There was something vaguely familiar about that grin— But before he could say a word, the cab shot off into the night.

"Son of wife number seven, no doubt," Agent 13 said to himself with a smile. By turning up his collar, crumpling his hat, and picking up an abandoned whiskey bottle, 13 turned himself into a drunken derelict. Then, weaving and singing a ribald song, he stumbled down the street toward his refuge.

Coming within sight of the lair, 13's song died on his lips. The American flag was flying over the warehouse!

The signal! Intruders! Someone had broken into the sanctum!

His mind raced. They could have found out the location of his lair from only two sources—Ray and Maggie! He immediately discounted Ray. Mystery man though he was, Furnow had proven his loyalty time and again. 13 trusted Ray now, as he trusted only one other person—Maggie.

Somehow, the Brotherhood must have captured Maggie! And they had made her talk. Bitterly, he cursed them. Maggie was strong. But no one was strong enough to hold out against the Brotherhood's hideous tortures. Even he had succumbed.

At least they had not caught him unprepared. Knowing that someday the secret of his lair might be revealed, Agent 13 had devised a safety measure in the elevator known only to himself. Unless the elevator remained on the fourteenth floor at least thirty seconds before descending to the thirteenth, a small lever would be activitated that triggered a network of defenses. One of these was the automatic hoisting of the American flag on the roof to warn him that the security of his lair had been violated.

Knowing that guards would most probably be positioned around the building, Agent 13 slipped into a tenement house across the street and climbed to the roof.

From that vantage point, 13 could see a black Chrysler stationed behind the warehouse with two triggermen holding grease guns. They watched over the back entrance, where yet another guard hid in the shadows by the frieght elevator door.

Despite the fact that they looked like typical thugs, they were probably the lowly but deadly members of the Jinda-Hai.

Agent 13's mission was delicate. He had to destroy the Jindas without killing the pointer. The one member in the group responsible for "pointing" the drugged Jindas on their mission, the pointer was normally *not* a member of the Brotherhood, but some recruit from the underworld who was paid well to perform a single mission. The pointer must be inside the warehouse, and 13 wanted the man alive!

Agent 13 was, of course, completely familiar with the area surrounding his lair, including the sewer system beneath the streets. Sneaking though a street grate like a rat, he was able to creep up on the two Jindas guarding the Chrysler from beneath.

Staring up through a storm drain, he targeted one of the Jindas with the barrel on his lighter pistol and squeezed the trigger. The Jinda's head exploded first with blood, then with flame.

As the body collapsed, the other Jinda whipped around. Too late. There was a crack. A second later, the Jinda's flesh turned to flame.

The Agent couldn't see what the guard at the door was doing, but he must have heard the shots. 13 ran through fifty yards of sewer system and emerged on the side of the warehouse. From this vantage point, he could safely observe the third Jinda by the freight elevator door.

Apparently the Jinda had heard the shots, but had chosen to remain in the shelter of the building. This was neither through cowardice nor tactical insight. This was the assignment he had been given. A drugged Jinda-Hai never deviated from his orders.

Knowing this made it easy for the Agent to dispatch his foe. Though the elevator had only one entrance, the building had many. Creeping through a window he purposefully left unlocked, 13 sneaked through the lower floor of the warehouse and caught the Jinda from behind while the man was staring out into the night.

A single shot turned him to ash.

Prying open the elevator doors, the Agent discovered that, as he feared, the elevator was stuck on the thirteenth floor. Grasping the elevator's steel cables, he began to climb up them.

Foot by foot he pulled himself up. Even to a man of his great strength, this was a remarkable feat of prowess. One floor. Two floors. His arms were growing weak. Three floors. Four . . . He suddenly heard footsteps enter the elevator car above him!

Then, he heard the loud whine of the engine. The cable he was climbing began to move, pulling him up on a collision course with the dropping car!

Faced with certain death, 13 formulated a desperate plan. With precise timing, he leaped from the cable to a small ledge just below the fifth-floor elevator door.

Seconds seemed minutes as he sailed through the air of the dark shaft. Then, slamming into the wall, his hands grasped frantically for anything! He missed the handle that would have opened the door, but his fingers gained a tentative purchase on the narrow ledge. Looking up, he saw the car descending toward him. Within moments, he would be knocked down the shaft!

With the last strength in his arms, 13 pulled himself up to the door and grabbed the outside lever. But the door, designed to be opened by the mechanical strength of the elevator and not by a mere human arm, moved only slightly.

Desperately, using the adrenaline surge that was flooding his body, 13 pried the doors apart as far as he could. Already he could feel the blast of air pushed ahead of the elevator as it bore down on him.

With a powerful lunge, 13 drove his body between the heavy doors an instant before the plummeting elevator would have sliced him in two.

His heart pounding, the Agent looked down the shaft at the moving freight elevator. Since it didn't have a ceiling, he could clearly see its deadly cargo. There were three men—two Jindas and the pointer. Apparently, they had found what they were looking for. Not losing an instant, 13 drew his pistol and leaped down the shaft into the descending car.

He had one instant to figure out who was who in the dimly lit elevator. The Jindas were probably the two with the Thompsons. The other man was armed only with a pistol.

The occupants of the slowly moving platform neither saw nor heard 13 as he dropped silently through the darkness. The first clue the Jindas had was the sensation of the Agent's slugs tearing through the roof of their skulls.

13 knew he had guessed correctly as he watched flames fill the elevator.

The pointer—a fat, disheveled thug—stared at the burning corpses in horror as the Agent landed lightly beside him.

"Who hired you?" the Agent demanded, shoving his pistol into the man's eye.

"I don't know, I swear!" the man whimpered, trying to squirm away from the flames and the gun at the same time.

"What was your assignment?"

"To find some kinda jewel and then rub out the guy that lived here. Tha-that's all I know!"

The pointer flailed about as 13 grabbed him by the throat.

The scum was probably telling the truth, 13 knew. He probably really had no idea who hired him. Pointers never did. Messages came by phone or through third parties. But 13 had to send a message, and the pointer was his best telegram. When the pointer went to get paid at his drop-off, someone would most assuredly be watching him.

"Where's the jewel?"

"He— One of those guys had it!" The pointer

gestured to a pile of ash on the floor.

"Tell your bosses I'll trade the stone for Maggie Darr."

"I don't know who the bosses are! I swear to God!"

"Don't worry. They'll find you. Tell them to meet me at the Palace of Illusion, four o'clock today with Maggie. Understand?"

"Sure! Sure!" the pointer groaned. Anything to get rid of the guy!

Then 13 struck a ring on his right hand hard against the brick of the elevator shaft. There was a loud sizzling sound as the magnesium in the special ring ignited. The inside of the elevator, thick with smoke and the stench of the burning Jindas, turned a blinding white as the ring began to glow. Wide-eyed, the pointer let out a terrified shriek.

Gripping the pointer by the neck, 13 brought his burning ring closer and closer. . . .

A moment later, the elevator shaft echoed with a terrible, blood-curdling scream.

When the elevator reached the ground, the pointer dashed to the waiting getaway car, holding his hand over his forehead and sobbing with pain. As he fumbled with the gears, the pointer peered into the mirror. The number 13 was branded forever on his forehead.

The Agent watched as the car sped away. Confident that his message would be sent, he spread around the smoldering ashes in the elevator. His foot hit a large object. Reaching down, he pulled it out. The Seer Stone.

Knowing that he would have neither the time nor the opportunity to move the contents of his lair and that he would never be able to return, Agent 13 began the grim task of burning the entire structure to the ground.

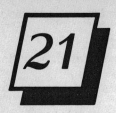

21

SLEIGHT OF HAND

When Harry Houdini died on Halloween in 1926, an era of American life came to an end. Attacked by the clergy, wounded by the Depression, magic began to die a lingering death. Sleight of hand became an almost forgotten art. The days of the grand illusion were past, and escape artists vanished from the scene, replaced by the more foolhardy but less artful daredevil.

If magic were truly dead, as many believed, then the Palace of Illusion was its tomb. Here, Blackstone had pulled rabbits from hats, the great Marmaluke had pulled fire from air, and numerous less famous illusionists had mystified, thrilled, and amazed. But the Depression, which had dimmed everything that glittered in America, had forced the closing of the Palace of Illusion.

Nobody was enthusiastic about entering the structure where were housed "The Cauldron of Horror," "the Casket of No Escape," the "Box with a Thousand Locks." Thus it was that the great structure stood, with seats and props intact, as it had on the night of the last show . . . except for some writing over the door, thought to be a curse.

China White gave the scrawl over the entryway an amused look as her agents broke into the building. Magicians? Amateurs, all of them. She herself had not only learned all the secrets in the Shrine, but many that would have astounded even Houdini himself.

"Hurry up," China said irritably, though she knew perfectly well that such things as picking locks put on by banks could not be hurried. She was looking forward to this night with as much anticipation—no, more—than she had looked forward to her debut at La Scala.

Tonight, China White would have everything she wanted—Maggie Darr in her control, Agent 13 at her mercy, and the Seer Stone. Tonight would be glorious. . . .

China brought along all that she needed for success. The six men opening the door were elite members of the Jinda-Gol. She had Maggie Darr—drugged and completely oblivious to what was going on—slumped in the back seat of the sedan.

China had no doubt that Agent 13 knew what he'd be up against. That left her with one question—What did he hope to gain? Standing on the steps of the Palace, she glanced back at the semiconscious woman in the back seat. Had 13 fallen for this woman? Anger creased her beautiful forehead as she remembered the bullet scar in her shoulder.

She had wanted to kill the woman when they brought her in last night, but the Masque had forbidden it.

"She will be of more use to us alive than dead," he said coldly.

"More use to *you*, perhaps!" China said, but she said it under her breath. She had seen the look in the man's eyes as he stared at the bound and gagged blonde young woman. China sneered. Two members of the Brotherhood smitten by this little tramp. Whatever she has, maybe we should bottle it, China thought with scorn. Because she wasn't going to have it much longer!

China looked at her watch just as the Jinda-Gol

succeeded in forcing the locks. It was three o'clock.

"Get the woman," she ordered one of the men. Bowing, he did as he was told. Dragging Maggie out of the car, he hauled her—stumbling and nearly falling—up the stairs and into the Palace behind China and her assassins.

"13," she called out into the darkness. It was early, but she knew he was here . . . waiting, hidden in the shadows of the mystical props.

She caught hold of Maggie and pulled her forward.

"I have an associate of yours, 13. She's unharmed—so far. I'm here to make a trade."

Still no response. She would have been surprised if there had been one. China turned to the Jindas. "Find him."

The fire in the abandoned warehouse had been a five-alarm blaze, and, by the time the firemen reached it, it was too late. 13, watching from a distance, saw that it was completely, totally destroyed. Everything in the lair, except for the small weapons and disguise kits that he had carried with him, was incinerated—years of research, a large cache of weapons he had used to fight the Brotherhood, an autogyro, and more. Turning away, he went to keep his appointment.

Sitting now in the darkness of the Palace of Illusion, waiting, the Agent sensed an aura of finality about the coming events. All the cards were in his enemy's hands. The Masque had Dr. Fischer's Lightning Gun, capable of reducing its target to ashes. The Masque had Maggie. But if, once again, he could throw a wrench into their works, keep them off balance, present them with the unexpected so they didn't have time to compensate . . . that was his hope.

Soon, President Roosevelt would deliver his State of the Union Address to the nation. Hanover and his other contacts in the White House were endeavoring to find out how Roosevelt would react, but—so far—the President had remained in seclusion. The Agent had strong misgivings. It would be political suicide to allow the Masque's threats and acts of terrorism to be made public. To go long with the Masque would cast the President in the role of a capitulator. But what havoc would be wrought by the Masque if the President failed to respond at all?

As 13 watched the six Jinda-Gol slip into the old building, flanking China White and Maggie, he realized how truly desperate his situation was. He hadn't had time to prepare the elaborate traps that would have been necessary to deal with these overwhelming odds. All he had was a plan.

Two Jinda-Gol guarded China White and Maggie Darr. He knew exactly what their orders would be—shoot the hostage first, himself second. The four other assassins were slowly and methodically working their way through the abandoned theater, checking each row of seats, each doorway. It was clear that they had no intention of trading the woman for the Seer Stone. But then again, neither did 13.

China heard the first gunshot at 3:55 p.m. In moments, her expertly trained agents had isolated the source. It came from the massive storage area in the basement of the theater. China could hear her men whistling instructions to each other in code as they disappeared down the stairs.

The Jinda-Gol slowly worked his way through the storeroom where props from the great magicians of past eras were stacked high on either side. He had determined that Agent 13's hiding place must be in one of two areas. The first area was sealed off by the other two Jindas. The second area was his.

The Jinda-Gol felt no sorrow when he found a pile of ashes—all that appeared to remain of his partner, who had obviously perished by the bullet they had heard fired. Sorrow was not a useful emotion to the Jinda-Gol. He was more concerned with trying to flush out the Agent.

Suddenly, the Jinda-Gol heard a scrabbling sound, the kind animals make when cornered and trying desperately to escape.

That wasn't like 13. The Jinda-Gol smelled a trap. Looking up, he saw a twenty-foot shaft leading to the stage above. At the top of the shaft there was a square of light which blinked suddenly, as if a figure had passed in front of it.

A trapdoor in the stage floor, thought the Jinda-Gol. The kind used by magicians for their disappearing acts.

Someone was up there. The Jinda aimed at the light and fired. There was a gasp of pain, then a scraping sound—like someone opening a door. Hurrying up the ladder leading to the trapdoor, he saw a shadow move above him and guessed what was happening.

He had wounded the Agent and now 13 was escaping through the trapdoor! The Jinda heard it scrape shut.

Whistling the code that meant success, the Jinda arrived at the top of the ladder, directly beneath the closed trapdoor. He reached up, into the darkness, to open it. . . .

Sitting in the dust-covered seats facing the stage and flanked by her two guardians, China White looked over at the groggy Maggie. The woman was barely conscious. Maybe an "accident" would occur. Surely the Masque couldn't hold her responsible if poor Miss Darr tripped and fell, breaking that pretty neck.

One of the Jindas stiffened suddenly. China heard what he had—movement on stage.

"Lights!" she cried out.

A spotlight glared, switched on by one of the Jindas guarding the back stage. China watched curiously as a wounded man staggered out of the wings. Blinded by the lights, he flung his arm up over his face. Then she saw blood on his chest. She saw, too, that he was not one of her Jindas! His clothes, his face. . . .

Leaping out of her seat, she ran down the aisle as fear built inside of her.

Suddenly a Jinda threw open the trapdoor on the stage. Climbing through it, he leveled the cold steel of his Thompson at the wounded man.

"Don't shoot!" China shouted frantically.

But the order came too late. The Jinda's Thompson began to sing, spitting out rounds. Agent 13's body danced for an instant like a marionette, as slug after slug tore through his body in an unending fury. But the body did not burn! So it was true—somehow 13 had managed to get hold of an antitode to the *mantha*. A lot of good it had done him.

"You fiend!" China screamed at the Jinda-Gol, who merely looked at her with that blank stare they all had. For an instant, she considered killing the assassin for failing to obey her command. Then she forced herself to calm down. It took years and enormous amounts of time and money to train a Jinda-Gol. One did not sacrifice them lightly. Besides, he had probably been following the Masque's orders.

They had no intention of letting 13 remain

alive.

Two other Jinda-Gol padded out from the shadows. They stood motionless on the stage, holding their machine guns cradled in their arms.

Kneeling by the body, China White reached gingerly into the blood-soaked pocket. Her hand emerged. The Seer Stone was in it, covered with the still-warm blood of Agent 13, the final confirmation of all she had feared.

Even though her mission was a complete success, the man she loved was dead. . . . But she couldn't think about that now. Time was crucial.

"Pick up his body and place it in the trunk of the car," she said coldly. Like the Jinda-Gol, she had been trained to keep her remorse and her sorrow bottled up inside of her—at least until she was alone in her room.

Several hours later, at the White House, the President of the United Sates was laboring over a crucial paragraph for his State of the Union Address. Short miles away, at one of the Masque's hide-outs, a dead body lay upon a cold slab.

Peering down at Agent 13's body, the cowled figure of the Masque nodded. One of his men reached down and lifted up the Agent's cold hand. Holding the Seer Stone, the Masque looked at the Agent's palm.

"I see nothing," he growled.

"He's probably using some kind of fake skin," China suggested, trying to keep from trembling.

"I've never seen one so lifelike before. Get me a knife."

Minutes later, the Masque peeled off what looked like a layer of skin from the hand. He held the Seer Stone to his eye once again.

"Ah," he purred in satisfaction. "There is the number 1 . . ." Continued scraping removed a second layer. He held the stone to his eye again.

"A 1 and a—" His voice caught in his throat, then turned into an inarticulate shriek of rage. "A 9! You imbeciles! 19! You have killed a Jinda-Gol!"

Reaching up to the corpse's face, the Masque's hand found the thin, nearly invisible line of the rubber fleshlike mask. Furiously, he ripped it off.

The Masque's grim gaze turned on China White.

"I-I don't understand," China faltered. "Why didn't the Jinda burn up? The body should have turned to ash! And what about the Seer Stone I found?"

"Fake, probably. Another one of *your* tricks, no doubt!" the Masque snarled. "Still trying to protect the man you love?"

"That's not true!" she cried, staring wildly at the body of the Jinda-Gol.

Though the Masque, like all Brotherhood agents, was expert at containing his emotions, his rage was apparent, even through the hood.

"You have failed me for the last time!" he hissed, motioning to two of his Jindas. "Take her away! You know what to do with her!"

He turned back to China, who was deathly white. "What a pity it had to end like this," he said without a trace of feeling in his voice. He watched the beautiful woman being led, struggling, away.

Whirling, he glared at the remaining Jindas. "Where did the others go?"

"To our rendevouz—the cannery—as you told them."

The Masque seethed in fury. "That means Agent 13 is there! With *it!*" His hands clenched. "Find him! Or I'll have your lives as well!"

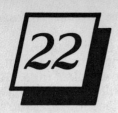

22

THE HORROR UNVEILED

Agent 13's eyes slowly adjusted to the tunnel's dim light. The passageways seemed to go on forever, with no apparent direction or purpose. He felt like a rat in a maze.

The lair was far bigger than he had expected, and it smelled strongly of fish—not surprising, since the building fronted as the Sea Breeze Fish Cannery. It covered several acres and employed vast numbers of workers who had no idea what terrible secrets lived beneath their workplace.

Disguised as China's henchman arriving with a group of her thugs, 13 was instantly waved on through by the guards at the outer doors.

Without hesitation, the thugs headed for a door at the rear of the building. They entered one by one, as 13 waited his turn. When it came, he found himself in a small, dirty latrine. There was no sign of the other thugs. His sixth sense told him he was being watched, most probably through the mirror that hung over the filthy sink.

The Agent feigned boredom. Looking at his reflection in the mirror, he pulled a toothpick from his pocket and began to pick his teeth. Immediately the entire room began to vibrate and hum. 13's inner ear told him that the latrine was actually an elevator, moving downward. After several seconds, it stopped abruptly. He opened the door and found himself in the main reception area for a large facility. Several uniformed guards were giving him the eye.

A guard caught his attention. "Where ya been? They're waiting for you in 4B." The disguised Agent disappeared around the corner. He had no intention of going to 4B. Instead, he took the first detour he came to, a roughly hewn stone staircase.

As 13 descended the stairs, he discovered a vast network of tunnels and rooms branching off from them. He kept going down, far into the bowels of the earth, until the staircase finally came to an end in a tunnel much larger than the others. 13 estimated that he was about three hundred feet beneath the surface of the earth.

The sheer size and complexity of the structure told 13 that he had found a headquarters of some kind, possibly the lair of the Masque himself. It must have taken years to carve the tunnels from the bedrock. 13 followed the tunnel downward, until suddenly it came to a dead end.

The Agent faced a pair of huge metal doors—obviously a new addition. It was also the only way out of the tunnel. 13 pressed his ear against the door's plate metal. Even through the thick fire door, the Agent's acute hearing was able to pick up a constant, rhythmic vibration.

13 recognized the throbbing rhythm as a Pratt and Whitney R-2800 Double Wasp airplane engine, an engine so advanced that it was available to the military on an experimental basis only. What would an experimental aircraft engine be doing far beneath the earth's surface?

The lock on the double door was no match for 13's talents. He had already bridged the major security barrier with his disguise. 13 silently slid the door open a crack.

Before him stood a hangar, similar to those used

to house the gigantic dirigibles at Lakehurst, New Jersey. But the hangar before him was entirely underground, carved from the granite bedrock! Its vast vaulted ceiling rose hundreds of feet above him. But even more amazing than the hangar was the airship contained in it. It was unlike anything 13 had seen before.

The saucer-shaped airship, the length of two football fields, was supported by massive, retractable legs. The Agent counted over twenty of the special Pratt and Whitney engines attached to the craft's sides. Considering the ship's sleek design, he surmised that the engines were enough to give it a considerable forward speed.

The airship's purpose was obvious. Plated with shiny black metal, it bristled with armaments and antiaircraft guns. 13 counted nine experimental-type fighter planes undergoing their final engine checks. How many had already been pulled into the waiting hangar doors beneath the ship?

Through an open, massive door set into the bottom of the craft, he saw a huge version of Dr. Fischer's Lightning Gun, the weapon that could deal instantaneous death to a tank . . . and more.

With all of its defenses, the airship would be impervious to attack. Once aloft, it would be invincible—a device of terror.

Suddenly it all made sense—the kidnappings of the scientists, the disasters to cover their disappearances. . . .

13 knew they were all here—Dr. Meinzner, the helium scientist who disappeared in the chemical factory explosion; Dr. Taylor, the physicist who disappeared in the train wreck; Dr. Fischer, the developer of the Lightning Gun; Dr. Heidelberg,the airship designer; Manny O'Brian, the test pilot; and Dr. Neilsen, the Nobel Prize win-

ner for chemistry. All had been forced by the Brotherhood to help build this death-dealing air-borne monster.

13 shook his head. It was a terrible weapon, but one of these ships alone couldn't be of much use against a nation as large and powerful as the United States. The Masque's plan must be deeper, more subtle. 13 had to find out what it was.

There was one person who might know—Maggie. He had to find her! Deep inside, he was beginning to realize that Maggie's loss meant something more to him than losing a trusted and valued employee.

Even as 13's mind weighed his options, his eyes and ears were absorbing the activities and shouted commands echoing through the vast chamber. It was obvious that the airship was in the final stages of preparation. The Brotherhood was preparing to make its move. He had to have his information quickly. . . .

Charlie Vickers was a petty criminal on the lam. Busted in Philly for a petty rackets operation, he was looking at five to ten in the big house. Charlie was already pushing fifty, so he skipped bail and took off.

Charlie tried to lie low, but word spread quickly—he was hot. Out of money, with no place to stay, Charlie was desperate. So when a Mr. Simons approached him with an offer of work and a place to stay, Charlie didn't bother to ask any questions.

The job seemed simple at first—installing steam pipes through a network of old tunnels beneath the Sea Breeze Fish Cannery on the shore somewhere in southern Virginia.

He noted a lot of people in suits and white lab coats, who looked out of place in a fish cannery, but they didn't ask questions about him, so he didn't ask questions about them.

But Charlie felt increasingly uneasy. He'd always figured he'd lived as long as he had by steering clear of the big boys. But now he had the feeling something really big was going on here. Charlie didn't know what it was, but he had the impression that these guys weren't to be messed with.

When the tunnels were completed, the next phase began—the construction of a giant cavern, which he later learned was to house a great airship. Charlie received a promotion. He was taken off the sweat detail and given a job in security.

The security job was easy at first. Charlie knew most of the crew in the building. But when work started on the airship, strange people began arriving—military types, Japanese, Germans, Italians. . . .

The job grew confusing. Charlie became flustered. The newcomers cursed him in foreign languages and looked at him as if he were a bug. This didn't sit well with Charlie. No one treated him as second class! But his uneasiness was changing into fear.

Then the prisoners were brought in. That's what Charlie called them at least. They seemed to have brains, but they looked either unhappy or angry most of the time. They were kept under constant guard, and it was obvious that they were being forced to work. Those who wouldn't cooperate were taken to the "special" rooms far below. Charlie was never allowed down there himself, but he had heard the horror stories.

Charlie would have been the first to tell you that he was no angel, but, for all his faults, there was a human side to him. He didn't like what he saw and heard. Even criminals had a code of honor. He was a patriot, and he didn't like all these guys talking about "*Der Fuhrer*" when they thought people couldn't hear them. He didn't like the rumors of torture chambers. He didn't like the way some of his coworkers began to disappear, particularly those who complained. Charlie felt trapped.

Maybe someone higher up sensed a change in Charlie's attitude, or perhaps it really was a transfer like they said, but Charlie was shifted back to the now-empty tunnels. Here he was told to patrol and watch for anything suspicious. He spent a lot of time alone, watching the airship take shape. And as it grew, more of his fellow workers vanished.

How much longer have *I* got? Charlie wondered as he patrolled the almost deserted tunnels.

Agent 13 stared at the motionless body, cursing. He hadn't intended to kill the young guard. Catching him unaware, 13 had quickly subdued him. Then, using *Shin Geseare*—an ancient form of mind probing—13 had attempted to search the man's mind for information. The probe was too much for the guard, however. He died quickly, of a sudden, massive hemorrhage.

Well, there was no help for that now. Quickly 13 exchanged clothes with the dead guard, then set about transforming his features to those of the lifeless face on the tunnel floor. Undoubtedly the dead henchman whom 13 had replaced earlier had been discovered by now. He would be safer in a new disguise.

As 13 was finishing turning himself into Scotty Cunningham, as the dead guard's name badge said, the Agent heard footsteps approaching. Their deliberate sounds told him that the person coming was older, possibly with a leg injury.

Maybe this man could supply the answers 13 needed. The Agent withdrew into a rocky alcove to await the man's arrival.

The approaching winter had made the tunnels cold and damp. Even the hot steam from the pipes couldn't help ease Charlie's bouts with arthritis in his left leg, the result of being "kneecapped" when he came up short on a gambling debt years ago.

Lost in gloomy thoughts, Charlie was just wondering when his "transfer" would occur—the one to the big pine box. . . .

Charlie felt a sudden, piercing pain behind his left shoulder. Reaching back in panic, he felt a man's hand. The strength ebbed from his body as he drifted into unconsciousness.

13 lost no time in probing Charlie's mind. *Shin Geseare* was a powerful force. With it, the Agent unlocked Charlie's subconscious, discovering a lot about the human side of Charlie Vickers. Immediately 13 realized that Charlie was a possible ally. Planting certain post-hypnotic suggestions, he short-circuited Charlie's criminal tendencies. Normally 13 would have spent more time with Charlie, but there was no time to spare. He would have to take his chances.

When Charlie came to, he was confronted by a man who seemed strangely familiar. The face resembled Charlie's arrogant assistant, Scotty Cunningham. He was wearing Scotty's uniform, with Scotty's name badge. But it wasn't Scotty!

Charlie tried to remember how he came to be lying here in the tunnel. The last memory he had was of the sharp pain in his shoulder.

"Who're you?" Charlie demanded.

"A friend," answered 13.

"Oh, yeah? Well, we'll just see about that!"

Charlie reached for his pistol. It wasn't there. "Where's my gat?" he demanded.

13 held up Charlie's gun. "We can be of use to each other, Charlie."

"How'd ya know my name? Where's Scotty?"

As 13 helped the confused man to his feet, Charlie said, "I'm dizzy. What happened?"

"You had an accident, but you'll be fine. Your life's in danger, Charlie. You know that, don't you?"

Charlie stared at the Agent in growing fear.

"They plan to kill you within the next twenty-four hours, to toss you away like a used dishrag, just like the others."

"N-no!" Charlie stammered.

"I can help you escape, Charlie, but I need your help."

"What do you know?" Charlie pulled away.

"I know I'm the only prayer you've got, Charlie. Look around you. Jack Yates, Tommy Meyers, Lou Tazaoli—they've all vanished. And you're next. You know too much, my friend. When that airship goes up, you're going down . . . if you follow my drift."

13 grabbed Charlie by the shoulders. "Take me to the room where they're holding the girl!"

"I can't," Charlie mumbled, trying to break free of the Agent's penetrating gaze, but he seemed to be fighting himself as much as the Agent.

"You can, Charlie."

The voice seemed to come from his *own head*! It was as if Charlie's mind was nothing but a radio speaker for the stranger's voice!

"No one's allowed down there," Charlie whined. "Those rooms are off limits—"

But the voice in his head said, "Come on, Charlie! You can get down there. And you're gonna take this stranger with you. He's a friend. . . ."

The large iron chair was bolted to the the chiseled stone floor. A woman sat upright in the chair, held by tight leather straps around her wrists, waist, and ankles. Securing her head to the chair was a masklike device with a tangle of electrical wires running from its back to a nearby generator. 13 recognized the device—the Helmet of Truth.

Devised by the Brotherhood, the helmet could, through a process of electrical shock and thought inducement, bring to excruciating reality its victim's worst fears. Too much of the "treatment" could lead to permanent brain damage or death. But in skilled hands, it could reduce the toughest hood to a whimpering child.

The woman had passed out. Her motionless body slumped forward, indicating that her "treatment" had already started. Around her stood three uniform-clad men who, quite clearly, enjoyed their work.

The fat one was called Axel. Sweat poured from his double chin, indicating his displeasure that the woman had passed out. "Revive her!" he commanded a skinny man with glasses. "The Masque said no rest. Bring me the Praxus!"

The skinny man repeated, "No rest! No rest!" as he shuffled off toward a box of tools.

The skinny man was Dr. Natchez, the renowned scientist in the field of missile warfare. He had been one of the top designers of projectile weapons for the army until his disappearence several years ago. He had been kidnapped to design a hellish weapon for the airship. But he refused to cooperate.

Being a man of high conviction, Natchez realized that turning his secrets over to his captors could mean horrible death for millions of innocent people. Try as they might, the Brotherhood couldn't break him. Finally, they decided to make an example of him. The higher-ups recommended the Helmet of Truth. So the rebellious man was placed in Axel's "care," and he was given free reign to "experiment."

It was during his fifth session with Axel that the change in Natchez occurred. In the middle of the most horrible of tortures, the essence that was Dr. Natchez departed. When Axel finally removed the helmet, he was confronted by a blithering idiot of the most vile nature.

Natchez's new disposition amused Axel, who felt that, in a way, he had "created" Natchez. Lexner, the hunchbacked dwarf who was Axel's assistant, welcomed Natchez as someone he could lord it over.

The woman's body jerked spasmodically from a sudden electrical shock. Axel spun to see Lexner turning various knobs on the generator.

"I said the Praxus, not more voltage, you idiot!" he screamed.

"Praxus, not voltage!" mimicked Natchez.

Shutting down the power, the dwarf fired an angry look at Natchez, but the deranged doctor was absorbed in his assignment. A large smile filled his face as he held up a devilish-looking tool.

"Praxus?" Axel looked at the device. It was a medieval-looking contraption, consisting of a long metal bar with several hooks, a belt, and balance weights. "Good. Bring it here. . . . Lexner! Prepare her!"

This was clearly a job Lexner enjoyed. He ripped open the waist of the woman's blouse. Her soft white stomach would be the target of the barbaric tool. Enthralled by the woman's soft skin, the dwarf continued to rip her blouse, touching her as he did so. Axel slapped him away.

"Enough!"

Axel grabbed the Praxus and fastened it to the woman's waist. The tips of the hooks pointed inward, the pressure against her skin regulated by the weights and balances protruding from the front.

Slowly Axel began to increase the weight. The woman started to moan as the pain increased.

"It's working!" yelled Lexner.

"Of course," replied Axel confidently as he continued to increase the pressure.

Suddenly the woman was awake, her piercing scream echoing weirdly from beneath the helmet.

"Shall we start again?" Axel said.

Disguised as a guard, with Charlie in the lead, 13 had no trouble getting past other guards and opening locked doors. The feverish activity everywhere, plus several overheard remarks about the transportation of carts filled with tanked gases, confirmed Agent 13's hunch. The airship would be launched within the next twelve hours.

Suddenly Charlie stopped. "Uh, it's through there," he said, pointing at an unlocked steel door. "But I'm not allowed in this area—"

Reaching out, 13 opened the door. Peering inside, he could see why no one had bothered to lock it—two hulking guards stood just inside.

"Let me do the talking," 13 whispered crisply.

With Charlie trailing along behind, 13 entered the door. The two guards eyed the newcomers suspiciously. The larger guard, who was built like a gorilla, immediately went for his gun.

"Turn around! Neither of you have clearance for this area!"

As he spoke, 13 heard the screams of a woman from a closed chamber off to his left.

Startled, the guard glanced around. Catching a quick glimpse of movement in front of him, he whirled, but it was already too late. Agent 13's fist slammed into the gorilla's throat. The man collapsed to the ground with a gurgle.

The second guard swung his .38, taking a bead on the Agent's heart, but the bridge of his nose was suddenly caved in. Reaching down, 13 ripped the pistol from the guard's hand.

It had occurred so quickly that Charlie was still trying to figure out exactly what had happened when he realized that 13 was gone. Leaping over the bodies of the guards, he caught a fleeting glimpse of the Agent running into the chamber.

Inside the room, the crackling sound of electricity filled the air as the dwarf manned the controls of the generator.

"More voltage!" yelled Axel as Dr. Natchez's screams mimicked those of the tortured woman.

"Kill her!" screamed Lexner excitedly, reaching for the dial.

Hearing a noise at the door, Axel turned in irritation just as a .38 slug hit him right between the eyes.

13 turned his gun on the dwarf, but Lexner managed to hit the alarm button, then flee the room. Screaming in panic, Dr. Natchez crouched in a corner.

"Maggie!" 13 gasped, recognizing her dress.

There was no reply. The woman had once more fallen unconscious. 13 tried to remove the helmet, but it was bolted in place. He turned to Dr. Natchez.

"Where's the wrench?" he demanded.

Natchez grinned idiotically. "Where's the wrench? Where's the wrench?"

Standing in the doorway, peering cautiously inside, Charlie's eyes grew wide.

"We've got to hurry!" snapped Agent 13. "Keep an eye on the door!"

Hurriedly 13 studied the Helmet of Truth. The machine was building power, and he knew that the next surge might be the last Maggie could stand. He studied the connections. The mass of wires were tightly bundled together. The slightest mistake could cause an electrical arc. Grabbing Natchez, 13 dragged him over to the chair.

"Shut it off!" 13 commanded.

The doctor rolled his eyes. 13 released him, realizing that the idiot could be of no use. He had to do it on his own.

With skilled hands, he started to disconnect the live wires. Suddenly he felt a sharp pain shooting up his leg. It was Natchez. Like a rabid dog, he had sunk his teeth into the Agent's leg. 13 froze, unable to move for fear of arcing the wires.

Charlie grabbed the nearest object he could find. Axel called it a Ripper, a razor-sharp instrument that could strip the flesh off living victims. Charlie wasn't versed in its use, but he had no doubt that it could be useful.

Natchez never saw it coming as Charlie brought the Ripper down hard on the deranged scientist's neck.

Charlie wasn't prepared for it when the facial muscles on the severed head continued to twitch. Horrified, he dropped the weapon and retreated to the corner of the room.

13 continued to work quickly. He knew the alarm would soon bring armed guards. His hands were steady, his steely eyes locked in concentration as he channeled his every thought to the cables in his hands. Every wire had a relationship, an interlocking code. Quickly he worked, making the needed connections to reroute the current.

"I hear 'em coming!" Charlie yelled.

Fortunately 13 was done. Gingerly pulling the

plug from the rear of the helmet, he freed Maggie from the fiendish machine.

"C'mon!" implored Charlie.

13 quickly unfastened the straps holding the Praxus in place, along with the ones binding the woman to the chair.

"Maggie?"

Still unconscious, she made no reply. Again he tried to remove the helmet. Though free of the generator, it still enclosed her head in its grip. The bolts held it firm. 13 could hear shouts in the distance. Charlie was dancing up and down with fear.

Running to the power box, 13 ripped off the metal panel, revealing a tangle of wires. Quickly he began sorting through the multicolored strands.

"Do you know the way out?" he asked Charlie.

"I helped build this place! I could find my way out with my eyes closed. But if we don't beat it now, every mug in this joint will be after us."

13 touched two wires together. The lights flickered, then suddenly went out, plunging the room and the corridor into an inky blackness.

Lifting the limp Maggie from the chair, he threw her over his shoulder. With Charlie in the lead, they raced from the chamber of horror, leaving only the grim remains of Axel and poor Dr. Natchez as testimony to their visit.

23

A Grim Surprise

Through the blackness Agent 13 and Charlie fled, the sound of their pursuers' boots close behind.

Charlie had learned the tunnels' patterns through his years of service. While the guards stumbled through the tomblike passageways, Charlie led 13—still carrying Maggie—twisting upward until the sounds of the Klaxons and shouting guards were merely echoes in the distance.

Finally they emerged onto a level where the lights were still on. 13 brought Charlie to a halt. They would have to slow down now, to move more sedately, as if nothing were wrong. The Agent's disguise and Charlie's presence might enable them to avoid a conflict.

Near the hangar level, most of the workers were busily preparing the aircraft for departure. Anyone who gave them a second look was reassured by Charlie, whom they all recognized.

They walked through the hangar area as quickly as they dared, then were back in the tunnels again. They were nearing the surface. Only the problem of getting out of the structure itself remained.

It was a question that had tormented Charlie. Suspecting that his own days were numbered, he had been searching for an escape route, only to find heavy security at all the exit points.

Higher and higher they climbed. Charlie soon fell behind, the increasing pain in his leg slowing him. Finally he had to call a halt.

"Hey, wait up!" he implored, collapsing against the side of the tunnel. The stranger stopped. Even with the woman slung over his shoulder, he had been pushing on at an untiring pace.

"How're we gonna get outta here?" Charlie asked. "Every guard and his brother will be looking for us at those exits."

"They won't be looking for me—only you and her," 13 replied from the shadows.

"Whaddaya mean?" cried Charlie suspiciously.

In answer, Agent 13 simply turned around.

"Jeez!" Charlie blurted, staring.

The face he saw was no longer that of Scotty Cunningham. It was thinner and better-looking.

"What in hell is going on?" Charlie demanded.

"It's unimportant. Where is the nearest exit?"

"Then what?"

"Let me worry about that."

But Charlie worried, with good reason. The ascent from the depths had exhausted him. He could have almost packed it in, here and now, but something about the stranger kept him going. With him, we've got a chance, Charlie thought. And any chance was better than what faced him if he stayed in the tunnels.

"The exit?" the Agent pursued, shaking Charlie from his thoughts.

"At the next intersection, turn right. Then up the stairs and a jog to the left."

"Where does it go?"

"I think it leads to a secret door in the back of a storage room. The storage room opens into the main area of the cannery. But they'll have guards at every exit—" Charlie stopped in midsentence.

The stranger's .38 was pointed at his chest.

"What's this?"

"You're my prisoner, Charlie. The dwarf will recognize you. Put your hands in the air."

"Why, you! I shoulda killed ya when I had the chance." Charlie scowled. "Ya think you'll skate outta here by layin' the smear on me?"

13 pulled the hammer back. "Start walking."

Looking into those intense eyes, Charlie knew the stranger was serious. Charlie's first thought was to make a break for it back into the tunnels, but that would be inviting a bullet in the back. Charlie had a vivid picture of himself lying dead on the cold stone floor.

He started to walk. "Ya think you're a slick operator, don't ya? Ya don't think they'll recognize ya, eh? Well, I got news for ya. If I go down, you and the skirt are going with me!"

13 shoved the .38 into Charlie's back. "Enough talk. Just keep walking."

Charlie did as he was told. As he walked up the stairs, he tried to figure out who the stranger was. Was he a field agent for the feds, a trigger for the mob, or just a hired muscle sent to rescue the moll? Charlie couldn't figure it. All he knew was that the man was a professional, and a good one. But even the best make mistakes, and when he did, Charlie would be ready.

When they reached the top, Charlie could hear sounds from the guard station ahead. There were no lights on here, either. Apparently it was on the same circuit as the lower tunnels. Charlie realized that the moment of truth lay just around the bend.

As they turned the corner, the beams of two flashlights suddenly hit them. There was the sound of clicking pistol hammers. Then a no-nonsense voice spoke from the darkness. "Hold it right there. What are you doing here creeping around in the dark? Let's see your clearances."

The Agent shoved Charlie forward with his pistol. "Call security," he said. "Tell 'em we caught one of the killers and the girl."

"Don't listen to him!" Charlie implored, stumbling forward. "It's me, Charlie Vickers!"

The guards sought his face with their lights.

"It's Charlie, all right," muttered one. His light played on the unconscious girl. "What are you doin' with a broad with her head in a bucket?"

"Yeah, Charlie, what's going on here?" demanded the one with the gruff voice.

Charlie was feeling a little more confident. He knew these guys. He might be able to get out of this after all. "Look," he said, moving forward a couple more steps, "I was workin' below when—"

A phone rang somewhere in the darkness. The gruff-voiced guard answered it. "Yeah?" he said. "Thanks for the tip." He hung up, then turned back toward Charlie. "That's close enough!"

The nervous guard's pistol took a bead on Charlie's forehead. Charlie stopped dead.

"That was a call from down below. Someone's rubbed out the fat man and that crazy old doctor. Now, you just back up nice and easy against that wall until we can figure this thing out."

"Put me through to security," the younger voice said into the phone.

Something hit Charlie from behind, knocking him sideways. Two pistol shots rang out in the darkness. There were two cries, two thuds, and then two flashlights were lying on the floor, their beams staring aimlessly into the darkness.

The stranger laid the woman down on the floor. Grabbing one of the flashlights, he began working on the lock to the door of the storage room. Within moments, it opened. Picking up the girl, he hurried inside.

Using one of the flashlights, Charlie managed to locate a guard's gun. Picking it up, he felt better. So, the stranger hadn't pulled a double-cross after all. Maybe the guy was all right. Charlie followed him into the storage room, slamming the iron door behind him.

A dim overhead light revealed rows of shelves containing canned sardines. "This way." Charlie motioned, hurrying to the end of the room. Here, the stranger paused and pressed his ear against a door. All that could be heard were the sounds of the cannery. Opening the door a crack, 13 looked through. The smell of fish was overwhelming. Outside, workers were cleaning, sorting, and packing fish in the immense work area.

"No guards," Charlie said behind the Agent.

"Not that we can see," 13 retorted grimly, looking around. "Bring me those smocks," he said to Charlie as he pointed to several fish-stained garments hanging in a corner. Then he laid Maggie on the floor while Charlie went to get the garments.

"Keep one for yourself and give me the rest."

Charlie quickly did what he was told. It was clear to him now that the guy really was trying to help save his life. He would obey orders.

The Agent rolled Maggie up in the smocks until she was nothing more than a pile of rags. Then he slipped his own arms into the remaining garment.

"Now listen carefully," he said to Charlie, staring hypnotically into his eyes. "We're going to pick her up and walk straight out that door. We're not going to stop till we're outside. Understand?"

"Just like we own the place?"

"Just like we own the place. If anyone says anything, you keep quiet. I'll do the talking."

"You're the boss."

Bending down, Charlie helped the stranger lift the bundled form. Then they casually walked out the door. In the distance, a large open freight door allowed sunlight in and fish fumes out. Their footsteps rang hollowly on the iron surface beneath their feet. Seeing the stranger pause and look at the floor with a puzzled expression, Charlie nodded.

"Queer floor, ain't it?" he said. "Always wondered why it makes that hollow sound. . . ."

The stranger's face cleared. "That's because it's really the ceiling of that huge cavern down below," he said. "See those gears and pulleys? When they're ready to launch the airship, they'll just lift up the floor and the ceiling above us."

Charlie gaped. "Jeez!" he whispered. "But why—"

"Shhh!" the stranger warned. Looking around, Charlie saw that they had become the object of curious stares from several workers.

Seeing the exit ahead and feeling the weight of the pistol beneath his jacket, Charlie felt a little better about their situation. He was good with a gat, though not nearly as good as the stranger. Still, he figured he could take down at least six of the workers if they got too curious. But that would bring the whole place down on them!

Charlie began to get nervous. Everyone in the place seemed to be looking at him suspiciously. He saw hands sneaking into pockets, and he knew they were going after guns! In a moment, he knew, he would have to drop the girl and pull out his gun and begin firing. . . .

A strange sensation swept over Charlie. He felt giddy, lightheaded. Suddenly he knew he had become invisible! He saw himself floating through the crowded factory, but he knew somehow that no one else could see him! And then he was strolling down New York's crowded Fifth Avenue on a warm, sunlit day. No one was paying the least bit of attention to him. He even stopped and bought a daily paper at the corner rag stand. He kept walking, past hotdog stands, pretty women with long legs, kids with balloons and flowers.

Suddenly Charlie felt overwhelmed with sadness. His life had been a waste. And now maybe he was going to die. Charlie did something in those moments he hadn't done in some twenty-odd years. He prayed.

He asked God for forgiveness and promised that if he ever made it out of that cannery alive, he would lead a good life. No more scams and ripoffs. All he wanted was one more chance to prove himself. He promised . . .

"Set her down here."

The command snapped Charlie out of his dream. He felt the heat of the sun's rays and cold, fresh air blowing into his eyes. He was in a forest. Dry pine needles crunched beneath his feet, filling the air with a sweet scent.

"We're safe, for the moment," the stranger said, smiling.

Charlie gasped. In his dreamlike state, he had apparently carried the woman through the crowded factory, past the guards at the door, and into the safety of the dense forest.

He gently laid the woman down. He could hear the sounds of the sea and the factory noises through the trees. He didn't understand what had happened, but he realized that there was a lot about this stranger that didn't make any sense.

"Thanks for your help, Charlie," the stranger said as he quickly unwrapped the unconscious Maggie. "I suspect they're aware of our departure by now. There's a train station a mile up the coast.

In your pocket, you'll find a hundred-dollar bill. Use it to buy a ticket and whatever else you may need."

Charlie reached into his pocket and pulled out the C-note. "I—I don't know when I can repay—"

"Consider us even. I suggest you leave while you can." With his head, the Agent gestured back toward the factory.

Charlie looked. Several guards with drawn guns were hurrying out of the distant structure.

"Say no more. Just remember that Charlie Vickers owes ya one. I'm good for it. Anytime." With that, he turned and fled through the trees, toward freedom and a new life.

24

BREAKING THE BONDS

The Agent watched Charlie disappear into the forest greenery. Satisfied, he shouldered Maggie and walked in a different direction to a muddy road hidden by large hedges. Laying Maggie down again, 13 removed loose brush from the largest hedge. Soon the sleek green hood of a Daimler Double-Six came into view.

During his drive to the lair, the disguised Agent 13 had thoroughly familiarized himself with the area, making notes of the towns, dirt roads, bridges, and even old Tuttle Field—now being used as a training base for pilots.

Slipping away from the thugs, 13 had made his way to the executive parking lot, had hot-wired the high-speed Daimler, and then driven it to one of the many firebreak roads he'd discovered. He had then concealed the auto with the thick brush before returning to his unsuspecting cronies.

The Daimler Double-Six clear of the shrubs, 13 placed Maggie Darr in the passenger seat, then climbed into the car and started the engine. He eased into gear, and moments later, the car stood poised at the end of a fire road, ready to spring out onto the asphalt highway.

13 waited several minutes, but there was no sign of pursuit. They were probably still searching for him in the lair. He smiled grimly, then slowly pulled out onto the road.

Next to him, Maggie began to stir. Moaning, her hands went to the mask on her head.

"You're safe now," 13 said, squeezing her hand reassuringly. "When there's a chance, we'll stop and get that thing off you."

Maggie nodded and slumped back into the seat, sighing in relief.

After several miles, the Agent pulled off onto a small, deserted side road. He went to the trunk of the car and found a wrench in the tool kit. Quickly he loosened the bolts securing the heavy metal helmet around Maggie's head. Then the Agent's powerful hands parted the hinged device.

"Maggie—" he began softly, but his features suddenly registered intense shock as a mass of black hair tumbled down over the woman's face. Beautiful, deep-blue eyes blinked open and looked up into his.

"China!" 13 gasped.

Shaking out her long, dark hair, China coolly pulled down the visor mirror to examine her make-up. "What a fright I must look!" she remarked glancing down at her torn dress. "I was wondering when you were going to get around to getting that thing off me."

Hearing a click, China looked over and saw a .38 pointed at her head.

"Where's Maggie?" 13 asked evenly.

"I don't think that's necessary," China said calmly, her eyes on the pistol.

"That's for me to decide. Now, where is she?"

Stretching sensually, China leaned back in the soft leather seat. "With the Masque," she said. Staring into 13's eyes, China tried to look into his heart, tried to read the thoughts of the man who once belonged to her. It was impossible. Shrugging, she continued. "Don't expect to see her again. It seems the Masque has developed a fondness for your blonde friend."

"Where's the Masque now?" Agent 13 demanded, still aiming the gun.

"At the cannery, with the airship."

"You know his plan?"

"Of course." She smiled lazily.

13 pocketed his weapon. "Well," he said nonchalantly, "perhaps things aren't so bad after all."

China watched him carefully. His act might have fooled others, but not her. He really cared for this Maggie Darr, but it was obvious that he still felt something for her as well, just as she felt something for him. How could they not?

He was the only one Carmarron had truly loved. It was against him, Tredekka, that all the others had been compared and been found lacking. After his escape from the Shrine, the Brotherhood had tried to erase all memory of Agent 13 from Carmarron's mind. But even with their most sophisticated techniques, they had been unsuccessful—the very fibers and essences of the two young people had become one.

"What's the Masque's plan?" 13 asked China, pulling her back to the present.

China looked away.

"You owe them nothing," 13 persisted, moving closer to her. "They tortured you, then threw you away, like a Jinda. There's no longer a place for you with them, China. They'll hunt you down and destroy you, just as they tried to destroy me."

China hesitated as she considered how to turn this to her advantage. Finally she answered, "He's going to bomb the Capitol building."

13's eyes narrowed. "Of course!" he muttered. "It all makes sense! Tonight, the State of the Union Address, all the top government officials present in one place—" The Agent fell silent, pondering, planning. . . .

China interrupted his thoughts. "They tortured me because I failed to kill you. They thought I was protecting you."

"And were you?" he asked.

"Yes!" she cried. But she could tell his mind was somewhere else, fighting an airship she knew couldn't be defeated, not even by him. She needed to command his complete attention.

"Believe me, there's nothing you can do! The ship is indestructible." Leaning forward, she gripped 13's hands. "This is the chance that was stolen from us years ago! Fate has brought us back together again. Together we might survive. But alone, we'll perish. Let's leave this madness and the Brotherhood behind forever!"

He looked at her.

"Yes, I love you!" She answered his unasked question. "I've always loved you!"

She could see him start to yield. He drew nearer, the passion in his eyes impossible to conceal. And then she was in his arms, kissing him with unleashed passion.

Suddenly he pulled away. Drawing a deep breath, he shook his head. "No," he whispered, "we can't go back! I have a new mission. I can't run from the Brotherhood—I must *stop* them! Can't you understand?"

Hearing the pain in his voice, China put her hands together and looked up at him pleadingly. Never before had any man resisted her. Never before had she been forced to beg. But now—

The low rumblings of an engine sounded in the distance. China looked around. Only the pines could be seen, lining the empty road. "What's that noise?" she asked, startled. "A car—"

"No. The airship," 13 said quietly.

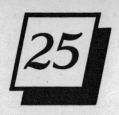

25

Storm of Darkness

Captain Kiffen McSpadden had been flying since the days of the Red Baron and the Lafayette Escadrille. A hero in France in World War I, the young pilot had returned home eager to be a part of the new United States Air Force.

McSpadden, and many more like him, was doomed to disappointment. Eager to return to peace, America dismantled the airplane factories and went back to building sewing machines. The training fields and airstrips fell into disrepair. More than one fighter pilot like McSpadden shook his head in dismay, knowing that the next war, if there was one, would be fought in the air.

By 1937, Kiffen McSpadden had been promoted to captain, but his outspokenness earned him only little-regarded Tuttle Field. He was rapidly coming to accept that his days and the field's were numbered. The money coming to the almost-forgotten airstrip was barely enough to keep the potholes repaired and seven trainers in the air.

Like all ex-fighter pilots, McSpadden followed the development of aircraft in other parts of the world. He cursed loudly over Hitler's announcement of the development of the *Luftwaffe* and wondered why no one else in this country could see what was going to happen.

McSpadden knew that a call for rearmament in the U.S. would eventually come. He only hoped it wouldn't be too late.

McSpadden did what he could with the tools he had to work with. His twelve bush-league pilots, even though they weren't the brightest, were of sound character and spirit. They practiced weekly in their P-12s, an outdated biplane that was scarcely a match for the deadly Messerschmidts and Stukas being tested in Spain. Even so, McSpadden's cadets took pride in their machines and mastered the basics of flight.

Now McSpadden stared gloomily at the ominous bank of clouds that had been building since noon. The P-12s sitting on the strip weren't about to go anywhere for a while. In disgust, McSpadden walked back into the pilot's lounge.

Twenty years ago, he thought, remembering the Great War, this room would have been packed with over fifty cadets, trying to earn their wings and get to the front. Now he looked at the four youngsters on call that day. There was Buck Dawes, a displaced cowboy who had fallen into the service because "it was the only job he could find."

Sitting next to Buck was Clay Lewis, busily replacing a tube in a radio. Lewis had joined up to escape a pregnant girlfriend in Pittsburgh.

A quick slapping sound came from the corner of the room. McSpadden didn't even have to look to know it was Juice Tanner, packing down his ever-present Luckies. Juice was a natural, as if he had been born with a pair of wings on his back. His only problem was his taste for whiskey. Juice said that if he could walk, he could fly. The problem was, McSpadden thought grumpily, Juice tended to have to crawl most of the time.

Finally there was Blake Carter, a happy-go-lucky kid who read nothing but trashy science fiction. Blake longed to be the first man on the moon, but since that wasn't possible, he had settled for the cockpit of a P-12.

"What was the last weather report?" McSpadden asked Juice.

"Scattered clouds, no precip expected."

"Bingo!" said Lewis suddenly from behind the radio as the device hummed to life.

"Ya get it fixed?" drawled Dawes.

"You bet!"

"Well," McSpadden said, glancing at the sky, "I don't give a damn what those weather boys say. It looks like we're going to be having a storm. Lewis, Carter—I want those planes tied down."

"Yes, sir!" Rising, the two grabbed their jackets and headed for the door. If the captain said there was going to be a storm, then they were going to have a storm. It was that simple.

McSpadden felt uneasy, but he didn't know why. Perhaps it was the approaching storm, or the chill in the wind, or the President's speech. He didn't know.

"Lewis?"

"Sir?"

"What time's the State of the Union Address?"

"Nineteen hundred hours. That's in three hours, sir."

Pacing, McSpadden hoped against hope that President Roosevelt would finally call "*Der Fuhrer*'s" bluff and start rearming. But McSpadden was doubtful. The more Captain McSpadden thought about the developing war in Europe, the more he paced and angrier he became.

Dawes found some swing music on the radio in an attempt to lighten the captain's mood. There was a sudden crack of thunder.

"Hah!" snorted McSpadden. "I told you so."

The wind was picking up, firing droplets of rain

like missiles onto the heads of the two young pilots as they ran across the airstrip. A drumroll of thunder pounded. Lewis and Carter grinned at each other. The captain was right again.

By the time they reached the planes, the rain was sheeting down, and they flung themselves under the wings for protection.

Lewis looked at Carter. "Damn!" he muttered. "So much for staying dry."

Carter was drenched to the bone and shivering. "Two degrees colder and this stuff'd be snow."

The thunder sounded again, this time closer.

"Almost is," replied Lewis, studying the sleetlike precipitation on his palm.

"Who ever heard of lightning in a snowstorm?" Carter muttered.

The plane rocked in the wind. "We'd better get these babies tied down, or they'll take off without us," Lewis shouted above the roar of the wind.

The two climbed out from under the wing into the rain's fury. Lewis walked to the wing tip, waiting for Carter to retrieve the tie-down straps that were stored beneath the fuselage.

"Hey, what's that?" Carter yelled suddenly.

They could see the headlights of an automobile driving down the airstrip in their direction. As it neared, Lewis and Carter could see that it was a sports car, an expensive rag-top model.

The Daimler skidded to a stop. A woman and a man were inside, the man driving. Opening the window, oblivious to the rain pouring inside, the driver motioned to Carter to come close.

"Who's your commanding officer?" the driver yelled over the sound of the pelting rain.

"Captain McSpadden, sir," answered Carter without thinking to ask why this commanding-looking stranger wanted to know.

"Where can I find him?"

"Pilots' lounge beneath the tower."

"Hey! Just a gol-darned minute!" exclaimed Lewis, just arriving at the scene. He eyed the pair inside the Daimler suspiciously. "Not so fast, buddy! What can I do for you?"

The driver didn't reply. He simply jammed the car into gear and roared off toward the tower.

Carter looked at Lewis shamefacedly and said hopefully, "Maybe it's brass from Washington."

"I don't like it—I'm going back," Lewis said, undoing the flap on his holster.

Captain McSpadden was still pacing when he saw the Daimler approaching through the rain.

"Looks like company," commented Juice, pulling himself up from the leather easy chair. The car stopped at the door, and a man and a woman leaped out. Running through the rain, they dashed inside.

"Captain McSpadden?" the drenched stranger asked with an air of authority.

"Yes?"

The man pulled out a badge and flashed it. "Richard Carol, Secret Service."

McSpadden took a good look at the badge. It was Secret Service, all right, but the guy had all the makings of a mobster—a stunning woman wearing a man's suit coat over her dress, a car that would've cost McSpadden two years' salary. Maybe the guy's a spy, he thought. One of ours.

"What can I do for you?" he said finally.

"I need to place an important phone call."

"The phone's over there." McSpadden replied, pointing to the table. He noted that the woman was shivering. "Dawes? Fetch some blankets and strong coffee."

"Yes, sir."

"Why don't you have a seat, ma'am?"

The shivering woman ignored the offer. She just stared out the window into the dark sky. The Secret Service man picked up the phone, frowned, then turned to McSpadden.

"The line's dead."

"The storm must've knocked down the lines."

"What about a radio?"

Lewis burst into the room, his hand poised over his pistol. "Everything all right here, sir?"

"It's all right, Lewis. Thank you." The captain turned back to stranger. "But why don't you tell me what this is all about?"

"No time. I need the radio!" the man said coolly.

McSpadden frowned. Secret Service agent or not, he wasn't about to let this guy push him around.

"I'm afraid there's nothing I can do, sir. That radio is for offical air traffic broadcasts only. Unless it's a dire emergency, I'm afraid—"

"The nation's Capitol is about to be bombed, Captain," the Secret Service man said, cutting him off. "Is that emergency enough?"

"Bombed?" repeated McSpadden in disbelief. "And just who and how?"

"An airship."

"In this storm?" McSpadden relaxed. This guy must be a nut. "I've got news for you, mister. The only things flying in this weather are sea gulls looking for caves. Now, why don't you and the lady have some coffee, and—"

There was a sudden flare of light, and they saw a large lightning bolt hurtle from the distant clouds and strike the power generator at the far end of the field. The explosion shook the room as the lights flickered, then went out.

"Jesus!" Dawes gasped and backed away from the windows. "That was some lightning!"

"It wasn't lightning," the man said grimly.

"Huh?" McSpadden started to turn away from the window to question the stranger when he stopped suddenly. "What the hell is *that*?"

A massive, saucer-shaped object floated into view. As McSpadden watched in disbelief, bright beams of light streaked through the air, striking the generator. Within seconds, it was nothing but a lump of twisted, blackened steel.

"What—what *is* that thing?" stammered Juice.

"The airship," replied the woman.

"I've been twenty years in the air," McSpadden said, "and I've never seen anything like—"

"The radio!" the man demanded.

"No good. It ran off the generator."

The generator destroyed, the airship began to move again.

"Are your planes in flying condition?" the stranger asked.

McSpadden stared at him. "Yes, but—"

"Then get them in the air—now!"

"It'd be suicide in this weather!"

"Captain, you and your men are all that stand between that device and the President of the United States!"

McSpadden looked at his fliers. They were young and inexperienced. Even if they managed to get their craft in the air, their chances of being able to do anything to stop that massive machine were next to zero. He could tell that they, too, knew the odds, but one look at their faces told McSpadden that they were behind him.

"All right!" McSpadden sprang into action. "Juice, Buck, you two are with me. We'll take the three P-12s with the Lewis guns. We're going to keep a tight formation and then come down on her from above, concentrating our firepower. Stay close and follow my example. Lewis?"

"Sir?"

"You and Carter fly to Fort Myers and let them know what's going on here. The moment you're in the air, try reaching someone on the radio."

"Yes, sir!"

"Now, let's get those birds off the ground!"

A static electrical charge suddenly filled the room, making their hair stand on end.

"Get out of here!" yelled the Secret Service man. Running forward, he grabbed the woman and pulled her out the door and to the ground as a bolt of energy burst into the tower above them. A flying board slammed into McSpadden, knocking him to the airstrip, unconscious. The captain wasn't going to be flying anywhere.

"Keep going!" 13 yelled. "Get those planes up!"

"But—the captain! Who'll lead—"

"He'll be fine!" 13 was already taking off the captain's goggles and flight jacket. Another beam struck the Daimler, sending it flying into the rubble of the burning lounge. "Come on!" 13 shouted. "Those planes'll be next!"

The pilots ran off down the concrete as the airship hovered above. Agent 13 quickly slipped into the captain's flight jacket, cap, and goggles.

"What are you doing?" China cried.

"I'm going up to lead those boys."

The deadly chatter of machine-gun fire began to rain down from above. "Let's get out of here! You've done what you can!" China implored.

"There's still a chance. . . ."

"Don't I mean anything to you?"

13 looked at her. "I didn't kill you, did I?"

She shrank away. One look in his cold eyes told her it was over.

"You have your freedom, China. Take it." The Agent turned and sprinted away.

26

SCRAMBLE!

Agent 13 was no stranger to airplanes. Under an alias, he had flown for the French in the Great War, racking up enough kills to qualify his fictitious alter-ego as an ace. Then before the publicity hounds could expose his true identity (or the fact that he was too young), he had disappeared as mysteriously as he had arrived.

By the time Agent 13 reached the captain's P-12, the other pilots were already grinding their engines up to full throttle. Through the dim light and the wind and the rain, they could see the stranger climbing into the cockpit.

13 glanced behind him. The control tower lay in ruins, and the airship was heading for the planes on the apron. Fortunately, the gigantic ship was slowed by the strong headwind. Even so, the direction of the runway would take the planes almost directly under the monstrous death machine.

His voice crackled crisply over the radio. "It's no good trying to use the runway! Sit tight, then follow me!"

"Like hell I will!" Blake Carter snarled.

13 watched as Blake's P-12 raced down the runway trying to become airborne. The airship hovered above, waiting for its victim.

As Carter's P-12 passed beneath the ship, he felt his wheels leave the concrete. A lightning bolt suddenly crackled from an open port beneath the airship, striking the fragile biplane's engine cowling. Instantly the airplane vanished, leaving in its place a searing ball of flame.

Buck Dawes was right behind Carter. Seeing what had happened to his buddy, fear and nausea welled suddenly in his throat. He quickly jammed the throttle forward and slammed the rudder pedal, attempting to stop. Unfortunately, he was too late. Gunners from the turrets ringing the airship opened up, and lead cut through Buck's P-12 like knives through melted butter. The plane nose-dived in a flaming ball of death.

"Follow me!" 13 repeated coolly over the radio, his plane finally ready for takeoff. The two remaining young pilots glanced over at the Agent, then shrugged and decided to follow him to what they felt was certain death. To their amazement, he motioned for them to follow as he turned his plane down a service road leading out of the base.

"He's crazy!" Juice gasped, bouncing and jolting over the rough surface, expecting his plane to shake apart any moment.

"Like a fox," muttered Lewis, suddenly understanding the Agent's plan.

After a rough quarter mile, the three aircraft reached the highway. The road was wide enough to accommodate the craft. The next concern was the possibility of crosswinds, which could force the planes into the tall pines lining either side of the road. But the Agent had no time to worry. The airship was right on their tails.

13 jammed the throttle forward, and the plane surged down the road. Lewis and Tanner immediately followed, breathing a prayer that nothing would go wrong.

Agent 13 felt his craft leave the ground. Suddenly a truck, loaded with lumber, appeared out of the fog directly ahead. 13 slammed the control stick back. The plane shuddered in response, then pitched upward, slowly gaining altitude. The driver of the truck hit the brakes as the aircraft's black rubber tires grazed the roof of his cab. Then the truck lumbered into a ditch.

The truck driver watched in disbelief as two more aircraft soared overhead. He froze for a moment, then stuck his head out the window.

"Jerks!" he screamed, shaking his fist. Reaching into the glove compartment, he pulled out a bottle of scotch, took a drink to calm his nerves, then got his truck back onto the road. Suddenly he slammed on the brakes again.

"Great jumpin' jehoshaphat!" he murmured in awe. The night was lit by flickers of lightning. Looking up, the truck driver saw a giant saucer-shaped airship. Lightning bolts streaked down from it, setting trees ablaze. He could see machine guns protruding from the great ship.

The death machine passed quickly overhead, disappearing in the direction that the planes had taken. Suddenly the night was still, except for the rumblings of the dying storm. The truck driver took another long look at the road ahead, wondering if perhaps Noah's ark would be next. But nothing came. He studied the scotch in his hand, then looked back at the sky. His wife had often told him he had a drinking problem. Maybe she was right.

"I think it's over between me an' you," he said to the bottle, tossing it out the window.

The P-12s climbed quickly into the thick thunderheads. Visibility fell to near zero, and the turbulence banged them around like marbles in a washing machine. But 13 knew that the clouds afforded them protection from their deadly pursuer. Higher and higher they climbed, flying on instinct and the dials of their control panels.

13 watched as his altimeter continued to spin through the numbers—one thousand . . . five thousand . . . ten thousand—and still they were in the inky clouds. The slushy rain had turned to snow, icing up their wings, sending arctic-like temperatures through their open cockpits.

Their faces grew numb, but they had no time to notice. They had a new fear—possible midair collision with each other. They were flying blind, the only light coming from the greenish streaks of lightning that ripped the murk apart, followed by earsplitting thunderclaps. But the sporadic flashes permitted them to see the dim outlines of their own frail craft. At eleven thousand feet, they finally broke through the cloud cover.

The full moon provided a celestial peace to the gray sea of clouds beneath them. Sheets of lightning rippled in the distance. But they weren't lulled by the beauty, knowing the sinister evil that was rapidly approaching them.

"Try to raise someone on the radio," 13 ordered as Lewis and Juice came up beside him.

"No, luck, Cap—uh, sir," Lewis stammered. "All I'm getting is static. Must be the storm."

"Not likely," 13 muttered. "More likely a jamming device. Make certain your guns work."

Both young pilots checked out their weapons, glad to have something to do to keep their minds off their fears and the intense cold.

They circled, waiting for the ship to appear. 13's mind drifted to Maggie. There was every possibility she was aboard the fortress he was about to attack! 13 drove the thought from his head. He couldn't let it interfere with his mission! The airship was somewhere in the storm beneath him. It had to be stopped—no matter what the price. Maggie would understand. . . .

Then, through the clouds beneath him, 13 saw lights, and a saucer-shaped airship appeared, rising up out of the clouds, coming into focus. He was Ahab, watching as the Great White Whale—his destiny—rose from the murky sea of clouds.

It was the first time Agent 13 had seen the airship from above. The bottom and sides tapered into a saucer configuration, but the top was flat. Along its center, like the spine of a serpent, was a lighted airstrip. Two elevators operated on either side of the strip, ferrying planes to the surface. Behind them were four autogyros, tied down behind small aerodynamically tapered enclosures. The entire runway was ringed with turreted machine-gun emplacements.

13 marveled at the evil genuis of the Brotherhood, but he had no time to waste in grudging praise. Below, he could see pilots scrambling in an attempt to get their planes in the air.

"Commence attack!" 13 signaled to Lewis and Juice as his own plane peeled out of formation.

Jamming the stick forward while tramping down on the rudder, 13 banked, then dove at the target. Slowly his thumb fingered the trigger button, holding his fire until the last possible second. Then the Lewis guns spat forth a short burst.

He watched as several tracers slanted off to the right, made the proper adjustment, then fired again. His guns began to shake and shudder, spitting forth spears of flame into the night.

Suddenly he scored a hit! Down on the airship, he could see a plane that had started to take off burst into flame. A dark figure leaped out of the burning plane, running for cover with 13's bullets following him. Two other pilots raced for the walls protecting the autogyros. The Agent fingered the trigger once more, and again the tracers found their mark. The dark figures spun and crumpled.

13's bullets merely ricocheted off the ship's armored surface. By this time, the turret gunners had gotten their bearings and were zeroing in on the Agent's craft. Their bullets tore through the wings as he pulled back on the stick, to end his dive.

The G-forces of the maneuver forced the blood from his head. The Agent struggled to maintain consciousness. Once out of range, he leveled off and glanced back. The plane he had hit was still burning. Live rounds from the plane's guns were exploding and firing in all directions.

Lewis was next into the foray, his guns ratatating like cracking whips as he descended. His bursts struck the autogyros, causing them to explode in balls of flame. His guns continued their deadly chatter until suddenly 13 saw him slump forward.

Lewis's plane began to tail off to the right. The airship's gunners kept him in their sights, the staccato impact of their 50-caliber slugs ripping through the fuselage of the P-12.

The wing of Lewis's plane suddenly broke away, sending the craft into a spinning nose dive. Blazing like a rocket, the craft disappeared in the sea of clouds while the remains of the broken wing drifted down lazily after it.

13 could hear Juice swearing in rage and grief.

"Keep calm, son," 13 commanded, though he knew it wouldn't do much good.

Furious, Juice dove at the airship with a vengeance. At five hundred feet, he opened up, aiming for the gun ports. The glowing barrels of his dual machine guns explored the surface of the ship with fingers of destruction. A machine-gun turret shattered in a hail of ruin as the gunner was sent twirling sideways. The flaming figure of another gunner suddenly leaped from the destroyed port.

Juice fired another burst as his P-12 dove past the airship's port side, obviously taking hits from the deadly fusillade. Somehow he managed to survive and fly out of range.

But he was in trouble. He was diving too fast. Summoning all his strength, he hauled back on the stick, attempting to bring the nose of the craft up from its sickening descent, but nothing happened. Juice glanced at his wings as he struggled to pull up. Half his fuselage had been opened like an eggshell, the control cables destroyed. He was still struggling for his chute as the shattered hulk hurtled to its fiery doom.

13 was alone. The airship was still practically unharmed. 13 knew what had to be done. Down he plummeted. Pushing the throttle full forward, he gave the craft everything he could. Blood rushed to his head and his temples throbbed with pain as he pushed his craft past its limit.

The wings vibrated in defiance, threatening to rip from their supports. Still 13 didn't let up. With every passing second, the P-12 picked up speed. The gunners had him in their sights, but they couldn't stop him. 13 aimed his plane at the center of the runway as the flames of lead licked at his wings. At twelve hundred feet above the airship, he undid his harness. Tracers suddenly ripped into the prop blades, splintering them into thousands of deadly fragments. Sparks and oil showered from the cowling, but the plane's momentum couldn't be stopped.

For 13, the world began to spin as up became down and time slowed to a stop. Images flashed before his eyes—the parents he barely remembered. A little girl playing with a broken tin soldier. The glowing temple of the Shrine. Carmarron, her body naked in the moonlight.

The skull of the Brotherhood, the Masque of death, dealer of destruction. Maggie in a delivery room. Cries of a newborn infant. Someone slaps it. The infant's head turns—it's him!

13 was suddenly jolted back to reality. He was inside a flaming cockpit, his head ringing with the explosions of the faltering craft. He felt pain, but it was a dull, unreal sensation. The wind screamed in his ears as his reflexes took over. Fighting the rushing wind, 13 grabbed his chute's D-ring and rolled out of the cockpit, disappearing into the black void of infinity.

The gunners heard the feverish whine of the approaching engine even as they saw the plane plummet from the moonlit sky. They had endured three previous attacks, but they weren't prepared for the speed at which the aircraft was descending. They opened fire in unison, their tracers arching into the blackness like crimson fireballs. Their murderous slugs tore into the craft, eating it away in jagged chunks of metal. But the pilot didn't veer. He seemed determined to crash his plane into their ship.

Nine hundred feet above them, the plane burst into flames, and the craft became a deadly fireball as it continued its path. But the gunners didn't give up. Their concentrated fire continued to find its mark until, less than two hundred feet above their heads, the remains of the marauder exploded in a blinding flash. The sudden concussion knocked the gunners to the ground, showering them with flaming debris. Moments later, they pulled themselves from the wreckage, half deafened and blind from the blazing light.

Thus they never noticed the parachute silk as it drifted silently off the port side of the ship like a ghost.

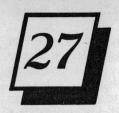

27

Belly of the Beast

When 13 landed on the airship, the runway was empty. Everyone had taken cover when the attack began. He knew, however, that they would soon return to deal with the damage. One look around told him that the P-12s' attack had been largely ineffective. The ship was still proceeding on course. The fires he saw were fueled by the debris of the destroyed planes and autogyros, not the airship itself. As 13 had foreseen, the ship was impervious to air assault. Even if 13 and the other pilots had managed to knock out the airstrip, the airship had other weapons just as deadly.

Slipping out of his chute, 13's first order of business was to gain entrance into the airship. On the port side, he found the gun turret that Juice had destroyed. Nearby were the bloody corpses of the two gunners. 13 quickly set to work removing the blood-soaked uniform from one of the dead men. Once done, he slid the naked corpse off the side of the ship.

Disguised as the gunner, he entered the smoldering gun emplacement. Here he found an iron ladder that led to the ship's interior. Grabbing the steel rungs, he grimly descended hand over hand, into the darkness.

The ladder led 13 to an iron catwalk, which in turn led him to a central gangway running directly beneath the airstrip. All around him was the austere coldness of the metal interior. The ship's basic design appeared to be similar to that of the USS *Akron*, an airship that had crashed in 1933 while at sea off Barnegat. The *Akron* was a ship of rigid frame construction. Its aluminum girders and bulkheads provided the structural support for the immense helium gas cells that filled ninety percent of the craft's interior. Lift and descent were achieved by changing the balance of gas against the water ballast located in the lower part of the ship.

Once airborne, *Akron*'s eight Maybach VL-II engines' 4480 horsepower could give it an airspeed of 79 miles per hour.

But 13 knew that the craft he was in now was vastly superior to the *Akron*. While *Akron* used aluminum for structural purposes, this new airship used a lighter weight metallic alloy whose superior strength was capable of supporting the armor-plated skin and the added weight of the airstrip above. The craft's saucerlike shape offered an aerodynamic advantage over the standard cigar-shape configuration of other airships. This, combined with the latest Pratt and Whitney engines, gave the airship greater maneuverability and an airspeed of at least one hundred and fifty miles an hour—nearly twice what the ill-fated *Akron* could achieve.

At that speed, the airship would be over Washington in less than two hours.

13 saw two chances to stop the flying leviathan. If he could locate the armory, he might be able to find a device capable of blowing the ship's bulkheads. Or, if he could gain entrance to the control room, he could empty the ballast, sending the ship rising into the air, out of control.

Logic told him that the service decks and flight centers would be located beneath the pressure of the gas cells, somewhere in the lower portion of the ship. Proceeding along the gangway, he was amazed that there seemed to be no response to their attack. Only the muffled hum of the Pratt and Whitneys reminded him that he was in an airship two thousand feet above earth.

The Agent came upon a large freight elevator, but ignored it—too many people. He preferred to take the less obvious approach, a ladder that descended into the bowels of the craft.

Reaching the bottom of the ladder, he was confronted by a hatchlike door. He pressed his ear against its metallic surface. The lack of activity above contrasted sharply to the buzz of activity on the other side.

13 cracked the door slightly. Technicians and mechanics hurried to and fro in preparation for their attack on the Capitol. Feigning the injuries that his blood-drenched uniform suggested, 13 stumbled out of the hatchway and into the lower gangway. His legs buckled beneath him as he collapsed to the steel-plated floor in apparent shock.

"Get him to the infirmary!" commanded a voice with a German accent. 13 was immediately lifted by two uniformed men and helped down the hallway. Though he appeared to be unconscious, he was in reality peering out from beneath his lashes, memorizing his surroundings.

One doorway especially caught his interest. In the glance he was afforded, he saw a large number of technical people working with many banks of electrical machines and generator-type equipment. As he was hauled past the next door, he saw what they were working on—a large towerlike apparatus bristling with capacitors, transformers, insulators, and other electrical equipment. It was a gigantic version of Dr. Fischer's Lightning Gun!

The same device had been responsible for the vaporization of Carter during takeoff, as well as the destruction of the airfield's generator and control tower. And it was the same diabolical device that would soon be turned on unsuspecting Washington unless he was able to stop it.

But even as he tried to concentrate on his prime objective, another thought intruded in his mind. What about Maggie? Was she somewhere on board? He tried to forget about her, but he caught himself trying to guess what they might have done to her and where she might be as the men carried him through a hatchway into the sick bay.

"Another one?" growled an old doctor, pulling a white cotton sheet over the charred remains of what was once a man's face.

"This one's still alive," responded one of the men as they placed the Agent on a steel table.

"Take this one away," said the doctor, gesturing to the corpse as he moved to Agent 13's side.

The doctor immediately went to work. First he checked 13's vital signs. Then he pulled back the unconscious man's eyelids. Nothing but whites. He felt the carotid artery. There was barely a pulse. Death couldn't be far away. He carefully opened the man's shirt, prepared to see his intestines spill out on the table. The doctor blinked in astonishment. No apparent injuries! Plenty of blood, but unscathed flesh. He opened the shirt wider. Still nothing.

"What the—"

The Agent's powerful, viselike hands grabbed the doctor by the throat. Leaping off the table, 13 slammed the baffled man against the wall, well out of sight of the open hatchway. "Let's talk," Agent 13 said grimly.

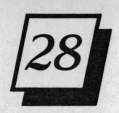

28

A CHANGE OF MIND

When Dr. David Fischer was captured by the Brotherhood, the reason was easy to understand—they wanted the Lightning Gun. They believed in him, having followed his lectures and attended his demonstrations. They had seen his proposals for a full-sized version of the weapon, and they knew it would work. So they had plotted to kidnap him.

It was because of the Brotherhood's influence that the United States Army refused to take Fischer seriously. Acting behind the scenes, the Brotherhood had destroyed his dreams and his career until finally he was a shattered wreck.

They enticed him aboard the *Normandie*, then kidnapped him as they had so many other crack scientists. But they didn't bother to torture Fischer. They figured they had already reduced him to emotional rubble. They came to him as friends.

"We can help you fulfill your dream!" the Masque said. "We have money, resources, manpower. We'll help you create this revolutionary device. You're a visionary, professor—a man ahead of your time. The ignorant masses cannot possibly see this. But *I* can! Together we will show the world!"

Fischer proved stronger than they'd anticipated. He knew what horrible power might be unleashed if his Lightning Gun fell into the wrong hands. He didn't trust this masked figure. He didn't trust any organization that had to resort to kidnapping, and he bluntly said so to the Masque. He then demanded to be sent back home.

As a result, Dr. Fischer ended up beneath the Helmet of Truth. After several sessions, the wretched man was more than willing to cooperate. To ensure his "enthusiasm" for the project, his sister and her husband were kidnapped and held at an undisclosed location.

Fischer began work. Whatever he needed, he received—including other scientists. After several months of forced labor, the device was finally finished, and a test was arranged. The cannon was fired at the USS *Trent*. After two direct hits, the ship simply ceased to exist.

The results exceeded even the Masque's expectations. He sent Fischer a congratulatory bottle of champagne, which the scientist promptly smashed. Even as the completion of the Lightning Gun was Dr. Fischer's dream, the hands that now controlled it were his nightmare. He wanted to destroy his demonic child. But how? He was guarded day and night.

When the airship was complete, the Masque's men loaded the cannon into a special chamber designed to house the gun. Large bomb-bay doors could be opened, permitting the cannon to discharge its tremendous power.

The Masque personally led Fischer and four other scientists on a tour of the awesome ship. As they stared at it in helpless horror, armed guards began prodding them up the entry ramp, forcing them inside.

"Surely you want to witness the tremendous capabilities of your wonderful weapon, Dr. Fischer," the Masque said.

"I'm a scientist, not a murderer!" Fischer protested helplessly.

"Precisely. And as a scientist, you will appreciate why I need you. Nothing must go wrong! If it does, I want you there to fix it."

There was nothing Fischer and the other scientists could do. Heavily armed guards watched them every second.

The airship had been in the air only thirty minutes when the command was given to open the doors beneath the Lightning Gun. Generators hummed, channeling power into the cannon's massive capacitors.

"What are you doing?" Fischer demanded.

"We've got orders to commence firing, Doc," said one of the workers.

"No!" Fischer began, but he heard the click of a rifle bolt behind him and could do nothing. He watched helplessly as a gunner donned goggles and began to operate the hydraulics that controlled the movements of the Lightning Gun.

Fischer watched in anguish as the gentle countryside rolled beneath them, wondering what their target was going to be. Breathing in the sea-scented air, watching the peaceful countryside drift by below, he thought of his past, remembering walks on the beach. Suddenly the picture stopped. Frozen below them, like a picture suspended in time, was a telephone relay terminal.

Suddenly the gun surged with electricity. A green light flashed, signaling that the power was sufficient to launch the deadly bolt.

"Fire!" a voice commanded. All heads turned aside as two hundred million volts filled the room and a plasmic bolt of electricity left the gun. A split second later, a thunderclap jolted their ears as the shock wave blew hot wind into their faces. It was an awesome display of power—except this time it wasn't a test.

Below the ship, the relay terminal lay in ruins. Fragments of twisted metal and wires were everywhere. All eyes in the room stared at the destruction they had wrought. No one spoke. It was as if the power of God had been harnessed.

A second order to fire snapped them back to their senses. They quickly turned their heads once more as the green light went on for the second time. Again the flash filled the room. As they looked below, they saw charred earth and a gaping hole where the station had once been.

The airship started to move as the Lightning Gun recharged for a third time. Storm clouds closed in, and rain blew through the open bomb-bay doors. Soon the gunner found a new target—the power generator of a distant airfield. The gun's tongue spat once more, and again came destruction. Next—a control tower. Next—a fighter plane. There was no end to the nightmare.

Dr. Fischer buried his head in his hands. What had he done? How many more deaths must he be responsible for? If he had only been stronger, if he hadn't submitted to their will . . .

Finally the bomb-bay doors closed, and the airship ascended into the clouds. The sound of an air battle above told Fischer that something was trying to stop the menace. Fischer prayed for the giant airship's destruction. He didn't care if he went down, too. All he asked was that his tormentors and the Lightning Gun go with him.

One by one, the sounds of the attacking engines swept past the ship, and one by one they were silenced. The men in the room began to cheer. Dr. Fischer started to weep. He knew that the attack had failed. The airship truly was invincible.

The guards shoved the shattered man into a corner. Alone, frightened, Fischer was considering hurling himself out the bomb-bay doors when suddenly he felt a hand upon his arm.

Startled, he spun around. A man wearing a gray technician's jacket stood beside him. He held a clipboard in his hand and appeared to be checking the settings on a bank of dials on a nearby generator. Fischer couldn't recall having ever seen this man before. The eyes, especially, were arresting—piercing, intense, intelligent.

"I'm a friend," the technician whispered.

"I have no friends here!" the scientist cried out.

At the sound of Fischer's voice, his guards turned. Who was he talking to? The only person near him was a technician, who looked at the professor blankly and moved away. The guards shook their heads and resumed talking.

"Dr. Fischer, listen to me!" The distraught scientist heard the whispered voice again.

He looked dazedly around. No one was even near him! Was he finally going mad?

"Who—" Fischer started to ask.

The voice cut him off. "Don't speak out again, Doctor. Just listen. I repeat—I am a friend."

Fischer spun around and looked. The technician wasn't even facing him!

"Don't be alarmed. I am able to ventriloquize my words so that only you can hear them. I have come to destroy the Lightning Gun and this airship, but I can succeed only with your help.

"If those who forced you to build this weapon are allowed to continue with their plans, thousands, perhaps millions, will die. The planet will be plunged into darkness such as it has never known. You and I are all that stand in the way, but I can't do it without you. If you will help me, cough softly. I will hear you."

Fischer's head whirled. Could this man be telling the truth? Or was this another trick of the Masque's? If it was a trick, it was a clever one. But why now? The ship was already in the air. If he had been going to sabotage it, Fischer surely would have done it before the gun was completed.

It only made sense if the technician was who he claimed to be. But how could he have gotten aboard? Questions spun through the professor's mind. He had to admit he didn't know the answers. Through his months of captivity, Fischer had learned to trust no one.

Fischer was about to decide to ignore the man when several guards suddenly burst through the door. A burly guard pulled out a pistol and, approaching the technician, shoved the cold steel of the barrel into the man's temple.

Another guard, tall and muscular, grabbed the technician by the hair and jerked his head around, holding his face up. Behind the guard, someone whispered, "That's him!" The ship's doctor was being held up by two guards, but after speaking, he slumped into unconsciousness.

"Hey, what's going on?" the technician cried, his clipboard clattering to the floor. "I—"

Without a word, the guard struck the technician on the temple with the barrel of his gun. Quickly they caught the unconscious technician and dragged him to the door.

"Back to work, everyone!" commanded a voice over the radio-intercom.

So it wasn't a trick! Fischer thought disappointedly as he watched the guards haul the man away.

"Hey!" One of the guards loomed up before Fischer. "What did that guy say to you?"

Dr. Fischer blinked and said, "Nothing . . . nothing at all."

29

A Sinister Scheme

Darkness. Nothing but darkness. His brain told him he was alive, as did the pain throbbing through his head. 13 automatically recited the ancient words that banished pain.

The vibrations set up by the repeated words enveloped his body in soothing waves of energy. Agent 13 could think again.

He recalled the events that led up to the moment he'd been struck. What had gone wrong? The ship's doctor should have died from the poison. Somehow, someone had gotten to him in time, someone who knew the antidote. . . .

The Agent remained motionless, his senses exploring his environment, assembling the facts.

A redness through his closed eyelids indicated there was light in the room. He was lying flat on a table apparently cushioned with leather. He was barefoot. His clothes appeared to be some sort of hospital gown. His watch and rings had been removed.

Elastic bindings held down his arms and legs. He could hear the din of the Pratt and Whitneys, so he was still in the airship. But his acute hearing picked up something else—someone breathing. And there was a scratching noise. 13 was not alone.

He opened his eyes slowly. The gray, slanted wall he faced contained large rectangular windows that afforded a sweeping view. He could see armor-plated shutters that could be shut quickly. It was dark outside the windows.

The Agent turned his head. He saw more blank gray walls, then a metal desk, cold and austere. Then he saw him.

The man was masked, as he had appeared in the filmed threats 13 had viewed in Washington. The Omega and Star symbol of the Brotherhood was affixed to his hood, and a Seer Stone hung from around his neck. The Masque!

He sat at the desk, fountain pen in hand, writing on paper before him. Except for the movements of his hand, he was motionless, deathlike.

His raspy breathing echoed through the chill room like the hiss of a reptile. He paused for a moment, as if in thought, then set the pen down.

All was still. Then 13 heard a low, dry chuckle.

The Masque rose from the desk, his face obscured in his hooded garment. "Welcome, Agent 13. At long last we meet. I congratulate you. It took an extraordinary man to spirit China White from my fortress, attack my airship, then manage to sneak on to it as well. You have been a worthy opponent—but the game is over!"

13 saw the Masque reach beneath the desk. There was a click, and the Agent heard the soft horns from Wagner's *Tannhauser*. The Masque rose and walked over to the bound Agent.

"Did you really believe you could stop me?"

13 did not answer but merely smiled.

The Masque stared out the windows. Flipping a switch, he turned on large spotlights outside the ship. The lights illuminated the cottony tops of the gray, puffy clouds below them. He seemed lost for a moment in his thoughts and the music.

"Beautiful, isn't it? The sea of clouds, so peaceful and serene. Yet capable of so much destruction—hailstorms, blizzards, tornadoes, thunderbolts . . ." He turned back to face 13.

"You are a fool. Our forces stand poised to strike. Soon we will be the earth's supreme masters, an opportunity we should have seized long ago. It was a destiny you might have shared—but you heard a different calling." He sneered. "All your efforts have been wasted, smashed like a grain of sand beneath my heel!"

13 stared hard at the hooded presence before him. "Why Washington?" he asked curiously.

"Because the United States stands in our way. We tried to achieve our ends by more subtle means, but your leaders refused. They've resisted long enough. Now they shall pay!"

"Your terrorism will unify the country against you."

"That's precisely what we plan. Tonight the governing body of this nation will cease to exist. It will be an animal without a head. . . ."

"For every one you kill, another will step forward with even greater resolve to oppose you."

"Exactly right, 13." He chuckled again. "And who do you suppose that other person will be? Who more qualified than—" The Masque removed his hood.

It was Kent Walters, the National Security Advisor! The entire plot was suddenly clear to 13. Kent Walters, supposedly still recovering from his wounds, would be the only major political figure who *wouldn't* be present at the State of the Union Address—and thus, the only survivor.

"With everyone else killed, you'll be able to take over the Presidency!" said the Agent.

Walters smiled. "Precisely. I've already laid the groundwork. I'm a hero to the public since the assassination attempt. With most of the members of Congress dead, I will step in and console a grieving nation. My first task as the new President will be to crack down on the terrorists responsible for the tragic deaths of the goverment leaders.

"The Masque will deliver yet another threat. This time it will be directed at a dam. The lives of thousands will be endangered. Would you like me to read it to you?" Grinning, Walters produced the sheet of paper that he was working on earlier.

"Not particularly," 13 responded dryly.

Walters returned the sheet to his pocket. "It doesn't matter. What's important is the result.

"At the last moment, the Armed Forces, under my direct command, will discover, then destroy, the airship and the Masque. It will be *I* who delivers the nation from the evil that threatens it. Once again, I will be the hero.

"And when war finally breaks out, the people will follow me blindly as I bring the United States to the aid of the misunderstood Axis powers. With the vast wealth of this nation, nothing can stop us from taking over the world! Then the Brotherhood will rise from the shadows and take possession for all eternity!"

13 said nothing. His mind raced through the scenario Walters had described. Once again, he marveled at the Brotherhood's genius. Their plan could work! Had he fought and struggled all these years only to fail now?

"It's a pity you won't be here to see it, 13. You are to be returned to the Shrine. There the brainwashing techniques will be continued. The Jindadii awaits. . . ."

13 went cold. He feared only one thing—and that was it! He would become the Serpentine Assassin once again! Who would he be instructed to kill this time?

Seeing 13 pale, Walters began to laugh maniacally. A red light began to flash on the wall above his desk. Turning, Walters pressed the intercom switch.

"Yes?"

"We'll be over Washington in thirty-five minutes," a voice crackled over the intercom.

"Good. Any sign of resistance?"

"None whatsoever."

"Good. Send four guards to my office immediately."

"Yes, sir."

Walters turned back to Agent 13, smiling grimly. "You will be given the same drug that was administered to you previously. The next face you see will be the face of the Jinda-dii."

"What about Maggie Darr?" 13 asked.

"Ah, yes, the sweet Maggie. What a treasure you found there. She's quite safe, I assure you."

"Is she aboard?"

"Oh, yes," he said, leering.

"I want to see her," 13 said.

Walters sighed. "I'm afraid that's impossible."

"I still have the Seer Stone. Let me see her and I'll tell you where it is."

Walters chuckled. "With your return to the Shrine, the stone is nothing but a worthless rock."

"If I fail to come back, I've left instructions with my agents explaining its use. They'll carry on the fight without me."

"And therefore I don't believe you, 13. You are too strong to compromise your agents for the sake of seeing a woman, no matter how sweet her flesh might be. No, you would give me a location, but I have no doubt that the Seer Stone would not be there."

"Can you afford the risk?"

"Indeed. You see, one of your first assignments, my fledgling Serpentine Assassin, will be to track down and destroy all of your own agents. . . ."

Four guards filed into the room and stood at attention in the doorway.

Walters looked at the Agent one last time. "I am disappointed in you, 13," he said coldly. "Look at you, carrying on like a lovesick schoolboy. Perhaps the Brotherhood was mistaken about you." Walters turned to the guards. "Take him away! Make sure he is given a full view of the coming event, then administer the drug."

The guards picked up the top of table that the Agent was strapped to. It turned out to be some type of stretcher.

"Good-bye, 13. I hope your journey to the Shrine is a pleasant one." Walters smiled.

The last thing 13 heard as he was carried off was laughter echoing from the cold, gray walls.

30

COOPERATIVE DEATH

Dr. Fischer didn't know who the man was that the guards had dragged away. It didn't matter. What counted was that someone finally had the courage to stand up against them!

The incident snapped Fischer out of his own shock. Perhaps something could still be done! Any doubts he might have had as to how they intended to use his gun had been quickly dispelled at the airfield.

The stranger was right. It was only going to get worse. He would be responsible for the deaths of thousands! He had to act quickly to stop it, before the next fiendish event occurred!

He was being watched constantly by three guards. Besides them, there were two technicians and two other scientists who, like himself, had been kidnapped.

So they outnumbered the guards. But what could they do? The answer was simple. They could destroy the gun. It would take some doing, but it was possible. He would need the help of the others, however, to deal with the guards.

"Uh, I don't think that dial is reading correctly," Fischer said, hurrying over to make an adjustment. Standing next to the dial was Dr. Floyd Stockwell, the designer of the massive capacitors that stored the charge for the cannon. Stockwell and Fischer had worked closely together for the last several months. Though Stockwell wasn't any more of a fighter than Fischer, he was resourceful. If there was one man that Fischer thought he could trust, it was Stockwell.

When Fischer approached Stockwell, the guards didn't give a second look. They were used to seeing the two involved in long technical discussions.

"We've got to stop this!" Fischer whispered.

"You're right," Stockwell replied in a low tone. "I don't care what happens to me anymore, but we mustn't let more innocent people die!"

"Can we take the guards?" Fischer asked.

"Get O'Brien," Stockwell suggested. "He's been in enough barroom brawls in his time."

Fischer looked dubious. Curly O'Brien was a large Irishman with a taste for whiskey. He was also the designer of the generators that created the power for Fischer's gun. But O'Brien believed that it was Fischer who had been responsible for his kidnapping and didn't trust him.

"Let me talk to him," Stockwell said, noticing Fischer's hesitation. "We've discussed escape before. We can trust him."

The technicians were another story. Two of them were small-time hoodlums with technical skills, who had become indebted to the Brotherhood.

"Don't worry," Stockwell said. "They'll follow whoever's got the guns.

"Dr. O'Brien," Stockwell called. "We have a minor problem here, but it could turn into something major. Could you come and have a look?"

O'Brien approached, scowling at Fischer as usual. In a low voice, Stockwell explained the situation. O'Brien smiled grimly.

"I've been waiting a long time for this!" he growled. "I never thought you lily-livered cowards would make up your minds. But, if you have—"

"We have, I assure you," Dr. Fischer said.

O'Brien thought a moment, then proposed a plan. Pretending that there was an emergency with the gun, O'Brien, Fischer, and Stockwell would assign the technicians jobs "of the utmost urgency." Once they were busy, a minor disaster would occur with one of the power cables. This would require the assistance of the three guards. When the guards were holding onto the cable, a switch would be thrown, sending two thousand pulsating volts through the cable.

The "accident" would take care of the three guards permanently. The scientists would then grab their weapons and seal the hatch leading into the room. Then they would destroy the gun itself.

Precisely on cue, the "emergency" occurred.

"Hey, you!" O'Brien bellowed at the technicians. "Check those readings!"

The technicians scurried off. O'Brien was about to create the cable "disaster" when he saw movement in the hatchway. The scientists turned nervously, staring as four more guards entered the room carrying a man strapped to a wooden slab, like a tabletop.

"That's him!" Fischer whispered to Stockwell. "That's the technician they hit over the head. He's the one who suggested this to me."

The guards carried the bound stranger into the room and were starting to set him down on the floor when a hunchbacked dwarf appeared in the doorway.

"Put 'im in the bomb-bay door!" urged the dwarf.

The guards gave a start as Lexner produced a submachine gun and leveled it at their chests.

"Do as I say!" the dwarf commanded.

"What's this?" a guard asked as the other three carried the man out onto the closed bomb-bay doors. "The Masque said we were supposed to give this guy a good seat, but this is ridiculous! When the gun goes off, the guy'll fry!"

"That's the idea!" cried the dwarf. "He killed Axel and Dr. Natchez! Now he's gonna pay!"

"But orders are—" the guard began.

"It'll be an 'accident,' " the dwarf interrupted. "And if there's any more arguing, the accident won't stop with him! Now, move!"

The scientists watched helplessly as the guards carried the man out onto the bomb-bay doors.

"Tie him to those hinges!" ordered the dwarf.

Stockwell glanced at Fischer, standing near the lever that controlled the doors. He made a subtle motion, as if pulling the lever. Fischer shuddered. He couldn't send those men to their deaths!

The guards set down the table, then went to work. Lexner stood over them, grinning widely. Fischer wondered about the stranger, who seemed resigned to his fate.

The guards lashed the stranger's wrists and ankles with heavy rope, then began to tie the ends to the door hinges. When the doors opened, he would be suspended directly in front of the gun. When the Lightning Gun fired, he would be vaporized instantly.

Fischer began to sweat. The four guards and the dwarf obviously weren't going to leave until they had achieved their sinister objective. The tension in the room was building. They couldn't take much more of this!

The stranger turned his eyes toward Dr. Fischer. "Go ahead," he told the professor silently. "Do it!"

The first guard finished his knots, and his

glance followed the stranger's gaze. The guard saw Fischer standing next to the lever and sensed what Fischer was planning to do. But it was too late!

"Hey! Get away fr—" The guard's words trailed into a scream as the bomb-bay doors suddenly swung open. Everyone standing on the doors, including the dwarf and the stranger, dropped from sight.

Fischer froze, horror-struck. But he had no time for remorse. One of the remaining three guards whipped out a pistol and fired. The slug slammed into Fischer's shoulder, spinning him back against the wall. The guard took aim again, intending to finish the job, when suddenly he was hit from behind with an iron wrench. The guard collapsed to his knees, clutching his head in agony as Dr. Stockwell stood over him, staring at him grimly.

The second guard reached for his gun just as an uninsulated electrical cable, thrown by O'Brien's powerful arms, wrapped around his neck. O'Brien threw the switch and it was over instantly. The man's hair stood on end as thousands of volts fried him to a crisp.

The third guard was still fumbling for his gun when the two technicians, seeing who was coming out on top, knocked him down and pummeled him into unconsciousness.

Grabbing the guns of the guards, the scientists suddenly found themselves in charge.

"Someone get the door!" barked Stockwell, hurrying to the injured Fischer.

"You—" O'Brien growled to the two technicians, "are you with us or not?"

Glancing nervously at each other, both technicians took this opportunity to beat a hasty retreat.

O'Brien slammed the door shut and closed the

locks. They were safe for the moment.

"You all right?" Stockwell asked, helping Fischer to his feet.

"I—I think so," Fischer breathed, looking at his blood-splattered smock. "It seems to have missed the bone."

"What about the bleeding?"

"It'll be okay."

Fischer felt pain, not so much from the wound, but from the knowledge that he had dropped the stranger and all the other men to their deaths. Unlike his Lightning Gun, when someone else pulled the trigger, this time it was his direct action that led to people's deaths. He had committed murder.

"I need help here!" yelled O'Brien urgently from the bomb-bay doors. Fischer and Stockwell ran to his side.

Looking down, Fischer gasped. The stranger, still strapped to the table, was dangling upside down beneath the ship by a single strand of rope secured to his ankle. Clinging to another rope, attached to the stranger's wrist, was one of the guards!

The stranger was unconscious. The strain on his leg must be tremendous, Fischer thought. The guard was screaming and kicking at the empty air in a desperate struggle to hold on to life.

"Someone give me a hand here!" yelled Stockwell as he dropped to his knees and began pulling.

O'Brien and Fischer reeled in the stranger, but as they did, the table caught on the door. They couldn't pull it up any farther. The guard began losing his grip on the rope as the rough hemp slipped and tore into the flesh of his palms.

"Hold on!" yelled Stockwell in a moment of compassion as he extended his arm down to the guard.

The panic-stricken man reached out with his hand, his fingertips only an inch from Stockwell's. Beads of sweat ran down the guard's forehead as he struggled to reach him.

"I—I can't . . ." he gasped.

"Reach!" yelled Stockwell, his fingers stretching for the extra distance.

The man slipped.

There was no scream, no yell, only silence as he plunged into the darkness, disappearing into the void of the passing cloud cover below.

"It's probably just as well," O'Brien muttered.

With the guard's weight gone, the scientists were able to pull the table and the stranger in the rest of the way.

Resting the table on the deck, they removed the straps from the stranger's wrists and ankles.

"Listen to the way he's breathing," said O'Brien. "Look at his face! He's not unconscious. He's in some kind of trance!"

Soon the strange, hoarse breathing subsided. The stranger opened his eyes. He was instantly alert. Instead of being contorted by fear or confusion, his face was calm and clear, his mind lucid.

Quickly he rose from the table, fully awake. It was almost as if he had just returned from a relaxing vacation, thought Fischer in amazement.

13 looked around him, quickly assessing the situation. The guards had been taken care of. The room had been sealed off, the scientists inside apparently united in cause and purpose.

"Tie up those guards. They'll be coming around shortly," 13 commanded.

Stockwell hurried to obey, but O'Brien remained behind, staring at the stranger suspiciously.

"Who is this guy?" O'Brien demanded.

"I don't know! He said that he—" Fischer's

voice faded as loud pounding and hammering began on the hatchways.

"Open up in there!" shouted a voice.

"Now what?" Stockwell looked alarmed.

"How do I destroy this gun?" asked 13.

Fischer stammered. "Well, there—there are several possible ways. The first would be—uh—"

13 impatiently cut him off. He didn't have time for long-winded explanations. He had but one purpose now—to destroy the gun.

As Fischer rambled on, O'Brien and Stockwell began shoving tables against the door. 13 quickly sized up the device, its massive capacitors towering upward in rings of iron and steel, the monstrous, snoutlike barrel pointing downward, waiting to be fired again. With several large coils of wire, he saw a way to create a back-surge that would destroy the gun. Unfortunately, it would also destroy everything else in the room, themselves included. Suddenly he had another idea.

"What kind of gases are in the cells?" the Agent interrupted Fischer.

The doctor blinked, thinking a moment. "It's a helium and oxygen mix."

The gas wasn't flammable.

"They're coming through!" Stockwell shouted.

The metal door was beginning to creak and bend under the repeated blows from what sounded like sledgehammers. "Put down your weapons and surrender!" a voice crackled over the intercom. "You are surround—"

The retorts of O'Brien's pistol, firing into the speaker, shut the voice up for good.

"God, that felt great!" O'Brien grinned.

Ignoring the commotion, 13 leaped into the gunner's seat and began spinning the cranks that controlled the Lightning Gun's movement. The snout began to tilt upward. The moment it started to swing above the bomb-bay door, however, it stopped. 13 looked down at the gears. There was a safety catch that prevented further movement. It could not, therefore, be turned inward.

Leaping away from the gun, 13 grabbed a pistol from Stockwell's hand.

"What are you going to do?" Stockwell cried.

"Stand back!" 13 yelled as he leveled the pistol at the gears.

13 fired four times, each spinning slug ripping away a pin that prevented the gears from swinging upward. The grim-faced Agent quickly leaped back into the gunner's seat and began to crank the gears once more. The cold black snout of the gun slowly rose toward the ceiling of the airship.

"What's he doing, for God's sake?" shouted O'Brien, backing up as the hatch door slowly caved in.

"Get ready to fire this thing!" 13 commanded.

The men in the room looked at each other, suddenly realizing that he was going to fire the gun into the airship itself.

"Let's do it!" yelled O'Brien to the others.

"We could all die!" Stockwell said, putting into words what they all knew. Without hesitation, all three men ran for their posts.

Slowly they brought the generator up to full power. Grabbing the protective goggles dangling from the gunner's chair, 13 watched the dials, waiting for the green light that would tell him it was ready to fire.

Suddenly bullets filled the air. 13 looked over at the hatch. The crew of the airship had managed to bend open one corner of it. One of the guards was taking potshots at anyone he could see.

Lifting his pistol, 13 fixed his eyes on the target, then fired.

The bullet's impact knocked the pistol from the

guard's hand and splintered his wrist into thousands of fragments. As the man withdrew the remains of his hand, 13 knew it would be a while before they tried that again.

The scientists, meanwhile, had never left their posts. They, too, affixed their goggles. The generators hummed, filling the capacitors with millions of volts. Suddenly the green light came on.

"Take cover!" yelled the Agent.

He waited seconds more while everyone else scrambled for safety. Unfortunately there wasn't much to hide behind.

The Agent squeezed the trigger. The blinding white light was instantaneous with the explosive concussion. Fragments and shards of twisted iron tore through the room in a fiery maelstrom of destruction.

13 was slammed back against his seat, his face blasted by the searing hot winds of the flames. The glass of the instrument dials cracked and sparked. The din of the explosion filled their ears.

Agent 13, who had been protected by the huge apparatus of the gun, took off his goggles and looked at the remains of the room around him. The blackened steel walls looked as if they had been peppered by shotgun blasts. A massive whirlwind of escaping gases spun through the room, creating a storm of debris. Shielding his eyes from the damaging splinters, he scanned the room.

Stockwell, his shirt torn to shreds, stood in a daze, his face covered with blood that gushed from a deep gash in his forehead. O'Brien rolled on the steel floor, groaning in agony, pulling at a five-inch shard of steel protruding from his knee. Fischer, apparently unharmed, knelt beside O'Brien, trying to help.

The efforts of the crew to get into the room had

stopped. There was no sound outside.

13 pulled himself from the wreckage of the gun. The entire device had been blown off its support stand and thrown backward by the force of the explosion. Freeing himself from the gunner's seat, he inspected the damage to the airship.

A fifteen-foot hole had been blasted through the ceiling. Girders and cables dangled like dead vines as the helium winds from the torn gas cells rushed past his face.

Staring upward, 13 could see no end to the hole. It disappeared into darkness. He wondered how many gas cells the blast had ruptured. He could see two. There might be more. Was that enough?

Then 13 felt something. His acute sense of balance told him the floor was beginning to list. Was it the ship itself or just a buckled floor plate, damaged by the explosion?

Suddenly, outside the door, he could hear pounding footsteps, voices shrill with panic shouting confused orders. Falling flat, 13 peered out the open bomb-bay doors. The ship seemed to be losing altitude, but it was hard to tell for certain. A loud, painful moan seemed to come from the airship itself. Was it collapsing?

"She's going to break up! Are there any chutes?" 13 asked.

"Yeah, I'll get 'em!" answered Stockwell, wiping blood from his face.

Hurrying to a supply compartment, he yanked it open and began pulling out belly chutes. Suddenly they heard what sounded like a rushing stream beneath their feet.

13 saw hundreds of gallons of water plummeting toward the ground. The crew was dumping the ballast of water in an effort to keep the airship aloft.

The craft shuddered. Everyone in the room

looked at each other. Even the injured O'Brien quit moaning. Fischer had managed to remove the sliver of steel and was wrapping a crude bandage around O'Brien's bleeding knee. He sat back. The slant of the floor was now plain to everyone in the room. The airship was beginning to list!

"Put on the chutes!" commanded 13.

Then, from deep in the hull's interior, came an ominous cracking noise like the breaking of matchsticks. The aluminum girders were snapping! Klaxon horns of alarm began to resound throughout the stricken ship.

Stockwell and Fischer helped O'Brien into a parachute. They were getting into theirs when a nearby beam supporting the bomb-bay doors suddenly snapped with a sickening crack. The beam dangled for a moment beneath the ship's hull, then wrenched itself free, tumbling end over end to the earth, thousands of feet below. The entire structure was breaking up!

Like a speared whale, the enormous craft began to screech and moan its death song to the heavens. The mighty airship was finished.

"Get out of here while you still can!" barked the Agent.

"What about you?" asked Fischer, noticing that 13 wasn't putting on a chute.

"I still have something to take care of! Now, get out of here!"

Fischer stared down into the inky blackness.

"I—I can't!" he moaned.

The Agent looked at Fischer's chute. It was fastened on properly. Grabbing the professor, 13 hauled him over to the bomb-bay doors.

"Count to three, then pull the ring!" 13 instructed, then he shoved Fischer out. The scientist shrieked, but 13 thought he could hear a faint voice counting. He turned around.

"Who's next?"

Stockwell jumped forward. When O'Brien limped, grimacing, to the door, the Agent stopped him.

"Give me your pistol."

"You got it," O'Brien said, happy to be rid of the thing. The next moment, he was gone, falling through the black void on his way to freedom.

13 was alone. He had two priorities—the first, to make certain the Masque did not escape alive; the second, to find Maggie.

Taking two of the parachutes, he hid them beneath some debris. Then, pistol in hand, he spun open the undamaged hatch door and ran out into the corridor.

31

For Whom The Bell Tolls

No one gave 13 a second glance as he hurried to the command room. He was only one of many who were rushing frantically through the stricken craft.

Passing the hangar, 13 noticed that the floor was listing so badly that the elevators wouldn't function. Planes were stuck down below, with no way to get them to the airstrip on top. Men scrambled for chutes as officers barked final commands.

13 noticed the planes beginning to slide along the floor, unbalancing the weight of the ship toward the bow. Everyone ignored them, too busy trying to save their own lives.

The stern of the ship began to rise upward. Oil drums broke free, rolling along the floor and knocking men down like tenpins. Flames erupted as the contents spilled over the hangar floor.

13 ran on, until he reached Walters's door. He kicked it open. It was dark inside, apparently empty. He dashed inside. Light from the corridor outside gleamed on something bright and shiny on Walters's desk—13's rings!

The Agent grabbed them. He would have a use for at least one of them, he hoped.

Racing out into the corridor, he grabbed the first body he saw. He shoved the pistol barrel into the crewman's chin with such force that it slammed the man's head back against the wall.

"Where are Walters and the girl?" 13 demanded.

"Wal—Wal—Walters?" the man stammered in panic.

13 pulled the hammer back. "The Masque!"

The man shook his head from side to side.

13 fired the pistol, missing the man's face by a quarter of an inch. Blood dripped down the side of the crewman's head, his eardrum shattered.

13 moved nearer, shoving the pistol into the man's throat. "Where?"

"The airstrip! He took her up on the roof!"

Tossing thc man to the floor like a used dishrag, 13 ran down the slanting corridor, heading for the iron stepladder he had used when he first entered the ship. As he ran, he wondered why Walters would go to the roof. The autogyros were destroyed. Did he have a plane up there?

Slamming open the hatchway, 13 grabbed the cold steel of the ladder. The ladder was tilting with the ship. It would be a difficult climb, but he had no choice.

Something caught his eye—movement! In the darkness above, he could see shadows moving upward. Was it them?

Seconds seemed like minutes, minutes like hours as 13 climbed hand over hand. The air was rapidly filling with smoke, becoming heavy with heat from the fires somewhere far below.

The weight of his body seemed to increase the higher he went. He tried to block out the fatigue, but his mind found it difficult to concentate. Finally he gave vent to his pent-up anger, letting it pump needed adrenaline into his system.

He was filled with a kind of madness, akin to battle-rage. The tilting of the ladder no longer affected him. He was a ravenous predator, stalking the game he must kill.

Consumed with fury, he climbed the ladder at an almost superhuman rate.

Suddenly he came to the top of the ladder and jumped off it, landing on the steeply pitched gangway. There was nothing in sight but an open hatchway in the distance. 13 sprinted down the pitched steel deck to the open hatch. Crawling through, he saw that it led to the airstrip above.

Sweat streamed down his face as he raced up the tilting stairs three at a time. Then, kicking open the final hatch that led to the airstrip, he was out in the open.

Chilled winds blasted at his face as he stared into the blackness of night. The airship's bow was pitched in a steep dive. The airstrip and surrounding surface were still littered from the debris of their earlier attack. Beyond that, the area appeared abandoned, the gunners who survived the attack having left their posts long ago.

Suddenly 13 heard the click of a bolt, then another. Whirling, he examined the pitching deck closely. 13 saw a huge steel device, strong enough to be pressurized, apparently buried in the deck. Explosive bolts were snapping back along its side, releasing it from the ship, raising it up. The device was ringed by thick glass portholes. What was this thing?

Then, through the portholes, he saw Walters, moving around in the greenish light within the capsule.

13 began to claw his way toward the device. The pitching deck made his journey difficult; one misstep and he'd slide to his doom. But he was like a fly. Every hairline fracture and rivet in the deck supplied him with the purchase he needed.

Then he heard the hissing of rushing gases. A large port cover exploded off the roof of the bell, and a canvas bag began to inflate and rise upward. It was a hot-air balloon! Walters was using a balloon with a pressurized gondola to escape!

The massive balloon inflated rapidly, slowly pulling the rounded escape bell from its protective cradle in the ship's deck.

13 lunged at the rising bell. For a moment, he was suspended in midair, the airship slanting away beneath him. If he missed, it was certain death, but it no longer mattered. 13 was consumed by one thought, one mission—to destroy Walters.

His hands closed over steel, and his body slammed into the side of the bell. Rivets bruised and tore at his flesh unnoticed. His hands, their knuckles white with anger and strength, clutched at a cable. Clinging precariously to the cable hanging from the ship's side, he hung on as the craft began its rapid ascent.

Slowly, using all of his incredible strength, 13 pulled himself up to the flattened top of the bell. Looking up, he could see the hemp ropes that held the pressurized bell rising upward to encircle the massive fabric balloon as it continued to inflate. The entire device rose rapidly into the heavens. The chill of the subzero winds tore at his flesh. 13 looked below him.

The airship was growing smaller. Flames poured from her inner ports as she began to sink, bow first, into the great sea of clouds. It was destroyed. It could hurt no one now.

Leaning over, he looked through the thick, round plate of a port window. 13 could see Walters clearly. His hands wanted to reach through the window and tear him apart, shredding him piece by piece.

There were two others inside the small bell, a

pilot—and Maggie! She seemed more angry than frightened, but she appeared to be uninjured.

Abruptly, 13 was aware of a new danger—anoxia! The air was thinning rapidly with the increased altitude. His oxygen was running out!

What could he do? There was no way to force himself into the bell. The small, thick glass portholes cranked shut from the inside and were designed to resist massive pressure. The glass was undoubtedly bulletproof as well.

The blood pounding in his head told him his body was screaming for air. He struggled to maintain consciousness, but things were beginning to blur. In addition, 13 began to freeze in the severe cold. He was getting lightheaded. Feeling weak, he slipped back against the top of the bell.

13 looked up. The stars were bright and clear. He seemed to be floating, journeying across the black void to those distant worlds. He looked down and saw himself lying flat on top of the bell. He appeared very small in the scheme of the universe—small and very fragile.

He no longer felt pain and torment, only peace. There were others around him, welcoming him into this strange new world.

13 felt a power directing him. Was it the dead leaders of the old, beneficent Brotherhood? God? He didn't know. Whatever it was, it was all-consuming and filled with warmth and goodness.

But something wasn't right. It wasn't time . . . not yet . . . not until his mission was complete. Then the answer was given to him in a moment of crystal clarity. He flew back to his body at a speed greater then light. A moment later, he opened his eyes.

13 pulled out his pistol, its cold grip like ice in his hand. He raised his hand, pointing the gun upward. His finger squeezed off two shots in rapid

succession. The bullets passed through the fabric of the balloon. The force of their passing tore a rip in the balloon. Within seconds, their ascent began to slow as gas began to escape from the bag.

His finger tensed again, and once more the pistol belched flames. He heard another tearing sound high above him, followed by the rush of air. The balloon began to descend . . . ever so slowly.

Then he heard another sound—the lever that opened the hatch. He ducked low as the *whooshing* of air told him the door seal had been broken. Someone was coming out to investigate!

A weathered hand groped for the iron hold only inches from 13's face. The Agent waited until he saw the pilot's eyes widen in surprise.

"What the—"

It was all the pilot had time to say as 13's hand snaked out. Grabbing the shocked man, he dragged him up onto the roof of the bell. Then he catapulted the horrified pilot out into space.

"What's going on up there?" Walters's angry voice called from inside.

"Problems! Get out here!" called 13.

He moved back away from the hatch and waited, his face tense, his frostbitten fingers clutching the pistol, his eyes cold with hatred and anticipation. He imagined his bullets turning Walters's face into crimson mush. It was almost too easy! Suddenly he heard a click.

Another hatch!

He turned quickly, but it was too late! Walters's arms grabbed him from behind. Encircling 13's neck, Walters pulled the Agent down to the roof. 13 struggled for a grip as his pistol clattered off the bell, disappearing into the dark sky.

Flinging 13 onto his back, Walters was on top of him in an instant. His clawlike fingers dug into 13's neck, trying to squeeze the life from him.

13 twisted and turned, struggling to hang on. But his opponent had also been trained by the Brotherhood.

"Say hello to your maker!" the Masque snarled.

A power suddenly welled up from somewhere inside 13. His ankle touched a tether line on the bell's roof, and he forced his foot beneath it. Then, with every last ounce of strength he had, he shot his knee upward with sledgehammer force.

The Agent's knee found home, ramming hard into Walters's gut. There was a cracking sound. 13 had hit the man's spine. Walters gurgled with infantlike sounds. His once-steely fingers relaxed and turned to Jell-o around the Agent's throat. His spine broken, he slid to the roof, a helpless—but still conscious—doll.

13 pulled himself to his feet. Leaning over Walters, he removed the man's belly chute. Walters's lips mumbled inarticulate words as his eyes pleaded for the mercy of a bullet.

13 looked down at the man. The battle-rage had subsided. 13 could easily have tossed the pathetic creature off the roof, but he didn't. Walters would pay for the untold misery and suffering he had caused with his own. He would leave him atop the falling balloon, let him linger to wonder just when the ground would slam into it, ending his misery forever.

Reaching down with his hand, the Agent struck the ring he wore against the metal surface of the bell. It began to glow white-hot. Then, leaning over Walters, the Agent pressed the burning ring against the man's forehead.

Walters's eyes registered shock as the mark of the Agent's continuing battle against the Brotherhood was branded onto his head—the number 13.

Turning away, 13 quickly slipped into the parachute. Then he leaned into the hatch. "Maggie!"

he shouted.

Her face looked up at his. He saw amazement, then swift, sudden joy.

"Thank God you're alive!" she cried. Tears streaming down her cheeks, she grasped his strong arm. He tried to pull her out of the bell, but the tremendous wind pressure caught her, holding her half in and half out. The whipping wind tore and shredded her shirt, exposing her legs and thighs to its biting chill.

"I—I can't!" she cried, struggling to free herself.

Faster and faster the balloon fell.

Holding onto the iron ring on top of the metal roof of the bell, 13 fought the winds as he climbed down inside the bell.

Grabbing Maggie about the waist, he added his strength to hers and they both struggled up the ladder.

"Hang on to my back!" he shouted.

Maggie flung her arms around him, and he leaped outward from the falling balloon.

Down they tumbled, through the blackness, freefalling toward the clouds below. Then suddenly the sensation of falling vanished. They had reached terminal velocity. It was as if they were floating.

"Hold on tight!" 13 yelled.

He jerked the D-ring with all his might. The parachute snaked out, jerking them sharply upward.

Maggie shrieked but managed to hold on as the chute jerked full against the rushing wind.

Then they were drifting slowly. Hearing a rushing, flapping noise above, they looked up to see the balloon hurtling past, the mouth of the paralyzed Walters open wide in a silent scream.

Maggie held 13 tightly. Tears froze on her cheeks as they floated lazily downward.

"I thought I'd never see you again!" she cried into his ear.

"I'm sorry it took so long," he shouted.

"Better late then never."

"I love you!" Maggie murmured, pressing her cheek against his strong back. He couldn't hear her, but it didn't matter to Maggie. She would never leave him. She would follow him to the bitter end, wherever that might lead.

They floated from the cloud cover toward the waiting ground below. For this brief moment, they were at peace.

AGENT 13™ THE MIDNIGHT AVENGER

The Hand Sinister sat on his huge throne. He was alone. Those minions who were fortunate had been able to flee his anger. Corpses of the unfortunate littered his stairs.

Itsu felt the emptiness of the aura that had been the Masque. He felt the triumph of Agent 13.

The Hand Sinister's elaborate plans were crashing down about him. And, what was worse, it was time—time for him to undertake the journey for the *Juvita-ta*, the ceremony of rejuvenation, the only time he ever left the safe, sacred grounds of the Shrine.

It was also the only time Itsu was vulnerable, and he could sense the aura of Agent 13 reaching out to destroy him.

"Jinda-dii," Itsu whispered into the darkness. "You must go. Find your pupil. Bring him back. . . ."

Be sure to read #3. . .

AGENT 13 AND THE ACOLYTES OF DARKNESS!

Caroline stumbled and a tear slid down her cheek

She brushed it away before it landed on her dress and spotted the material. "I can't stop crying," she said, running her hand under her eyes to catch another tear. "I keep thinking about what life's going to be like without the kids around–" She hiccuped and pressed her fingers to her lips.

She couldn't finish the thought, even to her best friend.

Without the kids around, what if there's nothing left between Nick and me?

A knock sounded on the door, startling her. "Mom?"

Her son's voice recalled her to her duties. She swallowed, hoping her voice sounded normal to him. "I'll be right there, Adam." She backed away from Patty's comforting embrace and steeled herself for the next few hours and what she had to do once she and Nick were alone....

Dear Reader,

I love listening to people's love stories. How did they meet? When did they fall in love? Why do they stay together? Because they're together when they're telling their stories, I know the couples have some variation of a happily-ever-after.

For me, the exciting part is finding out what happened from the time they met until the present. What ups and downs did they have to survive? How did they keep going through the different trials and tribulations that come in life? Their stories inspire my own stories–and help me keep my marriage alive and well. I walked down that aisle planning for a happily-ever-after…and I believe Caroline and Nick had the same intention!

Once they said "I do," they had to deal with twists and turns along their journey. I hope you enjoy finding out how Caroline and Nick deal with their marriage as much as I enjoyed writing about them.

Sincerely,

Tessa McDermid

P.S. I love to hear from readers! Please write me at tessa@tessamcdermid.com.

HR

WEDDINGS IN THE FAMILY

Tessa McDermid

HARLEQUIN®

TORONTO • NEW YORK • LONDON
AMSTERDAM • PARIS • SYDNEY • HAMBURG
STOCKHOLM • ATHENS • TOKYO • MILAN • MADRID
PRAGUE • WARSAW • BUDAPEST • AUCKLAND

ISBN-13: 978-0-373-71565-7
ISBN-10: 0-373-71565-X

WEDDINGS IN THE FAMILY

This edition published by arrangement with Harlequin Books S.A.

www.eHarlequin.com

Printed in U.S.A.

ABOUT THE AUTHOR

While Tessa McDermid writes fiction and nonfiction, she most enjoys writing about the love between a man and a woman. She and her husband live in the Midwest, along with their two sons, their Australian shepherd and several fish and lizards, proof that love takes many forms.

Books by Tessa McDermid

HARLEQUIN EVERLASTING LOVE

8–FAMILY STORIES

To Nadine and Paul; Steve and Nancy;
Alan and Catherine—and family weddings.

And to my husband, Bob,
who daily reminds me what a marriage should be.

ACKNOWLEDGMENTS

A special thanks to Suzanne Arruda, my critique partner, for being willing to read pages any time; to Dana Sanders, a friend and fellow mom, for sharing her professional expertise; and to my editor, Johanna Raisanen, who gave me great ideas for revisions!

REECIE'S WEDDING

The present

A PATCH OF LATE-AFTERNOON sunlight filtered into the room, giving it a slumberous feeling. Caroline settled into the deep leather chair, careful not to rest her head against the back and mess up the elaborate curls her hairdresser had deemed appropriate for the mother of the bride. The soft gray satin of her dress barely made a sound as she smoothed the material over her knees.

In less than two hours, her daughter would be married. By the time the sun went down, Caroline would be on her own with her husband.

Caroline's head throbbed, a dull ache behind her left eye. Gingerly, she rested her cheek against the cool leather and willed the pain to go away. She could do it; she'd done it before. She just had to concentrate on the center of the pain, visualize the ache flowing out of her body, dissolving in the air…

"Caroline? Are you in here?"

Patty's voice floated into the room. Caroline was tempted to ignore her, to wait silently in her chair until she was alone again.

But maybe it would help to talk to someone. And Patty had been there almost from the beginning.

"I'm over here."

Patty's heels tapped across the polished floor. Her dress was a soft green, the perfect foil for her auburn hair. Her hair's color had deepened over the years until it now had the patina of fine mahogany. Today she wore it in a smooth chignon at the nape of her neck.

I wore my hair like that when I was married, Caroline thought. *I walked down the aisle in the same dress that Reecie's wearing right now, with my hair twisted into a soft bun so it wouldn't tangle in the cape.*

The thought caused a pain to lodge in her stomach and she pressed her fist against the waistband of her skirt.

"Why are you sitting in the dark?" Patty rested a hand on Caroline's shoulder. "Are you doing okay?"

Caroline knew the question referred to her daughter's impending departure. She'd been asked variations of the question over and over during the weeks of wedding preparations.

Each time, she'd been able to blithely reply, "I'm fine." Having your youngest child and only daughter get married usually caused some turmoil in a person's life, but no one really expected you to say that.

Patty could stand the truth. Caroline tipped her head back and gave her friend a rueful grin. "Remember when we made those speeches at the beginning of each school year? How sending your five-year-old to kindergarten was the natural order of things, that as parents we were expected to watch our children grow up and grow away from us?"

Patty nodded. She and Richard had never succeeded in having children but she'd been as close as a parent to many of the students who had gone through her classroom.

"It's all crap." Caroline closed her eyes and sighed, feeling the air expand her lungs and then leave her body in a long release of misery.

"Caroline."

Caroline opened her eyes. "No, really, Patty. I don't want Reecie to go out into the big bad world, even if she does have a wonderful man at her side. I want her to be little again, sleeping in her crib where I can tuck her in each night."

"You didn't get this maudlin when Adam got married."

No, she'd been thrilled and excited at his wedding, dancing and smiling until her husband, Nick, finally had to drag her home so the caterers could finish clearing up and the DJ could leave.

But then, the rest of her life hadn't been about to change with her son's marriage.

A lump formed in her throat, making it difficult to swallow. Patty knelt down, the skirt of her gown swishing against the chair. "What's going on, Caroline? You haven't been yourself for days. It's more than Reecie getting married, isn't it?"

Caroline hesitated. She wanted to tell someone. But Nick deserved to hear it from her first.

A tic started behind her eye, the next stage of her headaches. She'd been getting them more and more frequently, partly, she knew, because she wasn't getting enough sleep. "I'm tired."

And she was. All the people in and out of the house, last-minute decisions. The trips and phone calls to clear up a misunderstanding about some aspect of the wedding.

"Reecie was in tears most of this past week," she said. "The florist called and had lost part of her order, could she remember how many flowers she wanted for the front tables? One of her bridesmaids left her dyed-to-match shoes at home." She shook her head. "Being the mother of the bride is very different from being the mother of the groom."

Patty rose to her feet. The sun coming through the paned window dappled her skirt with rays of pink and gold. "That's it? Just letting Reecie go?"

Caroline could hear the disbelief in her voice. Again, she was tempted to tell her everything. But she couldn't say a word to anyone until she talked to her husband. She owed him that much at least.

She pushed herself out of the chair and crossed the room with short, jerky steps, hindered in her urge to hurry by the long skirt of her gown. She linked arms with Patty. "It's harder to let them go than I thought it would be. I told Adam he couldn't go off to college until I put all his school pictures in that bus frame we bought from some school fund-raiser. He didn't think that was funny, especially since his junior- and senior-year pictures weren't in it. I just wish I had some way to hold Reecie back."

"You don't mean that."

No, she didn't. She wanted her children to be happy, to find someone they could love all of their lives.

That hadn't been her first goal. She was going to graduate from college, get her master's degree and change the world. A man hadn't been necessary for those dreams to come true. Then Nick had come into her life and she'd taken a detour.

And now she was going to ask him for a divorce.

The irony of the timing didn't escape her. How many times had she heard of couples who divorced after the last child left? She had thought they were overreacting about the empty-nest syndrome, but now she understood. Once the buffer of the kids was gone, it was so much easier to see what was missing in the relationship.

The sun dipped lower in the sky, only a few rays making their way onto the carpet. A bird flew by, its cheery song too loud in the quiet room. Soon she would have to paste on her party smile and join the crowd eager to see her daughter wed. And she did want Reecie to be happy.

Patty clasped Caroline in a light hug, her perfume wafting around the two of them, reminding Caroline of visits when they had sat on the guest bed in their respective homes, laughing and talking and catching up on everything since the last time they'd seen each other. "You're going to make it," Patty said. "You always do. You're one of the strongest women I know. You and Nick have years ahead of you."

Caroline stumbled and a tear slid down her cheek. She brushed it away before it landed on her dress and spotted the material. "I can't stop crying," she said, running her hand under her eyes to catch another tear.

"I keep thinking about what life's going to be like without the kids around—" She hiccuped and pressed her fingers to her lips. She couldn't finish the thought, even to her best friend.

Without the kids around and with nothing left between Nick and me.

A knock sounded on the door, startling her. "Mom?"

Her son's voice recalled her to her duties. She swallowed, hoping her voice sounded normal to him. "I'll be right there, Adam." She backed away from Patty's comforting embrace and steeled herself for the next few hours and what she had to do once she and Nick were alone.

Even though, deep down, she wanted to believe that maybe, just maybe, Patty was right.

CHAPTER ONE

Their wedding
Thirty years earlier

NICK SWUNG THE CAR off the highway at the Mustang, Kansas, exit. He slowed down at the stop sign at the top of the ramp and glanced over at her. They were sitting hip to hip and his face was only inches away from her. But instead of grabbing a quick kiss, as he usually did when they stopped, he studied her carefully. "You're not going to let your mother talk you into a big wedding, are you, Caro?"

"No." She scooted away a few inches so she could see him easier. "We talked about this. We're having a simple wedding with our families and a few friends. I haven't changed my mind about that, Nick."

His dark brown eyes were almost black in his intensity. "Your mom may try to change it," he said, his voice low and deep. "She may want to give her only daughter a big wedding. But we don't need a big wedding, right?"

She nodded. His family had money, she knew, much more than her family. Nick didn't want their wedding to be a burden on her parents and she loved him even more for that consideration.

She didn't care how they were married. She would have gone to the courthouse with him if she hadn't known it would hurt her mother. She wanted to start their life together and each day that they waited increased her desire to be alone with him.

He leaned forward and nipped at her lips. His musky cologne and the hint of the outdoors that always clung to him made her inhale deeply. He ran every day, rain, shine or snow. They had met when he almost knocked her down. He had been racing a fellow runner back to the gym and cut across campus. She had been walking to a history class and the next moment, she was stumbling to keep her balance. He had kept her off balance ever since.

His breath warmed her skin and she shivered, wishing they were anywhere but on the road to her parents' house. The college afforded them little enough privacy, the dorm rules stating that members of the opposite sex could only visit during certain hours of the day. Once in her house, her father would keep close tabs on their whereabouts.

So far, Nick had honored her request to wait until they were married before they went all the way. His patience was growing thin, though, and she couldn't blame him. If she hadn't been nervous that one of their roommates would return for a forgotten book or assignment, she would be tempted to go beyond their bouts of heavy petting.

A horn honked behind them. Nick pressed his foot to the gas and rolled through the intersection. Caroline slid across the seat until she could rest her head on his shoulder. "I love you."

He picked up her hand and pressed a light kiss to her palm, then linked their fingers together. "I love you. What do you say we skip your parents' house and drive to a motel for the weekend?"

Her stomach tightened at the thought of Nick and her in a motel room. "I—we—" She licked suddenly dry lips.

He chuckled. "I'm teasing, Caro. You already told your parents we're coming." Keeping his eyes on the road, he rubbed his chin against their joined hands. "Soon, though, I'm going to get you alone and naked. This waiting is killing me!"

She didn't answer, knowing her desire matched his. Sometimes she wondered why she was so adamant about keeping her virginity until her wedding night. She knew her parents expected it, even though nothing had ever been said out loud to her. But she and Nick loved each other, she wore his engagement ring, they had a wedding date picked out.

And yet a tiny part of her worried about what would happen if they made love and then didn't get married. Free love might be the norm for thousands of others in the country, but she had never been able to get that close to someone she barely knew. Making friends every time her family had moved had been difficult enough. The thought of letting someone into her pants had been excruciating, at least until she'd met Nick.

Nick was the right man, she knew it. And, soon, very soon, they would be married and she could satisfy the urges that were getting stronger and stronger every time they were together.

"WE'RE NOT HAVING A big wedding," Caroline said. Her father had taken Nick to the golf course and she had agreed to run errands with her mother. "Nick and I don't believe we need a lot of people around to prove our love for each other. Our family and a few close friends. That's all."

"I understand, dear. Your father and I are just thankful you aren't shacking up, like so many of these so-called modern couples, without benefit of any legalities."

"Mom!" Caroline sputtered. Had Evelyn Armstrong just said "shacking up"?

Her mother patted her hand. "Sweetheart, your father and I were young once, too."

Caroline sat silent in her seat. Where was the woman who had nervously told her about the birds and the bees, blushing furiously the entire time. Caroline's engagement had suddenly elevated her from the baby of the family into the secret society of women.

Nick's family had reacted differently to their announcement two weeks earlier. His parents had made it clear when he went off to college that they would not pay his tuition if he was living with a woman. He had thought that by getting engaged the situation would be more palatable. After his call home, he had reported that they had said little, except that they didn't know if they'd be able to travel to both his graduation and a wedding that year.

A letter from his father had arrived later that week, detailing all the reasons why Nick needed to reconsider getting married at such a young age. Reading the first few lines, Caroline had become so angry, she had crumpled the sheet into a ball and tossed it across the room.

Nick had hugged her close, telling her that it didn't matter what his parents said, they were going to get married. "I don't need his permission, Caro. Let's see what he says. We don't have to agree with him."

The letter had been addressed solely to Nick, her name never mentioned at all. Dr. Eddington had reminded Nick of the dedication that would be needed to complete his medical training. Being married would delay that and he wanted Nick to weigh his decision carefully.

"I'm not going to be a doctor," Nick told her. "They want me to follow in their footsteps and I'm not going to do it." He had tugged her close. "Instead of getting married at Christmas, let's plan a May wedding. I can finish my degree on their nickel."

She had reluctantly agreed. Now that she had decided to marry him, she wanted to get started on their life together. But he was right. It would be smart to let their parents pay for their last semester.

"How about we get married graduation weekend?" he asked, kissing her cheek. "They can't complain about travel time that way."

Her mother turned onto Main Street. The downtown area was being renovated and several new stores had sprung up over the last few months. Brightly colored awnings shaded the downtown sidewalk. Ornate lampposts identified the streets.

When her mother parallel parked in front of a shop with the name Radcliffe's discreetly lettered on the glass door, she said, "I thought we'd stop in and see Lily's shop first, and visit for a few minutes with her."

Caroline did want to see her best friend. Lily's aunt had bought the old dress shop that summer and from her mother's letters, she knew it had become all the rage in their small town.

"I'm not buying anything, Mom. I have a white linen suit picked out that I can wear later for church and special occasions."

"And I'm sure it's lovely, dear. You've always had impeccable taste." Her mother unlocked the car door and gracefully climbed out of her side. Caroline slid out and followed her mother across the sidewalk.

Her mother paused at the door. "All I want to do is see what she has to offer. You're my only daughter and this is the only wedding I can truly help plan."

A pang of guilt hit Caroline in the stomach. Her mom had been involved with the weddings of Caroline's three older brothers, but only in a superficial way as the mother of the groom. "I'll look, Mom. But that's all I can promise."

Lily rushed across the silvery-gray carpet as soon as the door opened. Her stunning red suit accented her curvy figure and slender legs. Caroline had only a second to wish she had put on something besides worn jeans and a peasant blouse before she was wrapped in a warm hug.

"Oh, Caroline! I still can't believe you're getting married!"

Neither could Caroline. Then Nick had asked her to marry him and she'd known she had to say yes.

Lily leaned back, her eyes roaming over Caroline's face. Caroline stayed still during the scrutiny.

"You look happy," Lily said.

"I am."

"Then I'm happy for you." She tugged Caroline over to an elegant gray sofa that sat perpendicular to the front door and perched on the armrest. "Let me see the ring."

Caroline held out her hand. The simple round diamond caught the ceiling lights, sending shimmers of rainbows around the room. The brushed-gold band sparkled.

Lily smiled at Caroline. "We were going to be career women. We didn't need men in our lives."

"I can still be a career woman," Caroline said.

Lily laughed. "Of course you can."

Caroline wanted to say that she had fought her attraction to Nick. She didn't have time for a romance. She was going to finish her degree and go on to graduate school. Shortly after they started dating, he had said something about their future together and she had broken up with him, alarmed at how serious he had sounded.

If she had been alone with Lily, she would have explained. How she had ignored him for two months, tamping down the feelings he had roused in her. Her plans didn't include a man. She had watched her mother move from place to place, packing up their belongings and her four children whenever her husband changed jobs. Caroline's father had been on a search for the perfect career and he had dragged his wife and children along with him.

But her mother was sitting with them and she couldn't say anything in front of her. Her mom had never complained about the moves and had seemed content with her volunteer work and homemaker status in each of their new towns.

Caroline wanted more. She had made it clear to Nick that she wanted a career, that she couldn't be happy staying home. He had agreed and she had accepted his ring.

"Do you have the drawings?"

Her mother's question interrupted her thoughts. "Drawings?"

Lily hopped up from her seat. "I have some drawings I want to show you. I'll be right back."

She disappeared through a light gray curtain at the back of the shop.

"What is she talking about?" Caroline asked her mother.

"Be patient."

Drapery in the same muted gray as the sofa flanked several alcoves, a simple backdrop for the dresses and suits that were displayed on faceless mannequins. Caroline had a feeling she couldn't afford any of the clothes in this shop. Her childhood friend had moved from giddy schoolgirl to savvy retailer.

Lily came back into the room and sat on the couch

next to Caroline, a large book in her hands. "The sketches are still pretty rough. When Evelyn mentioned that you were coming home, I immediately thought of all our conversations about weddings. I couldn't draw fast enough."

She bent the cover back, creating an easel, and flipped through the pages. She rested the book on the low glass table in front of the sofa. "What do you think?"

Caroline took one glance at the page and knew she was in trouble. "Oh, Lily!" she breathed.

"Do you like it?"

At the tremor of uncertainty in her friend's voice, she reached over and touched the back of Lily's hand. "It's wonderful."

"I knew you wouldn't like a lot of frills and ruffles so I kept the lines clean and simple." Lily ran a finger over the pencil drawing, trailing across the long skirt that flared out just before it touched the floor.

Lily had drawn two views, the front and the side. The sleeves were long and fitted, ending at the wrists with a tiny flare on the top that matched the hem. The smooth lines flowed over the natural curves of the body, without being too suggestive.

"I remembered you didn't like veils, so..."

Lily flipped to another page. The cape was as simple as the gown, a sheer column that flowed down the page. Caroline knew she wanted this dress. She would marry Nick at a wooded altar, forest animals their only witnesses, if that was what he wanted. But she would meet him in this dress.

She could feel her mother's satisfaction emanating from the seat across from her. She didn't care. The gown was gorgeous. Exactly like the dress she had always imagined she would wear when she met her prince.

Only better. Much, much better.

"I'll use soft, draped material, very sheer, for the cape," Lily explained. "And I found the perfect lace to edge it with. A delicate design with tiny purple violets tucked into every few inches. You always wanted violets at your wedding."

Caroline was touched at how much her friend had remembered from those late-night whispers. "I don't know where that thought ever came from. Something I must have read in a story or saw in a movie. I always thought violets would be the perfect flower."

Just like this was the perfect dress.

She glanced at the dresses hanging in the window, their elegance visible to anyone walking down the street. Lily and her aunt had brought city chic into their little town.

And with that, no doubt, they had brought city prices.

She sat back on the sofa, her head resolutely turned away from the sketches. "It's lovely, Lily, but Nick and I are going to have a simple wedding. No fancy wedding gowns."

"She has a white linen suit she can wear after the ceremony," Evelyn explained.

Caroline nodded, a lump in her throat. Her suit seemed terribly unromantic next to that lovely dress. But she had promised Nick.

"You won't have to pay a dime," Lily said into the

silence. "We'll want to take pictures, of course, and have it featured in the Living Section of the newspaper. This will be our first major design and could set us up for lots of commissions."

Caroline dared another peek at the dress. "Not a dime?" she whispered.

"Not a dime." Lily gave her a bright grin. "I know I shouldn't be helping a traitor to our cause, but you still are my best friend."

Caroline sighed. "I want the dress, Lily. But this doesn't change anything, Mom." She sent her mother a long look. "No big wedding."

"Of course, dear." Evelyn picked up one of the fashion magazines that were tucked into a basket next to her chair. "Now go with Lily and be measured. Your father and Nick will be home soon and we don't want to keep them waiting for their dinner."

Caroline followed Lily into a backroom. "I don't trust her," she said quietly.

Lily picked up her measuring tape. "I wouldn't either."

"Do you know something?"

"No." From beyond the curtain, they could hear Evelyn chatting with Lily's aunt. "But you're the only daughter and I can't see her letting you get away with a simple wedding." She nudged Caroline's shoulder. "Go in there and take off your clothes. We need to get you home so your menfolk don't go hungry."

"You wait," Caroline grumbled, stepping into the small changing room and closing the shuttered half door. "I'm going to be dancing at your wedding before long, too."

Lily chuckled. "Someday. Right now, I'm more than happy to be a bridesmaid."

Caroline peeked her head over the half door. "I don't know if I'll have any bridesmaids. We're having—"

"—a simple wedding!" Lily finished with her. "I know. I wasn't asking. Just saying that I have no one in the wings waiting to be a groom. I'm happy watching my friends get married."

Once again dressed, she told Lily and her aunt goodbye. Her steps were slow as she walked to the car and she tapped her head against the window once she was seated and buckled. "Nick is going to kill me," she muttered.

Her mother started the engine. "Why? How is he going to know about the dress unless you tell him?"

She swiveled her head. "What?"

"I didn't tell your father what I was wearing for our wedding. Bad luck, you know. The groom should not see the bride in the wedding dress."

"I know that, but..." Her voice trailed off. But what? She was doing Lily a favor by wearing that absolutely darling creation. She didn't have to pay for the dress, only have a picture of it put into the newspaper. And since her mother would expect an announcement of the wedding to be in the paper no matter what she wore or where she was married, she really had no problems.

"Okay, I won't say a word about the dress." A beautiful dress didn't mean a big wedding. She settled more comfortably into her seat.

Nick's used blue Ford was parked off to the side of her father's Buick. He sat alone in the living room, a textbook on his lap. He gave them both the lopsided grin that always made her stomach muscles quiver.

"What's the damage?" Evelyn asked.

He shifted until he could face her squarely. "Based on his mutterings on the way home, he shot his worst game ever. Mine wasn't much better, but I still beat him by at least three strokes."

"We'll pack and go back to school tonight," Caroline declared.

Nick laughed. "Come on, it's not that serious."

Both women stared at him and he shifted in his seat. "Is it?" he asked.

Caroline nodded, her hands on her hips. "Dad prides himself on his golf game. He wouldn't make it on the pro circuit but he almost always wins the local charity tournament. You didn't mention how few times you've golfed, did you?"

"It might have come up in conversation."

Caroline groaned. "Now. We have to leave now."

Her mother stepped forward and rested a hand on Nick's shoulder. "You're not going anywhere. Your father is a grown man and this was a friendly game. No reason to send his future, and only, son-in-law away before we've even had dinner."

Her footsteps faded away down the hall. Nick grabbed Caroline's hand and pulled her into his lap.

"Listen, I really did think I'd lose." His hand lightly stroked up and down her arm and she had to control herself not to start purring like a well-pleasured kitten. "You know how often I've played. I figured there was no way I'd come close to his score. Then I saw how quiet he was getting with each of my strokes. Your father was off, Caroline. If he does win the local tournament, he has to play a lot better than he did today."

She snuggled against his chest, her mind finding it hard to focus on a game that had been over for several hours. He traced lazy circles around her neck and under her ear. "He's good, Nick," she said, trying to stay with the conversation. "He really is. And I didn't even think to warn you because, well—"

He tipped her chin up with his finger and grinned. "You didn't figure I'd win."

She nodded and giggled when he tweaked her ear.

"Well, let me show you something I'm good at," he growled.

His lips met hers in a kiss that drove thoughts of golf games and wedding dresses right out of her mind. He nibbled and tasted her lips, her cheek, her jaw, blazing a trail down her neck and toward her low-cut top.

Her fingers clenched his arms, her head pressed against his shoulders. A soft moan worked its way past her lips and she felt his answering chuckle against her skin. His tongue and lips caressed and teased her, making it hard to breathe or think.

Footsteps sounded behind her and she jerked away, suddenly remembering they were making out in her family's living room. "Nick, stop!" she whispered. She jumped out of his lap, pulling her top back into place. She barely landed on the couch opposite his chair before her mother walked into the room.

If her mother noticed anything amiss, she didn't say a word. Caroline resisted the urge to smooth her hair back into place and sat up straight, her hands folded primly in her lap. Evelyn sat down next to her and gave them both a wide smile.

"Everything is fine. We're going out to dinner tonight, so why don't you both go freshen up." She cocked her head toward Caroline. "Maybe put on something a little less revealing, so your father doesn't have a reason to get any more upset at your young man."

At Nick's snort, she glanced down. A tiny love mark was visible just above the elastic of her top. She stood up slowly, keeping her dignity intact in front of the room. "Where are we going?" she asked at the doorway, her back to her mother. She would not look Nick in the eye. His humor was palpable from fifty paces away.

"The local diner. Can you be ready in thirty minutes?"

Nick followed her out of the room and caught her in a tight hug as soon as they were out of sight. "Stop it, you've caused me enough trouble." She pushed at his shoulders but he didn't release her.

"I like having my mark on you." He lowered his head and tickled her skin with his tongue.

She swallowed her quick giggle and renewed her efforts to get away. "If Dad sees us, he'll throw you out on your ear."

Nick lifted his head, his devilish grin sparkling in his eyes. "Your father isn't much different than me, Miss Caroline. How do you think you arrived in this world?"

She gave an enormous push and succeeded in backing away from him. "That, Nick, is just gross." She shuddered. "I do not want to think about my parents having sex."

Her shock at the easy way her mother had used the term "shacking up" still lingered.

"And they don't want to think about *you* having sex," he retorted. "Go on, get changed. I'll meet you in the living room. And I'll be the perfect gentleman all evening."

He was true to his word. He held the door open for her mother, waited for Caroline and her mom to be seated before sliding into the chair opposite Caroline, and leaned forward with rapt attention during all conversation. At one point, Caroline kicked him under the table, sure that his attentiveness would be seen as sarcasm by her usually aware father.

But her dad was intent on sharing information about their community with Nick, detailing recent developments, the progress the city council was making in marketing their community, and the many businesses advertising for employees.

"Your father wants us to live here after the wedding." They were several paces behind her parents as they walked back to the car.

"He's proud of Mustang." She wouldn't be surprised if her father had finally found the right place to settle down. Her parents had lived there since her freshman year in high school. Longer than anywhere else they'd lived.

Nick shook his head. "You're his little girl, Caroline. He wants you to live close by."

Caroline stared at her father's solid back. He was

holding hands with her mother and she felt an enormous wave of love flow through her.

Followed by a dull ache in her chest right below her heart. She'd be leaving them when she married. She'd always be their daughter, but once the vows were spoken, she'd be Nick's wife first.

Her vision blurred and she stumbled over the pavement. Nick caught her arm. "You all right?"

She nodded, ducking her head so he couldn't see the tears. How could she explain the feelings coursing through her? She loved him, she knew she did. Marrying him was the right decision and she could hardly wait to start their life together.

But she had never really considered what she was giving up by making a new family.

He bent down and kissed her cheek. "It's okay, sweetheart. We'll see them whenever we can."

"What?"

"Getting married is a big deal." His voice was as serious as the day he had proposed. "We'll have to work out all kinds of holiday visits between our two families. But you and me, we're going to be great together."

She cupped his cheek with one hand, all doubts washing away. "You're right. We are."

"I CAN'T BELIEVE YOU ended up getting married in the biggest church in town." Lily adjusted the filmy cape around Caroline's shoulders.

"I know." Butterflies danced in her stomach and she could hardly stand still. Twice, Lily had threatened to send her up the aisle with her panty hose showing to the world if she didn't stop moving.

Caroline held her head still while Lily tucked the hood of the cape around the braided bun at the base of her neck. "Mom kept saying it was our choice. But we all knew it wasn't."

Her mother had been clever, never outright asking them to use the church. Instead, she had casually mentioned that any elderly relatives they invited might find it difficult to stand for very long and getting chairs into the wooded glade could be a challenge. The lack of bathrooms and limited parking could also be a problem. Not a major one, of course, since the wedding would be short. And as long as it didn't rain and no one had to rush up the wood-chip path to their cars…

Nick had finally conceded defeat and told her mother to reserve the church. Caroline had said they didn't have to change their plans just because her mother was being manipulative. He had given a rueful laugh and hugged her close. "Caroline, you're her only daughter. It's one day. As long as we're married at the end of it, I don't care what happens."

Now Lily stepped back, her eyes narrowed. "Well?" Caroline asked. The mirror was across the room and she couldn't see anything.

The door opened behind Caroline and footsteps rushed into the room. "Caroline, your aunt…" Her mother's voice trailed away.

Caroline turned her head. Evelyn stood frozen in the middle of the room, her hand pressed against her mouth.

"What?" Was something the matter with the dress, with the way it fit? Her aunt?

Her mother advanced into the room, stopping next to Lily. Both women stared at Caroline for several long seconds and then her mom wrapped her arms around Lily in a tight hug.

"I assume that means everything looks good," Caroline said in a dry tone.

Her mom nodded, dabbing at her eyes with the handkerchief she had been carrying all day. By now, she could probably fuel Niagara Falls. "You look perfect, darling. Absolutely perfect."

"Can I see?"

Lily nodded. Lifting the hem, Caroline picked her way to the large mirror at the side of the room.

"Oh, Lily!" she breathed, staring at her reflection. She *was* a princess in a fairy tale.

"Oh, Caroline." Lily bent down and straightened the skirt. When she stood up, she had flickers of tears on her lashes. "Let's get you married."

Her father's reaction matched that of her mother. "You look lovely," he whispered.

She tucked her hand into the crook of his arm. "Thank you, Daddy. And thank you for being so nice to Nick."

"He's a good man." They started the march down the aisle. "As long as he remembers to take care of you."

The wedding passed in a blur. She saw Nick's eyes light up when she came into view and her lips curved into a wide smile that didn't disappear the entire evening. She danced with uncles and cousins she hadn't seen in ages. Her father whisked her into the father-daughter dance with old-world charm and then made her giggle when he swung her in a wide dip. Her brothers each claimed a portion of a dance, teasing her until their wives dragged them away.

The last dance was with Nick. His hands rested on her waist, their feet barely moving across the floor. She couldn't take her eyes off his face or the love she saw mirrored in his eyes.

"Happy?" he said.

She nodded. "Deliciously so." She had found words welling up in her mind all night, fulsome words she would never use any other time. In her Cinderella dress, with her handsome prince in his dark suit, the music playing around them, their family and friends surrounding them, she couldn't help thinking that no bride had ever been so lucky.

He deftly swung her out of the way of two little cousins dancing a jitterbug of sorts to the slow music. "How much longer before we can get out of here?"

The urgency and desire in his voice made her quiver. She had thrown the bouquet, he had tossed the garter. The cake was almost gone. "Now?" she murmured.

He stopped dancing and the cousins bumped into her hip. They scowled and jiggled around them. Nick grabbed her hand and dragged her toward the door.

She dug her heels into the flooring. "We can't just rush out. We have to tell our parents goodbye."

He growled but detoured toward the front tables and halted in front of her parents, his hand tight on hers. The wedding band she had slipped onto his finger felt smooth against her palm. "Thank you for a lovely wedding. We're leaving now."

Caroline's cheeks heated up. Without waiting for her parents' reply, he tugged her along to his parents. "Mom, Dad, we're leaving. Have a safe drive."

She caught his wrist with her free hand. "Nick."

He glanced over his shoulder at her. "Caroline, I'm not stopping again until we're at our motel. Do you have a problem with that?"

Desire shimmered in the air between them. A fine sheen glistened on his forehead and his lips were pressed together in a tight line.

They'd waited long enough. She leaned toward him. "How fast do you think you can get us there?"

A grin lit up his face. "Watch."

CHAPTER TWO

Career changes
Twenty-six years earlier

THE GARAGE DOOR slid closed behind him, but Nick made no move to get out of the car. Caroline's car occupied her space, sparkling from a recent washing. She must have stopped on her way home from school.

He inhaled slowly and then let the breath out just as carefully. He needed to go in, not sit noticing the lack of dust on her vehicle. He'd eat dinner, chat as if nothing out of the ordinary had happened and then offer to do the dishes. Once the kitchen was clean and they were relaxing in the living room, he'd bring up his news.

The door between the kitchen and the garage opened and Caroline hurried through, a cloth bag over her shoulder, her head down as she watched her step. She paused to push the garage-door opener. Halfway down the second step, she saw him, grinned and hurried over to his car.

"Hey!" She leaned over, tapping on his window.

Rather than roll it down, he opened the door, careful

not to bump her skirt, and climbed out. "You going somewhere?"

She nodded. "The school-board meeting, remember? I'm giving my presentation. I told you last night."

He had a vague recollection of listening to something about her third-grade class and the books they were reading, but sometimes Caroline rambled on about her school day in such detail he found it easy to ignore most of it. If he made a few "uh-huhs" or "reallys?" during the monologue, that sufficed.

"When will you be home?"

"I don't know. Most of the time, we can slip out after we finish our part. I'll see if I can do that without making a scene."

She took a step closer and leaned in, kissing him on the cheek and nuzzling his chin. "I won't stay a minute longer than I have to."

His body tightened at the promise in her voice. Four years of marriage and that whisper of longing in her tone still made him want to push her up against the wall.

His hand stole around her neck and he tugged her closer for a solid kiss. Her bag bumped against one hip and the door scraped his other one. He edged around the door, keeping their mouths melded together. With his free hand, he pushed the car door shut and wrapped his arm around her waist, catching his balance against the car.

A whimper slid over her lips and he swallowed the soft sound, using his teeth, his tongue, his lips to explore her mouth. She tasted of minty toothpaste and he wanted to devour her.

Her hands pressed against his chest and she backed up. He lifted his head. "I have to go," she whispered.

Her lashes were lowered, her cheeks flushed. "You sure?" he asked, a sense of satisfaction filling him. He had the same power over her that she wielded over him.

"Yes." She smoothed several locks of hair behind her right ear, then ran her hands down her skirt. "How do I look?"

He leaned back and gave her a once-over, moving slowly past the soft curves at her hips, her waist, her breasts, and back to her face.

"Not that way!" She gave him a push that knocked him against the car.

He grinned. The momentary pain had been worth the view.

"Do I look okay for my meeting? I don't have time to go back in and repair your damage." She brushed at the front of her blouse.

"You look fine." He patted her on the rear, chuckling at her squeak of annoyance. Nothing irritated her more than that patronizing action. She was back to her normal, public self. That half-out-of-bed look he wanted to keep for himself.

Whistling, he closed the garage door after her car turned into the street and wandered in to the house. The kitchen light over the sink was on, sending a soft glow into the room. Their rented town house was twice the size of the apartment they had lived in for the first three years of their marriage.

The silence of the extra rooms echoed around him.

He opened the refrigerator and peered inside. Grabbing a package of ham, he fixed a sandwich. He carried it into the living room, flicked on the television and plopped down on the couch.

The local sports announcer was giving a quick rundown of the coming baseball games, promising highlights during the special Friday night segment that ran during the season. The announcer added that the starting pitcher for the high-school team was considering several area colleges and that scouts from a prestigious university had been seen at the last game.

Nick frowned, the information bringing back the afternoon's conversation with his boss, the pitcher's dad. The opportunity to move up in the company had been handed to him, with a substantial pay increase. The only problem was that the promotion included a move out of state.

He slumped against the back of the couch, staring at the swirls on the ceiling. The extra money was secondary to the chance to head his own department. After months of following orders, he would be the one giving them.

The design in the ceiling formed itself into Caroline's face. Even before she saw him, he had seen excitement in her walk, in the way she swung down the steps. He couldn't have told anyone about the program she was going to discuss for the school board that evening, but he did know it was something that had involved most of her waking free moments for the past school year.

Good teachers are needed everywhere, he thought. Her principal would be sad to lose her, but he'd give Caroline a glowing recommendation. The man had been full of praise for her abilities when they met at the school's Spring Fling. Nick had been proud she was his wife.

"Nick?" Caroline's voice sounded from the kitchen.

"In the living room."

"What are you doing sitting in the dark?" She clicked on a lamp and dropped onto the couch next to him.

"Did you wow them?" He muted the television, now in the middle of a weekly variety show, and draped an arm around her waist.

She leaned her head on his shoulder. "Yeah." Her lips briefly touched his neck. "The kids were so good. The board members asked several questions and not one of the kids faltered in their answers."

"Did you think they would?"

She shook her head, her hair rustling against his shirt. The silky movement brought a clench to his groin, reminding him of the unfinished business between them.

He looped his arm around her and tugged her into his lap. She giggled, her skirt flipping up and baring her legs to the tops of her shapely thighs. "What are you doing?"

"Celebrating your wonderful performance." She wasn't wearing stockings. His free hand caressed the soft skin under her knee and her giggles shifted to a lower pitch.

"Tell me what happened at the meeting," he murmured, his index finger tracing lazy circles over and behind her knee.

She swallowed and licked her lips. "After a couple short announcements," she managed to say in a higher-than-normal voice, "the vice superintendent introduced me."

He added another finger to his tracing and navigated a few inches higher on her thigh. “And?” he asked.

She shifted, her hand tightening on his waist. He followed her leg, alternating his tracing with gentle squeezes on the soft thigh muscles.

“I, um, I told them about the books that we use, how much we read each day, some of the activities—”

He watched the skin of her throat ripple as she swallowed. Using the pad of his thumb, he trailed down the faint ridges, slowing at the hollow at the base of her throat.

“I bet they were impressed.” He leaned in and kissed the pale skin at the curve of her neck. “You’ve been working on this all year.”

“Yes, well, I—Ms. Russell—” She swallowed and the skin danced across his lips. “She mentioned that they’re considering—Oh! Nick!”

He grinned, his mouth hovering over the nipple he had just kissed through her shirt. “Do you want me to stop?”

“No, I—” Her hand caressed the hair at the nape of his neck and gently, slowly, she eased his head and mouth back to her breast. “I’ll tell you the rest later,” she murmured.

CAROLINE LOUNGED AGAINST his shoulder, nestled between his body and the back of the couch. Their clothes were scattered on the floor, her panties resting precariously on the edge of the lamp shade. She shivered and he tucked her closer.

Her hand twirled the hair on his chest, her fingernails lightly dancing over his skin. “Did you eat something?”

"Yeah." His fingers tangled in the curls above her ear and he leaned in for a long kiss. "A sandwich," he managed to say when he could breathe again.

She was wedged between the cushion and his arm. With every breath she took, her body rubbed against his skin. He clamped his teeth against the surge of desire that raced through him. No matter how many times he was with her, she could start the reaction all over again with a simple smile, a touch of her hand, her skin against his.

Instead of giving in to the desire, he knew he had to tell her his news. The temptation to wait until the next day was balanced by the thought that their current bout of lovemaking had left her in a mellow mood.

"I had my formal review," he began.

She jerked upright and he had to press his foot to the floor to keep from sliding off the couch. "You got your promotion, right?"

He nodded and she yipped, her face lighting up as she threw herself on top of him. "Oh, Nick! That's wonderful. Now we can look for a house, finish paying off your school loans. You'll have your own office, right? With a window? We can decorate it, add some personal touches. That cubicle you have now—"

"Wait." He interrupted her with a hand on her lips and at her waist to keep her still. Her bouncing was causing parts of him to respond and he had to keep his wits about him.

She frowned. "You didn't get a raise?" she mumbled against his fingers. "No new office?"

"No, I'll get a raise." He glanced at the ceiling, at

the flickering lights of the television, toward the glass door leading to their small patio. Anywhere but at her shining face.

"Nick." Her hands framed his cheeks and turned his attention back to her. "What is it?"

He'd never been a coward. She'd understand. She loved him. She wanted what was best for both of them and this was a grand opportunity for his career. She was a wonderful teacher, she'd find another job…

"The new office is in Missouri."

Her stunned silence bounced off the walls. From the corner of his eye, he could see the comedian speaking to his cohort in the sitcom that had replaced the variety show, their mouths moving wordlessly. A branch scraped across the glass door of the patio.

"Caro?"

She pushed against his shoulders, climbing to her feet. She scooped up her clothes and hugged them against her body, crossing the space to the stairs.

"Don't walk away. We have to talk about this."

She glanced at him over her shoulder, dignified in her posture. For a moment, he was distracted by the lean length of her, the tight buttocks, the slender legs.

But her words snapped him back to the conversation. "You're asking me to move, right? Did you hear a word I said earlier? No, of course you didn't. I didn't finish because you distracted me."

She leaned forward. "Well, let me tell you the rest. Ms. Russell wants to develop my program for the entire district. The vice superintendent of curriculum, Nick!"

She flung her hands out, her stance a belligerent, naked goddess. "She wants me to work with the other teachers next year and go into their classrooms. The administration talked about it at their work session today and are willing to give me a stipend for the extra hours. Are you asking me to give that up?"

"No." He stopped. How could she develop her program here in Iowa if they moved to Missouri for his new position?

Her eyes narrowed. "I'm not going." She took another step toward the stairs and rested a hand on the railing. "This is what my mom did, Nick. She followed my dad everywhere he wanted to go. Not once did she get a chance to be her own person, someone other than George Armstrong's wife."

"Caro." He sat up, his arms crossed over his thighs. She had looked fierce and commanding standing in the middle of the living room, her eyes intense. He felt vulnerable, arguing his case naked. "Good teachers are needed everywhere. You'll get a great recommendation. You can start your reading program in Missouri."

"You don't start changing things as soon as you move into a new district." She stomped toward the stairs, her body disappearing around the bend.

"We're not done talking about this," he called after her.

All he heard in response was the sound of her feet treading up the steps.

THE BEDROOM DOOR WAS shut when he made it upstairs. He had locked the doors, checked the windows, turned off all the lights. Stalling, to let her have time to get ready for bed, to calm down and realize that the promotion was good for both of them.

The lights were out in the room when he pushed the door open. "Caro?" he whispered.

The streetlight shone through a crack in the curtain and illuminated the bed, showing her curled on the farthest edge away from the door. He could hear her light breathing, but he couldn't tell if she was asleep or faking it so she didn't have to talk to him.

He crossed the room and entered the small bathroom, brushing his teeth quickly. He clicked off the light and made his way through the dark room, climbing onto his side of the bed.

She tensed up and he sighed. "Caro, we have to talk about this."

Silence.

He touched her shoulder. "Caro."

She rolled away and he waited for her to tumble from the bed. She paused and he knew she was clinging to the edge of the mattress.

"Fine." He stretched out on his side of the bed, his back to her. "We'll talk tomorrow."

Breakfast was a quiet affair. He had awakened in the night, expecting her to be spooned around his back. Instead, he had felt only the wide chasm of the empty mattress between them. Hurt and angry, he had settled back into his pillow, determined to wait her out.

"I have a meeting tonight, so I'll be home about six." Her voice was neutral.

"Do you want me to start something for supper? I should be home at five-thirty."

"There's hamburger for tacos in the refrigerator."

He nodded. Anyone observing them would see two people going about their before-work activities. No raised voices, no angry glares.

No kiss goodbye.

HE WAS CHOPPING TOMATOES into fine pieces when she came home. "Hi." He kept his voice low. "How was your day?"

"Fine. We had a meeting with one of my parents. I think we sorted out the problem."

"That's good." He slid the chopped tomatoes into one side of the divided bowl. His back to her, he unscrewed the lid on a jar of black olives and drained them before adding them to the other side of the bowl.

Caroline reached over his shoulder and snagged an olive, popping it into her mouth. Her other hand rested on his shoulder.

"Sorry about last night," she said softly, her breath a whisper against his ear.

He relaxed and turned around, placing his hands on her waist. "It's okay. I didn't mean to spring it on you like that."

She tilted back, her eyes narrowed. "You weren't hoping that making love would keep me from yelling at you?"

"I didn't plan it that way, but afterward, I did think it might help." He kissed the tip of her nose and then edged away, giving the hamburger sizzling on the stove a stir. "I didn't accept the promotion yet, Caro. I wanted to talk to you first."

"I figured that out after I calmed down this morning." She carried the condiments to the table and spread out the dishes he had stacked in the center. "I made a list."

His bark of laughter echoed around the room. She faced him, her hands on her hips. "I know you think my lists are crazy, but they let us see all the options. I'll show you after supper."

He nodded and dished up the meat. Caroline was always easier to talk to when she was well fed.

After dinner, with the dishwasher humming quietly in the background, Caroline lit a candle on the kitchen counter. The soft scent of apple cinnamon cut through the spicy aroma of the tacos they had just eaten. Outside, a neighbor mowed the common area in front of the town houses, taking advantage of the light now that daylight saving time had started. Two children raced past the window on big-wheeled tricycles, their voices high and shrill over the loud whirring of their tires.

"I listed the pros and cons of two options," Caroline said.

He turned away from the scene outside. "Two options?"

She pulled a tablet out of her bag and opened it to the first page. "Not what you think."

He frowned. The only two options that came to his mind were taking the job or not taking the job.

She laid her hand on top of his. "You need to take the job, Nick. That's a given. You've worked hard for the promotion. I know we didn't consider a move, but that doesn't have to be a bad thing. We just have to look at what's good for both of us."

He glanced at the paper she had turned toward him. The heading at the top caught his eye. "You stay in Iowa?"

"Yes. Wait—" she said quickly, lifting her hand. "Just listen before you say anything."

She pointed to the first two items on her list. "Pros. You get the experience and job you deserve. I can develop my program with the teachers."

He tapped the right side of the paper. "We won't be together."

"During the week." She ran a finger over the words she had written on the first line of the con entry. "Four days."

"Four days? We both work Monday through Friday." How could she calmly suggest that they be apart four days each week? They hadn't slept away from each other since their wedding night. Even angry last night, they'd been in the same bed.

"You'll come home every Friday night. And I checked the mileage. If you left early Monday morning once in a while, you'd still get to your office on time. So, you'd really only be gone Tuesday, Wednesday and Thursday." She raised a finger with each day.

He bent over and kissed the raised fingers. "Three days, four days. It doesn't matter, Caro. That's a lot of days to be apart."

She tapped the paper. "But, Nick, it's only during the school year. We'll have the summer and holidays together. I can visit you on my breaks."

He sat back in his chair, his arms folded over his chest. He didn't like her reasoning, but he was willing to hear her out. "Okay, go on with the list."

"With the raise you'll receive and my stipend, we can save toward our house." She lifted her hand again when he opened his mouth. "I know, I know, it doesn't sound like we'll save money, with two places to live. But if we can find you an apartment close to your office, we'll save on gas money."

The pros took up the full side of the paper. Only one item was on the con side. "You don't mind living apart for the year?" he asked.

She fixed him with her look that was just a fraction short of being disgusted. "Nick, it's just for a few months. And we'll see each other every weekend."

She scooted her chair over until she could frame his face with her hands. "Honey, what if this job doesn't work out? Or you don't like the town? I'll have given up this great opportunity for no reason. I want to try it for one year."

She wasn't pleading, but he could hear the tremor in her voice. "If I do move with you, I'll have to get another certificate to teach in Missouri." She sighed and he felt the motion all the way to his feet. "You know what happened when we moved to Lawrence. I had to work as an aide for a year before a job came open."

He nodded. "You're right." He scooped her into his lap, holding her close. "But what am I going to do when I come home and you're not there?"

"We'll talk on the phone. And we're both always so

busy during the week, we hardly see each other in the evening anyway."

He couldn't put it into words, but he liked knowing that she was sitting at the dining-room table, her school papers spread around her, while he read through a report or checked on figures. She was always there when he prepared for bed, eager to tell him about her latest meeting or some funny story from her day.

Right now she was warm in his arms. How would he deal with the long nights without her?

"I MADE A COUPLE OF CASSEROLES and put them in the freezer." Caroline stood next to her car, watching him add her last suitcase to the trunk. "And you have bread and sandwich fixings for the week."

He caught her shoulders and kissed her mouth, silencing the rest of her words. "Caro, I can take care of myself."

"Maybe this wasn't such a good idea." Her brow was puckered in a frown, her gaze darting from the car to the door of the apartment building. "I mean, you lived at home, then we got married and I took care of you—"

His kiss was rougher and when he lifted his head, he was pleased to see the dazed look in her eyes. "I can take care of myself," he repeated. "Now, you? What will happen if you need a clean blouse in the middle of the week?"

She grinned and tossed her head. Dressed in cutoff shorts and a Mickey Mouse tee shirt, her long blond hair pulled back in a simple ponytail, she looked more like a high-school student than a teacher heading back for a new school year. "I'll buy a new one and wait until you come home to do the laundry."

He laughed and spun her around, giving her a soft pat on the derriere when he put her down. "No shopping." He marched her toward the car, leaning down to open her door. "We're saving money here, remember? We want to buy a house we can live in together."

"Okay, okay." She stood on tiptoe and planted a long kiss on his mouth.

He held her close. The last two months had been a whirlwind of furnishing his small studio apartment and training at the new office. He liked the people and they had responded well to him. The local manager, the oldest son of the company's owner, had invited them over for dinner. Caroline had discovered a mutual interest in authors with Mrs. Abbott. Their youngest child, an almost kindergartner, had crawled into Caroline's lap and stayed there until sent to the family room to play with her older siblings.

Caroline had spent her days while he was at the office putting together school materials. Their nights had involved making memories that would last them through the days ahead. In a new place, a new town, she had lost any inhibitions and he sometimes wondered what his neighbors on either side of the apartment thought of the new tenant.

"I feel like your lover and not your wife," she had whispered to him last night, arms and legs wrapped around each other in the dark, tiny space he would call home for the next ten months. "Grabbing every minute together, until we can sneak away again."

He had held her close, savoring her scent, her soft skin, committing them to memory for the lonely nights ahead.

Now he tucked her into the car and reached across to fasten her seat belt. “Call me as soon as you get home.”

“I will.”

He shut the door and she rolled down the window. “I love you, Mr. Eddington.”

“Ditto, Mrs. Eddington.”

He watched the car head down the street, waiting until she disappeared from view before going back to his apartment. The place was functional, one large room with a kitchenette built into the wall under the window. They had pushed the double bed into the opposite corner and hidden it behind a wooden screen Caroline had found at a garage sale. She had positioned the flowered couch at an angle from the front door. An easy chair, coffee table and simple entertainment center with a TV and his stereo created the illusion of a living room separate from the other areas.

The apartment felt empty without Caroline. He wandered around, touching the leaves of the potted plant she had placed on the table, straightening a picture she had hung from their honeymoon in Colorado. He had snapped the shot from their cabin porch, the sun casting shadows on the canyon walls across the river. She had surprised him and had it enlarged and framed for their last anniversary.

“So you don’t forget me,” she had said, sitting cross-legged on the bed. They had been eating pizza, the only food available in the town by the time they finished celebrating between the sheets.

"I won't have time to forget you." He fed her the last bite of pepperoni. "I'm going to be so busy at work, I won't have time to think of anything else. Once I'm home, I'll drop off to sleep."

He sank onto the sofa, his feet stretched in front of him. He wished he was tired enough to fall asleep right now. The long nights of boisterous lovemaking should have worn him out. Instead, all he could think about was his lonely bed and the long drive ahead for Caroline.

He changed into running shoes and shorts and jogged through the neighborhood, under the shade of the thick oak trees that lined the yards. The apartment building was nestled at the edge of a residential area, the five units catering to those few people in town who didn't have a house of their own.

A dog barked at him from the back fence of a two-story frame house and he gave a jaunty wave. He hadn't had time to meet any of his neighbors yet, too eager to savor the time he had with Caroline. He would spend the next few days getting to know them, to become part of this town.

His shower over, he turned on the evening news and slumped on the couch. When the phone rang, he dashed across the room and grabbed the receiver from the wall. "Hello?"

"Hi. I'm home."

He glanced at the cheery kitchen clock she had placed over the refrigerator. Everywhere he looked, touches of her. He didn't know if they would provide him with solace or make him regret their decision. "Didn't take you long," he said.

"I didn't stop. And I didn't speed, thank you very much."

He grinned and sank to the floor, his back against the wall, the cord of the phone wrapped around his wrist. "Did I say you did?"

"No. But you can't let it go that I was stopped on our honeymoon. The only time I've ever been pulled over, I might add. And I didn't even get a ticket!"

"The officer gave you a warning ticket." The yellow slip was packed away with their wedding pictures and license, a reminder of that first trip to Colorado. She had been nervous when the Kansas highway patrolman had come to the window, stating that she had just been married and the name on her driver's license hadn't been changed yet. The young officer had given her a warning and said they would be watching her.

Her sniff of indignation sounded over the line. He could imagine her sitting with her legs crossed, her back against the headboard of the bed. "What time do you have to be at school tomorrow?" he asked.

"We're working in our classrooms. We can go whenever we want. I'll go in when I wake up."

"The afternoon, then?"

Another sniff. "I'm not sleeping in that late."

"Maybe I should call you and wake you up before I go to work."

"Don't you dare!"

The bantering went on for several more minutes. He was prone on the floor, the phone pressed against his ear as he said outrageous things to make her laugh. "I should hang up now," she finally said.

"Yeah." They were talking late on Sunday night, but the bill would still add up.

"Love you."

"Ditto."

"Nick! At least say it over the phone."

"I did."

A long sigh. "Sleep tight," she said. "And have a good day tomorrow."

He crawled into bed and lay on his back, watching the shadows from the streetlight flicker over the ceiling. Her scent lingered on the pillow next to him and he tugged it into his arms, feeling foolish but comforted at the same time. He was a grown man. He could survive a few days without his wife next to him in bed.

The days at work passed quickly. The owner of the heating and air-conditioning company had opened this second branch three years ago, putting the main responsibilities in the hands of his oldest son. Nick had been chosen to head the marketing department and improve their sales in the region. He pored over reports, looking for ways to help grow the company, papers covering the dinette table he and Caroline had found at a secondhand shop.

He talked to Caroline each evening, after he ran down the streets of his new neighborhood. His running had been relegated to the bottom of his priorities over the last few years. Work and marriage had taken up his time. Now he found the exercise necessary, the sweat and heat he generated helping him forget the empty apartment and the emptier bed.

After covering several miles, he would shower, dial the number of their town house and crawl under the covers. He had replaced the short phone cord with one that reached to all corners of his temporary home. Listening to her chatter about her day while he lay in bed brought her closer.

Not that he could ever tell her how he felt. Except for her "I love you" at the end of each conversation, Caroline never expressed any emotion and certainly never let him know that she missed him. He knew it was foolish, but his pride wouldn't let him say that he missed her first.

"When are you coming home tomorrow?" she asked after a detailed description of her open house the night before.

He kicked off his running shoes. The phone had been ringing when he came in from his run and he had grabbed it before she hung up. "About tomorrow night—"

"No!" she interrupted. "Nick, you don't have to work late, do you?"

He dropped his sweaty clothes on the floor and grabbed a towel off the rack, mopping up the sweat dripping from his forehead. "They're having a picnic to introduce the new employees to the community. I'm expected to be there."

"Why didn't they have it earlier? Your boss knew I was going back to Iowa."

"The picnic isn't just for our company. The chamber puts it on every year to welcome any new employees that have been hired by the different businesses. They have it in the fall to include the new teachers. I have to be there, Caro. It's a big deal around here."

"Fine. Can you leave after it's over?"

He wanted to. He'd planned to show up, eat a few hot dogs, chum around with the people he was starting to know by name and sight. Then leave and be home by midnight at the latest.

"I don't think so. There's a dance, some speeches, lots of mingling. Most people don't leave until around eleven, I'm told." Too late to drive three and a half hours. Even if he wanted to see his wife after four days without her.

"Can't you explain you have to get home to your wife?"

It was the closest she had come to saying she missed him in all of their phone conversations.

"I wish I could, honey. I'll leave first thing Saturday morning. I'll be there before you wake up." He would crawl into their bed, nuzzle the soft skin of her neck, wake her up just enough to rekindle those fires they had been burning all summer.

Her sigh sounded over the line. "We have a fund-raiser for school. A car wash. I took the first shift, from nine to eleven, figuring I'd be there and back before you woke up."

He stretched out on the bed, the towel wrapped around his waist. "Then I'll be waiting for you when you come home."

THE WEEKEND WAS BUSY. Except for several hours in bed after she came home from the car wash, her hair wet and her skin slippery and soapy from the kids' antics, their time together was spent on household chores. He caught up on the bills, ran a few loads of laundry, helped her stop a leak in the shower. She made what she expected to be a quick trip to the grocery and ended up stuck in the weekend crowd. They had considered a movie but decided Saturday date night wouldn't give them any privacy.

"I'm coming to you," she announced over the phone the next Wednesday. "When you come here, you work on the house. I want to have you all to myself, no chores."

"About this weekend—"

"What this time?" Her voice was resigned.

"We have a retreat to determine the direction for the new year. Mr. Abbott is coming himself." The boss had been in communication with him during the summer months, but this was the first time he had shown up at the office since Nick's move.

"I'll come home next weekend, no matter what," he added.

Her long sigh echoed over the line. "All right. I can't go two weeks without you, Nick."

The longing in her voice warmed his heart. They might not say how much they missed each other, but he knew the need was there. He felt it every night when he crawled into his lonely bed.

THE RETREAT WAS DEEMED a success, Mr. Abbott calling him aside to praise the work he was doing. Nick was certain the business would continue to thrive if they took advantage of the growth spurt that was happening in the town. He was in daily contact with the home-builders' association, working with the contractors developing new neighborhoods. He had heard a rumor that a large company was considering the area for its latest factory and he was following up on that possibility. Abbott's Heating and Air could benefit from both the new factory construction and employee housing that would be needed.

He missed talking with Caroline about the progress that was being made. After the first month and the arrival of their phone bill, they had curtailed the long evening phone calls in favor of shorter calls each morning. He'd call and wake her up, they'd chat for a few minutes, and then both rush off to get ready for their day.

Little talk had gone on during the two weekends he made it home. He had tossed in a load of laundry and they had jumped into bed. Once, Caroline had started to tell him about her latest workshop, but he had been distracted by the movement of her lips and they had fallen back into bed, surfacing only when it was time for him to leave.

"Come down next weekend," he urged at the end of September. He had an important meeting on Friday with the factory manager that would no doubt last late into the night. If she drove to Wheeler, they could salvage the rest of the weekend. "I'll make sure nothing interrupts our time on Saturday. We'll hide away from the rest of the world," he whispered into the phone. "Have that affair you talked about."

"Isn't that what we've been doing when you come back here?"

He laughed and then glanced around the small space he was calling home. The current state of his apartment couldn't be further from a secret love nest. Clothes from his week were spread on the chairs and couch. His running shoes and shorts trailed a path to the bathroom. Papers from the current project were piled on the dinette table and chairs. Dirty dishes littered the small sink, and old newspapers were stacked against the overflowing trash can.

He had a week to clean up or she would leave him for being a slob.

"Just come," he begged. His adrenaline over winning the bid for the factory's heating and air-conditioning systems threatened to overtake him and he needed to release steam. With his wife.

He arrived home late Thursday after an intense meeting with the department heads. Hammering out their figures before the next day's meeting meant the team worked through dinner. He was confident the final negotiations would go well for both parties.

Now he needed to spend some quality time with his apartment. The days had blended into the nights and the mess had grown. He planned to crank up some rock and roll and get down to the dirty business of straightening the place before Caroline saw that their love nest had deteriorated into a sloppy bachelor pad.

Whistling, he walked up the two steps to his front door, his tie loosened and the top button of his shirt undone. The suits were the worst part of his day. Who had ever decided a man needed a cord tied around his neck to be successful? He stuck the key in the door and pushed it open.

"Surprise!" Caroline jumped from the couch and wrapped her arms around his neck.

He staggered and caught the edge of the door to keep his balance. "What are you doing here?"

She blinked and he shook his head, sorry his voice had sounded so rough. "I didn't mean it that way." He dropped his tie and hooked an arm around her neck, tugging her close. "I didn't expect you until tomorrow."

"I gathered that." Her voice was dry and he glanced around the room.

She had washed and dried the dishes, putting them away in the open cupboards that flanked the kitchen window. His clothes were gone from the various places he had flung them each night. The covers on the bed were smoothed down and he saw a wad of bedding in the hamper. She had even changed the sheets.

He sat down on the couch, keeping her close to him. The citrusy perfume she favored wafted over him and he inhaled deeply. "I expected you tomorrow night. Did you take the day off?"

She shook her head. "Fall break. I forgot to tell you and then decided to surprise you."

Her scent was causing his insides to twist and he had a strong desire to check out the clean sheets.

Her fingers were busy on his shirt. He sprawled against the back of the couch, watching her work her way down his shirt and onto his belt through half-closed eyes. When she slid the zipper down on his pants, he stilled her hand. "I've had a long day."

"Oh." Disappointment shone in her green eyes.

He laced his fingers through hers, tugging her to her feet. "I think I'd do better in the bed. Just in case I fall asleep."

Desire flickered again on her face. "I don't think you'll be falling asleep."

"Really?" He backed her to the bed and gave her a light push, grinning when she bounced on top of the spread.

She raised her arms, holding them wide. "Not right away. After I'm through with you, though, you may wish you had tomorrow off."

He dropped onto her, rolling them over and over the bed. The meeting with factory management flickered through his mind. No, he had to be there. But a few hours' wrestling with his wife could only heighten his ability to negotiate the final terms. He buried his hands in her thick curls and prepared for the next day.

"MR. EDDINGTON? YOUR WIFE is here."

Nick lifted his head from the budget report he'd been studying and frowned at Mildred, his secretary. "Caroline is here?"

He didn't wait for her response, pushing his chair back and rushing across the room. Why was Caroline here in the middle of the week?

She rose from her seat on one of the soft chairs.

"Hi, Nick." Her cheeks were flushed and her voice sounded nervous.

"What are you doing here?" His hand cupped her elbow and he ran his gaze over her quickly.

He grabbed her other arm, turning her so she faced him fully. "Is everything okay? Your family?"

She glanced over his shoulder at Mildred. "Can we talk in your office?"

"Yes, yes, of course." He paused at the open doorway. "Hold my calls, please, Mildred."

He settled Caroline on the couch and sat down next to her, his hand still on her elbow. His heart had kicked up a pace and he couldn't stop checking to see if she was okay.

"Oh, Nick, you won't believe what's happened!"

She didn't sound upset. Excited, bubbly. "Your presentations are a success?" he guessed. Would that be enough to send her to his office in the middle of the week? Or had she forgotten to tell him about another break?

"Well, yes. In fact, I've been asked to present at a state conference next month. But I wouldn't drive all the way here for that." She giggled and shook her head before placing both hands on his thighs. "Nick, we're having a baby!"

Outside the open window, a tractor rumbled over the farmland that adjoined the main building of Abbott's. A few of the trees that bordered the two properties had bare branches, their leaves giving way to the cooler weather of fall. Others wore the bright red and gold of late October. Lazy clouds floated past in the bright blue sky.

A perfect fall day.

"Nick?"

He ran a hand over his face, across his chin. What had she said?

"Nick, did you hear me?"

"You said a baby, right?" Maybe he had misunderstood. Maybe it wasn't *their* baby she was talking about—

"Yes! Can you believe we're having a baby?" A burble of happiness sounded in every syllable.

A baby?

"A baby?" he said out loud.

She nodded, her eyes dancing with excitement. "I thought I was sick or had the flu. I was eating everything in sight, going to sleep about the time I came home. Moody." She glanced down at her hands. "Then I thought maybe I was just missing my man."

He grinned and nudged her chin up with the flat of his hand. "I like hearing that. I miss my woman."

"Well, you're a barbarian. I saw the way you live when I'm not around." She laughed and slipped her arms around his neck. "We're having a baby, Nick! Can you believe it?"

A baby. Caroline was carrying his baby. He knew she would accuse him of being sexist and behind the times, but he liked the thought of his woman round with his child.

"I couldn't just call with the news. When the doctor gave me the test results this morning, I knew I had to tell you in person. So I told my principal I was going to use a full day of sick leave and drove up here as fast I could."

"You didn't speed, did you?" His arms tightened at the image of her car mangled at the side of the road, the result of taking a corner too fast.

"No. I was careful." She snuggled against his chest. "I'm driving for two now."

Caroline. A mother. She'd be a good mother. Her patience and compassion would benefit a child. She'd know what books to read, the schedule a baby should have. And she had more than enough love to lavish on a dozen children.

"I'm going to turn in my resignation for the end of the semester," she murmured against his shirt.

"What?"

"I thought about it on the drive here. They shouldn't have any trouble finding my replacement. They have candidates waiting for openings all the time."

"What about your reading program?"

"The baby's due this spring. I'd leave in April or May anyway. I probably would have figured out I was pregnant earlier but I never even dreamed that was what was going on with me." Her cheeks were red and she couldn't meet his eyes. "I know this wasn't in our plans, and we've been careful..." Her voice trailed off.

"Birth control isn't a hundred percent effective."

He couldn't believe they were talking about birth control. If she was serious, they had a dozen decisions to make. He wanted to know how she felt, what the doctor had said, when she could move to Missouri with him, where they were going to find a house.

The phone rang on the other side of the door, reminding him they were in his office. He jumped to his feet, pulling her with him.

"Come on, we have to go."

"Where?" She draped her purse over her arm as he yanked open the office door.

"Somewhere to celebrate."

He paused at his secretary's desk. She was filling out a phone-message form and he waited until he had her full attention. "Mildred, cancel my meetings for the day."

"Of course, Mr. Eddington."

He tugged Caroline next to him, his arm tight around her waist. "We're having a baby, Mildred."

His secretary stared at them for a moment and then hurried around her side of the desk, her face beaming. "Oh, Mr. Eddington! Mrs. Eddington! That's delightful news." She shook Nick's hand and hugged Caroline. "You'll be a wonderful father, sir. And Mrs. Eddington, how delightful!"

Nick grinned, basking in the congratulations.

He was going to be a father. And, soon, he and Caroline would be living together again.

CHAPTER THREE

The newspaper column
Twenty-one years earlier

REECIE WHIMPERED and kicked her feet in her pink booties against Caroline's arm. She readjusted and tucked the tiny feet closer to her chest. "Just a few more minutes," she whispered, inhaling the soft baby scent, the fresh odor of the laundry detergent that promised to keep clothes "baby soft all day long."

Her lips touched the pert nose poking out from under the blanket she had wrapped Reecie in. The blue and red colors proclaimed the favorite basketball team of her daddy. Reecie's big brother had passed the blanket to his new sister, saying that his daddy would like the baby to have it.

Caroline smiled as the big brother walked onstage, his hands clasped tightly in front of his waist. His eyes were round and his lips pressed together.

He stopped at the edge of the trees that had been painted by the preschoolers with long streaks of brown and green paint. She had soaked his clothes for hours after that experience and Caroline had a feeling the T-shirt he'd worn that day would never be completely free of the bright green hue.

"We give thanks for our family," Adam stated in a loud voice.

"Your brother's talking about you," Caroline whispered in Reecie's ear.

"We give thanks for food," the girl standing next to Adam said.

The other three students gave their lines and then exited the stage. Adam didn't follow.

Caroline glanced at Nick. "What's he doing?" she mouthed.

Nick shook his head. She stared at the stage, waiting, and then grinned when Adam hollered, "Hi, Mom! Hi, Dad!" He sent them a big wave before galloping after his classmates.

"I forgot to say hi to Reecie," Adam said on the way home. His feet kicked a tattoo against his seat.

Caroline leaned over the front seat and patted his shin, stopping the pounding. "It's okay, she doesn't know."

Reecie waggled her feet in her car seat, sending a bootie flying toward Nick's head. Caroline caught it in the air just before it landed.

Adam giggled and tickled his sister's bare toes. "You're silly," he told the baby.

Reecie waved her hands at her brother, her mouth open as she gurgled. "Still no teef," Adam announced.

"Not yet. But one of these days, you'll see a tiny white speck that's the start of a tooth."

Adam leaned over as far as he could, strapped in his own seat. Reecie grabbed his hair. "Let go, Reecie," he said patiently. "My hair isn't a toy."

He tugged her hands away and sank back into his seat. "We done good today, didn't we, Mama?"

"You did great." She slid her arm across the empty space between their seats and rubbed Nick's shoulder.

He slid a quick glance her way and smiled before returning his attention to the road. Behind her, she heard the soft coos of their baby daughter and their son's answering soft chatter. A lot to be thankful for, she thought.

"SHHH, SHHH." SHE PACED around the room, jiggling the crying baby up and down in her arms. "Hush, hush, hush."

The baby only wailed louder at her crooning. Caroline ran a finger over the bottom of the little girl's gums, feeling the tiny bud of a tooth. "I know, baby, I know. Shh, shh."

She hummed a lullaby, swishing Reecie back and forth, dancing around the living-room carpet. Her nightgown swayed against her knees, reminiscent of a fancy evening gown.

Normally, the motions soothed Reecie in just a matter of moments. But Caroline had been dancing and pacing for more than an hour, with no relief.

"Mama?" Adam's plaintive voice sounded from his room down the hallway.

"I'm sorry, honey. Reecie's mouth hurts."

"My ears hurt."

Mine, too, baby. She kissed the forehead of her other sad child, wishing she could take away the pain.

"I can't sleep, Mama."

Caroline waltzed down the hallway, her arms cradling Reecie against her chest. She pushed open his door, letting the light from the living room filter into his room. "Come dance with Reecie and me," she coaxed Adam.

He lifted his head from his pillow. Dark hair spiked around his face, the same shade as his sleeping father's.

Not that she blamed Nick. He had been working early morning to late at night, organizing bids that would win them jobs. They were heading into their slow season and Nick had been on the lookout for inside jobs that would keep them from laying off any employees, a constant worry during the winter months.

At the first whimpers from Reecie, she had slid out of their bed, careful not to disturb him. The door had shut behind her with an almost silent click.

Adam leaped out of bed. They danced down the hallway and back into the living room, away from Nick.

He had slept through Adam's bouts with teething and colic, too. Then they had both been working. Nick had tried to share the late-night duties with her, but Adam had only cried harder when his father marched around the room with him. They had soon realized that if they wanted any sleep, Caroline would be the one to sing and pace with their new baby.

Back then, she'd been lucky if she managed a few hours of sleep before the alarm went off and she had to get ready for school. Nick delivered Adam to the woman who watched him during the day, while she taught other people's children and Nick managed the office at the Abbott Heating and Air-Conditioning Company.

She had resigned the minute she found out she was pregnant with their second child. "I'm not teaching next year," she had told her teaching partner and friend.

Patty had given her the big toothy grin that brightened the lives of her kindergarten students. "I knew it."

"What?" Caroline poured herbal tea into Patty's cup. Since the discovery of her pregnancy, she had cut out all caffeine.

"I knew you wouldn't go back if you got pregnant again."

Caroline sipped her tea. They were enjoying the spring weather in her backyard while Adam napped. The baby monitor sat on the table between them. "I don't want to have my children taken care of by someone else while I'm taking care of other people's children."

"You don't have to explain, Caroline. If you want to stay home, do." Patty broke off a piece of shortbread. "It's your choice."

She thought of Patty's words as she dipped and swayed with Reecie. It was her choice. She had talked to Nick about her decision and he had said that whatever she decided was fine with him. Once the kids were older, she'd go back to teaching. She wasn't like her mother, letting her life revolve around her husband and children. She just wanted to give Adam and Reecie the best start in life by being with them during their early years.

Adam danced around her legs, grabbing the hem of

her nightgown and swooping down to the floor when she dipped. Reecie's eyes were still round, filled with big fat tears, but she had a tiny grin on her face as she watched her brother.

"You're a sweetheart," she whispered, feathering her lips across her daughter's smooth forehead.

"Kiss me, Mama, kiss me!"

She ducked and smacked a kiss on Adam's cheek. "You're a sweetheart, too. Look how Reecie's watching you. You're helping her forget how much her tooth hurts."

Adam jumped up and down. "Let me see her toof. Is it there yet?"

Caroline leaned down and gently held Reecie's lower lip away from her gum. "No tooth yet. But see that little white spot? That's where it's going to be."

He pressed his nose against his sister's tiny button of a nose. "You're going to be okay, Reecie. My toofs are all in my mouf now and none of them hurt."

He raised his eyes to his mother's face. "Right, Mama? That's what I should tell her, right?"

Caroline shifted to hold Reecie with one arm and smoothed her free hand over Adam's curly head. "Exactly right, honey. See? She's happier already."

"What's going on out here?"

Nick's voice was gruff. He rubbed a hand over his eyes and across his chin, his mouth widening in a big yawn as he came into the room.

"We're dancing, Daddy, 'cause Reecie has a toof coming in." Adam spun around the room, landing in a heap at his father's bare feet.

Nick scooped his son into his arms. "Dancing, huh? In the middle of the night?"

Adam's head bobbed up and down. "It's what makes Reecie stop crying. Mama did it for me, too, didn't you?"

Caroline caught Nick's gaze over the heads of their children. The corners of his eyes crinkled in a sleepy smile. He yawned again and Caroline swallowed to keep her own yawn from breaking out.

"Mama likes to dance. Hang on, Adam."

Nick stepped up to her, Adam's arms around his neck and the sturdy legs around his waist. With a flourish and a small bow, the little boy hardly hindering his movements, he encircled Caroline's waist with his hands.

Nestled between her mother and father, Reecie tucked her head down. A fat fist went into her mouth and Caroline could feel her suckling the tiny fingers.

"What are we dancing to?" Nick asked, his body moving from side to side.

"'The Elephant Song'!" Adam piped.

Nick grinned. "'The Elephant Song'?"

"I'm working through the alphabet. It's been a long night."

They swayed back and forth, their feet shuffling in tight circles. Adam's head slowly lowered to his father's shoulder, gentle snores emanating from between his lips. Reecie curled in a ball, her feet drawn up to her chest and her mouth moving rhythmically against her knuckles.

"Why didn't you wake me up?" Nick asked softly. His breath feathered against her cheek.

"You have to work tomorrow." Her head was on his shoulder, Adam's baby-fine hair soft against her chin.

"So do you."

She lifted her head at that, looking into his eyes. Her nipples tightened and need pooled in her middle. She was the mother of two children, both of them in her arms. Yet one look from their father, and she was a teenager again.

She tried to remember what they had been talking about. He'd said she had to work in the morning. "No, I don't." For the first time in their marriage, she was not going off to a classroom every morning.

He traced her cheek with one finger, the lightest of touches. A shiver started at the top of her spine and traveled all the way down her back. "Yes, you do. What you do with our children is as important as what I do in that office every day."

Reecie gave a hiccupy sigh, her body rippling with the effort. "I need to tuck her into bed," Caroline whispered. "Before all this dancing is lost."

He stepped away from her and she felt bereft. He must have seen it in her eyes. "I'll put Adam down and meet you in our bedroom."

She nodded, her tongue thick in her mouth. They hadn't been together in their bed except to sleep since before Reecie was born. She hadn't meant to wait so long, but she was so tired by the time she settled both of the children and finished picking up the living room and loading the dishwasher. And Nick would be asleep, the bedside lamp left on for her.

She expected him to be sleeping when she went into their room, but he was sitting up, his back against the headboard. His arms were crossed over his bare chest and she licked suddenly dry lips.

"Lock the door," he said softly.

"What?"

"Lock the door. We don't want Adam wandering in."

She nodded and closed the door quietly, pushing in the button. Nick patted the bed next to him. "Come here."

She gave a nervous giggle and walked toward him on wobbly legs. Where were the graceful moves of earlier with Adam and Reecie? Now that she was alone with him, her legs could hardly manage to cross the room.

She sat down on the edge of the bed. He leaned forward, his elbow denting the mattress next to her hip, and ran his fingers lightly over her arm, from her elbow to her wrist and back again.

The fine hairs on her arm rose up and she shivered. "Problem?" he murmured.

The gleam in his eyes told her he knew exactly what he was doing to her. "I'm so tired from dancing with Reecie." She gave a delicate yawn and patted her mouth. Two could play at the teasing game.

"Maybe you'd better crawl under the covers. Stretch out and rest." He turned down the sheet behind her hip.

She tilted her head, her lips curved together in a soft smile. "Good idea."

She never made it as far as the covers. Nick's mouth captured hers, his unshaven skin rough against her jaw. She reached her arm around his neck and pulled him closer, needing to know that she was more than the mother of his children, that somewhere deep inside her still lurked the heart and body of a woman.

"You have too many clothes on," he growled in her ear.

She grinned and shifted, helping him tug her nightgown over her head. He had discarded his pajamas after putting Adam to bed and she ran her foot up and down his bare calf.

He shuddered and she moved her foot higher, over his knee, past the muscles of his thigh. He caught her foot before she could go higher. "Stop. I don't have much patience right now."

"Really?" She wiggled her other foot, heading for his calf and points beyond, freezing when his hand dipped down and cupped her between her thighs.

She gasped. "Everything okay?" he whispered, his breathing ragged.

"I—I— Nick, please…"

She didn't know if she was begging him to stop or to continue the exquisite torture. His touch was making her body arch on the bed. He kissed her again, his tongue dancing with hers, his fingers playing her as rhythmically as they had danced earlier.

When he edged on top, pushing the covers out of his way, she welcomed his weight. She wrapped her arms around his broad back, guiding him inside. Her lips nibbled at the sensitive skin beneath his ears, her tongue darting in and out to taste him.

He moved within her, slowly at first but that wasn't enough. She dug her heels into his back, urging him to move faster, to satisfy her growing need. He panted in her ear and she kissed his cheek, murmuring to him until his back arched and he froze. Her own release followed soon after.

She lay beneath him, listening to his breathing return to normal. "I need to move," he muttered after several long seconds.

She rubbed her hand over his back, tracing the strong muscles, the neat line of his spine. "You're fine."

"If I fall asleep on top of you, I'll crush you." He stayed still and then rolled over with a loud grunt.

"Hush." She pressed her hand over his mouth. "Don't wake up the kids."

He kissed the pad of her fingers. "Sorry. You make me forget we have kids."

Her heart warmed at the compliment. Her breasts felt heavy and she knew Reecie would be waking soon for her morning feeding. But for the last few minutes, she had forgotten that she was a mother, reveling in being a woman.

A rattling at the door woke her. Sunlight streaked through the light curtains at their window. She glanced at the clock on the nightstand next to her side of the bed and pushed at Nick's shoulder.

"Nick, wake up. It's seven-thirty."

He groaned and shifted his weight from his back to his side, his arm coming over her waist. She nudged at his elbow. "Nick, you have to get up. We missed the alarm." He was expected in the office by eight.

"Mama?"

She scrambled out of bed, grabbing her nightgown and tossing it over her head. Shrugging it down her body, she buttoned the two middle buttons before unlocking the door. "Hey, buddy." She scooped Adam into her arms. "What is it?"

"Reecie's crying. I went into her room and she's banging on the sides of her crib."

"She's hungry." She carried Adam over to her side of the bed and dropped him with a little bounce. He giggled and snuggled under the covers. "Wake Daddy up. He needs to go to work."

She left the room, confident their son would be able to rouse Nick. He had pulled on his pajama bottoms sometime during the night so they wouldn't be subjected to curious questions.

"I'm leaving." A while later, Nick stood in the doorway of the nursery, his eyes on their nursing daughter. Reecie patted her hand against Caroline's breast, her mouth pursed as she suckled. Mewing sounds came from her throat.

"All right. Will you be home for lunch?"

He shook his head. "No, I had planned to go in early this morning. I'll have to make up the time during lunch." He crossed the room in three strides and bent down, catching her chin under his hand and raising her mouth for a long kiss. "Not that I mind after last night."

"Neither do I." She smiled and settled Reecie at her other breast. "Shall we schedule another night like that?"

"You bet." He gave her another swift kiss and left the room.

"I THOUGHT OF YOU AS soon as I read the advertisement." Patty handed her a packet of paper held together with a bright red paper clip.

Caroline skimmed the top page. "A newspaper column?"

"Yes. You answer questions people send in about their kids, education, family life. Two or three letters a week."

"But I've never written a newspaper column." She pushed the papers across the table toward Patty.

Patty pushed them back. "Caroline, you'd be perfect. You know education, you write well and you have contacts."

"What contacts?"

"All of us at school, for one." She lifted her hands, palms up. "The materials you created for your reading program are great. If you'd ever take the time to put a packet together, I bet you could get it published with a company that makes teacher resources. A lot of teachers would love to have your plan available to them."

She had toyed with the idea of submitting her reading program to a publisher, but finding the time to organize the idea into a legible manuscript hadn't happened yet. Once Reecie was weaned and Adam was in regular school… She knew she was making excuses, but with Nick working so many hours, she barely had time to get a shower in every day.

"How does that relate to this column?" she asked.

"You're an expert on education. You wrote your own curriculum, you have a teaching background and you know kids." Patty waved her hand around the living room, taking in Adam on his stomach coloring a picture and Reecie playing with a stuffed toy in her playpen. "Why not apply? You either get the job or you're rejected. One changes your lifestyle, one doesn't make a difference at all. You'd be good."

"Fine." She felt a flurry of excitement at her friend's confidence, but she kept her face bland. No sense in getting worked up and then having her plans dashed. Being the calm, collected parent had become her calling in life.

Oh, but to be more than a parent for even a couple hours each week. She loved her kids, she loved being with them every day. But except for Patty's visits, Sunday-morning church and the few times Nick was able to get home for dinner at a decent hour, she was surrounded by children and their needs.

"I should probably talk to Nick first."

"Why? Is he going to tell you no?"

She had no idea. They had so little time to talk to each other. No repeat of their late-night dancing had occurred. Reecie's tooth had popped through and two nights later, the second one had shown up with very little fuss. Caroline had heard her whimpering in the night but when she checked, her baby's eyes had been shut tight. Not until the morning's nursing had she discovered the second sharp tiny tooth.

Caroline slid the clip from the papers and riffled through the pages, pulling out the application form. The column couldn't take that much time each week. Nick wouldn't even realize she was employed unless she told him.

"You have to help me answer the questions," she said. "And you'll have to help me figure out my credentials."

"Okay." Patty hitched her chair closer to the table. "I've always wanted to write fiction." She grinned at Caroline's glare and handed her a pen. "We can stick to the truth, if that's what you want to do. But one of these days, I'm going to write a book that will keep people guessing if it's really my life story or make-believe."

"I GOT THE JOB." Caroline stared at the single sheet of paper she'd taken out of the envelope.

"What, Mommy?" Adam did a semicartwheel and landed upside down on the brown grass.

"Stand up, bud, it's too cold for you to be on the ground."

Adam lunged to his feet and almost fell again as he tried to wipe off his bottom. "I can flip all the way on a mat. Miss Burton showed us how."

"That's nice," Caroline answered absentmindedly.

Adam tugged at her hand. "Are you listening to me?"

She lifted her head from the letter she was rereading and focused on her son's face. "Yes, Adam, I'm listening."

He sneezed and brushed his hand under his nose. "I'm cold." He tipped his head back and stared at the sky. "I think it's going to snow again. Is it going to snow again, Mama?"

"I don't know, honey." The winter had been long, and while a few hardy crocuses had poked their heads out of the ground, nothing else proclaimed that spring was on its way.

She followed him across the lawn. For the past week, she had hurried out the door as soon as the mail truck arrived. Until today, she had collected nothing but bills and flyers for local stores.

The envelope was slender, the size of a single sheet of paper. She had been certain it was a "thank you for your interest but we've found someone else" letter. Instead, the editor had invited her to come down to the office at her earliest convenience to sign papers for her new position as the education columnist.

"Caroline Eddington, journalist," she whispered as she helped Adam up the front-porch steps.

Adam looked at her over his shoulder. "My name is Eddington," he said.

"I know. That's my name, too."

His brow furrowed and he shook his head. "No, your name is Mama."

She opened her mouth to tell him her real name and then snapped it shut. Only two people in the world could call her Mama. She was not going to give one of them any information that would make him choose to call her by her given name.

"You're right." She opened the screen door and waited while he struggled up the last step into the house. "Let's see if Reecie is awake and then we can take a drive downtown."

He grinned and skipped down the hallway. "Can we stop and get ice cream?"

One afternoon after school, Patty had volunteered to take Adam for a couple hours to give Caroline a respite.

Reecie had been napping and Caroline had enjoyed a long bath and a short book. When the two returned from their expedition, she learned that Patty had introduced Adam to the ice-cream parlor on the edge of downtown. Since then, whenever anyone mentioned downtown, he begged for ice cream.

Today he would get his wish. A new job called for a celebration. "We can get ice cream. But you have to be good while I make a quick stop."

"I will, I will, I will!" He pushed open Reecie's door and ran across the alphabet carpet, pausing at the crib to stare through the slats at his sister. "Reecie, we're going downtown. And we're going to eat ice cream!"

Caroline didn't think she could be any more excited.

"Do not touch anything," she warned Adam later that afternoon. She had paused outside the door of the *Wheeler Weekly* newspaper office and smoothed down her hair with a nervous hand. "We'll get ice cream after I talk with Mr. Frazier."

The secretary behind the wooden counter looked up as they came. "I'm here to see Mr. Frazier," Caroline said. "I'm Caroline Eddington."

"Oh, good! He should be here any minute." The young woman looked frazzled. Her curly hair was clipped back with a large barrette and she had a pencil tucked behind her ear. Adam kept looking at it and Caroline hoped he didn't decide to climb over and snatch it. With Reecie in her arms, she wouldn't be able to stop him.

"Leave it alone," she whispered when his hand inched toward the young woman's desk.

He dropped his hand back to his side. "She shouldn't have a pencil on her ear," he said in a loud stage whisper.

The woman plucked it out with a laugh. "That's where I put it. I swore I would never do that. My old grandmother used to stick pencils behind her ears and her glasses on her head and then forget where they were. I never wanted to be that forgetful and here I am, doing the same thing. And I'm way too young."

Caroline didn't think she was much older than the secretary. But she felt ancient, with one child on her hip and the other clamped around her leg.

The door banged open behind them, the cold wind blowing a stack of papers off the counter. "Amber, Harrison didn't deliver the papers again today."

Adam's fingers bit into Caroline's leg as a broad-shouldered man stormed into the room, his salt-and-pepper hair disheveled. The glass door clicked shut behind him.

"I'll take care of it." She waved a hand toward Caroline and he swiveled around, noticing them for the first time. Adam scooted behind her, his face hidden against her thigh. "This is Caroline Eddington, Matt. For the education column."

"Mrs. Eddington? Thank you, God," he said, tilting his head to the ceiling. "At least one thing's going right today."

At the sound of her name, Adam came forward. "She's Mama!" he stated.

Caroline patted his head and ran her fingers down his cheek until she could touch his lips, shushing him. "I hope you don't mind I brought my children. I didn't have a sitter."

He held out a hand and she extended hers. "Matt Frazier." His grip was tight, the skin chapped and rough. Not a man who sat around writing all day, she gathered. "No problem about the kids. I'm thankful you're here to take the job." He bent forward and peered into her face. "You *are* here to take the job, right?"

She nodded. "If you're still offering."

"Oh, yeah." He released her hand and raised one portion of the counter so they could walk through. Adam slipped away from Caroline's leg, his eyes wide as he studied the hinges that opened the space.

"Wow. We could put these in our counter," he said to Caroline, his earlier fear of the large, blustery man disappearing in the wake of a new discovery.

"Maybe." She turned to the man leading them through a maze of desks covered with papers and a few computers. "We're remodeling an older house. Adam has ideas all the time about what we can do."

Matt ushered them into a small office, the desk and bookshelf piled high with papers, books and other items Caroline knew Reecie would enjoy tackling with her new toddling skills.

He picked up a stack of newspapers and several books from a straight-backed chair. "I don't get company much," he explained, indicating the empty seat.

"That's fine."

"Our last columnist retired and moved to California to be closer to her grandchildren." He handed her a fat folder, the pages inside held together with a thick rubber band. He leaned against the desk, his legs crossed at the ankles in front of him. "I've included her last couple of columns and the letters we've received this month. The column's published every Thursday, which means I need your copy no later than 5:00 p.m. Tuesday night. Go through some of those letters, pick two or three, and answer them."

"All right." Bemused, she watched him straighten and head out the door. "That's it?"

He paused and looked over his shoulder at her. "Do you need something else?"

"Well, I—" What did she need? "The letter said I had to come to sign some papers and pick up my assignment."

"Amber!"

His shout caused Reecie to jump in Caroline's arms. She patted her on the back, hoping she wouldn't start to cry.

"Yeah?"

"Did you say Mrs. Eddington needed to sign something?"

"Yeah." The younger woman appeared in the doorway. "Thought you'd have a contract or something to make it official."

He shook his head several times, his hair flying around his face. "When I ask you to write a letter, just put in the words I tell you." He turned back to Caroline. "Here's the deal. You write the column, if it's good I publish it, if not, it's canned that week. You miss a couple weeks, I look for somebody new."

"Okay. Am I paid for the column?"

He smacked his hand against his forehead. Reecie

laughed and hit herself in the forehead with her hand, tossing her head back so quickly, Caroline had to grab her around the waist to keep her from falling to the floor.

"Yeah, it's not much." He named a sum and Caroline nodded. She would have taken the job for half the price, just to remind herself that she was more than a mother.

She felt guilty for her thoughts as she helped Adam into his car seat five minutes later. Her new boss had retraced their path through the maze, Amber had waved goodbye, the phone at her ear, and they were on the sidewalk. Reecie had given a gurgling wave and Adam had hopped on one foot back to the car, chanting "ice cream! ice cream!" all the way.

They ate dishes of ice cream at the 1950s-style diner. Reecie banged her spoon against the metal tray of her high chair in time to the bebop music. Adam laughed at his sister, and Caroline couldn't help smiling. She loved her family but she was going to have a paycheck again.

NICK WAS WORKING LATE, so she ordered burgers and fries to take home for her and Adam. She fed Reecie a jar of macaroni and cheese and bathed them both. After they were down for the night, she sat on her bed and sorted through the folder of letters, waiting for Nick to come home. Now that she had the position, she had to tell him what she had done.

He came into the bedroom and went right to the closet, shrugging out of his suit coat and hanging it on its wooden hanger. "Did the insurance statement for the house come today?" he asked.

"Yes, I put it with the bills." She tucked the letter she had been reading back into the folder and laid it on her nightstand. "I have a job," she said quietly.

He paused, his back to her, the blue and red tie she had given him for Christmas from the children in his hand. "What?"

"I have a job. I'm writing a column for the *Wheeler Weekly* about education."

He draped the tie over his tie rack and leaned against the doorjamb to take off his shoes and socks. He lined up the pair on the closet floor and unbuckled his belt. "You're writing a column for the paper? When did this happen?"

"Patty brought me the application last week." She pulled her knees to her chest. He hadn't looked at her since he came into the room, methodically undressing and putting his clothes away. "The editor sent me a letter hiring me and I went down to the office today."

He creased his slacks and slid them onto a hanger. "I thought you didn't want to work while the kids were little."

"It's only a couple hours a week, Nick. I can write while they're asleep." Why wouldn't he look at her?

He unbuttoned his shirt and peeled it off his shoulders, dropping it into the hamper. Clad only in his boxers, he crossed the room to the bed and sat down next to her.

She reached over and kneaded his shoulders with her knuckles. Watching him perform the slow striptease had caused her pulse to race. "The kids are asleep," she murmured, pressing light kisses to his back.

"Mmm." He lowered his head and scrubbed his hands over his face.

She leaned around until she could see his eyes. "Is something the matter?"

"Mr. Abbott came to the office today."

From his tone, she knew he meant Mr. Abbott Senior, the owner of the heating and air-conditioning company. He had hired Nick right out of his MBA program, coming down from Iowa to interview prospective candidates at his alma mater of KU. During their three years in Wheeler, he had visited a few times, trusting his son to run the Missouri branch while he took care of the Iowa region.

Panic welled up in her chest, making it difficult to breathe. She was overreacting, she had to be. But Nick didn't usually rebuff her invitation to make love. "He asked you to move again, didn't he?"

"No." He shifted until he was facing her and took her hands in his. "That is—" He took a long ragged breath, the air blowing gently against her cheek. "He's replacing me with his nephew, Caroline."

"What?"

His hands clenched hers, his fingernails digging into her palms. "His nephew graduated at Christmas. He interned with us last summer and now he's been offered a job in the business. The family business," he said with a bite to his words.

She rose to her knees, her hands on his shoulders. Outside, the shrill siren of a police car and the hoot of an owl split the night. "He's firing you? How can he do that? After all you've done for the company!"

"He's giving me a strong recommendation."

Her eyes widened. "Nick! Are you defending him?"

She punched his shoulders. "This isn't right! We bought this house. Adam starts school next year."

She ran her hands through her hair. "I don't want to move! I like it here." She'd started to hang pictures on the walls and she'd picked out paint for the bathrooms. Minor details for some people but a huge step toward the future for her.

"Caroline, nothing's definite yet." He pulled down the covers and sprawled on his side of the bed. "I can't talk about this tonight. I'm too tired to think."

She stared at him. How could he drop this on her and then just crawl into bed? He rolled to his side, his cheek pillowed on one hand, his eyes already closed.

She watched his chest rise and fall with his steady breathing. *Talk to me, dammit!*

Sighing, she climbed off the bed and left the room, flipping off the ceiling light at the door. She checked that the doors and windows were locked. She wandered down the hall to the kids' rooms, running her hand over the maple wainscoting they had attached to the lower half of the walls at Christmas. She had painted the top of the walls a creamy yellow, bringing the sunshine into the narrow space. A single picture hung on the wall.

She studied the picture in the hall light. Adam held Reecie in his lap, his arms locked tight around his little sister's tummy. She had fussed and wiggled, but he had not let her go until the photographer had snapped several pictures. Caroline had framed the one with both faces lit up with giggles. Every time she saw it, she felt a surge of love and amazement that she was the mother of two such delightful children.

She didn't want her kids to move around the way she had. Making friends became harder with each move. The older she grew, the more she was left out. The other boys and girls had busy lives and they didn't have time to add someone new to the mix. She had found it easier to stay aloof rather than run the risk of being snubbed. She found solace in her schoolwork and books, earning top marks in all of her classes.

Reecie had kicked off her blanket, so Caroline draped it back around the sleeping form of her daughter. Adam was sleeping upside down, his feet on his pillow. She readjusted him, kissed his cheek, and went back to the room she shared with Nick, crawling into bed next to him.

He mumbled in his sleep and rolled over, tucking her against his chest. His hand slid over her waist, locking their bodies together. She rested her hand over his, feeling the band of his wedding ring. She ran her finger over and over the smooth metal. She loved him, she did. But could she make another move?

"NOT BAD FOR A FIRST time." Matt nodded his head and handed her the column she had labored over for the past week. Nick had been filling out job applications at the kitchen table while she sifted through letters and drafted answers.

"You need to cut the second answer by half and drop the third letter."

She widened her eyes in surprise. "But that letter is the most common problem parents have."

"Then it should be the first letter." He grabbed a page from his desk and went to the door. "Amber! Did you put Pickett's Car Sale on the front page?"

"Yes, Matt. I always do."

Matt walked back to his desk and leaned against the edge, his legs stretched out toward Caroline. He ran his hand through his hair, causing the ends to stand up. That's why his hair always looks so wild, she thought.

"Advertising has top priority," he said. "That's what pays the bills. If I have to cut your column or any of the articles, I'm going to start from the bottom and work my way up. If you want something to stay in your column, put it at the beginning. Your lead is the most important piece of your article."

She scribbled notes as he gave her a crash course in newspaper writing. "Where are your kids?" he asked suddenly.

"A neighbor girl just completed the hospital's baby-sitting seminar. She's watching them."

"A babysitting seminar?" Matt's voice boomed around the small room. He seemed to have only one level. Loud.

She nodded. He grabbed a tablet and wrote on it for a few moments. "Do an interview with your sitter and contact the hospital. Make your next column about proper care for children."

She was getting used to his lightning-quick changes of subject. They talked for a few more minutes and then she left. If she hurried, she'd be home before Nick arrived.

His car was already parked in the driveway when she got there. He sat in the living room, Reecie in his lap and Adam playing with his cars on the floor. "Nick! You're home early." She dropped her briefcase on the antique oak pew she'd refinished last summer.

"I need to talk to you." He carried Reecie over to her portable playpen and carefully set her down, handing her a stuffed bear.

Caroline perched on the edge of a chair. He walked to the window and faced outside, his hands clenched behind his back. Adam's soft *vroom-vroom* punctuated the ticking of the mantel clock.

"I received a job offer today."

She waited. He turned around, his eyes dark. "Aren't you going to ask any questions?"

"No. You'll tell me what I need to know."

The moment the words were out of her mouth, she wished she could take them back.

"What does that mean?" he asked.

She tilted her head toward Adam. "Adam, go play in your room, please," Nick said.

Adam frowned at his father, his lower lip pushed out in a big pout. "I want to play here," he said.

"Adam."

He gave a big sigh and gathered his cars in his shirt. His feet pounded down the hallway and she heard the cars crash to the floor in his room. Reecie jabbered to herself in the playpen.

"We're moving, aren't we?" she said.

He sank onto the couch. "Caroline, it's a great offer. And it's the only one I've had so far."

"But you just started applying." She reached over and grabbed his hands between hers. "We have some money saved up, we can wait a little bit. See what's around here."

"Caroline." He brushed his thumb over her knuckles. "There's nothing here. You know that."

She did. The town was small. The downtown consisted of a single block with a limited number of shops and a pizza parlor. Most of the people shopped out of town on the weekends, patronizing the larger cities of Springfield or Joplin for their major purchases. The local grocery store provided staples for those times when someone ran out of milk or eggs.

The heating and air-conditioning company succeeded because it didn't rely on the community for its business. Nick had spent hours traveling to other towns, dealing with contractors from the surrounding counties.

"Where is it?" she asked. Listening to him didn't mean she had to accept the move.

"In Kansas. South of your folks a couple hours. A construction company. They need someone to do bids."

She knew the marketing aspect of his job had grown to include making bids for jobs that had come their way. He was good with numbers and his boss had complimented him often on how accurately he was able to predict the cost of a project.

Too bad he hadn't been able to predict that his job wouldn't last for more than a couple years.

"Caroline, I know this is hard. I had no idea this was coming." He flexed her fingers back and forth, his eyes on their linked hands. "Will you at least go to Kansas with me this weekend and check out the place, let me see what the job is like?"

She drew in a breath and let it out slowly. "Yes." What else could she do? He was her husband.

"Thank you." He leaned forward and kissed her, his lips warm against his mouth. "I love you," he murmured against her mouth.

Heaven help her, she loved him, too.

"YOU SEND ME PICTURES of those kids, you hear me? I want to see how they're growing." Patty wrapped a glass in newspaper and carefully placed it in the box she was packing. Dishes and pans were stacked on every inch of the kitchen counters.

"Okay." Caroline layered hot pads in her box.

"And during the summer, we can get together when I'm not at workshops."

"Mmm-hmm."

"Hey!" Patty held up a hand. "What's with you?"

"Nothing." Caroline wrapped several plates and stacked them neatly in the box.

"You're acting like we're not going to stay in touch. You're not moving out of the country, just a few hours away."

"I know." She closed the box and sealed it with tape.

Patty dropped the newspapers off her lap and scooted over until she was next to Caroline. "Are you dumping me?"

Caroline snorted. "What?"

"Are you dumping me?" Patty repeated. "I know when I'm being dumped, it's happened enough with guys. But to have my best friend dump me!" She scowled. "I'm not letting you dump me."

"You're crazy, you know that." She unfolded another box, not looking at her friend.

"Yeah. And I know when somebody is trying to get rid of me." She slung her arm around Caroline's shoulders. "What's the matter with you? Why are you pushing me away?"

Caroline sighed. "I just don't want you to think you have to keep in contact with me. I know you'll get busy with your life, with school—"

"Stop right there." Patty gave her a shake. "I'm not a fair-weather friend. I'll write to you, we'll visit. Who else is going to corrupt that little boy of yours? And just wait until Reecie gets big enough to hang out with her auntie Patty."

Caroline blinked several times. Patty slewed around until they were face-to-face, her hands on Caroline's shoulders. "It's about all those moves you did as a kid, isn't it?"

Caroline shrugged. "It's easier to make a break now, rather than drag it out. You know, rip a bandage off quick."

Patty stuck her fists on her hips. "I'm a bandage?"

"You know what I mean."

"Yeah, I do. And, personally, I'm offended." Patty sat on the sofa, her lower lip pushed out in a pout reminiscent of Adam at his most irritated.

"Patty, I don't want to make you mad. I've just done this so many times. It's the best way, trust me."

"No, you're not getting off that easy." Patty shook her head, her red curls bouncing around her cheeks and shoulders. She had tied them back with a bandanna but that hadn't lasted long. "Because some grade-school kid forgot you twenty years ago, you think I'm going to write you out of my life? That's insulting. We're not eight years old, Caroline."

"I know it."

"Then act like it." Patty got up and walked over to her box and picked up a glass, twisting paper around it with sharp, quick jabs. "Do you know how many friends I have left from elementary school? None. Oh, I see some of them around town. But we're not in and out of each other's houses like we were in fourth grade. It doesn't matter if you live in the same town all your life or not. People drift apart."

Caroline sat silent. They had cupboards to empty, drawers to wipe out. The moving company that had been hired would arrive first thing in the morning and after the kitchen, the bathrooms still had to be packed up.

"I'm sorry." Her voice came out small and weak.

"Oh, honey." Patty wrapped her arms around her again and hugged her close. "We're soul sisters. You can't get rid of me. I'm like a burr on your pants."

Caroline bit her lip to stop the tears that were threatening to blur her vision. "You'd rather be a burr than a bandage?"

"Oh, yeah." Patty released her and snapped the tape

over her box. "'Cause no matter how hard you try to get rid of a burr, it just keeps coming back."

How did she get so lucky in her friends? "I love you."

"Yeah, I know." Patty carried the box she had finished over to the stack by the door. "I love you, too," she said over her shoulder. "Which means you're never going to get rid of me."

They finished packing the kitchen and moved into the bathrooms. Her life in Wheeler was coming to a close. This time tomorrow, she'd be in Kansas.

The trip to Freeston had been a formality. Nick wanted the job. She could tell from his voice as he told her about the company on their drive. The construction company was growing and the two older men who owned it were impressed by Nick's credentials and the recommendation he'd received from Mr. Abbott. They'd offered him a substantial raise over his current salary and offered to help them with the purchase of a home in the town.

"Until we sell the house in Wheeler, we don't have to make any payments," he'd said. "I should have been looking before this happened. The Abbotts had a good deal with me."

She hadn't been able to answer him. She'd gone through it before, the search for the perfect job. Her parents, though, seemed to have finally settled down. During her last phone call with her mother, she'd been informed that her father was running for the city council of Mustang.

She wiped down the empty drawer and sat on the

edge of the tub. She had given Reecie her first bath in this room. Adam had been potty trained here. Memories were etched in every inch of the house.

She'd just have to pack them up with the rest of their belongings. Her mind started a mental list of the positives of their move. They were closer to her parents in Freeston. One of the state universities was an hour's drive from their house. She could work on her master's degree, think about going back to teaching when Reecie entered school.

Once again, the pros outweighed the cons.

CHAPTER FOUR

The master's degree
Eighteen years earlier

"THE SCHEDULE CAME for my master's program. The first class starts next month."

She and Nick were enjoying a quiet few minutes in the living room after dinner. Adam was in his room, ostensibly completing his homework, and Reecie was writing a thank-you letter to Grandma Armstrong for her new school outfit.

Nick flipped a page of the newspaper and shook the paper to straighten it. "I thought you decided not to do that."

She couldn't see his face over the paper. "Not do what?"

He lowered a corner of the paper. "Get your master's degree. You decided not to teach anymore, right?"

She bristled. "I didn't say I wasn't going to teach anymore."

"After your last sub experience, you said you weren't going back in the classroom."

Once Reecie entered kindergarten, she had applied

to substitute in the local school district, planning to be available only for the elementary school. The administrative office had called several times during the first month, asking her to reconsider and cover a class at the middle school or high school. She had accepted one time at both places and then decided she did not want to sub, except as a special favor to the teachers in her children's school.

"That's not what I said." His newspaper still provided a barrier between them. "Could you put that paper down while we're talking?" she asked in exasperation.

He lowered the paper, his gaze wary. "Okay. What do you want to talk about?"

She hated when he used that overly adult tone with her. "My master's program."

"Listen, Caro, if that's what you want to do, go for it. It's your choice." He lifted the paper.

She reached across and grabbed the page, hearing a rip. "Don't read while I'm talking to you!" She took a deep breath and exhaled slowly, counting to ten and forcing herself to be calm. "Nick, this affects all of us. The classes meet on Saturday in Pittsburg and one evening a week here at the high school. You're going to have to help with the kids."

"All right. Just tell me what to do and when. We're a team. May I finish my article now?" He picked up the paper and returned to his reading without waiting for her response.

She stared at him so intently she was surprised a hole didn't burn through the newsprint. A team! He said that all the time, but a team would talk about plays, discuss winning strategies. He was leaving everything on her shoulders.

"Just like he always does," she grumbled, carrying her papers through the kitchen and onto the back porch he had renovated into a study for her.

"Did you say something?" he called.

"No, dear, just read your paper."

She sat down at her desk and stared into the backyard. A squirrel ran up the oak tree, chattering all the way. Two crows squawked their reply and then flew to the back fence, their claws catching the top rail.

Their chocolate Lab lay in the doorway of his doghouse, ignoring the animals cluttering up his yard. Nick had brought the pup home last spring. He'd been checking on a project when a client mentioned the litter of pups that had been born that afternoon. He'd told them about the puppies at supper and taken Adam and Reecie over to see them while she did the dishes. She hadn't been surprised to hear that Nick had agreed to buy the puppy. Since their move to Freeston, he'd talked about getting a dog for the kids.

She didn't mind dogs. She just never had been around one. Rental properties weren't keen on pets and by the time her parents purchased a house, she was off to college. Her mother and father had a poodle now, a yappy little thing that piddled every time she saw Reecie and Adam.

The squirrel leaped across the yard onto another tree. Corky lifted his head and gave a halfhearted bark.

Without slowing, the squirrel scampered down the tree and under the fence to the neighbor's yard.

"I hope you do a better job with burglars," she told him through the closed window. His eyes were shut again, his head flopped down on his paws. At his last checkup, the vet said he probably had some more growing to do. At the rate he was eating the dog food she purchased in forty-pound bags, she expected him to grow as big as Clifford, the Big Red Dog in Reecie's favorite books.

She flipped a pencil over and over. She missed teaching. The thrill of watching students finally connect over a skill, their eyes bright with understanding. Teaching third grade had been fun, but her favorite years had been in kindergarten. Nothing had been more exciting than introducing the five- and six-year-olds to stories they hadn't heard before, pushing them to try something new, exploring the world of nature around them.

The day she walked Adam into his kindergarten room, she knew she had to go back. The smell of the chalk, the color of the walls, the alphabet lined up across the wall, all had drawn her in. She loved that world and she wanted to be part of it again.

She volunteered at the school and was an officer on the PTA. She helped organize fund-raisers and was at the school every day of the book fair. Reecie toddled along beside her, flipping through her toddler books, playing with the quiet toys that Caroline packed for her.

She'd kept her column with the *Wheeler Weekly* when they first moved. Every few days, a stack of letters would arrive from Amber. Caroline would sort through them, write her column and mail it to Matt. The finished column didn't always resemble the one she had sent in, but most of the time she had to admit that Matt's editing resulted in a better article.

Matt had been the one to call it quits. The postage for the packets of letters, on top of the payment for her column, had been cost prohibitive for the small weekly. Caroline had suggested that Patty take over her spot and her friend had been pleased at the recommendation. Every time they got together, Patty thanked her again for thinking of her.

She hadn't quit writing. A local writers group met monthly in Pittsburg and she traveled there whenever she could. They gave her suggestions for markets and she had sold a few short educational articles. Patty had been after her to submit her reading program and she had been toying with the idea of finally getting started when she heard about the master's program.

The university program had been created with classroom teachers in mind. Eighteen months of intense courses, with a project due at the end. The students who started the program would move through the courses as a class, forming study groups and working on assignments together.

Adam's fourth-grade teacher had suggested Caroline take the course with her. "I've applied," Sylvia Ralston had said. "Two of the other teachers are also considering the program. We can carpool to classes and you can help us all with our writing assignments."

"Mom, how do you spell 'especially'?"

Caroline turned at the sound of her daughter's voice. Reecie stood in the doorway, her blond hair in two pigtails.

"Come here." Caroline gestured her forward with a wave of her hand.

Reecie skipped over and leaned an elbow on the desk. She plopped down the card she had been working on and pointed to the last word she had written.

"I want to tell Grandma Armstrong that I *especially* like the skirt because it's flippy." Her enunciation told how much she appreciated her gift.

Caroline grinned. Her daughter had inherited her feminine side directly from her grandmother. Flippy skirts had never been part of Caroline's wardrobe. A dress for church now and then, a skirt if necessary for a wedding. Otherwise, give her a pair of slacks and a comfortable blouse and she was ready to go.

She slowly spelled the word, watching Reecie carefully add each letter to the card in her first-grade penmanship. After the letter "a," Reecie ran out of room on the line. She made a hyphen and continued her writing on the next line.

"Miss Sullivan showed us how to do that," she explained without lifting her head from her task. "When a word's too long, you have to make a hyphen."

"I see." Caroline didn't have the heart to explain where the syllable break should occur. Her mother wouldn't mind. She'd tack the card to her refrigerator, where she displayed the work of all her grandkids.

"Like...the..." Reecie murmured, her tongue caught between her teeth as she wrote, "skirt..."

She lifted her head. "How do I spell 'skirt'?"

Caroline pressed a hand to her throat at the expression on her daughter's face. She was Nick's child, no doubt of that. Her hair might be blond, the same shade Caroline's still managed to be through bimonthly visits to the beauty shop, but her eyes were pure Nick. A deep, dark brown, with lashes that were going to be the envy of all her friends when she was older. And the same intense look when they were concentrating.

Caroline bent down and kissed her nose. "Mama!" Reecie ducked away, scrubbing at her nose with her pencil hand. "I'm trying to finish this card. I want to play a *little* bit before bed."

"Okay. Sorry."

Caroline helped her with the rest of the words. Reecie drew a picture of a happy girl with a flippy skirt on the front of the card. "See these lines?" Reecie explained, pointing to the curved lines on either side of the skirt. "That shows it can flip up. We learned that in art."

Caroline made a mental note to call her mother after the card was mailed to explain the lines to her.

Her task completed, Reecie licked the envelope, stuck on the stamp Caroline handed her and wrote her name on the upper left-hand corner. She had already printed "Grandma Armstrong" in large block letters in the middle of the envelope. Caroline trusted the post office would be able to read the much smaller address she squeezed underneath.

Caroline kissed the top of Reecie's head and sent her

off to play for a half hour before bedtime. "Remember to lay your clothes out for tomorrow," she reminded her.

"I know." Reecie's long-suffering reply was to be expected. She never went to bed without agonizing over her outfit for the next day. Often, she laid out two sets of clothes, just in case she woke up in a different mood.

Adam, on the other hand, would forget what he was doing by the time he opened his dresser drawer. He would find a shirt that he liked, put it on the chair where he laid his clothes, and then see a toy or book on top of his desk. If she didn't check with him before bed each night and ask if he had a shirt, pants, socks and underwear, he'd get up in the morning with only half his clothes ready for the day. He'd dig through his dresser for the rest and leave his room looking as if it had been burgled or in a tornado.

Gazing at the piles of paper on the windowsill, the stacks of books on the love seat that was tucked under the window, she had a hard time faulting him for being entranced by a book. The same thing often happened to her.

Reecie liked having books read to her, but her first love was clothes. Caroline still wasn't sure why she had borne a daughter fascinated with fashion. Books, critters, nature, travel. Those were all interests she had hoped to share with her children. Her daughter wasn't completely caught up in the materialistic world, but her fashion sense was already more developed than that of her mom.

The scent of roses wafted into the room and she glanced outside at the last few blooms climbing on their backyard fence. Maybe she wasn't being fair to Nick.

She *had* complained last spring after her experience substituting at the high school.

"But I still love teaching," she said out loud.

She leaned forward, her elbows on the desk and her chin resting on her clasped hands. She would have to explain to Nick again. Just as he loved his job but sometimes griped about the day-to-day grind, the same thing happened with her. Teaching was in her blood. Getting a master's degree would get her back in the classroom faster.

"MOM, I CAN'T FIND MY Cougars shirt for school!"

Adam's frantic voice sounded down the hall. Caroline draped her blouse over her shoulders and stepped into her pumps. "Did you check all of your dresser drawers?"

"I did! Mom, I have to wear it today! We're going to the zoo and they said we have to wear a school-spirit shirt."

Caroline hurried down the hall to his room, her fingers fumbling on the last buttons of her blouse. "Adam, you were supposed to lay your clothes out last night." She couldn't help the frustration in her voice.

Nick was already gone, having left before she was even out of bed. He had to meet with a subcontractor, he told her. They were already behind on their schedule due to rainy weather. They didn't need any more delays.

Adam stood in the middle of his room, tearstains on his cheeks. "I did lay out my clothes, Mom, honest. But I forgot about the field trip."

She had, too. Recently, it seemed that everything was being done on the run, with no time to think about what was coming next.

"Calm down, Adam, we'll find it."

"Mom! We're out of milk!" Reecie's shrill voice traveled up the stairs from the kitchen.

Caroline closed her eyes and quickly counted to ten. "Then have a banana and bagel for breakfast. Or make some toast."

"Mom, I already poured the cereal into my bowl."

This problem she could solve. "Pour it back into the box, Reecie. I'll buy milk on the way home from class tonight and you can have cereal tomorrow."

Silence emanated from downstairs and Caroline breathed a sigh of relief. One almost crisis averted.

Five minutes later, she found one of Adam's school shirts wadded up against the corner of his room, on the far side of his bed. Squelching the desire to remind him where his dirty clothes belonged, she crawled back over his mattress and stood up. She shook out the major wrinkles and handed the shirt to him. "By the time you get off the bus, your wrinkles will either be gone or everyone will look like you."

She leaned down and kissed his forehead. "Have a great time, buddy. Tell the monkeys hi from your dad and me."

Adam lifted his head, his eyes wide and bright as he looked at her. "Can you come with me, Mom? I know Mrs. Ralston wouldn't mind having another mom with us. She likes you a lot. She'd be happy to see you."

A pang clutched her stomach at his eager question. Her son would be the happiest one if she could say yes.

"No, honey, remember? I have to go to Pittsburg

today for my class." Once each semester, they were required to spend a day at the university for a mandatory session. This time, a national speaker had been brought in to discuss learning styles on the same day as the yearly fourth-grade trip to the Topeka Zoo. Sylvia had to go on the field trip with her class. Caroline was bringing back any handouts for her.

His eyelids dropped and he lowered his chin. "Okay. I just thought, maybe…"

"Not this time, squirt." She tipped up his head and looked deep into his eyes. "But I promise, I'll see what I can do with the next trip. I'll check with Mrs. Ralston and find out what's coming up." She kissed the tip of his nose. "Now, grab a jacket and let's get you to school. You don't want to be left behind." The weather was sunny but the past week of October rains had chilled the air.

He scampered down the hall and she followed, wishing she could lose her feeling of guilt as easily.

SHE WAS THE LAST ONE to the parking lot, squealing into an open space and jumping out of the car before the engine completely shut off. "Problems at home again?" The young woman stood next to the school van they were using for their trip.

Caroline hefted her school bag over her shoulder and walked to the van. "Not really," she said with a hearty smile. "Just hard to get all three of us off to school at the same time."

"My mom always had us lay out our clothes and

school supplies the night before," the woman suggested with a somewhat patronizing air. "She was a lawyer and had to be sure not to be late to the office, especially on court days. We always knew how important her job was and made sure not to slow her down."

Well, wasn't this a great way to start her morning? Advice coming from a svelte barely-over-twenty-year-old.

The driver honked his horn and leaned out his window. "Come on. We don't want to be late. Parking's clear across campus from your building."

The speaker was interesting and told stories of actual children to illustrate his points. Caroline found herself comparing her former kindergarten students with the ones he described, noting that some things didn't change. She wrote notes in her tablet, circling several points he made that would relate to Reecie and Adam.

Near the end of his first session, she had a thought for an article. When the other students stood up to leave for the fifteen-minute break, she waved them on, her head bent over her paper. "I need to finish this."

She scribbled and scratched, flipping back to the notes she had written down, drawing stars where she would need more information. If she could get a direct quote from the speaker to beef up the article…

"Working on an assignment, Mrs. Eddington?"

Her head shot up at her professor's voice. "I—no, just, something he said—" She broke off at the humor she saw in Dr. Cole's expression.

"I had an idea for an article I could submit," she

admitted. "Nothing major, just some tips that parents could use."

He sat down in the seat next to her. "What kind of writing do you do?"

"A little of this and that." She snapped her book shut. She had the main points written down and would be able to recreate the thoughts later that night, after the kids were in bed. "And I was taking notes for our class," she added belatedly.

He laughed. "I'm sure you were."

He asked her about the articles she had published and she listed the few bylines she had accumulated over the last three years, warming under his attention. When the other students joined them, she left to find a bathroom and a cold drink before the second session started.

The speaker was already talking when she entered the auditorium. She slipped into the back row and took out her tablet. Just as she wrote her first note, she felt a tap on her shoulder.

"Caroline, you have a phone call," Dr. Cole whispered.

She pressed her hand against her chest and followed him out of the lecture hall. "You can take it in the secretary's office." He pointed to the room several doors down.

She hurried toward the indicated door, her heart pounding. Reecie? Adam? Nick?

"Hello, this is Caroline Eddington."

"Mrs. Eddington, this is the nurse at Reecie's elementary school. She's all right but we needed to contact you. We tried her father first but his secretary said he was out of the office."

"Yes, he had a meeting." He always had meetings. "Reecie's been hurt?" She pressed a hand to her forehead and sank into the chair next to the secretary's desk.

"She fell at recess. Her knees and palms are skinned. I cleaned her up and don't think she needs stitches. We wanted to let you know before she came home with bandages all over her."

"Thank you." She hung up the phone and sat in the chair for a moment, trying to regain her breath.

"Everything okay?"

She glanced at the secretary. "Yeah. My daughter fell at school. Skinned her knees and hands. They couldn't get her dad so they called me."

"It's hard being a working mom," the woman agreed. "But we're teaching our daughters how to be independent."

Caroline nodded and stood. Yes, but was she ready for her six-year-old to be independent?

"THEY GAVE ME A POPSICLE and I missed PE and music," Reecie said at home that night. She sat on a stool at the kitchen counter while Caroline finished putting a salad together.

She knew it was foolish on her part, but she always felt driven to fix a big meal made from scratch whenever she had to be away for the day. The kids didn't care, gobbling down whatever she set in front of them. Sometimes Nick was home with them, but more and more, especially with the number of houses going up around town, he would call and say he'd be late.

"How did you fall?" Caroline added the chopped tomatoes to the bowl.

"It was Bobby Miller's fault!"

Caroline glanced over her shoulder. Reecie's face was scrunched up, her hands on her hips. "Did he knock you down?" If her daughter had encountered a bully, she would take it up with the principal.

"No!" Reecie heaved a big breath. "He wouldn't stop. I kept chasing and chasing and chasing him and he wouldn't stop. I ran right over the gravel and I fell on my knees."

"You were chasing him?"

"Yes." Reecie crossed her arms over her skinny little chest, her bandaged hands hidden against her shirt. "I wanted to kiss him and he wouldn't stop."

Oh, my. Caroline pressed a hand against her mouth to stifle the smile that would only inflame her daughter more. Nick, we are going to have such trouble with this child.

"Honey, you can't make someone kiss you." She carried the salad bowl out of the kitchen and into the dining room, swallowing her smile as she went.

"Why not?" Reecie hopped off the stool and followed her. "You kiss me when I don't want you to."

Caroline centered the bowl on the table. She had set four places. Nick hadn't called yet and she could only hope he would be able to join them for dinner. The kids had been asleep the last three nights by the time he'd come home.

She turned to her daughter. "When?"

"At night. I want to go to sleep and you kiss me anyway."

Caroline tried to think of any time when she had kissed her daughter under duress. "Do you tell me you don't want to be kissed?"

"No, I just—" Reecie heaved another big sigh. "I want you to kiss me. But why doesn't Bobby Miller want me to kiss him?"

Caroline squatted down and hugged her daughter tight. The little body wiggled and squirmed, but Caroline held on for a moment longer before releasing her. "Because he's six. And boys that are six don't like girls that are six to kiss them."

"I'm almost seven."

Oh, honey, you just turned six, Caroline thought. Don't rush to grow up, sweetheart. It's happening fast enough.

"One day you'll understand." She stood up and patted Reecie on the head. "For now, don't do any more kissing at school. Go wash up and call your brother for supper."

"SHE'S KISSING BOYS?" Nick was propped against the headboard, a building magazine in his hands.

Caroline rubbed the rest of her moisturizer into her face and turned off the bathroom light. "No, she wasn't kissing him. That was the problem. She was chasing him so she *could* kiss him."

Nick sighed, the sound similar to Reecie's earlier frustration. "She's only six, Caroline. I do *not* want to deal with boys in elementary school."

Caroline leaned over and kissed his cheek, easing the magazine out of his hand. "You won't. How old were you when you finally let girls catch you and kiss you?"

He wrapped his arms around her, tugging her onto his chest. "I never let a single girl catch me until you came along."

Caroline groaned. "Right."

"Hey, are you calling me a liar?" He slid her along his body until they were eye to eye. "I was never caught before you walked in front of me and tripped me up."

"If I remember right, you tripped me." She nibbled his jaw, moving her lips over his chin and stopping just before his mouth. "You had some pretty good moves when I met you. I'd say you'd done your fair share of kissing."

He pinched her bottom. "Ow!" she said, trying to shift away.

His arms were steel bands holding her in place. The gangly kid she had first fallen for had been replaced by a solid man. He's been working out, she thought. Or hauling equipment at those job sites he visits.

"You want to see moves?" he growled in her ear.

"What do you have?" she dared him.

He flipped her onto her back, his legs straddling her and his hands still holding her arms. Looking into his eyes, seeing his passion for her, she didn't care if he worked out, if he lugged entire buildings from place to place, if he had kissed a dozen girls before she came into his life. She had caught him and she was going to keep him around.

CAROLINE WALKED INTO THE empty house and dropped her keys on the counter before sinking onto the couch. She'd picked up groceries, paid the water and electric bills at their offices so they wouldn't be charged a late fee, and returned movies and books to the library. The groceries were still in the trunk but she needed to sit for just a minute. The spring weather wouldn't hurt the milk and eggs.

Adam was going to be ten years old at the end of the month. The date had hit while she was writing her check at the water department. Double digits. He'd mentioned something about a party at the local arcade the other night and she'd stalled, telling him they'd talk about it with his dad. Her baby was growing up and she couldn't do a thing about it.

Knowing the groceries wouldn't empty themselves, she pushed herself off the cushion and went outside, carting in the three bags she had purchased. She put the bread into the basket on the top of the refrigerator, scooted leftovers out of the way for the milk and eggs, and thought about calling for a pizza. It was crazy to spend money on groceries and then order takeout, but Nick had a dinner meeting and she was too tired to think about cooking.

"ADAM WANTS TO HAVE his birthday party at the arcade this year. I told him I'd talk to you. I can't believe he's turning ten! Before you know it, he's going to be a teenager, Nick!"

She plumped the pillow behind her back and watched Nick moving around the bedroom. He'd come home a few minutes earlier. The kids had been bathed and in bed for hours. She'd spent the quiet time to catch up on her reading assignment for her next class.

"Mmm-hmm." Nick slid his shoes under his side of the bed. "You did get my suit, didn't you? I'm representing the company at the Chamber breakfast tomorrow."

Caroline clapped a hand over her mouth. "Oh, Nick, I'm sorry! It slipped my mind, with everything else."

"That's my only suit."

She hopped out of bed and opened the closet. "What about this?" She held up a charcoal-gray jacket. "With your black pants, you'd look great."

She ran her hand over his back and down his rear end, hugging him close. "Of course, you always look great."

He backed away from her touch. "Caroline, the company's the host for the Chamber breakfast. I can't show up in a mismatched suit."

She bit her lip. He worked for a construction company. He could show up in work boots and a tool belt and look fine. "The dry cleaners opens at six."

"Great. If you're back by six-thirty, that'll give me time to get to the breakfast."

She stared at his back, disappearing into their bathroom. "You want *me* to get your suit in the morning?"

He popped his head around the door, his toothbrush in his hand. "You did forget the dry cleaning."

"And will you help get the kids up while I'm running this errand?" she asked with deceptive calmness.

"They don't get up before six-thirty, do they?" he asked around his toothbrush.

She pressed a hand against her chest. "Nick Eddington," she called, padding across the thick rug they had placed on top of the wooden floor. Nick had spent hours last summer sanding the floor, bringing out the natural beauty of the oak that had been hidden under carpeting when they moved in.

He stuck his head out the door, a towel at his face. "What?" He finished drying his face and hung the towel on the rack by the shower.

She leaned against the wall opposite the bathroom door. Peeling paint hung over the top of the shower. His next project, he had told her. Paint the bathroom. She'd been waiting since Labor Day.

"I'm not picking up your dry cleaning tomorrow morning. I'm working at the book fair tomorrow. I have to get myself ready and the kids."

"And I have to go to the Chamber breakfast."

He turned off the light and walked back into their room. He crawled into his side of the bed and draped the blankets over his chest. "Come on, Caro, it's not that big a deal. If the kids wake up while you're gone, I'll help them get ready."

She shook her head. "Nick, it *is* a big deal. I ran all over town this afternoon taking care of family errands."

"And one of the errands was to pick up the dry cleaning."

She stared at him. He was tucked up in bed, all cozy and comfortable. She fought down the urge to grab her pillow and thwack him on the head.

"Fine." She stomped over to her side of the bed, snapped off her bedside lamp and scooped up her pillow.

"What are you doing?" His voice was muffled by the thick quilt he'd tugged around his ears.

"Sleeping on the couch."

"Caro." He rolled over and reached his hand toward her. "Come on. Get in bed. It's just the one time."

No, it's not, she thought, ignoring his hand and walking out of the room. He said he would help, but he came home late four nights out of five. She picked up the kids, fixed their dinner, helped them with their homework. By the time he did make it home, he was almost too tired to eat and usually fell asleep before she finished closing up the house and crawled into bed.

In the living room, she twisted and turned, trying to get comfortable on the bumpy couch. They needed a new one but were waiting until the kids were older and less apt to jump on every piece of furniture. She reminded them constantly, but Adam and Reecie couldn't seem to slow their bodies when they made it to the couch.

She punched her pillow into a ball and wrapped up in the blanket she'd unearthed in the hall closet. It smelled like dog. She sniffed and groaned. She'd picked the blanket they used to take Corky in the car with them.

She flopped over. Her face pressed against the back of the couch, she closed her eyes and willed herself to sleep.

A hand touched her back. She jumped and flipped over, catching herself before she landed on the floor. A thin strand of streetlight filtered into the room, illuminating Nick's silhouette.

"What are you doing?"

"I can't sleep with you on the couch." He slid his arms under her legs and shoulders and hefted her up.

She grabbed his neck. "Put me down! You can't carry me down the hall." One of her yearly resolutions was to lose the weight she'd gained with the birth of the children, but she hadn't succeeded yet.

"Yes, I can."

"Nick, come on, put me down. I'll come back to bed."

"No, I can do this." His breathing was labored and he was bent at the waist, her body perilously close to the floor.

She wiggled, trying to get her balance. He shifted her weight and she grabbed on to his shoulders. "Hold still," he growled into her ear. "I don't want to drop you."

They were outside the kids' bedrooms. Reecie was a light sleeper. Caroline didn't want to explain why her father was carrying her mother down the hall in the middle of the night. "Nick, put me down," she hissed.

"Nope. Almost there."

He staggered the last few steps across their bedroom and dropped her on the bed. She rolled away just before he landed with a loud groan.

She cuffed him on the shoulder. "You could have broken your back, carrying me like that."

He rubbed his arm. "I thought women liked to be swept off their feet."

Being scooped into his arms had been a little thrilling. But she was no featherweight. "Next time, just ask me to come back to bed."

"Next time?" He raised himself on an elbow.

The room was lit by the night-light she kept on in the bathroom in case she had to get up for one of the children. Shadows deepened the crease in his cheek, the brown of his hair and eyes. A ripple ran down her spine.

She swallowed. "I, um—"

He leaned forward and nipped at the delicate skin under her ear. "Sorry I was so stubborn about the dry cleaning. Guess I'm nervous about speaking in front of everyone tomorrow morning."

Her heart clenched. "Oh, honey, you're a great speaker."

He was nibbling his way under her jaw and over to her other ear. "Um, is the door locked?" she managed to say.

"The kids are asleep." His finger had slid one sleeve of her nightgown off her shoulder and he was pressing warm, moist kisses onto her skin.

"Reecie wakes up in the night." She was finding it difficult to think and if she didn't concentrate, they'd find themselves interrupted.

He gave a heavy breath and crawled over her to the edge of the bed. She scooted up to the pillow, tore her nightgown over her head and slipped under the covers.

"Now, where were we?" His voice was a low growl and the tingle in her spine spread throughout her body.

He stopped at the edge of the bed. "Where did you go?" he asked in his normal voice.

She giggled. "I'm under the covers."

He pounced on the bed, making the headboard bang against the wall. "Shh!" She grabbed the top and held it still. "You're going to wake the kids up."

"Can you put the kids out of your mind for a little while?" He yanked back the covers and slid into his side.

His hand touched her bare thigh. "Hello." He walked his fingers up her leg and into the curve of her waist.

"Nick, about tomorrow..." She licked her lips. His other hand had found its way to her hip.

"Hmm? What about tomorrow?"

"Um," she swallowed. "Your suit at the dry cleaners?"

"You know what? You're right about my jacket and dark pants. They'll be fine." His head was under the covers and she was finding it hard to concentrate or breathe. "And I'll pick up the dry cleaning after work."

"Okay."

Those were the last words either of them spoke that night.

CHAPTER FIVE

His own company
Sixteen years earlier

"NICK! WHAT ARE YOU doing home in the middle of the day?"

Caroline turned away from the kitchen sink, her hands dripping soap on the floor.

"Something came up at work." He advanced into the room, his eyes darting from the dirty dishes stacked up to be rinsed, the prism of light shooting off the glass hummingbird hanging in the middle of the window, her rings resting in the ceramic dish Adam had made her years ago in some art class.

Anywhere but at her face.

He'd expected her to be on campus, teaching one of her classes or available for office hours. She'd given him her schedule, but since he didn't have much cause to be home during the day, he hadn't worried about it, instead tacking the half sheet of paper above his desk in case an emergency came up and he needed to contact her.

Now he wished he'd spared a moment to look at the

sheet. After he'd met with Claude and Joe, the small construction office had been too congested for thinking. He'd driven around town for the last hour, passing their current projects, sizing up possibilities for the future. Without worrying too much about his direction, he'd ended up on his street, cruising past the neighbors before he pulled his truck into the driveway behind Caroline's minivan.

"Are Joe and Claude okay?"

"Yeah, they're fine." His elderly bosses were the reasons he was home.

He paced around the room, running his hand over the granite countertop, past the stainless-steel lip of the sink. He paused next to her and glanced into her eyes.

He'd needed to be home, with her. She always helped him make sense of what was going on in life. "Joe wants to retire. And Claude's wife says that if Joe retires, Claude has to retire, too. She wants to move to Florida, get out of the cold. They're selling the business," he finished.

He hadn't meant to be so blunt. The news they had dumped on him at their weekly morning meeting had come as a shock. They were getting on in years, but no one would know it from their activity. Maybe they didn't do as much physical labor as they had in the past but the two men were prime examples of keeping young through steady employment.

Their banter recently had included more talk about getting away from the daily grind of their job. Sitting around shooting the breeze. Fishing. Learning how to golf. But he hadn't expected them to decide to shut down and move away. They were born to build houses. Claude had the eye for design; Joe the knack for financing.

He liked the old guys and appreciated the training they had given him over the past eight years. The Abbotts had done him a favor, bringing in their nephew and squeezing him out. He hadn't thought so at the time and he'd been worried about what it would do to his marriage. But if it hadn't happened, he would never have met Claude and Joe.

And now they wanted to retire, certain he could make it on his own.

"Joe and Claude are leaving Freeston?" The shock in her voice echoed his own sentiments. "They're part of the town. They can't leave!"

He almost smiled at her vehemence. "They're getting on in years," he said. "They want to enjoy whatever time they have left, visit grandkids, travel. Claude says Verna wants to go on a cruise."

"A cruise? Oh, Nick, can you see Claude in a flowered shirt and Bermuda shorts?"

The image of his slightly overweight, gray-haired boss on the deck of a cruise ship, his girth covered by a flowered shirt and khaki shorts that exposed his bony knees, brought a quirk of a grin.

"I bet we have a postcard sometime next year," he said.

"What does this mean?" Caroline moved a few steps away from him, pausing next to the kitchen table, her hands clutching the back of one of the wooden chairs she had refinished in a soft oak to match the cabinets. "Are we going to have to move again? Nick, we can't. Not now. Adam's in middle school."

She whirled around the room, her hands spread out. "And what about me? Every time I get settled, you want to pack up and move. How many times do I have to reinvent myself?"

He caught her arm as she sailed past. "Caro," he said softly.

She shook his hand off. "No, Nick, I'm not doing this anymore. You can move all you want. Find another great job in another town. Go ahead. But the kids and I are staying here!"

He stared at her. "You wouldn't come with me?"

"No." Her hair danced around her face at her emphatic answer. "Not this time. I know I married you for better or worse, but I can't go this time. I gave up my column but I'm not giving up my job at the community college."

He sank into the chair she'd been holding. She wouldn't move with him? She was willing to split up their family? The last time they'd been separated, it had been just the two of them. That had been hard enough. But to take his kids away from him…

"Caroline, this is ridiculous. I'm not asking you to leave Freeston."

She frowned at him, a crease appearing in the center of her forehead. "Then what? Do you have another job lined up? Did you know this was happening? Why didn't you tell me?"

His head hurt. He lifted a hand to his temple and rubbed at the ache that was growing with each angry phrase. When had they stopped talking to each other and started yelling without listening?

"Caroline, sit down." He raised both hands when she opened her mouth. "Please, just sit down. Let me tell you everything before you get angry with me."

She flopped into a chair opposite him, her elbows on the table and her chin in her hands. Her eyes were still narrowed at him.

"I didn't know anything about their decision." He kept his tone light, his voice low. "They've made joking remarks for as long as I can remember about retiring, getting out of the rat race. I've told you that. Today's comments didn't seem any different."

Her hands had fallen into her lap and her eyes had lost their angry glare. "Honest, Caroline, I didn't have a clue." He ran his hands through his hair. "The news that they were selling came as a complete shock."

She reached her hand across the table and lightly touched the back of his wrist. "I'm sorry I yelled. I just—" She broke off, shaking her head. "Go on."

He hesitated but she didn't finish her thought. "They want me to buy the company."

She stared at him, her eyes reflecting the blue of the sky outside the kitchen window. "They want you to buy the company?"

He nodded. "Yeah. Nobody in their family is interested. Except for Joe's daughter, none of them even live in the state."

She jumped out of her seat and raced around the table. She peppered his face with kisses, her hands clutching his shoulders. "Oh, Nick, this is wonderful! We don't have to move, the kids can graduate from high school here, I can keep my job." Her lips rained kisses over his cheeks, his nose, his lips.

"Hey, stop!" He held her at arm's length. "Does this mean you're okay with me buying the company?"

"Oh, Nick!" Her grin lit up her entire face. "This is the best news you could have given me."

HE SPENT THE REST OF the afternoon in his work shed, measuring and cutting boards for the gazebo he planned to give Caroline as a surprise. They had talked until Caroline looked at the clock. With a cry of dismay, she'd grabbed her briefcase, given him a quick peck on the lips and rushed out the door to make her class. Her excitement had been hard to contain but now he needed time to think about the decision.

The thought of owning his own company had been in the back of his mind for years. But he'd always been an employee, letting someone else carry the risk while he put in his time. He knew he couldn't get ahead as quickly working for someone else—he heard that enough times from his own father.

Now the opportunity had fallen into his lap. The terms of the loan were generous, with Claude and Joe willing to give him three years before he had to borrow from the bank. Their reputation and goodwill would help him get jobs and his own work in the area would stand him in good stead.

Caroline's feelings had been the only unknown in the equation, and her response in the kitchen had made it clear she would support him. He'd been worried, after the way she'd reacted to his other career changes. Staying in Freeston had been her only criterion.

Corky nuzzled his leg, the Lab's wet nose poking under his shorts. "Hey, boy." He rubbed his hand over the dog's head. "Come to keep me company?"

The dog moaned and bounced his head, as if he was answering Nick's question. Nick gave him another pat and picked up a piece of shingle, notching it so it would slide into place with a minimum of effort. His plan was to have all the pieces cut and ready to put together for the next time she went to her parents' house. She didn't come out to the work shed very often and if she did, she'd just see a pile of wood in the corner.

She liked sitting on the back stoop, sipping a cup of tea, watching the seasons change and the animals that visited in spite of Corky's presence. A gazebo would give her a comfortable place to observe and, when he was finished with the electrical, a place she could work on her writing.

He liked working with his hands. He'd enjoyed the challenge of the marketing he'd done with Abbott's and he liked coming up with the bids for the JC Construction Company. Watching a project come together through his own hard labor was his passion. Once the transfer of the company was complete, he'd see about taking on some small renovation jobs that he could do himself.

A bird flew past and Corky ran out the door, barking and jumping at the intruder. "Good for you, old boy." Caroline was sure the dog had latent couch-potato genes. He seemed to spend most of his time lounging in his doghouse. He'd have to tell her that the dog could chase birds.

"SO WHAT'S OUR NEXT STEP?" Caroline was sorting through the mail that he had just brought in.

"I have to check on the licenses I need." A few he already had. Joe and Claude had warned him that he might need a few others, since they'd been around long enough to be grandfathered in on some of the city council's more recent decisions.

She tossed an envelope into the fireplace without opening it. "How many credit-card companies are there in this world? And do they all have our address?"

She handed him a magazine intended for home builders and leaned down to kiss his cheek. "I'm so excited. Are you going to keep the name or change it to something else?"

He hadn't considered a name change. "People know JC Construction," he said. "They have an excellent reputation around here."

"But it doesn't represent you." She tossed in the empty envelopes and knelt in front of Nick, her elbows on his knees. "When are we going to tell the kids? And I want to call Mom and Dad, let my brothers know."

He looped his fingers around her wrists. "Caro, you realize this is going to be a lot of hard work? Long hours, even more late nights than now."

"I know." She raised up and pressed her lips to his.

"But we don't have to move. I can live with anything if we don't have to move."

He thought of those words several times a day over the next six months. Joe and Claude walked him through the paperwork needed to transfer title to his name. They helped him set up his own business account at the bank and introduced him to the leaders in the community that he didn't already know. They did everything they could to make the transition smooth and then they packed their bags and moved out of Freeston.

The company had won several bids before the two left and Nick spent his time making sure the jobs were being completed up to the standards that had been established by Joe and Claude. He had to let a plumber go when he found him using inferior materials on a new house and two electricians walked away when he wouldn't give them the raise they demanded for staying with him.

Caroline didn't complain about his late nights. Often he came home to a quiet house, the light over the sink on for him. His dinner would be in the refrigerator, ready to be warmed up. If he was hungry, he'd eat the meal. Other nights, he sat on the stoop and fed portions of it to Corky so she wouldn't know her work had been done in vain.

His first project earned solely on his own was a complete remodel of a two-bedroom bungalow on the edge of downtown. Mrs. Renfro, the head librarian at the public library, had inherited the small house from an elderly cousin.

"Can you make it habitable?" she asked Nick as they walked through the rooms.

The place had been neglected for years. He jotted down measurements and made a list of supplies that would be needed in each room. He had listed an ad in area papers for someone to help with bids. Until he found a suitable candidate, he was responsible, in addition to his other tasks.

Mrs. Renfro accepted his bid and he went to work. Adam and Reecie helped him strip wallpaper after school. Adam liked ripping the huge chunks off the wall, jumping up and grabbing a loose piece of the flocked paper, riding it down to the floor. Reecie picked at the tiny pieces stuck to the wall, scraping them off with the wedge Nick gave her. She had the patience to not gouge the wall.

Caroline came by in the evening and brought them supper. They'd take a break and sit on the front stoop, watching the neighbors walk by with their dogs. A fire truck drove by one night, the firefighters driving around town to check on addresses in case they were ever called in an emergency. The driver honked at Reecie and Adam and sounded his siren in a short burst.

"We should live down here," Adam said one evening as they were cleaning up their mess for the night.

"I thought you liked our house." Nick swept the pile of debris into the bag Reecie was holding.

"I do. But it's pretty quiet around our place." Adam did an over-the-shoulder toss of a wad of wallpaper. The ball landed next to the trash bag.

He grabbed it off the ground and slam-dunked it into

the bag. Reecie staggered and let go of the bag, dislodging all of the litter she had just collected onto the floor.

"Adam!" Nick sighed in frustration.

"Sorry, Dad, sorry." Adam scrambled over and started to scoop the trash into it with his hands.

Nick took the bag away from him. "Stop. You're going to get a nail in your hand. Or a splinter."

Adam's shoulders drooped and he went outside. Nick finished gathering up the trash and followed, locking the door behind him.

Adam stood in the middle of the sidewalk, scuffing his shoe along the center crack of the concrete. Nick grabbed him around the neck, tugging him close. "Hey, bud, it's okay. It was an accident. You just need to slow down and pay attention if you're going to work with me. I don't want you hurt on a job site."

Mrs. Renfro came by the next day. She cautiously stepped over the tarps Nick had placed on the floor. "How much longer until I can move in?"

Nick looked around the room, at the wallpaper still clinging to the walls, the floor that needed to be ripped up and replaced. The plumbing fixtures were old and corroded. He had hired a plumbing contractor to come in and replace them.

"Another month, Mrs. Renfro." If all went well. The plumber was supposed to be available in a week, when he finished one of their other jobs.

She placed her fists on her hips. "A month! You've already had a month."

"The place was in bad condition," he explained carefully. The customer was always right, Joe had said. Even when they were completely wrong.

"I talked to a fellow over in Pittsburg who said he'd have me living in this place already. And for a fraction of your cost."

"You don't say?" He'd already discovered that his bid was too low and he was going to lose money on the project. He had a feeling the quality of the work she would get from this "fellow" wouldn't be up to the standards that Joe and Claude had instilled in him.

Caroline was still up when he walked into the house, grading papers on the living room couch. "Hi. The kids said Mrs. Renfro was coming over tonight."

"Yeah, I didn't want her to know they were helping me." He sank into the wingback chair and rubbed his shoulders. "She wants to know why I'm not done yet. Says there's a fellow in Pittsburg who claims he'd be finished by now and for less money."

Caroline put her papers on the couch and came over to him. She replaced his hands with her own, kneading the knot at the base of his neck. "Relax," she ordered, pushing at the pain with the heel of her hand.

"I can't. The project's going over budget, we may not be finished even in another month, I have two bids to finish this week—"

She leaned down and worked at the tension in his shoulders with her arm and elbow. "Who's in charge of this project?"

"What?" Her ministrations were lulling him into a doze.

He blinked and started to rise, but she held him down, her fingers working magic on his stiff muscles. "Who's in charge?"

"I am." She knew that.

"Then don't let the Mrs. Renfros of the world run over you." She leaned down and kissed him on the forehead. "Your bid's realistic, right?"

"Too low. I didn't realize how much floor damage there was."

She shrugged. "You live and learn. Come on, Nick, you did know that having your own business was going to come with some headaches and back pains."

He snagged her around the waist and pulled her onto his lap. "When did you get so smart?"

She stretched and curled her arms around his neck. "I've always been smart. You've just been too busy to listen to me."

A big yawn escaped him. She climbed to her feet and pulled him out of the chair. "Come on. You need to sleep. You'll feel better in the morning and able to handle Mrs. Renfro."

"No, I won't. She's a tough old bird. You ever know anybody to get out of a library fine? She's not going to leave me alone until she's in her new place."

Even then, she didn't leave him alone. He finished her house a day after the initial completion date he'd given her. He had walked her through the completed rooms and waited for some comment expressing her appreciation at the work that had been done. The place had been transformed and he would have been happy to move into it himself.

She said nothing during the tour. Three days later, she called. The toilet wouldn't stop running at night.

He jiggled the handle and settled the ball into place.

A few nights later, his phone rang again. The new door he'd hung on her bedroom scraped against the floor.

He sanded the bottom until he could see light under it when he was in the hallway.

Saturday morning, he was playing catch with Adam in the backyard when Caroline called him to the phone. The backdoor screeched when Mrs. Renfro opened it to let her cat out.

He squirted it with a can of WD-40.

"She's making me crazy," he said after he returned from oiling her door.

"She's lonely. I'm going to invite her to dinner."

Nick turned appalled eyes on his wife. "No! I can't have that woman in my house. I spend too much time with her as it is."

Caroline patted his hand. "Trust me."

He had a week's reprieve. On the weekend, Caroline took the kids to Mustang to visit her parents. Nick begged off, saying that he could use the time to catch up on some paperwork. She had kissed him goodbye, told him not to work too hard and driven off. He had spent the weekend working in his shed and the backyard.

Monday night, he drove over to Mrs. Renfro's house. He didn't understand why he had to pick the woman up. She had a perfectly good car in the garage he had repaired. Caroline had just patted his hand and sent him on his way.

In addition to Mrs. Renfro, she had invited the librarian from the Freeston Community College. "He's been widowed for five years," she had told Nick as she tucked her hair into a neat bun at the nape of her neck. "She's been alone for ten years."

"This is going to backfire," Nick cautioned. "You can't set people up."

Caroline had just given him an enigmatic smile.

By the time she served apple crisp for dessert, he had to admit that she was right. The two older people enjoyed the same books, had visited several of the same countries during their summer vacations and agreed completely that computers had no place in a library.

"Next thing you know, people will expect to read books off a computer," Marguerite Renfro said. Nick had seen her full name on the contract but never considered using anything but her title during their dealings. When she arrived, Caroline had paused in her introductions until Mrs. Renfro had given permission to call her by her first name.

"And how do you curl up with a computer in front of a fireplace?" Roger Petry had asked.

When Roger heard that Nick had picked her up, he graciously offered to drive her home. "That's why you had me pick her up," Nick said, locking the door after they'd left. "You're a genius."

"I keep telling you that." She wagged her finger at him. "She's lonely, Nick. That's why she keeps calling you. I wonder, though, if Joe or Claude would have gone to her house to fix a running toilet."

He looped his arm through hers and headed her toward the backdoor. "Joe, maybe. Claude. No. His wife wouldn't let him."

She stopped at the edge of the kitchen. "What are you doing? I have class at eight in the morning."

"You can take a moment to walk with me." He unlatched the door and held her arm as they walked down the steps to the yard.

Corky ambled across the grass and met them, his head butting against Caroline's knees. "Hey, you, careful. You're going to knock me over." She scratched his head. "Are we visiting Corky?"

"No." Nick paused to get his bearings in the dark. The neighbor's tree hid the streetlight from their backyard, creating a shadowed landscape that was completely different from the daytime one.

"Do you want me to look at the stars?" She tipped her head back. "It's too dark. There's not even a moon."

He didn't answer, just propelled her across the yard. Corky snuffled along beside them, his head bumping their legs every now and then. She took several steps beside him before she stopped, bending down to touch the flagstones he had spaced two feet apart. "Wait a minute. What is this?"

"A path."

"You put a path in the middle of the yard? Won't that make it hard to mow?"

"No, they're low enough the mower will go over them." He linked their fingers together. "Come on. You're almost there."

The clouds blew away from the moon as they reached the steps to the gazebo. The shimmery light sparkled on the shingles and lit up the inside of the octagonal room.

Caroline stared at the structure in front of her and then at Nick, twisting her head back and forth. "What is this?"

"A gazebo."

"I know that. But where did it come from?"

He shrugged. "Elves. Or fairies. I'm not sure. It just cropped up while you were at your folks' house."

She swayed toward him, her hand on the railing. "You built this for me?"

"Yeah. You like to sit outside on the stoop and watch the leaves change. I thought this would be more comfortable."

"Nick, you are the most incredible man."

Their lips fused together. An owl hooted behind them. Clouds drifted back over the moon, obscuring the light and sending the yard into darkness. A breeze tossed her hair over his hand where it rested on her neck.

She lifted her head and gave a satisfied sigh. "This is the nicest present anyone's ever given me."

"Better than the kids?"

"They're not presents, they're treasures." She trailed her fingers over his lips. "And you're the best treasure of all."

"Hmm. What do you say we christen your gazebo?"

"What?"

"I put some cushions on the floor. I deserve something after putting up with Mrs. Renfro all evening, don't you think?"

"She said you could call her Marguerite."

"I think I'll stick with Mrs. Renfro." She reminded him of a former elementary teacher.

Caroline ascended the three steps. He felt, rather than saw, her twirl around.

"Ouch!"

He hurdled the steps, hesitating inside the door. "What happened?"

She chuckled from somewhere near his shoes. "I tripped on your cushions." A loud thumping sound alerted him to her location. "Join me down here."

He lowered himself to the floor. Outside, he could hear Corky sniffing around the base of the building before he turned back to his doghouse. "I ran electrical under the flagstones," he said, his hands searching in the dark for the cushions he'd layered on the floor. "You can work out here in the evenings."

His hand touched a soft cushion, but it wasn't one that he'd brought out earlier. "Are you in a hurry?" she asked, laughter lacing her voice.

He slid his hand from her breast to her hip. "Not at all. Your class is at eight tomorrow morning, right?"

"I can't stay out here until—"

He silenced the rest of her words with his kiss.

"I can stay a little longer," she murmured against his lips when he raised his head.

"I thought you'd reconsider." He settled more comfortably on the cushions, keeping her close. The night was made for loving and he was more than willing to oblige.

CHAPTER SIX

The supper club
Fourteen years earlier

THE HOST OF THE EARLY-morning TV show invited listeners to the upcoming Maple Leaf Parade. "Are you marching in that?" Caroline asked Adam. He and Reecie were eating breakfast before school.

"Yep." He poured milk into his glass and splashed a dollop on the table.

She sighed and handed him a sponge. "I stayed up late last night cleaning for the supper club. I don't have time to straighten again before they show up tonight."

He lifted his hands shoulder high. "Hey, why are you warning me? Reecie will be home before I am."

She glanced at her daughter, calmly finishing her breakfast, the area around her bowl neat and clean.

"Not a speck of clutter," she added. "No book bags in the living room, no shoes in the middle of the floor."

"Fine, treat me like I'm a class-A slob." He clumped across the kitchen and dumped his bowl in the sink.

She grabbed his shoulder before he could exit the

room. "That is what I'm talking about," she said, pointing to the bowl in the sink. "Do we have kitchen elves who come in and wipe up the table or rinse your bowl? Put your dishes in the dishwasher, please."

His sigh echoed around the room. Caroline caught Reecie's smirk out of the corner of her eye and swung around so her son didn't see her own smile. He was so predictable sometimes.

SHE WAS LATE LEAVING the campus. Two students wanted help with their writing projects. She was tempted to remind them their projects weren't due for three more weeks, but they were so enthusiastic, she didn't have the heart to cut them off. She finally managed a goodbye when one of the girls took a breath, and hurried out of the building before they could say any more.

The lights were off in the living room and kitchen, a good sign that the kids had stayed away from the two areas. She breathed a sigh of relief and raced into her bedroom, tossing her briefcase on the bed and throwing her jacket on top. Hopping on one foot, then the other, she kicked off her pumps and slid out of her slacks, leaving them on the floor where they fell.

"Isn't *this* a nice sight?" Nick's arms wrapped around her waist, his fingers toying with the lace at the top of her panties.

"We don't have time." She batted at his hands, only succeeding in having him catch her fingers with his own.

"Nick, we have company coming in—" she leaned around him to peer at the clock "—less than thirty minutes. I have to set the table, make the tea..."

"Relax." He swept her hair off her neck and nuzzled the tender skin below her earlobe. "I set the table at lunchtime, the iced tea is already in the refrigerator, and the coffee will be ready in the next fifteen minutes."

She slewed around in his arms, her eyes wide. "You set the table?"

"Mmm-hmm." He leaned in and nibbled at her earlobe. "Don't you think I deserve some sort of reward?"

She was finding it hard to breathe, let alone think. A worry niggled at her brain. "The door's open, Nick. One of the kids is going to come in."

"Nope." He was working his way down her shoulder, loosening the sleeve of her blouse with his teeth. "They're downtown having pizza," he murmured, his breath heating her skin. "They have enough money to go to a movie afterward."

He lifted his head and gave her a wolfish grin, waggling his eyebrows. "I'm a needy man, Caro. I figured nothing would get you in the mood faster than a table that was set and no kids."

She laughed and hugged him around the neck. He tugged at her thighs and pulled her legs around his waist. The motion toppled them both onto the bed, Caroline poised above his hips.

"Now, *this* is interesting." His hands slid from her waist and under her top, slowly caressing the bare skin up to her bra.

She swallowed. "Nick, we still have company coming over. I need to change clothes—" She swallowed again. His finger was lazily circling a nipple. "Um," she tried again. "And you know the Rutledges are always early."

"They aren't coming tonight." Another finger joined the first and he adroitly shifted the bra so her breast was bare under the blouse.

She jerked away from him, his hand catching under the cotton of her blouse. "Art and Stella aren't coming over?"

"Nope." He reached for her, but she rolled away, jumping to her feet and out of his reach.

"What happened?"

He shrugged and crooked a finger toward her. "Come back here. We can take care of this in five minutes, get you into the kitchen in plenty of time to finish whatever you need to do."

"Five minutes. Aren't *you* a smooth-talking man."

His hand snagged the edge of her shirt and toppled her onto the bed before she realized what he was about. "Nick!"

"Five minutes used to be all I needed with you, woman," he growled in her ear, his hand smoothing up her bare leg. "Against a wall, on the couch, on the dining-room table."

His breath whispered across her skin. "I'm older now," she managed to say. His words had conjured up those early years, when they had been ready for each other every minute of the day. "More mature."

"And why does that matter in the bedroom?"

He had succeeded in sliding her panties to her knees. She scooped them off with one foot, flicking them across the room with another long sigh.

"You're going to have to answer the door," she muttered, rolling over and undoing his pants. "Give me time to get myself back together."

He grinned from his new position above her, his hands cupping her face. "Whatever you say, darling. Now stop fussing and kiss me. I'm on a deadline here!"

"WHAT DO YOU SAY WE LET the womenfolk take care of the dishes while we check out the ball scores?"

Caroline tilted her head toward the man sitting beside Nick. "I take it that's some sort of lame joke, Pete?"

The balding man grinned. "Now, honey, I know you'd much prefer to gossip with the wimmen in the kitchen than bother your little head with numbers of players."

His wife stood up and stacked several plates in her arms. "Do not even answer him, Caroline. He's been in this strange mood for the last week, ever since he read some kid's class assignment. The thing was full of clichés, bad grammar and extremely sexist ideas."

"They were not sexist, Ellen." Pete added his plate to her stack. "They made good sense."

"If these weren't Caroline's best dishes, I'd use one to whack some sense into you. Right over your head."

The other couples chuckled. "We'll take care of the dishes tonight," Caroline informed him. She wanted to find out more about Art and Stella and she was certain one of the women in their group would know what was going on. "Next time, you guys clear."

"And after the kitchen is cleaned up, we're coming

out to watch the ball scores with you." Ellen gave her husband a sweet smile. "I may not care about the numbers of their jerseys but oh! the way those fellows fill out a pair of pants."

Caroline was still chuckling when she opened the dishwasher. Her interlude with Nick before the company arrived meant she hadn't had time to put the clean dishes away. She opened the cupboard above the counter and popped the glasses on the shelf.

"That bread pudding was delicious!" Wanda stacked plates on the table, staying out of Caroline's way. "And the lemon sauce was perfect on it."

"Don't look at the ingredients." Marie took the clean plates from Caroline's hands and stashed them in the cupboard. "You'll kick yourself for having another piece." Since she had eaten at least three helpings, no one said anything.

Caroline unhooked the silverware rack and carried it to the drawer at the right of the sink.

"I'd be careful about nagging Pete," Wanda said.

Caroline glanced over her shoulder at the women working behind her. "The old coot knows what I think when he gets all macho on me," Ellen said. "I wasn't nagging him."

"That's probably what Stella thought, too."

Caroline froze, a dirty glass in her hand.

"Stella and Art didn't split up because she nagged at him," Ellen scoffed. "Art traded her in for a coed. He moved in with her last week."

The glass Caroline was holding slipped out of her

fingers. It bounced on the small rug she kept under the sink and rolled to a stop at Wanda's feet.

Wanda bent down and picked up the glass, handing it back to Caroline. "You didn't know?"

Caroline shook her head. "I had no idea. Nick said they weren't coming tonight, but..." She gave her head another toss. "Art and Stella."

Art and Stella had been married longer than any of the other couples. Their two sons were grown and married, living at opposite ends of the state. Years earlier, Stella had organized the supper club. Each month they experienced cuisine from other cultures and met together to visit. Caroline had received an invitation as soon as she began teaching at the community college. She had convinced Nick that it would be a good way for her to meet other faculty and he had reluctantly agreed to attend the first dinner.

The only ones left from the original group were Art and Stella and Pete and Ellen. Caroline looked forward to the monthly gathering. Nick might grumble, but he never scheduled anything on the supper club night. The couples were their friends, people they didn't see often, but people they counted on for a good time and a pleasant meal together.

"ART RAN OFF WITH A student," Caroline told Nick in their bedroom later that night. The kids had been tucked in, their prayers said. Reecie had wanted to talk about the movie, but her eyes had drifted shut right after Caroline's kiss good-night.

"Anything you need to tell me?"

She punched him on the arm. "Nick! This isn't a joke! Art and Stella have been married for years!"

"Caro, I don't have time to look at another woman…even if I wanted to. Which I don't," he added quickly. He massaged his arm. "You'd probably kill me if I did."

"For starters."

He chuckled and tugged her close, his arms tight around her waist.

Caroline tipped her head against his shoulder, savoring the warmth of his skin, the comforting scent of his cologne. Her hand crept up his chest and she caressed the firm line of his jaw. "You aren't tempted by any of the women at those houses you're building?"

The deep rumble of his laughter warmed her further. "Honey, once someone's nagged you a dozen times about a light fixture that isn't exactly right, you have no desire to get any closer."

There was that nasty word, *nagging,* again. Why was it a woman was nagging if she asked a man to do something, and a man was just making a request? The double standard irked her.

She raised herself until she could see the deep brown of his eyes. A few flecks of gray peppered his hair. He was the same handsome man who'd caught her attention all those years ago. He ran at least twice a week and had only gained a couple pounds since their marriage. She didn't want to consider how much she'd added to her wedding weight.

She nipped at his mouth, catching his lower lip between her teeth. His eyes widened and then narrowed. "Hmm," he murmured against her teeth.

"The kids are asleep and it's too late for anyone to call." She slid her other hand up his chest, caressing him slowly. "Deadlines are good some of the time. Right now, I'd like to work on quality."

In one quick motion, he flipped her onto her back. His arms pinned her to the bed. "If you're trying to make me forget other women and promise to stay with you," he whispered into her ear, "it's working. Of course, I might need to be reminded every night."

She laughed and locked her arms around his neck, her legs encircling his strong waist. "That could be arranged. Now suppose you show me why I don't need to be checking out any of those college guys?"

Their lovemaking before the supper club had been fast and frantic, a race against the clock. Now he used his hands and his lips to explore her slowly. By the time he maneuvered himself on top of her, she was writhing with need.

"Too slow?" he murmured.

"No." His hand lazily caressed her thigh, coming closer and closer to her center and then pulling away again. "Okay, yes, too slow," she panted. "I need you now."

"I thought you'd never ask."

Conversation ceased in the room. She arched her back, taking him inside, helping him find the rhythm that was theirs alone.

"I'M GOING SIMPLE THIS month," Ellen said over the phone. "With Stella out of the picture, I had to go back to some of our older recipes. The southwestern menu looked good and it shouldn't be too hard for anyone."

Caroline agreed to make the mini tacos. "Any news about Stella?"

The student wasn't in any of Art's music-appreciation classes, so he had only received a verbal reprimand from the administration. Caroline had been surprised the student's parents hadn't descended on the college. She could imagine Nick's response if he ever found out a married college teacher was living with their daughter.

"She left town," Ellen said. "Her mother lives in Oregon and Stella's packed up and moved there. The house is on the market."

Caroline had driven by their house, Stella's pride and joy, while taking Reecie to a friend's house. The air of abandonment saddened her.

She hung up and finished fixing the macaroni and cheese she was making for the kids' supper. Nick was attending the city council meeting. She planned to have a quiet, romantic dinner for just the two of them when he came home.

"I do not! Stop it!" Reecie ran into the kitchen, her hands over her ears. "Make him stop!" she shouted at the top of her lungs.

"Reecie and Bobby sitting in a tree. K-I-S-S-I-N-G!" Adam sang.

"That's enough." Caroline reached out her arms, holding the two of them at arm's length. "Adam, stop teasing your sister."

"I'm not teasing. It's true."

"It is not!" Tears filled Reecie's eyes.

"Adam, stop. No more," she said when he opened his mouth. "You're being a bully."

He turned around and stomped out of the room. "It's not being a bully when you're telling the truth," he muttered.

"Come here." Caroline hugged Reecie, feeling the tears soaking the front of her shirt. "What was that all about?"

Reecie sniffed and rubbed her nose against Caroline's blouse. I'll need to change this before Nick comes home, she thought.

"Bobby Miller said he likes me. But I don't like him!"

"Hmm." Caroline stroked a hand over her daughter's soft curls. "Not at all?"

"Uh-uh." Reecie shook her head back and forth. "We had to pick partners for our reading circle and he picked me! I asked Mrs. Ralston if I could change, but she said he got to choose."

She lifted her tear-stained face, her bottom lip pushed out in a big pout. "If I have to work with him, Mama, everyone will think he's my boyfriend! And I don't want a boyfriend!"

Caroline reached around and tugged a paper towel from the rack, wetting half of it under the faucet. She mopped at her daughter's red cheeks and held the other half up while Reecie blew her nose.

"Go get your brother and let's eat supper. I won't let him tease you," she said, stopping her complaint before it was voiced.

She watched her daughter walk out the door, shaking her head at the changes a few years could bring. Reecie had a scar on her palm from the scrapes she'd received falling after chasing Bobby Miller for a kiss in first grade. Three years later, she didn't want to be in his group.

"She was very upset," she told Nick that night, ladling soup into his bowl. By the time she settled both of the children, her romantic evening had turned into soup and sandwiches with candlelight.

"Over the same boy?"

Caroline nodded. "Yeah. One minute, she's chasing him around the playground. The next, she's crying about him picking her for a reading-group partner."

"How did Adam find out?"

She handed him the platter of chicken-salad sandwiches.

"Somebody's brother rides the bus with Adam. I told him he should be protecting his sister from gossip like this, not spreading it. He said he only teased her when they were alone together."

"I'll talk to him tomorrow. He doesn't need to be spreading gossip about anybody anywhere." He scooped up the last of his soup and gestured toward the candles with his spoon. "What's the occasion? I didn't miss an anniversary, did I?"

"No." She felt foolish stating her reason out loud. "I just wanted to have a date with you. Since you're working so much in the evenings, I figured this would be the easiest way."

"Work's going to slow down one of these days, Caro. I've hired a guy to help with the bids."

She'd heard that before, but she wasn't going to complain. As long as he was spending his time with nails and two-by-fours, she didn't have to worry about him checking out other women.

"WE'RE MEETING AT OUR HOUSE," Ellen said over the phone two nights before the supper club was scheduled to get together.

"Okay." Caroline nudged the tomatoes she had diced off the cutting board and into a bowl. "Why?"

"Wanda and Chuck have separated."

The knife clattered to the floor. "Wanda and Chuck?"

Chuck was a favorite in the math department. The students found his lectures easy to follow and lined up to get into his classes. Wanda had been the children's librarian at the Freeston Public Library for the past eight years.

"Yeah. He moved into the same apartment complex as Art. No roommate yet, but there was a coed involved. This is getting to be an epidemic."

Caroline didn't find her friend's comment funny. "Ellen, this isn't good."

"I know. I'm not laughing. Who's going to be next?"

SUE MOVED OUT OF THEIR house, taking their three children back to her hometown in Illinois. Carl stayed in Freeston, splitting his time between his science courses at the community college and helping to rally support for the conversion of unused railway tracks into bicycle and hiking trails.

"No hint of another woman or another man," Ellen said when she met Caroline for coffee at the student center. They had canceled that month's supper club with the news of another split.

Caroline sipped her coffee and stared at the students and faculty scattered around the room. "Is there something in the water?"

She didn't mean to be flip, but the sudden rash of separations was uncanny. Out of six couples, three were now separated. They were living the national average for divorces.

"You and Pete are doing okay, aren't you?" she asked.

Ellen nodded. "He knows that if he even thinks of leaving me before he's in a casket, I'll put him in one myself."

Caroline choked on her sip of coffee. She patted her lips and grinned at her friend. "I said something similar to Nick."

"There you have it. The secret to a long and happy married life. Communication. They know exactly where they stand. We didn't marry stupid men."

Caroline relayed Ellen's comments to Nick later that week. They were sitting in the gazebo, a pitcher of iced tea on the low table he had built into the wall. A single bug light illuminated the space. Adam and Reecie were working on homework in the house.

"You're saying Pete and I are staying with you two because we're afraid of you," he said.

"Funny." She sipped her tea. The bitter cold slid down her throat. "Why are we together, Nick? I mean, how do we know something isn't going to creep up and tear us apart?"

He shrugged. "Caro, sometimes you have to take things on faith."

His answer wasn't good enough. She wanted assurances of his love, his need for her. Sometimes she watched him sleeping and wondered what had possessed her to marry him. They'd been so young and she'd known so little of him. She'd packed up her belongings and let him drag her from town to town before they'd settled. Even now, she found it hard to understand how she could live with a man who was a stranger to her in so many ways.

He stood up and stretched, his fingers touching the ceiling beams. "Ready to go in?"

She folded her arms under her breasts and settled back in her chair. "You go on. I want to sit out here a little longer."

He bent down and pressed his mouth against hers, the kiss soft and tender. His hands held on to the arms of her chair, trapping her within. The scent of his cologne mingled with the scent of the lilacs blooming alongside the back fence.

"I love you." He rubbed his lips over hers, as if he was branding the words into her mouth. "Remember that."

"I know."

He stood up. "I'll get the kids to bed. You come in when you're ready."

Through the windows, she could see him enter the

house and move into the living room. Adam passed by the kitchen window, heading down the hall. Reecie walked by with her father, her face and hands animated as she talked. Lights winked on in their bedrooms and then disappeared as they shut their drapes.

She didn't know how long she sat there, staring into the shadows of the yard, watching Corky patrol his territory. The owl that lived in one of their trees sailed by, searching for his evening meal. Stars twinkled above her.

"Caro?" Nick called from the backdoor. "Phone call."

She uncurled her legs and walked the short distance. "Who is it?

"Marie."

Marie? Why would she be calling so late?

"Hi, Marie." From behind her, she could hear Nick putting their glasses into the dishwasher.

"Sorry to call so late, Caroline. I thought you should hear the news before you went into school tomorrow."

She gripped the receiver. "What?"

"Ellen left Pete."

Caroline slid down the wall and landed on her bottom. "Ellen?"

"Yeah. I just heard and wanted to let you know. Pete's beside himself."

Her tongue felt thick. "I— Thanks, Marie."

"Caroline, there's more."

More? What could be more? All the time that she had been spillng her guts to Ellen, worrying about their friends breaking up, Ellen had been planning to leave her husband. She had said that he could only get away from her if he was in a casket.

Of course, Ellen had never said anything about her leaving.

"She moved in with Carl."

Caroline didn't remember what else was said. Nick pried the phone from her fingers and spoke into it before hanging up. He reached down and caught her under the elbow, raising her to her feet. "Caroline."

She lifted tear-stained cheeks. "Ellen lied to me, Nick. All those days we visited, sat together and talked about our husbands, she was fooling around with Carl! We had them both in our house and they were cheating with each other!"

He led her down the hallway, his touch gentle. "We didn't know."

She stopped inside their door, staring at the bed where they made love. Nick's wallet and keys were tossed on top of his dresser. A book she'd been reading lay on the nightstand.

Ordinary signs of an ordinary life.

She whirled around, almost clipping Nick in the stomach with her elbow. "How can you believe anyone, trust anyone? I thought she was my friend."

"Honey, Ellen walked away from Pete, not you."

Caroline shook her head. Ellen had also walked away from her friends. They had to choose sides and she couldn't choose Ellen.

The next day, she left campus as soon as her classes were over and drove the three hours back to Wheeler.

On the way, she stopped at a pay phone and called Patty's school, leaving a message for her friend to meet her at a local coffeehouse, if she was available, when she finished for the day.

"THIS IS A PLEASANT SURPRISE." Patty slid into the booth across from her and shrugged out of her jacket. "What's going on?"

Caroline leaned her elbows on the table and fixed Patty with a long look. Patty met her stare for stare. Satisfied, Caroline leaned back in her seat and rested an arm along the top of the booth.

"You and Richard doing okay?" Patty had married a high-school science teacher two years after their move. Caroline had come back to be a bridesmaid and Adam had been the ring bearer. No children yet, but Patty hadn't ruled out the possibility completely.

"Yes." Patty picked up a menu and scanned the list of coffee drinks available. "You and Nick?"

"I think so." He was in the middle of his busy season so they didn't see each other much. But he did slide into bed with her and several times a week they connected under the sheets.

"Everything good at work?"

"Yes and no." Caroline waited while the waitress took their orders, coming back a few minutes later with their drinks. "Lot of divorces going on." She spilled the details of their supper club, relaxing somewhat at each of Patty's astonished oh no!

"When I heard about Ellen and Pete, I lost it,"

Caroline admitted. Her mango smoothie sat in front of her, untouched. "I sat down on the floor and cried and cried. Nick had to practically carry me to the bedroom."

They sipped their drinks in silence. "I'm not going away," Patty said quietly, smiling at Caroline over her cup of mocha latte. "You can't get rid of me that easily."

Caroline glanced up, licking whipped cream from her lips. "I'm not going to disappear from your life," Patty added. "I'm dancing at the kids' weddings, remember?"

"I—" A lump formed in Caroline's throat.

"I know." Patty reached over and rubbed the back of Caroline's hand where it rested on the table. "You have to stop worrying that someone's going to leave you. It happens in life. You're strong enough to deal with it, Caroline."

"I had no idea."

That was what rankled the most. She had met with Ellen or talked to her on the phone at least once a week since the divorces started. Ellen had seemed as flabbergasted as anyone else when she reported the news. She had even stated that there was no hint of another woman involved in Sue's reason for leaving Carl.

And all the while, Ellen had been the other woman.

"Would you have dumped her first if you'd known?" Patty asked.

Caroline stilled and her gaze darted to her friend's face. Patty was watching her with a clear-eyed look. "Maybe," she said slowly.

Patty finished her drink and put the cup on the table. "Here's some free advice. People are going to leave you. Their lives are going to intersect with yours for a while and then go a different direction. It doesn't mean anything's wrong with you."

She glanced at her watch. "Do you have to be somewhere?" Caroline asked. She knew she'd been taking a chance coming this far on such short notice.

"No, but you do." Patty threw down tip money and slid out of the booth. She bent down and kissed the top of Caroline's head. "Go home. Your best friend is waiting for you."

Caroline sat in the booth after the door closed behind Patty. When the waitress asked if she needed anything else, she shook her head, thanking her with a distracted smile. The only thing she needed was several hours to the west.

Driving the winding road that led from Missouri to Kansas, she pondered Patty's words. The years in Freeston had eliminated most of her worries about moving. Nick was firmly entrenched in the community, JC Construction expanding on its previous reputation and growing each year. The kids were doing well in school and Nick had expressed no desire to uproot them from their friends.

She had to quit living on the edge, as if she was waiting for the people she knew to jump off or push her off. Life was a series of changes, she knew that. She dealt with the start of a new school year and new students without a second thought.

By the time she drove into her driveway, she had collected herself. No one was home yet. Adam had gone to a friend's after school to work on a project and she had made arrangements for Reecie to go home with a neighbor after the bus arrived.

She trailed her fingers over the backs of the furniture, the shelves that Nick had built into the living-room walls, the mantel. She paused at their wedding picture displayed prominently in the center, other family pictures scattered around the sides.

Next year they'd celebrate their twentieth wedding anniversary. Twenty years! Lily was the only friend she'd had any longer and she only saw her high-school friend if they both happened to be in Mustang at the same time. They exchanged Christmas cards, called each other on their birthdays. Lily had finally found the right man, marrying him four years earlier, and Caroline had danced at her wedding.

The front door opened behind her. "Hey!" said Nick, as if she'd conjured him while staring at his picture.

She spun around. "Hey!"

He walked into the room, dropping his briefcase on the pew, unknotting his tie as he came closer. He pulled it from his neck and draped it over his shoulder. "What are you doing?"

"Just thinking." She looped her arms around his neck. "Are you ever sorry we got married?"

His arms eased around her, holding her in a light hug. "No." He kissed her nose. "Are you?"

She shook her head. "I'm surprised sometimes that we've lasted so long. We're kind of different, you know."

He ran his hand up her side and slowed at one of the differences between them. She shifted at the surge of desire brought on by just his touch.

The door banged open. "Hi, Mom! Hi, Dad! Saw your cars so I came home."

They backed away at Reecie's exuberant entrance. "Later," he whispered, giving her a hard kiss.

She knew he'd keep his word. He always did.

CHAPTER SEVEN

Children
Eleven years earlier

"CAROLINE!" NICK DROPPED his briefcase in the entryway and walked down the hall toward the kitchen.

"She's not home yet. She called and had me put a casserole in the oven for dinner." Reecie lifted her head from the page she was studying at the kitchen table.

"What are you working on?" He ruffled her hair and she ducked away from his hand.

He could imagine the grimace she was sending his way. How many times had he rolled his eyes at his mom and dad? Life was a cycle and now it was his turn to be the parent.

"Algebra. We have a big test tomorrow."

He popped the lid on his soda can and sat down across from her. "Need some help?"

She shook her head, her attention again on the paper in front of her. She had smoothed her hair back into a semblance of its original style, the bangs draping over her eyes, shading her face from anyone's attention.

He felt a pang at how grown-up she looked. Thirteen already. Didn't they bring her home just yesterday? He knew he was showing his age thinking that way, but Caroline would understand. Instead of two tiny tots who needed them, they were housing teenagers poised on the verge of going their own way.

He sipped his drink, silently watching her scribble her way toward the answer of her problem. That was the way it had to be, he thought. Parents prepared their children for the world and then let them go out on their own. The only way the species could survive.

He finished his drink and stood up. Reecie cringed away from him and he laughed. "I won't muss up your hair again," he promised. "At least not tonight."

"I'm too old to have my dad ruffling my hair," she argued.

He almost broke his promise, his hand hovering over her hair. But a promise was a promise. He leaned forward and kissed her cheek.

"You'll always be my little girl," he said. "Just ask Grandma. Mom will never grow up around her."

He chuckled at her sniff and left the room, heading for the living room and a few uninterrupted minutes.

An hour later, the front door clicked open. He glanced up from the newspaper and smiled at Caroline. "Hi. Did you have a late meeting?" She usually beat him home from her classes at the community college.

"Is Adam here?"

He shook his head, surprised at her gruff response.

"No. He's probably still at practice. Isn't he riding home with Josh this week?"

Adam had been nagging for a car since he started his junior year. They had agreed that if he worked during the summer, they would help him find a good used car for his senior year of high school. Until then, either Nick or Caroline took him to school each morning and he found a ride home with one of his teammates.

"Adam hasn't been going to practice."

Nick dropped the newspaper in his lap. "Adam hasn't been going to practice? He'll be cut from the team if he doesn't practice."

"He *was* cut from the team."

Nick stared at her. "Adam was cut?" He knew he sounded like a parrot, but he couldn't make sense of what she was saying. "From the baseball team?" His son lived for baseball.

She nodded. "I don't know if he was cut because he didn't make practices or never made the team to begin with. I ran into Coach Blackmore this afternoon. I asked about the first game." She frowned and dropped onto the couch opposite him. "He said he was glad we were still supporting the team, with Adam not playing this year. That's when I found out our son wasn't on the team."

"Adam isn't playing baseball."

She leaned forward, her hands clasped between her knees. "Focus here, Nick. If Adam isn't going to practice every afternoon, where has he been?"

Nick lifted his head, the enormity of what she'd discovered registering. "I don't know."

"Exactly. For two weeks, he's been lying to us, talking about practice at dinnertime like he's working out with the team. And not once has he been there."

The front door clicked open. Nick clenched his hands together to stop from jumping up and shaking his son, demanding the truth. He could see Caroline struggling to control herself.

Adam stopped in the doorway, a wide grin on his face. "Hi. Supper smells good."

"Thanks." Caroline gracefully rose to her feet and crossed the few yards to his side. "How was school?"

"Not bad. Have to finish that English paper for Thursday."

She looped an arm around his neck and turned them both toward the kitchen. "I'll look over it after supper if you want me to."

"That'd be great." His grin widened. "Sure helps to have a mom who's a writer when you have an English paper due."

Nick followed in their wake. He knew Caroline was lulling Adam, putting him at his ease before she forced the truth out of him. He hoped she succeeded soon. He didn't think he could maintain his control for long.

Reecie turned from taking the casserole out of the oven. "Finally," she huffed. "I've been working on supper all by myself."

Caroline shifted a trivet to the center of the table for the casserole dish. "You're a sweetheart, Reecie. Your brother can take care of the dishes."

"Hey, I have that English paper to finish!"

"Which you said is due Thursday." Caroline brought over the glasses of water that Reecie had already filled. "Today is Tuesday. You can spend a few minutes loading the dishes into the dishwasher."

"Fine." His earlier shining mood gone, he slipped into his seat with his head bowed.

Caroline caught Nick's eye. He relaxed. Whatever Adam had been doing the last few days couldn't be that bad. He was still the same moody kid they loved and tolerated. Maybe he'd been embarrassed to tell them that he hadn't made the team.

Playing sports had always been Adam's joy and interest. They had spent hours at soccer matches, baseball games, hitting the basketball courts. In middle school, he had played a sport every season, relishing the hours practicing and playing. His grades had been good and they had encouraged him, believing that the extracurricular activities kept him out of mischief.

Not that he wasn't basically a good kid. But a few of his elementary-school friends were prone to trouble. Once he went to middle school, they'd hoped he'd find some other friends. Friends who cared about school and good grades. Where Reecie was hardworking and determined to keep her grades at the top of the class, Adam did just what was needed to make a passing grade and no more.

"When's the first baseball game?" Caroline handed Adam a piece of apple pie. The dinner conversation had been general, Nick and Caroline chatting about the weather and how it was affecting Nick's construction work.

"Next Tuesday. Starts early, before school's out, since the JV and Varsity both play. The team won't be very good by then, so you probably won't want to go." He picked up his fork and cut off a piece of the flaky pastry that was one of Caroline's specialties.

Reecie passed a plate to her father before accepting her own. Nick picked up his fork and then carefully placed it on the side of his plate with a tiny clink of cutlery.

"Okay, this has gone far enough." His voice boomed around the room. Caroline froze, her fork poised halfway between her plate and her mouth.

She gave a tiny shake of her head. Nick hesitated and then glanced toward their son.

He was calmly chewing his pie, his head bent toward the table. The sides of his hair hung down, creating a curtain that hid his face from view. Nick cursed himself for not noticing the length of his hair earlier. Coach always expected his ballplayers to keep their hair trimmed short during the season.

Adam's continued nonchalance grated on Nick and he half rose in his seat.

"Nick," Caroline cautioned.

He frowned. "What? You want me to ignore this charade your son has been perpetrating for the last two weeks?"

"You told them?" Adam's fork clattered to the table and he glared at his sister. "Thanks a lot."

"I didn't say a word." Reecie picked up her fork and dug into her pie, ignoring her brother and the drama that was unfolding around him.

"Your sister had nothing to do with our discovery. But I am disappointed, Reecie, that you didn't say anything to us."

She shrugged, her hair hiding her face. Did neither of his children frequent hair salons? "Wasn't my news. And I didn't know if it was true. I just heard it from somebody at school who heard it from her brother."

Nick opened his mouth and then shut it. His daughter's code of honor might be questionable from an adult's point of view. She was in middle school. Her brother was in high school. Ratting on each other was not acceptable.

He sighed. His children had grown up faster than he expected. He supposed all parents felt this way at some time.

But now he was tired from the day at work and he had to make a decision about Adam.

Caroline sat ramrod straight, her hands folded on the table. His call, she was saying. She would support his decision.

"When were you cut?" he asked.

Adam scooped up the last crumbs of his pie. "After the first tryout. Lot of good players this year. I couldn't keep up with the drills. And my hitting sucks."

His voice was matter-of-fact. Nick swallowed, determined to maintain an even tone. "What have you been doing after school for the last two weeks, Adam?"

"What do you care?" Adam's voice rose a fraction at the end of the sentence. At last a reaction, Nick thought. He wasn't as calm as he pretended to be.

"I've been home in time for supper," Adam snapped. "So what if I haven't been practicing ball?"

"What *have* you been doing?" Nick repeated, with the slightest inflection in his voice.

"I've been with my friends." Adam's voice was sharp. He was losing his cool. "Just hanging around, talking."

"Where?"

"Around town. At their houses. That's all, Dad." His tone had changed and become the wheedling tone reminiscent of his younger days.

Nick wasn't swayed. "You're grounded for the next two weeks, Adam. You go to school and you come home. If we go somewhere as a family, you may go with us. Otherwise, you're in the house."

Adam scowled. "I'm grounded? For getting cut from the baseball team? That's crazy!"

Reecie carefully slid out of her chair, carrying her dishes into the kitchen. Nick knew she would disappear into her bedroom, away from the anger emanating from her brother.

"You're being grounded for lying to us, Adam. We had no idea you weren't practicing at the school." He glanced at Caroline, but her eyes were on her lap. "What if something had happened to you while you were with your friends? We wouldn't even know where to begin looking for you."

Adam pushed away from the table. "This is really lame. My grades are okay. All I did was go off with my friends for a couple hours after school. And now I'm being treated like a criminal."

Adam's outrage drained away Nick's irritation. "You lied to us, Adam." He lifted his hand, weary of being the grown-up but knowing he couldn't back down. "A lie of omission is just as bad as an actual lie. Now you have to deal with the consequences."

Adam didn't say a word. He stomped down the hall. A few moments later they heard his door slam shut.

"That was nicely done." Caroline stood up and began stacking the dishes.

"You could have said something."

She paused, a plate in her hand. "Why? You were doing just fine. Anything I said would have diverted his attention from you. He'd have tried to pit us against each other."

She was right. The kids knew the consequences were severe if they asked one parent after the other one said no, but Reecie and Adam had tried every so often.

Nick followed her into the kitchen. "What do you think he was doing with his friends?"

She shook her head, rinsing off a plate and stacking it in the dishwasher. "I don't know. I want to believe they were just hanging around, talking, like he said. Maybe getting a snack at some fast-food restaurant. He's always been a good kid, Nick. I want to believe he hasn't changed."

Nick leaned against the counter. "Why didn't he tell us he was cut? We've never been the kind of parents to get upset if our kid didn't make the team. It was his choice, after all, to play."

"I know." She leaned on the counter next to him. "Did you keep secrets from your parents?"

"Sure. What girl I liked. Which kids got into trouble at school. But I never snuck around. That's what he was doing, Caro."

She snuggled under his arm and he tucked her against his chest. He felt better with her warmth seeping into him. Being firm with his children was never easy for him.

"You did the right thing," she murmured, as if she knew the torment he was suffering. "He'll live, Nick. We both had consequences and survived. He has to know he can't just come and go when he wants to. Not while he's living under our roof."

Adam was sullen the next morning at breakfast. He plunked down at the table, not looking at either of his parents. Caroline chatted with Reecie about the dress for her final middle-school concert. "We can look after school Thursday," Caroline said. "I'm finished early that afternoon. I'll pick you up and we'll go shopping."

She slipped the strap of her briefcase over her shoulder and rested her hand on Nick's shoulder, giving him a quick peck on the cheek. "I have my one o'clock class and then I'm coming right home to finish that proposal. It's going out this week." After years of talking about it, she had finally decided it was time to submit her reading-program idea to a publisher. He knew Patty's success at selling a selection of her columns to a publisher was the impetus.

Adam shoved back his chair. "Aren't you picking me up?"

Caroline gave him a startled look. "Oh, of course. Wait for me out front."

The glance she gave Nick was rueful. Their son wasn't the only one being punished for the next two weeks. They would have to make their own sacrifices to pick him up each day.

"HE'S BEEN FINE," Caroline said a week later. They were in their bedroom, getting ready for the first baseball game. Adam had said he didn't want to go, but Nick needed a night away from his business. Cheering on the home team would relieve some of the adrenaline from keeping up with the growing demands on his time at work.

"Pleasant?"

Caroline grinned at him from her seat in front of her dressing table. "I wouldn't go that far," she said, pulling her thick hair into a low ponytail at the nape of her neck. "He's offered to help around the house, though, and I've let him. In addition to his regular chores, he's gone through the junk drawer in the kitchen and organized the gloves and boots in the front closet."

"You're not cutting his time down due to good behavior?"

She zipped up her sweatshirt emblazoned with the school mascot on the back. Nick and Adam had given it to her the previous Christmas. The sun might be shining, but the spring days were still chilly. "No. I don't like the fact that he was lying to us any more than you do, Nick."

He rested his hands on her shoulders and smiled at their reflections in the mirror. A glass replica of a hummingbird caught the overhead light, a present from the kids during a Colorado trip.

No one would guess she was the mother of two teenagers. Her skin was smooth, a few lines around her eyes and mouth corresponding with her laughter. Her hair was still as thick and honey-blond as the day he met her. She might touch it up—he didn't know what happened when she went to the beauty shop—but she had the fresh, natural look he had fallen for years earlier.

"Should we let him go to the game without us?"

He grinned at the look in her eyes. "Why, Mrs. Eddington, are you propositioning me?"

She reached up and clutched his neck, tugging him down until their mouths were inches apart. "Could I?"

Their kiss was long and sweet, a taste of what they were together. He twisted around, his hands tight on her shoulders, his lips never leaving hers. He could relieve the stress of the day right here, in the comfort of his own bedroom…

"Eww! Geez!" Adam's disgust rang through the room loud and clear. "Could you at least shut your door? I thought we were going to the ball game."

Nick eased away from her lips, smiling at the dazed look in her eyes. They might be an old married couple, with teenage kids who were probably going to be the death of them, but he could still make his wife forget how to breathe. His own burst of lust was taking its time fading away.

"We're going." He straightened and hooked a hand under Caroline's elbow, helping her to her feet. "Tonight," he whispered in her ear.

She chewed on her lower lip, her eyes still glazed from their kisses. The temptation to stay home with her, to erase the craziness of his day with her gentle loving, was almost more than he could ignore.

"Mom, Dad, let's go!"

The moment was shattered by his son's aggravated voice. They could send him to his room for the night, but Caroline wouldn't agree to make love with the kids awake and aware. For all his desire hadn't completely diminished, he wouldn't feel comfortable either.

He grabbed his sweatshirt from the bed. Screaming at a ball game would serve two purposes now. At least he had the promise of the night ahead.

"DO I HAVE TO SIT WITH YOU?" Adam asked as they turned in to the parking lot.

"No." Nick backed into a space near the end of the lot, away from the backstop. Sitting with his parents would ruin the game for all of them. "Meet us here after the last out."

Adam sprinted toward the gate as soon as the car stopped. "It will be strange watching the game without Adam playing," Caroline said, following their son at a slower pace.

Nick nodded. Now that they were at the ball field, he wasn't sure who was being punished.

"Adam isn't playing this season?" The woman sitting in front of them slewed around until she could face both of them.

"Not this year," Caroline answered calmly. The air was nippy and she tugged her hood over her head.

"Give them no more info than they ask," she whispered. "If her son didn't mention that Adam was cut, then we don't need to say anything either."

Nick agreed. Watching the other boys stand in the middle of the field, their caps held over their hearts while the national anthem was played, brought a lump to his throat. He didn't want to be one of those dads who lived their lives through their kids, but Adam's natural interest in the game and innate ability had been a thrill he had never been able to put into words.

He sighed and settled into his seat to watch the game. The home team's pitcher wound up and threw the first ball. A strike, clean across the plate. The excitement caught him and soon it didn't matter who was playing, only that the ball was in motion, with the teams battling for the lead, inning after inning.

"Dad, come here."

He blinked. Reecie leaned over his shoulder. "What?"

"Come here." She tugged on his sleeve. He checked the scoreboard. Bottom of the eighth inning, with two outs for their side. Tied with four runs each. They needed to add another run or two to the score and then make three quick outs…

"Honey, can it wait?"

"No." Her tug was stronger.

"Where's your mother?" Now that he thought about it, he hadn't seen Caroline in a while. She had been talking to a woman on the other side of her, discussing something about the school. He had turned his attention to the game, focusing on the speed of the runners, the curve of the pitched balls, the calls from the umpire. The players didn't seem that much faster than Adam or that much stronger in their swings. Maybe if he talked to the coach…

"She sent me to get you."

The fear in Reecie's voice registered. "Where?" he asked, climbing over the two people seated near the aisle with a hurried "excuse me."

"Just come on." Reecie grabbed his hand and practically raced him down the steps to the exit.

Her hold on his hand intensified his worry. His children never physically connected with him in public. "Your mom?" he breathed, hardly able to imagine Caroline hurt.

"No." Reecie gasped the word and led him toward the exit gate. "It's Adam."

An image of his son, on the ground, wounded, caught at his heart. His legs churned up the distance, barely letting Reecie give him directions.

They skidded to a halt at the edge of the parking lot. Two police cars were parked at angles to the curb. Nick's heart slowed a fraction when he saw Caroline and Adam standing upright, all limbs appearing intact.

A police officer stood on either side of Adam. Caroline was gesturing with both hands. As he came closer to the small group, he saw tears shimmering on her cheek.

"Caroline?" He slipped an arm around her shoulder, presenting a united front to the officers.

"Oh, Nick, I'm glad you're here! There's been some sort of mistake—"

"No mistake, sir." The officer closest to them stepped forward. "Mr. Eddington?"

Nick nodded. "Your son was found with a marijuana joint in his pocket," the officer said.

"My son? Adam?" Nick shook his head, trying to clear his thinking. Adam was accused of having marijuana?

"Dad, listen—"

He knew in that instant. That tone. The wheedling one that tried to erase a bad incident after the fact. Whatever excuse Adam may have given his mother, he was guilty. Where he'd gotten the drug Nick didn't know. That wasn't the issue right now. His son had been caught and had to pay the consequences.

"What happens now?" he asked the officer.

"Dad!"

He shifted, separating Caroline and Reecie from Adam's pleading face. Caroline's words at the beginning of the game, to only give the minimum answer to questions, came back to him. He hoped Adam would stay quiet. He was in enough trouble as it was.

"Nick?" Caroline plucked at his sleeve.

"Let's hear what the officer plans to do," he said softly.

"We've already contacted the juvenile authorities," the officer informed him. "This is his first offense…"

He paused and Nick nodded, aware the officers had already run a background check on Adam.

"We have the authority to make a decision regarding your son's situation." The second officer had been silent until now.

"Which means?" Caroline moved closer to Nick, her fingers clutching his back belt loop.

"That we can take him down to the juvenile center or release him to your custody."

Nick scowled. His anger at Adam had been simmering below the surface since the discovery of his lying about practice. The temptation to encourage the officers to take Adam to the juvenile center was strong.

He passed the center each day on the way to his office. Its brick sides and lone front window showed a sterile place, a prison of sorts that he did not want his son to experience. They would mete out their own punishment for him.

Nick hesitated, fighting the urge to have Adam face his actions. Caroline's fingers tightened on his loop. "If we take him home, what happens then?" he asked.

"We would recommend that he have an evaluation at the local drug-rehabilitation program. This may be an experimentation phase he's going through," the officer said, "but it's important that he understand a second offense could require more drastic consequences."

Nick glanced at his son's pale face. He stood stiff and tall next to the police car, his eyes wide. "I believe he understands that. Don't you, son?"

Adam gave a jerky nod. "I'm sorry, Dad. It was stupid and I—"

Nick cut him off. "We'll talk about it later."

Reecie tugged on her dad's sleeve. "Can we go home, Dad? Everybody's staring at us."

He became aware of the curious faces peering over the bleachers. Most people were focused on the game, but a few had decided the scene in the parking lot was more interesting.

Judgment was being passed about them and he had to curb his furious retort that they were good parents, dammit!

Then he remembered that Adam had been lying to them, hanging out with friends while they thought he was playing ball. The same friends who had no doubt helped him find the drugs he had now been caught with. Nick's fingernails dug into his palms as he swallowed his pride. "Officer, what's our next step?"

"You can take him home." The first officer nodded toward Adam. "We don't want to see you again, understand, young man?"

Adam's head bobbed up and down. "I'm sorry, Officer, I'm sorry. I know drugs are bad, I was just—" He stopped, his voice hitching on a sob.

"Let's go, Adam." Nick took his arm and hurried him after Caroline and Reecie.

He bundled his family into the car, a subdued Adam in the seat behind him. Reecie huddled in her corner, a muffled sob emanating at intervals.

No one spoke until they reached the driveway. "I'm sorry," Adam mumbled, making no attempt to exit the car.

Nick shifted the car into park and shut off the engine. "Go to your room, Adam. We'll discuss this tomorrow."

Adam scurried out of the car and up the steps just behind Reecie. His sister pulled the door open. Adam didn't pause, just raced into the house. A moment later, Nick saw his bedroom light go on.

"What now?" Caroline hadn't moved from her seat, her belt still attached over her shoulder.

Nick caught her hands in his, surprised at how cold they were. He felt as if he would explode with the heat of his rage and frustration. "We make some calls tomorrow, find out about a rehab program."

She nodded, her fingers clenching his so tight he feared circulation would be cut off. But he relished the contact. He was drifting in unknown waters and she was his only source of stability.

"How could he do this?" she asked. "We've talked and talked about not using drugs since he was little, he's always been so careful to keep his body in shape for sports..."

Her voice trailed off, her eyes wide. Nick loosened his hand and tugged her against him. "We'll get through this, sweetheart. He's a good kid. He just lost his way for a little bit."

He hoped he was right. If not, it would kill Caroline. And he could not stand the thought of her in pain.

"WE CAN'T GO TO COLORADO." Caroline had repeated the phrase for the last four days.

Nick added another pair of socks to his suitcase and snapped it closed. "We're going to Colorado." His reply had become just as much a constant refrain.

"But Adam isn't finished with his program."

Nick sighed. He dropped the suitcase on the floor at the end of the bed and sat down next to Caroline. "Honey, we've gone over and over this. His counselor said it was perfectly all right to leave town."

The day after the ball game, they had contacted the community rehab program. Adam had been accepted and spent the last six weeks meeting with a counselor and small group of boys twice a week. Nick didn't know the details of their sessions, but he did know that they were discussing positive ways to spend their time instead of using drugs.

"He'll miss two sessions, that's all." She knew the procedure as well as he did but that hadn't stopped her from arguing that they needed to stay in town. "His counselor thinks it will do Adam some good to get away for a while, to refocus on his priorities."

"He's not a drug addict, Nick!"

"I know, honey." He ran a hand through his hair, wishing he could speak as clearly as she did. Words didn't come easily to him and explaining his need to get away, to find a way to recharge his batteries, was more than he was able to do.

"Caroline, we need this time in Colorado." Now more than ever. The last few weeks had been torture for all of them. No legal charges had been lodged against Adam, but they had all been called into a closed session of the school board. The administration had enforced their new drug policy, banning Adam from any extracurricular activities for the rest of the school year. His behavior for the last few weeks of school would determine if the ban would be carried out for the next year also.

Their neighbors and friends had been sympathetic. Nick knew their caring had been tempered by a sense of relief it wasn't their child.

All for a stupid mistake that Adam could regret for the rest of his life.

"We're going to Colorado," He stated again.

"We can't." Her voice was low.

He rose off the bed and picked up his suitcase. "Caroline, it's one week. Once we're in the mountains, everybody will be able to relax and maybe we can regain a semblance of normalcy."

"I don't mean we shouldn't go. It's just that I—I—I canceled our cabin."

He swung around, staring at her. "What?"

"Heidi called last week to confirm our reservation and I canceled it. I didn't think, with everything going on, that we'd be going."

"You canceled without talking to me?"

"Yes." She met his look steadily. "You made the reservation without talking to me."

"Because we'd already talked about going to Colorado."

"And then Adam got into trouble." Caroline fisted her hands on her hips. "Nick, I don't think this is a good idea."

"And I think it is."

"Mom, I—" Reecie skidded into the room and stopped in front of Caroline. "Are you two fighting?"

"No," Nick snapped.

Reecie blinked, tears shimmering in her eyes. "You're always so mad. I hate this family!" She ran out of the room, her noisy sobs echoing off the hallway walls.

"That's why we need to go," Nick said. "Reecie needs some normalcy in her life."

Caroline glared at him. "And we'll get that cooped up in the car together for a day, trapped in a small cabin for a week?"

"Is that what you think this will be? Then Reecie and I will go without you."

"Fine."

He walked out the door and down the hall to Reecie's room. "We're leaving in fifteen minutes."

"I don't want to go!" She had thrown herself onto her bed and had her face buried in a pillow.

"You and I are going alone."

She shifted and glanced at him from under her arm. Blotchy red spots covered her cheek. "Just you and me?"

He nodded. "Yes. I'm going to call about our cabin."

Reecie scampered off the bed. She had been quieter since the ball game, tiptoeing around the house, her head lowered when she had to pass by her parents, skittering in surprise when anyone talked to her. Getting away from the oppressive atmosphere would be good for her.

Caroline came out to the car as he was loading his fishing gear into the trunk. "You're going without us?"

He shrugged and carefully tucked the tip of the fishing pole into the corner. "You said you couldn't go, that Adam needed to stay for his sessions. Two parents, two kids."

"We've never taken separate vacations."

He could hear the bewilderment in her voice, but he would not back down. Reecie had suffered enough. She needed to get away from the whispers, the sympathetic looks. Heidi had found him an empty cabin and said they were eager to see the family again. He hadn't told her he was coming alone with Reecie.

"We'll be back on Sunday."

Reecie bounced out of the house. She froze when she saw Caroline. "Mom?"

Caroline bent down and kissed her cheek. "Have fun with your dad. You can tell me all about your trip when you get back."

Reecie flung her arms around her mother's waist. "I don't mind if you come, too!"

Caroline untangled herself from the hug. "You'll have a great time with your dad." She patted her on the shoulder. "Keep him awake on the road and don't let him stop every time he sees a deer."

Reecie giggled. "Hey," Nick said, appreciating Caroline's attempt to keep things normal. "It's not every day we see a deer."

"It is when we're in Colorado!" Reecie said. She hopped over to the front seat. "I can ride shotgun the whole way."

Nick stepped to Caroline's side. "Are you sure?" he asked quietly. "The cabin's big enough for all of us."

She shook her head. "I can't ruin Reecie's trip. She's so excited about having you to herself."

He wrapped his arms around Caroline, holding her close. Making a point, leaving her behind, seemed foolish now.

She moved away first. "Drive careful. And call me when you get there."

THE TIME AWAY FROM home was good for him. Reecie chatted nonstop in the car, enchanting him with stories of her friends, her ideas about what her high school years would be like, her quick bursts about things she saw outside. She dozed a few times and would jerk herself awake, chastising him for letting her sleep. "I'm supposed to keep you awake," she said. "Not sleep."

They made it to their cabin the second night. He had planned to drive straight through, but with only one driver and their late start, he had decided it would be better to find a motel. They left early in the morning, Reecie yawning as she carried her suitcase to the car.

Once in the mountains, they hiked, carrying sandwiches and fruit up the trails and stopping to view the panorama below them while they ate. Reecie sat patiently on the bank of the river while he fished, a book in her hands. He offered to teach her how to cast but she gave up after several snagged attempts.

"You fish, Daddy," she said, resorting to the name she had called him before her middle-school years. "I'll just read."

They left their cabin early in the morning, their unspoken desire to get home loud as they packed the car. Nick had enjoyed spending time with his daughter and didn't regret their trip. Now he wanted to be back with his wife.

The house was dark when they pulled in to the driveway. Reecie was curled on the passenger seat, her cheek resting on her hand. He patted her awake.

"Reecie, we're home."

She sat up slowly. "Did I fall asleep?"

He popped the trunk. "You slept for a little while." He handed out her suitcase. "Go in quietly. It's late. Looks like everyone's asleep."

He dropped his clothes in the hallway, padding quietly into the room in his boxers. He slipped into bed next to Caroline.

She rolled over, her hand brushing against his side. "Nick?"

"Were you expecting someone else?" His body was reacting to the scent of her shampoo and the warmth of her body next to his.

She chuckled sleepily. "No. I missed you." Her hand slid across the sheet and caught his fingers.

He laced their hands together. "I missed you. I had fun with Reecie but I wanted my wife at night."

Their voices were hushed in the dark room.

"Adam talked to me a little," she murmured. He had to lean close to hear her words.

"Did he tell you where he got the drug?"

Adam had refused to name any of the others involved or where he had gotten the marijuana. For a while, they had been worried that this would keep him from getting the maximum benefit of the program.

"No. He said it was his own choice and the other guys will have to deal with their own consequences." She curled against Nick's side, her head on his chest. "I didn't push him. He said it was the one time and that he hasn't seen any of the kids again. I believe him, Nick."

He wanted to believe him. He had seen real fear in

his son's eyes, and his counselor said that he was serious in their sessions.

He and Caroline had drawn up specific requirements for Adam and were keeping tabs on him. They would take those before the board in the fall and talk about the need for Adam to have something positive to do with his time, and explain that this had happened after his cut from the ball team. His counselor's report would also carry weight with the school board.

He pushed aside thoughts of their son and his problems. He had been away from Caroline for six long nights.

"I love you," he whispered.

He could feel her smile against his skin. "Hmm."

He caught her chin between his fingers and gave her a rough kiss. "I love you," he growled.

"Ditto."

He laughed and rolled on top of her. "What's it going to take to get you to say you love me?"

"I don't know. What do you have?"

He was more than happy to show her. And by the time they were both worn-out and ready to sleep, her whispers of love were more than satisfactory.

CHAPTER EIGHT

Mothers and daughters
Nine years earlier

"WHY DO WE SPEND every Thanksgiving with Grandma and Grandpa? Why don't they ever come here?" Reecie plunked down on the kitchen chair, her elbows thumping on the table.

Caroline wrapped foil around the pumpkin-pie tin and carefully added it to the box of goodies already packed. "Because it's easier for everyone to get to their house. We're the only ones who live any distance away."

"My days off and I have to be traveling."

Caroline dropped a kiss on her daughter's hair. Reecie shifted, but she had always been faster than her children when it came to kisses. She had to grab them when she could. "We'll be back on Friday afternoon. You have the entire weekend with your friends."

"Fine." She stumbled to her feet. "What needs to go to the car?"

Caroline handed over the box of food she'd packed. "Have Dad put this on the very backseat. Adam said he'd keep an eye on things."

Reecie froze in the doorway leading to the driveway. "Mom! What are you thinking? He'll eat everything before we even get there."

"That's why I double bagged all the containers. We'll hear him if he gets through the first layer."

Reecie grinned and Caroline grinned back. Her daughter was so like the little girl in the poem, she thought, watching her happily sashay out the backdoor. She could be so good…and so horrid.

Adam sauntered in, his jacket over one arm. "Need any help?"

"Your sister carried the box out to the car." She wiped down the counter and rinsed out the dishrag, draping it over the faucet.

"I'll just see how Reecie's organizing things in the car." He gave her a grin and a jaunty wave as he walked out the door, looking so carefree, she felt a nostalgic pang in her stomach for the days when she could swing him in her arms and make him laugh.

She did a last check of the kitchen and hitched her purse over her shoulder. "Nick! You ready?" she called.

He entered the room and snagged her around the waist. His kiss landed on the side of her jaw. "Yep."

"Not for that. We should have left the house an hour ago."

He nuzzled her neck, his fingers creeping up her waist. "We always have time for this."

She wiggled out of his hold and tugged her sweater back down. "Come on. If Phil beats us there, I'll never hear the end of it." They might have to drive the farthest, but her brothers were not known for punctuality.

Three hours later, she waved at the two cars parked in front of her parents' house. "Oh, look! Phil and Dan *both* beat us."

Nick neatly parked behind her father's pickup truck. "Carter isn't here yet."

"Is Megan coming with Uncle Carter?" Reecie unbuckled her seat belt and opened the door.

"I don't know." Most of the cousins were years older than her children and had their own families, but her youngest niece was still single and had been protective of her father since his divorce.

The divorce had caught the family by surprise. Last year, the month before Megan left for college, Priscilla stunned the family by stating that she had never been happy in the relationship and she wanted to discover who she was on her own. Carter and Priscilla had seemed perfect together, both athletic, active in the schools of their three children, successful in their respective careers. She had walked out of the marriage without a backward glance.

First the supper-club friends and then Priscilla and Carter. Caroline couldn't help checking with Nick, making sure he was happy, that he wasn't just going through the motions of marriage because that was easier than walking away.

"Being married to you isn't easy," he told her one night. She had followed him out to his workshop in the backyard.

"What's that supposed to mean?"

He had tipped up his goggles and leaned forward, planting a long kiss on her pursed lips. She had all but fallen over when he finished.

"You make me crazy with your questions and then you look at me like that. That's what I mean." He had dropped his goggles on the workbench and spent the next half hour showing her how satisfied he was, that he had no reason to go looking for his life anywhere else.

"Are you coming in or checking out the neighborhood?" Her father stood on the front stoop, the door open wide behind him.

"Hi, Grandpa." Reecie skipped up the steps and stretched to kiss his weathered cheek.

"Hello, sweetheart." Her grandpa patted her shoulder and then turned toward Adam. "And look at you, young man. You get taller every time I see you."

Adam ducked his head and gave his grandfather a one-armed hug, his other arm around the box of food. "Hi, Grandpa."

"Go inside, both of you. Your grandmother's been watching the clock for the last hour. And watch out for Fifi. She's even more excited than usual."

Caroline climbed the three steps to the porch. "Hi, Dad." She kissed his leathery cheek, noting that he hadn't shaved yet. That wasn't like her father. He was always up early and ready to go before most people had left their beds.

"We wondered where you were." He held the door for them and then latched the bolt closed after her family entered the small house. Shrieks and hollers sounded from the living room, battling with the sounds of the television set. Tiny yips let her know that the poodle was in the house.

"Keeping people out?" She couldn't remember ever locking the door in Mustang. One of the few things she'd liked about the small town after they moved there.

He shrugged. "Doesn't stay shut all the way otherwise."

She studied him but he was already walking down the short hallway to the living room.

"Hey, look who finally showed up!" Her oldest brother grinned at her as she came into the room.

Strands of gray dotted Dan's light brown hair. "The best for last," she retorted.

He laughed and tossed a throw pillow at her. She caught it easily. She greeted her other brothers and her two sisters-in-law, trying not to be obvious as she calculated the signs of aging in them.

They weren't that much older than her. She had noticed a few more wrinkles in her face. Not unexpected with teenage children, she'd told herself. But if her brothers were getting older, that meant she wasn't far behind.

In the kitchen, her mother looked much the same. A small, neat woman with tidy gray hair. She was bent over the stove, a frilly apron tied around her waist.

"Hi, Mom."

"Hello, darling." Her mother placed the long-handled spoon in the ceramic rest in the middle of the stove and moved forward to kiss Caroline's cheek. "Your father was about to give up on you."

"Now, Evelyn, you know that isn't true."

Caroline turned around in surprise. Her father had followed her into the kitchen, not staying with the others to watch the football game. He picked up the spoon and gave the stuffing a stir.

"You're cooking?" Caroline asked.

"Don't sound so surprised. I've always helped around the kitchen." Her father moved the pan off the burner and shut it down. He picked up another large pan and carried it over to the sink, carefully shifting the lid so he could drain the potatoes.

"Really?" Caroline didn't mean to be rude. Her father's presence in the kitchen was not part of her childhood memories.

"Okay, not always." He finished draining the liquid from the potatoes and poured a premeasured amount of milk into the pan. Setting it on a hot pad, he adjusted the beaters into the portable mixer. "I'm helping now, okay?"

"He helps all the time now, Caroline." Her mother opened the oven.

Her father's indrawn breath caught her attention. Evelyn glanced at him over her shoulder. "I'm not taking the turkey out, George." Her mother snapped the door shut. "For heaven's sake! You're treating me like I don't even remember how to cook! I'll go set the table and let *you* finish the meal."

She marched out of the room, her apron swaying from side to side.

Caroline stared at her father. "What was that all about?"

"Nothing." He flipped on the mixer and blended the milk and melted butter he had added to the potatoes.

Caroline edged closer to him. "Dad," she said, raising her voice slightly to be heard over the mixer.

"If you want to help, dish up the stuffing into a bowl. And make sure the green beans are heated through."

She wouldn't get any more out of him. Determined that she would find out what was going on before she left their house, she followed his directions as they finished preparing the meal.

The talk at the table was loud and boisterous. Fifi had been banished to her bed in the master bedroom or her voice would have been added to the ruckus. Reecie and Adam were the only children present and sat opposite each other in the middle of the table. Megan had gone to her mother's house for the holiday. Caroline was glad she didn't have to think about seeing only one child at holidays. That day was coming soon enough.

Her brothers talked about their work, asked Adam and Reecie about school and brought up stories from years gone by.

"Caroline followed us around everywhere," Carter told her children.

"I don't know why!" she snapped. "If you were half as obnoxious as you are now, you weren't worth the bother."

Adam snickered and she glared at him. "I was a little girl," she said. "They were my big brothers and for some reason, I thought they were pretty cool. Thank goodness I've grown up."

"Dinnertime sure hasn't changed." Her father shook

his head and gave Reecie a rueful grin. She giggled. "I'm sorry you have to witness this. Their mother and I thought we did a better job."

Evelyn was quiet through much of the meal. She asked for food to be passed to her or offered a dish when someone's plate was empty.

Her brothers good-naturedly complained when told they had to do the dishes since Caroline helped with the preparations. "We'll be in there for hours," Phil said. "Look at this pile of dishes."

"I'll help clear," Caroline volunteered.

"Is Mom okay?" she asked once she was alone in the kitchen with her brothers.

"I think so. Why?" Dan ran water into the sink.

Caroline stacked the plates next to the sink and leaned against the counter. Phil and Carter were putting the leftovers in the refrigerator. "She's been so quiet. And Dad was cooking. Mom never lets him in the kitchen."

"He helps now that he's retired."

"He's been retired for years. I don't remember him helping this much."

"They're getting older, Caro. That's all. Now, scat." He waved a soapy hand at her. "Go sit in the living room and relax. We'll do the dishes and then we can have pie."

She slowly walked into the living room. She didn't want to think of her parents getting older. They had always been there, a fixture in her life.

Her parents sat together on the love seat, her father's arm draped along the back, his fingers on her mother's shoulder. They'd often sat that way. When she was little, she'd loved to wiggle between them and rest her head on her father's chest, her feet in her mother's lap.

She sat on the arm of Nick's chair. "Another game?"

He nodded, his eyes glued to the set. "Who's winning?" she asked.

"The wrong team," her father grumbled.

Her mother struggled to stand up. "I need to fix the pie."

George tugged her back down. "The boys are doing the dishes and then they'll bring in the pie."

"The boys?" Evelyn pushed at his hand and straightened. "The boys are here? They'll be hungry, want some sandwiches."

The game conversation paused. Reecie and Adam glanced at Caroline from their sprawled positions on the floor and then over at their grandmother. Fifi was curled in a ball against Adam's hip, asleep, the only creature in the room oblivious to the uneasy atmosphere.

"Mom, we already ate," Caroline said quietly. "You and Dad made a wonderful Thanksgiving meal."

Her mother frowned, her teeth chewing at her lower lip. "Did I?"

Caroline nodded, watching carefully as her mother's gaze darted around the room, lighting for a moment on her grandchildren, the other women, Nick, and then back to Caroline. She smiled. "That's right. I don't know what I was thinking."

"WHAT'S GOING ON WITH Mom?" Caroline asked, cornering her father after everyone had eaten their fill of pie. Her mother and Reecie sat at the dining-room table, poring over picture albums together. Caroline had taken the empty spot on the love seat.

He rubbed his hands over his stomach. "We're not sure, Caro." He lifted a hand as she opened her mouth and she snapped it closed. "I'm not keeping anything from you, honey. The doctor's still running tests. As soon as we have some answers, we'll let you and the boys know."

She bent down and kissed his cheek. "Are you okay?"

He rubbed his knuckles against her jaw. "As okay as I can be. I love your mother. It's not easy watching her like this."

Caroline nodded and blinked. His worn face showed signs of weariness. She looped an arm around his shoulders. "What can I do to help, Dad?"

"Say a couple extra prayers," he whispered.

"DAD CALLED THIS MORNING," she told Nick a week after New Year's. They had spent Christmas at home, celebrating quietly just the four of them. A winter storm had blanketed the area, creating a Currier and Ives effect that made traveling risky.

She followed him down the hall to the bedroom. "A meeting's been scheduled with Mom's doctor for this Thursday. He wants us to come. I can go on my own if you're not able to get away."

"I can go." He stripped off his shirt and dropped it into the laundry hamper. "What time do we need to be there?"

She felt a rush of relief. She had been afraid that Nick had a prior commitment. But he hadn't hesitated.

"The appointment's at eleven. We can leave right after Reecie and Adam go to school. Dad didn't think it would take that long, so we should be home before the kids."

He sat down on the bed and tugged her next to him. "Honey, don't upset yourself like this. Let's wait and hear what the doctor says."

She nodded, blinking her eyes to force the tears back. "Mom's never been sick. And, now..."

The tears threatened to escape. Nick tucked her against his side and she leaned into his strength. He kissed the top of her head. "Let's wait and hear what the doctor says," he repeated.

"THE TEST FOR ALZHEIMER'S is more a test of elimination," the doctor explained to them on Thursday morning. Phil and Dan had arrived with their wives, Carter the only sibling without the comfort of a spouse. Caroline sat between him and Nick on a large, overstuffed couch in the psychologist's office. A social worker joined them, her papers spread in front of her on a table at the back of the room.

Evelyn sat on a low couch across from them, her hands folded over her purse in her lap. She had greeted them pleasantly, thanking them for coming in the middle of the week. Their father had sat down next to her, one large hand covering both of his wife's hands. He said nothing, letting the doctor give them the results of the weeks of tests.

"She's disoriented to place and time," Dr. Oppenheim continued. "She's agreed not to drive anymore and given your father her keys."

"She never was very good with directions," Phil said.

Dan nodded. "We always had to help her get anywhere in town."

"You don't have to give away all our family secrets," Evelyn chided.

Caroline sniffed at her brothers. "Stop!" How could they joke at a time like this?

"Humor is a good way to deal with this situation," Dr. Oppenheim said, as if he could read her thoughts. "There's going to be some changes in your life, but for the most part you want to continue as before."

"Can she stay at home?" Caroline asked.

"That would be best for now." Dr. Oppenheim shifted toward Caroline. "The less change, the less strain on her mind. We don't know all the ways that she'll change over the next few years, or even months, but we do know that familiarity can slow down some of the process."

"Is there any medicine she can take?" The questions had piled up in her mind over the last few days. Now that she had a possible diagnosis, she wanted to know everything she could.

He shook his head. "Not right now. There's some experimental drugs in the works and when they become available, your mother's regular doctor can see if she's a candidate."

He crossed his arms over his chest. "I wish I had more positive information to give you, but we're looking at a long road ahead. Not much is known about Alzheimer's at this time. You'll have it easier than most, with your close family relationship. Keep your sense of humor, work together. And please don't hesitate to ask any questions of me or your mother's regular doctor."

He gave them more medical facts, the social worker handed them a book with information and suggestions for community support, and then the family was left alone in the room.

No one spoke after the door closed. Phil cleared his throat and Caroline looked at him expectantly, but he didn't say anything. "What are your plans, Dad?" she asked when no one else spoke.

"We're going to stay in the house for now," he said. "I've added some locks to the doors that take a key."

She remembered him setting the dead bolt at Thanksgiving. "Does she slip outside?" she asked, appalled to think of her mother roaming the streets in the winter cold, not knowing where she was supposed to go.

"I'm right here, Caroline," her mother said. "I can understand what's being said."

"Sorry, Mom."

Evelyn stood up and moved to the center of the room. "I know this is a big adjustment for all of you. It's more than I can handle sometimes. After talking with the doctor, we wonder if your grandfather was in the beginning stages of Alzheimer's when he had his car accident."

Caroline gasped. Her grandfather had died in an accident after he'd turned down a one-way street the wrong way. The driver of the other car had swerved to miss him and her grandfather had hit a pole at the edge of the road. He'd died instantly. She had been six months pregnant with Reecie.

"It's possible," her father said. "That's one reason your mother was so willing to give up her keys. We want to keep her around as long as possible."

Evelyn reached for his hand and linked her fingers with his. She smiled at her children. Caroline could see a glimmer of tears on her lashes. "We'll get through this, kids. It's hard and I hate that I'm losing parts of my mind. But I'm still with you. I'm going to see those children of yours get married, Caroline."

Caroline nodded, a lump in her throat. "Okay. Just let us know what we need to do and we'll do it."

"Treat me the same as you always have and keep me posted on what's going on." She inhaled a deep breath and exhaled slowly. "And pray like you've never prayed before."

"WHAT TIME IS IT?" Caroline rolled over in bed, squinting at the red numbers on the clock.

"Almost 3:00 a.m." Nick picked up the receiver. "Hello?"

Caroline leaned against his shoulder, trying to hear the conversation on the other end.

"What is it?" she asked when he hung up the phone.

He took her hands in his. "It's your mom. She's in the hospital."

Caroline shot up, her head bumping the headboard. She rubbed the ache with her hand. "In the hospital? But there's nothing physically wrong with her."

She had talked with her mother every other day since their joint visit to the doctor two months earlier. Her last conversation had been about the Sunday crossword puzzle and a clue that had stumped her. Her mother had easily identified the actor from the 1940s that Caroline needed to finish the puzzle.

"This has nothing to do with her Alzheimer's. She had an aneurysm in her brain and it burst last night. Your father wants everyone to come to the hospital."

Caroline dressed by rote, tugging on her slacks, buttoning her shirt. Adam and Reecie were silent as they all filed into the garage and the car. The streets were deserted, the streetlights small circles of light on the road as Nick drove them toward Mustang.

The bright lights of the hospital were glaring after the darkness of the outside. Caroline wrapped her arms around her children and held them close as they waited for the elevator doors to open.

"Caro." Phil met them in the waiting room of the fourth floor.

She collapsed in his arms. "What's going on?"

He patted her back. "She's in a coma. She hasn't responded to any of their tests. She didn't want to be resuscitated and Dad wants to honor her wishes."

She squeezed her eyes shut. "What about Dan and Carter?"

"They're here, too."

Her chest heaved with her sobs. She couldn't catch her breath. Phil ran his hand up and down her back.

"I know it's hard, honey." His voice was ragged and she could feel his pain through her entire body.

"Why did this happen now?"

"We don't know. The doctors found the aneurysm when they were doing the earlier tests. It wasn't in a place that could be operated and they were watching it. Not sure what triggered it now."

She gave a shuddering breath and lifted her head from his shoulder. "Can I see her?"

He nodded. "Dad wants everyone in there as much as possible. We've been talking to her, to each other. They have her on oxygen and gave her some morphine to be comfortable."

She squeezed her eyes shut again, holding the tears back. "Let's go."

Nick and the kids followed her down the hall. She paused outside the room and Nick pressed a hand on her shoulder. "We're with you," he whispered.

A bedside lamp lit the private room. Dan sat next to the bed, one hand holding their mother's hand, his wife at his side. George sat on the other side of the bed, his arm under Evelyn's shoulders. Carter leaned against the end of the bed.

"Oh, Daddy." Caroline knelt at his side and buried her head in his lap.

He stroked her hair with his free hand. "Shh, sweetheart. She's not in any pain and much as we'll miss her, this may be best."

How could he say that? She lifted her head, tears streaming down her cheeks. "I just can't think about not having her around." She sniffed and dashed at her tears with her hand.

"She'll always be with you, honey, you know that."

Caroline rose to her knees and gave her mother a watery smile. She lay on the bed, her hair smoothed back from her pale forehead, her eyes closed. Her chest rose and fell with each staggered breath and Caroline thought her own chest would burst with the pain.

"Talk to her, honey. Let her know you're here."

Caroline swallowed and took a deep breath. Releasing it slowly, she curved her lips in a soft smile. "It's Caro, Mom. Nick and the kids came with me. We made good time. The snow's been cleared from the streets, so driving wasn't bad. Only a few trucks on the road. Passed a lot of them parked at the rest stops and entry ramps."

She was babbling, talking about the traffic while her mother was dying. She couldn't concentrate, couldn't think how to tell the woman who had borne her and raised her, how much she loved her, how much she valued the words of wisdom she had been given over the years. She had never voiced the words before, never thought she would need to. And, now, with such a limited time before her, she couldn't think what to say.

She felt her father stand up. "We're going to leave you alone for a few minutes," he said. "The boys each had some time alone with her already."

A sense of panic rose up in her. "I can't," she whispered.

Her father kissed her cheek. "Just talk to her, Caro."

The room emptied. She sank into her father's chair, her fingers clutching her mother's hand. Already she could feel the life slipping away.

"Adam graduates this year, Mom. Wasn't sure he would, after that trouble he had with drugs. You were such a help, reminding us of all the good things he did. He really is a good kid. He reminds me of Carter sometimes. Especially when he gets that goofy grin on his face."

She sniffed and swiped at her tears with her shoulder. Both hands were wrapped around her mother's hand. "Reecie has a boyfriend. I didn't want her to start dating yet, but I also didn't want her to think she'd found the love of her life because I kept them apart. I don't know how you did it with four kids, Mom. Two keeps me hopping all the time."

Her mother gasped, a long breath that shuddered through her body. Caroline held her breath and relaxed when Evelyn's breathing returned to the steady inhales and exhales.

"I should have called more, Mom," she whispered, leaning her cheek against her mother's shoulder. "Let you know what was going on with all of us. We've been busy, but that's no excuse. We should have visited more. You always made sure we saw Grandma and Grandpa even when we moved so far away. I should have done the same, brought the kids here more.

"We always had so much fun! Remember that trip we all took together to Colorado? The kids still talk about Grandpa George and his huge fish. Too bad nobody could hold on to it long enough to put it in the basket. We could have all had trout that night for supper."

She rambled on, reminding her mother of the good times at holidays, how much she appreciated the late-night phone calls when the kids were little and she didn't know how to stop Reecie from crying or Adam from sticking everything into his mouth. Tears streamed down her cheeks and she brushed them away as she kept her hands tight on her mother's.

"I need to let the rest of them come back. I love you so much, Mom. You and Dad are why I wanted to find a good man, a loving husband."

She kissed her mother's forehead. "Thank you for being part of my life, Mom. I love you and I'll never let the kids forget you."

She slid her hands out of her mother's hand and rose to her feet. Her head felt light and she rested a hand on the wall to gain her balance. At the door, she paused a moment and smiled at the beautiful woman lying in the bed.

They left George alone with his wife and sat in the waiting room. Reecie curled up next to her on the couch, her head in Caroline's lap. She stroked her daughter's hair over and over, reliving those moments right after they brought home their new baby. Her mother had stayed with them for several days after each birth, helping with the housework, playing with Adam when his little sister arrived.

"At least we have good memories," Dan said softly.

Caroline couldn't bear the thought of being without her mother and pressed her lips together to stop from shouting at her brother. She didn't want memories, she wanted her mother to stay with her. What happened to watching her children get married?

"She was lucid the last time I talked to her," he added. "She repeated her questions several times, but other than that she was her usual self."

"It's going to be hard on Dad." Phil's voice was gruff.

Caroline inched toward Nick. He was sitting in the chair next to her. Adam's head leaned against his dad's shoulder, his eyes closed. Caroline didn't think he was asleep, just trying to absorb what was happening to his beloved grandmother.

Nick reached over and linked his fingers with hers. How would she live without him? They shared so much, even when they weren't together. He knew her dreams, her hopes, her fears. He loved her in spite of her angry words, her foolish frustrations.

She vowed to be a better wife, to show him how much he meant to her. She wouldn't wait until they were alone in a hospital room to spill out her feelings. He was her soul mate, the man she had married on faith more than two decades earlier. They had raised two children together, moved to new towns, changed careers.

Nick nudged her shoulder. She lifted her head. Her father stood in the doorway, his face haggard, his eyes sunken. "You need to come back in," he mouthed, as if speaking was too difficult.

They were all together when Evelyn took her last breath. They stood for a moment in silence and then let their father say his goodbyes alone. Nick took Reecie and Adam to their grandparents' house, Caroline staying with her brothers to help with last-minute arrangements in the hospital.

"I love you," she whispered, her arms holding Nick tight.

"I love you." His lips crushed hers, the kiss affirming the life that they shared. "Do you want me to come back after I settle the kids?"

"No, stay with them." She clung to him, her arms around his shoulders, reluctant to let him go.

Finally she released her hold. Her eyes hurt. How many more tears could she shed? "We can't do much right now, but Dad shouldn't be alone."

The funeral arrangements had been finalized years ago by both of her parents. Their minister sat through the meeting with the funeral home and helped organize the memorial service that was held in the church for an overflowing crowd. Friends and neighbors brought food to the house and Caroline struggled to find places to store all of it.

"You have enough food for at least two weeks," she told her father as they prepared to leave. Her brothers had left the day before, needing to return to their jobs. Nick had been able to have his assistant step in on the current projects. But now he needed to go home and the kids needed to get back to school.

"I'll be fine, honey." Her father stood on the front porch, his hands on the railing. Fifi sat patiently beside him. She had wandered around the house, her big eyes forlorn as she searched for her mistress. Now the little dog wouldn't leave George, her tiny feet padding along beside him wherever he went.

She hated leaving him like this. He looked bewildered and she had heard him wandering around the house last night, Fifi's toenails clicking on the wooden floors. Nick had told her to let him be for now, that he had to adjust to sleeping alone in the bed. "It's not easy," Nick had whispered. "That year we were separated was the longest year of my life."

Now her father was going to have to spend the rest of his life alone in bed. Her heart lurched and she wrapped her arms around him. "Call if you need anything."

He phoned twice after they returned, asking for suggestions about what to do with her clothes. "You don't have to do anything yet, Dad."

"I can't be in the house with her things, Caro. I need to box them all up and give them away."

She convinced him to wait. "I'll come up and help soon," she promised.

The second time, he wanted to know if she wanted any of the books. "A fellow said he would come and buy the whole lot. What do you think?"

"Nick, I have to go up there," she said after that phone call. The kids were out with their friends. She and Nick had shared a pizza in the living room, a game show on TV.

He nodded. "I know."

"I already talked to the dean about getting my classes covered," she added. "Just in case."

She couldn't remember the last time she drove to Mustang on her own. If they didn't go as a family, she had one of the kids with her. Driving along the familiar roads, the radio tuned to an oldies station, she tried to block out what she would find when she arrived.

Her father opened the door at her knock. "Caro?"

"Hi, Dad." She carried her suitcase into the house. "I'm here to help you go through Mom's things."

"You don't have to do that."

"Yes, I do."

She called Lily to help her sort through the clothes. The dress shop had expanded and she now owned several around the state. The publicity with Caroline's wedding gown had garnered her attention from as far away as New York City and for several years, she worked with a designer there. When her aunt decided to get out of the business, Lily returned to Mustang to take over the management of the stores. Being her own boss, designing dresses for local and area celebrities, was more in keeping with her plans.

"I don't know what to do with Dad." They were packing up her mother's sweaters to send them to a consignment store in Kansas City.

"He's going to survive. Caroline, his neighbors are going to take care of him."

They were. Every day, someone showed up with a casserole, a roast, a pot of chili. Her father graciously accepted each offering and shared it with her for suppper.

Lily added another sweater to the box and taped it shut. "You can't stay here forever, Caroline. Your family needs you."

"They're fine."

"Caroline, Adam graduates at the end of this year. What about prom?"

"Nick helped Adam rent a tux. And Reecie's not going this year. She's a freshman." Her daughter had begged and pleaded, but Caroline had held firm. Her boyfriend was a sophomore and they could go next year, if they were still together.

Nick had not asked her when she was coming home. He asked about her father, what she was doing, and told her about his jobs. He had a big job coming up with a new housing development and he had taken Reecie to the site with him. Adam had filled out the paperwork needed for the community college and was enrolled for the coming fall term.

They didn't need her.

"DAD SAID I COULD GO to the prom."

Caroline's head jerked up, the phone cord going taut with the movement. "What? You're not going to the prom, Reecie. We talked about this. Next year, when you're a sophomore."

"Dad said that it's okay. Other freshmen are going."

"I'm not their parent."

A huff of air sounded over the line. "Well, you aren't my parent, either. I haven't seen you in a month."

A month? Caroline stared at the calendar dish towel hanging on the kitchen wall. Every year, her mother bought a new one. Caroline didn't know where a person would begin to look for a calendar dish towel.

April. If Reecie was right, it was now April. Outside, she could see blue sky and buds on the trees in the backyard. A rainstorm had awakened her, the drops hitting gently against her bedroom window. April showers, she thought.

Which meant the next month would be May. Adam's graduation. Her anniversary.

She slid down the wall and sat on the floor, her feet splayed in front of her. What was she doing? She had a family in Freeston and she was pretending she was a child again, sleeping in her old bed, using her old dresser, sitting at her old dining-room table.

"Reecie, you are not going to the prom. I don't care what your father said," she added, breaking into her daughter's sputtering. "You played us against each other. I'm coming home tonight and I'll talk to your dad."

"Mom, wait! No! I didn't— I'm not going— He didn't say—"

"Your father didn't give you permission?"

"No." The answer was wrung from Reecie's lips. "I just said that, hoping you'd change your mind and I could tell him you had. I don't understand why I can't go."

Caroline smiled into the receiver and stood up. "You will someday, honey. When you're a mom."

She was a mom. She'd been a daughter long enough. Now it was time to go to her own daughter and continue the cycle.

Her father was puttering around the back garden. He wore a straw hat and had a rake in his hand. Fifi nosed around in the bushes, her little tail bobbing up and down as she walked.

He leaned on the handle when he saw her. "I'm going home," she announced.

"Good girl."

"Why didn't you send me away earlier?"

He shrugged, the loose strands of straw fluttering with the movement. A yellow butterfly floated by, landing on an early tulip. "You're a grown woman, Caroline. I figured you knew when it was time to go. And I liked having you here."

She wrapped her arms around his shoulders. He was thinner, his bones sharper. "You eat after I'm gone, you understand?"

"Yes, ma'am."

"And don't stay up all night watching television."

He tipped his head and studied her. "I don't know about that one."

"Dad."

He propped the rake against the shed wall and slipped an arm around her waist, leading her toward the house. "Caro, I have to get through this on my own. And you have to go home to your family. I'm surprised Nick hasn't been up here to take you off."

She had wondered about that herself. "Busy, I guess."

"Caro."

"I don't know, Dad, really. I told him I needed to be here."

"And now you need to be there."

Her suitcase was packed and sitting on the front porch. He picked it up and carried it to her car. She unlocked the trunk, stowed it away and slammed down the lid.

"Take care of yourself," she whispered.

"I will." He rubbed his nose against hers.

Lights shone from all of the windows when she

pulled in to the driveway. She carried her suitcase to the front door and tried the knob. It opened under her hand.

She set her case by the stairs and walked down the short hallway to the kitchen. Reecie looked up from the table, her math book in front of her. "Hi, Mom."

"Hi, sweetie." She bent down and kissed Reecie's cheek. "Where's your brother or dad?"

"Adam's studying at the library. Dad's in his workshop."

Caroline crossed the kitchen. "You won't tell Dad what I said, will you?" Reecie called after her.

"No more fussing about the prom?"

"No more," Reecie promised.

"Then it's between you and me."

Walking across the damp grass, she thought of the times she had kept a secret with her mother. Her wedding dress. The ding on her dad's car. Mothers and daughters.

Corky shuffled over and butted his head against her knees. She petted his head. "You would eat your cousin Fifi in one bite," she told him. Leaving her father with the poodle had given her some consolation. His late-night meanderings wouldn't be completely alone.

Nick lifted his head when the workshop door opened. "Hey," he said softly.

"Hey."

He dropped his hammer and goggles. "I didn't expect you home today."

His grip was tight around her waist. "Why didn't you come get me?" she asked.

"You needed to be there." He leaned back and used the

back of his hand to tilt her chin up so he could see her eyes. He smelled of sawdust and cologne. "Didn't you?"

"Yes." She tucked her head against his shoulder and savored the feel and scent of him.

And now she needed to be here.

CHAPTER NINE

Adam's wedding
Five years earlier

"WHAT TIME ARE YOU coming home?" Caroline's voice sounded over the telephone. "Adam's here. He said he needs to talk to both of us."

He glanced at his watch. "Give me an hour and I'll be there."

"Nick."

"I need an hour, Caroline. We've finished the McIntyre house. She's walking through it with me tonight."

He shut off the cell phone and tucked it into his pocket. Reecie looked up when he came into the newly painted garage. She wore the yellow hard hat that all his employees were required to wear while on the job. "Hi. You ready to walk through the place?"

He grinned. "Yes. Let's do this."

The owner met them on the front porch. The house had taken almost two years, with the additions and changes to the original plans. The place was beautiful, a showcase for Mrs. McIntyre's lifetime collection of nativity sets. She had been widowed and used a portion of her husband's insurance money to build a home that would let her start anew and continue her hobby.

A Yorkshire terrier padded along beside them. The late-afternoon sunlight sparkled on his rhinestone collar. The dog had been there every time the owner showed up, well behaved and only vaguely interested in the new smells being created at the house.

Nick had considered getting another dog after Corky passed away last spring. But with Adam off to college, Reecie busy with her school activities and he and Caroline gone most of the day with their work, they decided that was no life for a dog.

"We've gone through everything, Mrs. McIntyre." Reecie held open the door to the kitchen. "You're going to be very happy here."

The older woman smiled at Reecie. "You've been a big help to your father, I'm sure."

Reecie beamed. "I'm going into the family business when I graduate."

"After college," Nick reminded her. He and Caroline were agreed on that.

"Dad."

He lifted one eyebrow and she stopped. No arguing in front of the client, he had drilled into his children.

Mrs. McIntyre signed off on the house. "I'll be sure to tell everyone of my wonderful contractor. And his daughter," she added. "Have him include you on his signs—Eddington and Daughter."

He still wasn't used to the name Eddington Construction and often had to correct himself when he answered the phone. When Claude had called three years earlier to let him know that Joe had died peacefully in his sleep, the former owner had added, "Time for you to change the name of the company, Nick. Let people know it's your business now."

For a time, he'd felt trapped. He knew it was irrational. They hadn't moved in twenty years. He liked the town, they were part of the community. People recognized him when he walked down the street or drove one of his trucks to a construction site. But for some reason, changing the name of his business had made the move more permanent.

"Eddington and Daughter," Reecie said out loud. She sat in the passenger seat of his truck, her arm on the open window.

"What about Eddington and Children?" He shifted into reverse and rested his hand on the back of the seat as he left the driveway.

"*Pfft!* Adam isn't going to build houses."

"How do you know?"

"He said so. He's getting out of Freeston as soon as he can."

Adam attended Pittsburg State University. This semester, he'd rented a small apartment near the campus and came home most weekends to do his laundry and pick up his mail. Over the past two years, he'd declared several majors. They were still waiting for him to decide on one.

Adam's car was in the driveway when they pulled in. "I'm going to shower before supper." Reecie slammed her car door shut and raced across the sidewalk.

"Nick?" Caroline called out to him as soon as he entered the house. "We're in the living room."

He toed his boots off in the entryway and padded down the hallway in his socks. Adam perched on the edge of the couch, his hands dangling between his knees. His brow was puckered and Nick had a sinking sensation in his gut.

"What's going on?"

"I don't know." Caroline gestured toward Adam. "He wouldn't tell me anything until you were here, too."

He sat down on the arm of Caroline's chair. "Adam?"

His son was twenty, an adult in the eyes of the law. For a moment, his mind darted back to that night when Adam was questioned by the police about drugs. They'd been fortunate that time, with just a warning. If he'd gotten into trouble this time, things wouldn't go as easy.

"I'm getting married," Adam said.

"What?" The word was jerked out of him.

"Next weekend. Nothing fancy. Just a simple ceremony at her mom's house."

Nick could feel Caroline's confusion rolling off her. He felt just as stunned.

"You're getting married?" Caroline asked. "Who? When did this happen?"

"Shannon McIntyre. You know her. We went to high school together. She started at PSU this semester."

Nick thought of the house he had just toured. "Shannon McIntyre?"

"Yeah."

Caroline grabbed Nick's hand. "He can't just get married like this. Nick, say something."

He shrugged and stood up, pacing to the fireplace. He leaned an elbow on the mantel and stared into the empty cavern. "She's pregnant, isn't she?" he asked quietly. No other reason precipitated such a hasty wedding.

Silence. He turned around slowly and saw the answer on his son's face.

"One time, Dad." Adam lifted both hands. "We just did it one time. I didn't have anything with me because we weren't planning to go all the way—"

Caroline gasped behind him. "When's the baby due?" he asked.

"This summer. She's going to move into my apartment after we're married and we'll keep going to school."

"Oh, Adam!" Anguish sounded in Caroline's voice.

"I know, I messed up." He straightened his shoulders. "We're going to make this work."

Nick thought of the woman he had just escorted through her new house. "Does her mother know?"

Adam shook his head. "We're going over there later tonight."

At least he wasn't letting his girlfriend take the heat by herself. Nick couldn't imagine how Mrs. McIntyre would react. Her joy in her new home would be buried under the news that her only child was pregnant.

She'd talked to him over the past two years. They'd spent a lot of time discussing her desire for a new house, somewhere that didn't echo with the voice of her late husband. She'd known her daughter would eventually move away but that hadn't been expected for years.

Shannon was going to live at home, get her degree at PSU, figure out where she wanted to go with her life.

"We thought we couldn't have children," Mrs. McIntyre had confided. "Then, when I was almost too old, we found out Shannon was on her way." Her voice had beamed with pride at her daughter's name. "Her father adored her. She was definitely Daddy's little girl."

His death from a heart attack when Shannon was a freshman in high school had devastated both of them. They had struggled to live without him in their old home and then Mrs. McIntyre had come to Nick for help in designing a new home.

And now his son was taking her daughter away.

"What do we need to do?" Caroline asked quietly. She had turned to the practical, accepting the reality of their son's marriage. Nick could almost see the lists forming in her mind.

"Nothing. We have the license, we're going to ask her mother if we can have a simple ceremony in her living room. Just you and Dad, Reecie, Shannon's mom and a friend for each of us as witness."

Adam rose to his feet. "I know I've disappointed both of you again. But I'm willing to pay the consequences. I like Shannon a lot. Even if this hadn't happened, I could see asking her to marry me."

He left, saying that he would return after their visit with Mrs. McIntyre. From the back of the house, Nick could hear Reecie rummaging around in the kitchen. He had lost his appetite.

"They're too young to get married!" Caroline paced

around the room, her fingers tapping on the back of the couch, a chair, the fireplace mantel.

"They are. But Adam's right. They have to deal with this themselves."

"But, Nick, he can't get married! He has his whole life ahead of him—"

He tugged her to a halt, his hands tight around her wrists. "What do you want him to do? He can't abandon her. Are you suggesting they get rid of the baby?"

Her head snapped back. "Nick! No!"

"Adoption?"

"No." Tears were streaming down her face.

He gathered her close, stroking his hand over her hair, down her back. His anger wasn't directed at her. He'd wanted so much more for his son. "I'm sorry, sweetheart, I didn't mean to snap at you. Adam's made the best decision he can under the circumstances. They'll survive. He's a smart kid."

Smarter than he usually showed. He'd graduated from high school with better grades than they'd expected, working hard the last semester to make up for the year before. He'd received a scholarship from PSU and agreed to live at home his freshman year. That summer, he worked with Nick, putting in long hours, and earned enough to pay for his apartment.

THE WEDDING WAS SIMPLE. Both mothers cried during the service, mopping at their eyes as the minister talked about the sanctity of marriage and had Adam and

Shannon recite their vows. Reecie stood next to Caroline, her usual exuberance tempered by the solemnity of the situation. A college friend of Adam's was his best man and a local girl that Nick knew by sight was the maid of honor.

After the service, the minister excused himself and left for another appointment. The wedding party adjourned to the dining room that Nick had finished only the week before. A lighted hutch on the back wall illuminated the crystal nativity sets that Mrs. McIntyre had collected through her years of travel with Shannon's late father.

A light buffet sat on the dining-room table. Nick filled a plate with shrimp, fresh fruit and triangles of sandwiches. He didn't feel like eating, but it would be churlish to ignore the attempt to make the event festive.

"I know this isn't what you wanted for Adam." His new daughter-in-law stopped in front of him.

"I'm concerned about how things will work out for both of you."

He'd had little chance to talk with her before the wedding. Adam had brought her over to meet them. They'd stayed a few minutes, the conversation stilted and awkward, and then Adam and Shannon had left to complete more of their plans.

She was slender, her brown eyes large in her pixie face, her dark hair loose around her shoulders. Her ivory dress was simple in design, with only a silver necklace as accent. He had no doubt the dress had cost more than Adam's income from his summer job.

He didn't begrudge the McIntyres their money. A large chunk had gone into his business account over the past two years. His concern was whether Adam would be able to provide for his new wife in the manner she'd been accustomed.

"I like Adam a lot," she said now. "He tutored me in algebra when we were in high school. I always hoped he'd ask me out, but I was too bashful to say anything."

Adam had been a tutor? Nick hadn't known that. He glanced at his son, deep in conversation with his best man.

Adam lifted his head, his eyes searching the room until they lighted on Shannon. A smile lifted one corner of his mouth. Nick turned and saw a blush creep up Shannon's cheeks.

They care for each other.

More than just liking and lust. A sense of possibility swept over him. Maybe his son would be all right.

"Lois suggested they move in with her next semester," Caroline said on the drive home. Reecie sat silent in the backseat, a piece of wedding cake in her lap.

"Shannon said I have to put this under my pillow," she told Nick when she was getting into the car. "So I can dream about my own groom."

He had been tempted to toss the cake into the trash. Reecie was only seventeen! She had no need to be dreaming of husbands at her age. He'd let her work full-time at the business if it would stave off her marriage.

He struggled to focus on Caroline's statement. "Live here in town?"

"Yes. She said she has that big house and no one to

share it with. They'd have to pay the gas for the trips back and forth to class but in the long run, that would be cheaper than rent."

"Adam's car guzzles gas." Adam had bought the car with his own money his senior year, working on the engine with his friends, getting it repainted. A reminder that he could be responsible.

Caroline didn't say anything. "What?" he asked when he'd crossed two streets and she'd still made no reply.

"She's giving them a new car as a wedding present."

He nodded, his lips pressed together. They'd given them a microwave and dishes. "So Adam's landed on his feet once again."

"Nick!"

He flicked on his indicator, making the turn onto their street. Their house was the last one on the block, a neat four-bedroom rancher with an acre of land. The house they'd moved into when they first came to Freeston. He'd remodeled, added the porch for her study, built the gazebo in the backyard. A good solid home half the size of the house he had just left.

"I'm happy for them, Caroline. Shannon's mother can afford to be generous. And it will be good to have them close by. Are they planning to stay there after the baby's born?"

"Maybe."

Reecie had jumped out of the car as soon as he parked, stating that she had homework to do. He doubted she was studying on Saturday night. She didn't want to listen to her parents argue.

Caroline rested her hand on Nick's arm. "Please don't be upset with him."

He leaned his head against the back of the seat. "I'm not." He closed his eyes. "They've got a tough road ahead of them, Caroline. You know that."

Her breath feathered against his skin. They weren't touching, but she was close. His safe harbor in the constant sea of change.

"I know they do," she said. "I wish they hadn't started their marriage this way, but they're both good kids. Lois wants to make sure they finish their education."

So did he. A college education was no guarantee of a successful life but it would give Adam and Shannon an advantage.

By Christmas break, Shannon's condition was evident. She missed several days of classes the last week of school, staying in bed with an upset stomach and then crawling into campus to take her finals. Caroline had been concerned that it was more than the typical morning sickness but the doctor had told Adam and Shannon it wasn't uncommon for young mothers to suffer more the first few months.

Lois traditionally opened her home for tours of her nativity sets the two weeks prior to Christmas and this year was no exception. Nick had built in several lighted display cases in the living room and dining room. Caroline went over the day the local TV station filmed a segment, telling Nick and Reecie about the experience at supper that night.

Nick and Caroline opened presents with Reecie in the

morning, conscious of Adam's absence. The two families had gone together to the Christmas Eve service at church the night before, singing carols and listening to the story of another baby's birth. Adam had then gone home with Shannon and Lois, spending his first Christmas away from them since he was born.

Nick, Caroline and Reecie went to the McIntyres' house for Christmas dinner. Decorations covered the trees in the front yard, the front door, the staircase in the entryway. Nick had never seen the nativity sets displayed and was caught by how many she had collected.

"How did you start collecting?" Reecie asked at dinner.

"Shannon started me off." Lois handed around the platter of ham. She had a cleaning service take care of the maintenance of the house. The cooking was her domain. "She wanted to know why I put away the nativity after Christmas, if we were supposed to remember Jesus all year long." She smiled at her daughter. "Next thing I knew, I had a shelfful of nativity sets. I bought one every time we traveled with her father."

"Dad used to complain about how many stops we made." Shannon's voice was breathless and Nick slanted her a concerned look.

Her eyes were ringed with dark shadows, her lips a natural deep red against her pale skin. Her skin was translucent and he worried a strong wind would blow her away. No one else seemed concerned, listening to the conversation and passing around the food.

Lois chuckled. "He complained out loud but he also

made sure we didn't miss a single Christmas store. He was a good man, your father." Her voice was wistful.

Nick had met Tad McIntyre at city events, visited with him as they stood around a table of hors d'oeuvres. Otherwise they hadn't traveled in the same circles. Tad McIntyre had been the bank's vice president, and while Nick did all his banking there, he'd had little reason to meet with the vice president.

They spent New Year's Eve with Caroline's father. He had gone to Dan's house for Christmas, spending three nights in Saint Louis. Fifi had gone with him. The top of her head was gray now and she moved slower. "Like me," George said when Caroline commented on the dog's aging. "Two old codgers rattling around the house."

"Don't talk like that. You're not old."

"I'm a great-grandfather, Caroline. Your brothers are grandpas. My baby girl's going to be a grandmother. I'm getting old. Nothing you can do about that."

"Well, that was a cheerful visit," she said as they drove home.

"He's right, you know. Grandma."

She nudged him with her elbow. "Hey!" He gave her a scowl. "Be careful. I'm the driver. An old-grandpa driver."

His cell phone chirped and he dug it out of his pocket. "It's Adam. You answer it."

She pushed the button. "Hi, honey."

Nick waited. She was listening, her body hunched over with the phone to her ear. "Where are you?" she finally asked.

"We'll be there as soon as we can."

She clicked the phone shut. "Shannon's lost the baby," she said quietly.

"What?" The car swerved and he tightened his hands on the steering wheel.

"She woke up this morning in pain and Adam rushed her to the hospital. They've been there all day. They couldn't save the baby."

He didn't know how he made it to the hospital. Reecie sobbed in the backseat and Caroline sat stiff and silent beside him. His mind refused to grasp what she had told him. They were going to be grandparents. They'd been joking about it when the phone rang. It was a mistake. She'd misunderstood.

Lois met them at the entrance. She collapsed in Caroline's arms. The two women stood together, their tears mingling for the loss of their first grandchild.

Nick kept a tight hold on Reecie. Her face was red and blotchy from crying. "Where's Adam?" she asked.

Lois lifted her head from Caroline's shoulder. "He's in the waiting room. They took Shannon up to surgery."

Caroline rushed into the room, scooping Adam into her arms. His eyes were rimmed with red. "Oh, honey, I'm so sorry."

"She wasn't feeling good at Christmas," he said. "I wanted her to go to the doctor, but she just thought it was more of the morning sickness."

Nick remembered how pale she had looked. Caroline had always glowed with her pregnancies, the picture of health. He should have insisted Shannon go to the doctor, but hindsight was always wiser.

A white-coated doctor came to the door. "Mr. Eddington?"

Nick started forward until he realized the man was referring to Adam. He stepped back, watching his son steel his shoulders and cross the room.

"Your wife's in recovery. She's had a hard time of it but everything looks good. This shouldn't affect her ability to have other children."

Lois moaned and Caroline helped her to a chair. Nick wanted to throttle the doctor. He knew the man believed he was giving them good news, but they had just lost their baby. It was too soon to even consider another one.

Shannon spent three days in the hospital. Adam didn't leave her side. She was wan and listless when she came home, lying on the couch in her mother's living room, drifting off to sleep and then awakening with a startled cry. Caroline shared nursing duties with Lois, staying at their house during the last few days of her holiday break from the community college.

Adam showed up at the office one afternoon a month after Shannon had come home from the hospital. "We need to move," he said.

Nick set aside the plans he had been studying. The winter snows had slowed down construction and he was considering several bids for the coming spring. "What's the matter?"

"Her mother is smothering her."

"Your mother's there, too."

Adam shook his head. "Mom reads and watches TV, talks to Shannon, tries to get her to think of something besides the baby." His voice caught on the word and Nick had to swallow his own pain.

"Her mom is babying her," Adam continued. "Shannon's sleeping on the couch, getting special meals. She won't get better that way."

"Adam, give her time. Her entire world's crashed down."

"So has mine," Adam reminded him.

Nick felt a guilty start. They had been so focused on Shannon's physical health, they'd forgotten two people had been involved.

He reached out a hand, but Adam was already walking toward the door. "If something doesn't change, it's going to get worse," he said before he left.

In the end, they separated. Shannon couldn't look at Adam without remembering their baby. He stayed with her through the spring and into the summer. On July 2, the due date that their doctor had first given them, he moved into his old room.

"They're not going to work it out," Caroline said. They were sitting in the gazebo, leaving Adam some privacy in the house.

"No, they aren't." He'd talked to Adam the night he'd returned to the house. Shannon was going to file for divorce. Her mother was selling the house and they were moving to Wichita, near an aunt and uncle. Adam was going back to Pittsburg to finish his senior year.

"I ache so much," Caroline said. "If I could have saved them this pain, I would."

"I know, sweetheart." He pulled her close. The owl

that had lived in their oak tree for years, or possibly a descendant, swooped past them, its voice screeching in the night air. A fitting sound for his mood.

"What would we have done if we lost a baby, Nick? Would we still be together?"

Would they? They'd gone through so many other trials. The divorces of their friends, Adam's troubles, her mother's death, his father's illness and death last year. But losing a child was different…

His grip tightened on her. "They were so young," he murmured against her hair.

"Only a couple years younger than we were, Nick."

The McIntyre house sold to a young family. They contacted Nick for renovations and he referred them to a company in Pittsburg. Adam graduated with a degree in business and found a job with the electric company in Kansas City. Caroline missed him, even more so after Reecie graduated from high school and headed to Lawrence for her own business degree.

Adam announced his engagement the week after his twenty-fourth birthday. They'd met through a mutual friend and dated for a year before deciding to get married. Caroline had danced and laughed at his wedding until Nick finally had to drag her away so the caterers could clear up and the DJ could go home.

"He's happy now, isn't he, Nick?" She dropped her dress on the floor and flopped onto the bed in their hotel room.

He draped her dress over a chair and hung his suit coat on a hanger. "He is. She's sweet."

Kelly was a year older than Adam, a stocky blonde with a ready smile. She worked at her family's flower shop and was being trained to take over the business. Her father wanted Adam to come into the business with them and Nick had a feeling he would make that jump soon.

He didn't mind. Adam had to find himself, decide who he was going to be. Reecie still planned to be part of her dad's construction business.

Caroline gave a soft snore. She'd fallen asleep in the middle of the bed, still wearing her slip and high heels. He eased her shoes off her feet and tucked a blanket around her, watching her sleep.

The mother of his children. The love of his life.

CHAPTER TEN

Reecie's wedding
The present

LILY MET HER as she came out of the small room with Patty at her side. "There you are! Reecie's getting frantic." She looped her arm through Caroline's elbow and dragged her down the hall.

"I just needed a quick break."

"You get the break *after* Reecie's married." She opened the door to the room she had commandeered as Bride's Central.

"Mom! Where have you been? The wedding starts in half an hour."

"Sorry, sweetheart." She walked across the room, stopping several steps in front of her daughter.

Lily had added a gentle flounce and short train to the dress to compensate for Reecie's extra inches. The line of the gown was still flawless and flowed over Reecie's healthy figure, the result of work around the construction sites and the miles of running she put in each day.

"What do you think?" Reecie dipped and swayed in

front of the full-length mirror. "Aunt Lily did a great job, didn't she?"

Caroline grinned in the mirror at her daughter's reflection. All grown up and still the little girl who had adored a flippy skirt. Who knew she'd go into the construction business, wearing hard hats and tramping around worksites in big heavy boots? *Can you see her, Mom? Is this how you felt when you looked at me?*

"No flipping on the way up the aisle," she said, covering her sudden desire to cry. "You'll trip your dad. You can flip it all you want at the reception when you're dancing."

"Oh, I forgot all about my flippy skirts!" Reecie stepped back from the mirror and gave one experimental flip, using the tip of a matching satin heel.

The flounce fluttered a few inches off the ground and then settled back at her heels.

"That's enough." Lily adjusted the cape over Reecie's shoulders. "Do not listen to your mother another minute. She's just babbling so she doesn't cry."

Caroline stuck out her tongue. Patty laughed and Lily ignored her, straightening the drape of the gown and smoothing the cape.

She backed up, studying Reecie with a critical eye. "All right. You look lovely, Reecie." She gave her a peck on the cheek. "We're going to leave you alone with your mother for two minutes."

Lily raised two fingers. "Two minutes, Caroline. Then she's getting married."

The door closed behind the bridesmaids and Lily

and Patty. Caroline faced her daughter, tears blurring her vision.

"Please don't cry now, Mom." Reecie clutched her bouquet, the ribbons fluttering in her unsteady hands.

"I won't." She leaned forward and brushed her cheek against the soft skin of her second child. "I love you, sweetheart. I want you to be so happy. Troy's a good man."

Reecie nodded. "He is. And he loves me. We're going to have a marriage just as good as yours and Daddy's."

Caroline clenched her fingers together at her side. Have a better one, she wanted to say. Don't come to the wedding of your child and realize you have no life ahead of you together.

She swallowed the words and pain. "Let's go before Aunt Lily storms back in here."

Nick waited outside the door. His eyes widened and he opened his mouth several times before words came out. "You look beautiful, princess."

Reecie gave him a curtsy and tucked her hand into his elbow. "Thank you, kind sir."

Caroline walked down the short hallway, turning toward the foyer of the church. Troy waited for her at the back of the pews and grinned when she came into view.

"Are you ready?" she asked him. He had already escorted his mother down the aisle to her seat on the groom's side. Once Caroline was seated, he would take his place at the front of the church in preparation for his bride.

"Yep." His steps were measured, his mood solemn. "I'll take good care of her," he said.

They pledged their vows in front of the congregation,

kissed as husband and wife. Caroline stood next to Troy's father in the receiving line, introducing him to friends and family he didn't know, accepting congratulations. She smiled in the pictures, holding on to Nick's arm when directed to, stepping away as soon as possible.

The crowd cheered when Troy dipped Reecie during their first dance together as husband and wife and laughed when Reecie fed him the first piece of wedding cake. Caroline resisted when Nick held out his hand to her and then stood up, resigned to carrying on the charade for the sake of their daughter.

"She was beautiful," he said. They swayed around the room, the floor getting crowded as more and more couples joined them.

"I told her she couldn't flip her skirt on the walk up the aisle." Her stomach was reacting to his arms around her. When had they last been together like this?

He laughed. "She didn't. She's making up for it now."

Caroline glanced over his shoulder. Reecie had looped the train of her skirt over her arm, slipping her hand into the cord Lily had sewn into the train for just that purpose.

"That's so she can dance."

"Hmm." Nick leaned his head down, his cheek resting on the top of her hair. "She was beautiful," he repeated, "but her mother was even lovelier."

Caroline stumbled over her feet. Nick caught her against him, his arms strong and solid.

"I can't do this." She struggled to get away from him, her breath shallow and frantic.

"What's the matter with you?" He loosened his hold and she took advantage, breaking away and threading through the crowd to the open door at the edge of the reception hall.

"Caroline?"

She pushed past Lily, seeking the sanctuary of the room she'd discovered earlier. Her feet were silent on the carpeted hallway and she was almost there when her arm was grabbed and she was whirled around.

"What are you doing?" Nick's eyes blazed in his face. "The entire room was staring at your mad dash out of your daughter's reception."

She pressed her hands against warm cheeks. "I can't do this anymore, Nick. I can't pretend everything is perfect between us."

He leaned a hand against the wall by her head. From behind him, she could hear the fast pace of a popular song and the chatter of the wedding guests. Her dash out the door had not stopped them from enjoying the party.

"Nothing's ever been perfect between us, Caroline. Why should it start now?"

"This is serious! I'm not joking!"

Two girls in their fancy dresses ran down the hallway, sliding past them on the way to the bathroom, their giggles echoing off the walls. Nick reached around her and opened the door next to her hip. His hand between her shoulder blades, he gently pushed her inside. "Let's talk away from the crowd."

She didn't want to be alone with him. Not yet. Her plan had been to get through the wedding, send all the guests home and then talk to Nick in their house. She had a bag packed, ready to leave for her father's house as soon as she broke the news of the divorce to him. She hadn't said anything to her father, but she knew he wouldn't turn her away.

"What's going on with you?"

She decided to brazen it out. "Wedding nerves. You know how crazy things were with Adam's wedding and we were only the parents of the groom. This time, it's been everything. The cake, the flowers. One mishap after another."

"Something happened with the cake?"

"Well, no, not the cake."

Marguerite Renfro had baked the cake, pleased to be able to repay Nick for those times he came around her house to help with repairs. The matchmaking Caroline had tried all those years ago had lasted for several weeks. Then a single mother of three young children had decided to finish her college education, gone into the library at the community college for an assignment and caught Roger Petry's eye. He had married her, helped raise her three children and added two more of their own.

Marguerite had retired from the library and taken up cake decorating. Nick had added to her bungalow, designing a kitchen that was worthy of a four-star chef. Her wedding cakes were prized around the area and Caroline had counted herself lucky to get on the list for Reecie's wedding.

"Marguerite loves you. And Reecie." Their daughter

answered as many calls from the former librarian as Nick did. "She wouldn't do a thing to cause either of you any problems at her wedding."

Nick folded his arms over his chest and leaned against the door. "I didn't bring you in here so we could talk about Marguerite." He frowned, his eyebrows pulled together almost to his nose. "You haven't been yourself recently. What's the matter? It's not just the wedding preparations. I know you. A wedding wouldn't throw you off."

She thought of what she'd told Patty, that she didn't want Reecie to move away, that she wanted to keep her daughter safe and protected at home. She knew Nick would understand that. And then he would tell her it was their job to send their children out into the world.

"I don't want Reecie to leave," she managed to say.

He shifted from his position at the door and moved toward her. She backed up, not wanting him to touch her, and he paused, a puzzled look on his face. "I know you don't," he said after a moment. "I don't either. But we'll see her all the time. She's still working at the business."

Troy had a job at the bank as a loan officer. Nick was turning more and more of the responsibilities over to Reecie. He wasn't ready to retire but he wanted Reecie to be ready when he stepped aside.

"Yes, but she'll have her own life, her own friends." She still regretted the times she hadn't called her mother, let her know about the changes occurring in her grandchildren. She had consoled herself with the fact that staying in touch had been harder then, without cell phones and the Internet. But writing a letter once a week should have been doable.

She pressed her hand against her stomach. Between the lack of sleep and worry, she was causing herself physical pain. Patty had slipped her two aspirins in the bride's room and her headache had receded. But her stomach still churned and the piece of wedding cake she'd eaten felt as heavy as a piece of lead.

Nick's hands settled on her shoulders. She jumped. She hadn't realized he had moved so close.

"Caro, talk to me. I'm your husband and for the rest of our lives, we're going to be the only two people rattling around in our house. We can't keep secrets."

She stared at the tips of her shoes poking out from under her dress. "I want a divorce," she whispered.

His hands fell from her shoulders and she could feel him jerk back. His shoe kicked at a chair leg, sending it scuttling over the wooden floor.

"A divorce?"

She nodded, unable to look at him. She hadn't wanted to tell him here.

His hands grabbed her shoulders again and he shook her until she lifted her head. "What are you talking about? I'm not giving you a divorce!"

"I'm not asking you to *give* me one. I'm taking one."

Now that the words were out in the open, she felt light-headed.

"Why?"

She shrugged out of his hold and paced to the

window, stopping and turning around, her hands gripping the back of a chair. "Except for the kids, we have nothing in common. You have the construction business, I go to the community college. Now that Reecie's gone, what is there to keep us together?"

"Our past!" His voice roared through the room. He ran his hand through his hair. "Caroline, this is crazy! Do you want me to sell the business and come teach at the college with you? Or maybe you could quit teaching and come work at the office."

The fury in his voice barely concealed his pain.

"It's more than different careers."

"Then tell me what it is." He sat down in the chair opposite the one she was holding, his legs spread out in front of him. His arms were folded on his chest, his eyes hard. "I deserve to know why, on this day that we're celebrating our daughter's wedding, her mother wants to leave me."

"I don't want to leave you." She mumbled the words and crawled around to sit in the chair in front of him.

"Then don't." His voice had lowered.

"It's not that easy." She wished she hadn't sat down, that she could pace away from the wounded look in his eyes, the pain that barely simmered under his voice.

His eyes were intense, watching her with the single-minded purpose he gave to one of his projects. She felt vulnerable and she wanted to leap out of her chair and run away.

"You're leaving me before I leave you," he said. The anger was gone, replaced with a firm confidence.

"What? No!" She shook her head emphatically.

"Yes, that's it." He crossed his legs at the ankles. "You've decided that the kids are the only reason we're together and now that they're gone, we have no reason to stay together. You think I'm going to walk away, look for someone else."

He stood up and paced around the room, his long legs eating up the distance. She sat huddled in her chair, her hands clasped in her lap, her heart pounding at what she had started.

"If I didn't love you so much, I'd wring your neck." His pacing had brought him back to her chair and he squatted in front of her, his hands on her knees.

"Look at me."

She lifted her lashes, keeping her chin pressed against her chest. He reached out and tipped her head up with one finger.

"Caroline, you have to stop worrying so much about people leaving you. People are going to disappear out of your life all the time. It's the way life is."

She sniffed, blinking away the tears that had gathered on the ends of her lashes. "It's so hard, Nick. And it hurts each time."

"I know, babe." He shifted and gathered her against his shoulder. "But you can do it. You have done it. You're one of the strongest women I know."

His echo of Patty's earlier sentiments dislodged the tears that had been gathering since she first saw Reecie standing in the bride's room with her wedding dress on. They tumbled down her cheeks and over her chin.

He leaned back. "Hey." He bent down and kissed away the tears. "Shh. Honey."

"I just—" She shuddered. "I'm not that strong, Nick."

"Yes, you are." He held her close, her cheek tucked against his shoulder. "And I'm not going anywhere. You can serve me all the divorce papers you want, I'll fight you every step of the way."

A tiny hiccup slipped over her lips. "I'm glad I stepped in your way that day on campus."

"About that."

She lifted her head and looked at him. "What?"

One corner of his mouth was quirked in the grin that had enticed her all those years earlier. What had she been thinking?

"You didn't exactly step in my way," he said.

"Yes, I did." She nodded and felt the soft silk of his dress shirt against her skin. "I wasn't looking where I was going and I stepped right in your path when you were running back to the gym. I know it was a long time ago but I haven't forgotten."

She might have fought her attraction to him back then, told him it was over before they'd gone too far, but nothing would erase the memory of him staggering back after she rushed down the steps, his long legs clad in running shorts that barely covered his rear end.

"The thing is—" He twisted his neck back and forth a couple times. "I was waiting for you."

She frowned. "Waiting for me? What do you mean? You were running past me and I almost tripped you."

"I wanted you to think that." His grin was devilish.

"I've always let you tell the story your way, but the truth is..." He hesitated again. "I saw you leave that class several times. We met once at a party. I wanted to ask you out, but I couldn't get up my nerve."

He had been nervous about talking to her?

"I, ah, planned the whole thing."

She stared at him. "You made up the story about racing a friend to the gym?"

He nodded.

"No shortcut across campus?"

He shook his head. "I started around the next building. Timed it so I would bump into you just as you came down the stairs."

She leaned back, her eyes scanning his familiar face. His dark hair was streaked with gray and deep lines bracketed his mouth. The tiny lines that fanned out from his eyes were as much from his love of laughter as from age.

And yet she didn't know all his secrets. "I can't believe you kept this from me all these years!"

He shrugged. "I didn't mean to. The first time you told your version, I thought it would be rude to correct you in front of others. Then it just became easier and easier to let you tell it your own way. It didn't seem to matter."

"Yes, it does." She looped her arms around his neck. "I wasn't just an accident to you. You made *plans* to meet me."

She peppered his face with kisses. "Yeah," he said slowly.

"Nick, all the time I was growing up, whenever we moved, I had to make the first step to make friends. I was the new kid and I had to walk up to some girl and introduce myself. I had to make them like me."

"You're very likable." His hands hitched under her bottom and tugged her closer.

"Yes, well, it would have been nice to know someone wanted me for myself."

His grin faded. "Caroline, I always wanted you."

Her face heated at the intense gleam in his eyes. "I know—"

"No, you don't." He placed his fingers on her lips, silencing her. "You think you do. I know I don't say it enough and I'll try to change. I love you, Caroline. I love who you are and who you were. And I'll love whoever you become."

The tears threatened to spring forth again. She swallowed and sniffled, willing them to stay back. She did not want to cry all over him.

Why had she ever thought she could leave this man? Their lives were so bound up together, they could never be untangled. He was her past, her present, and he had just promised to be her future.

"What do you say we pack a couple bags and disappear for a few days?" His voice was gruff in her ear. "Find a cabin in the mountains where we can hole up with no cell-phone connection, e-mail or TV. Just you and me, away from it all."

She smiled. Her bag was already packed. She'd just been confused about her destination.

"Lead on," she said. "I'm right beside you."

* * * * *

In honor of our 60th anniversary, Harlequin® American Romance® is celebrating by featuring an all-American male each month, all year long with MEN MADE IN AMERICA! *This June, we'll be featuring American men living in the West.*

Here's a sneak preview of THE CHIEF RANGER by Rebecca Winters.

Chief Ranger Vance Rossiter has to confront the sister of a man who died while under Vance's watch...and also confront his attraction to her.

"Chief Ranger Rossiter?" The sight of the woman who'd stepped inside Vance's office brought him to his feet. "I'm Rachel Darrow. Your secretary said I should come right in."

"Please," he said, walking around his desk to shake her hand. At a glance he estimated she was in her midtwenties. Her feminine curves did wonders for the pale blue T-shirt and jeans she was wearing. "Ranger Jarvis informed me there's a young boy with you."

The unfriendly expression in her beautiful green eyes caught him off guard. "Yes," was her clipped reply. "When we arrived in Yosemite the ranger told me I couldn't go anywhere in the park until I talked to you first."

"That's right."

"Knowing you wanted this meeting to be private, he offered to show my nephew around Headquarters."

So this woman was the victim's sister.... "What's his name?"

"Nicky."

The boy who haunted Vance's dreams now had a name. "How old is he?"

"He turned six three weeks ago. Were you the man in charge when my brother and sister-in-law were killed?"

"Yes. To tell you I'm sorry for what happened couldn't begin to convey my feelings."

The woman's gaze didn't flicker. "I won't even try to describe mine. Just tell me one thing. Was their accident preventable?"

"Yes," he answered without hesitation.

"In other words, the people working under you fell asleep on your watch and two lives were snuffed out as a result."

Hearing it put like that, he had to set the record straight. "My staff had nothing to do with it. I, myself, could have prevented the loss of life."

Ms. Darrow's expression hardened. "So you admit culpability."

"Yes. I take full blame."

A look of pain crossed over her features. "You can just stand there and admit it?" Her cry echoed that of his own tortured soul.

"Yes." He sucked in his breath.

"I work for a cruise line. Aboard ship, it's the captain's responsibility to maintain rigid safety regulations. If a disaster like that had happened while he was in charge he would have been relieved of his command and never given another ship again."

Rachel Darrow couldn't know she was preaching to the converted. "If you've come to the park with the intention of bringing a lawsuit against me for negligence, maybe you should." It would only be what he deserved.

"Maybe I will."

In the next instant, she wheeled around and hurried out of his office. Vance could have gone after her, but it would cause a scene, something he was loath to do for a variety of reasons. In the first place, he needed to cool down before he approached her again.

The discovery of the Darrows' frozen bodies had affected every ranger in the park. A little boy had been orphaned—a boy whose aunt was all he had left.

* * * * *

Will Rachel allow Vance to explain—
and will she let him into her heart?
Find out in
THE CHIEF RANGER
Available June 2009
from Harlequin® American Romance®.

COMING NEXT MONTH

Available June 9, 2009

#1566 A SMALL-TOWN HOMECOMING • Terry McLaughlin
Built to Last
The return of architect Tess Roussel to her hometown has put her on a collision course with John Jameson Quinn. The contractor has her reeling…his scandalous past overshadows everything. Tess wants to believe that the contractor is deserving of her professional admiration and her trust, but her love, too?

#1567 A HOLIDAY ROMANCE • Carrie Alexander
A summer holiday in the desert? What had Alice Potter been thinking? If it wasn't for resort manager Kyle Jarreau, her dream vacation would be a nightmare. But can they keep their fling a secret…? For Kyle's sake, they *have* to.

#1568 FROM FRIEND TO FATHER • Tracy Wolff
Reece Sandler never planned to raise his daughter with Sarah Martin. They were only friends when she agreed to be his surrogate. Now things have changed and they have to be parents—together. Fine. Easy. But only if Reece can control his attraction to Sarah.

#1569 BEST FOR THE BABY • Ann Evans
9 Months Later
Pregnant and alone, Alaina Tillman returns to Lake Harmony and Zack Davidson, her girlhood love. Yet as attracted as she is to him, life isn't just about the two of them anymore. She has to do what's best for her baby. Does that mean letting Zack in—or pushing him away?

#1570 NO ORDINARY COWBOY• Mary Sullivan
Home on the Ranch
A ranch is so not Amy Graves's scene. Still, she promised to help, so here she is. Funny thing is she starts to feel at home. And even funnier, she starts to fall for a cowboy—Hank Shelter. As she soon discovers, however, there's nothing ordinary about him.

#1571 ALL THAT LOVE IS • Ginger Chambers
Everlasting Love
Jillian Davis was prepared to walk away from her marriage. But when her husband, Brad, takes her on a shortcut, an accident nearly kills them. Now, with the SUV as their fragile shelter, Jillian's only hope lies with the man she was ready to leave behind forever.…

HSRCNMBPA0509